8

Nemesis of the Dead

Nemesis of the Dead

Frances Lloyd

ROBERT HALE · LONDON

Robert Hale Limited
Clerkenwell House
Clerkenwell Green
London EC1R 0HT

www.halebooks.com

2 4 6 8 10 9 7 5 3 1

Typeset in 10/13½pt Sabon
Printed by the MPG Books Group in the UK

PROLOGUE

Now there is a rocky isle in the mid sea ... a little isle

The Odyssey Book IV – Homer

Ten people are bound for Katastrophos, a hypnotic Greek Island steeped in superstition and ancient myth. Ten disparate travellers whose lives will never be the same again, for not all are what they seem. Some have objectives much more sinister than a quiet holiday in the sun. And as the island slowly begins to work its timeless magic, even the most prosaic become disengaged from reality and capable of indiscretions they would never have believed possible. But on Katastrophos, anything is possible. Who could have guessed that of the ten who travelled so hopefully, not all would return?

THE COP AND THE CATERER

It was going to be the perfect honeymoon. What could possibly go wrong this time? Detective Inspector Jack Dawes and his wife, Coriander, had already postponed one honeymoon – Jack to head up a murder investigation and Corrie to attend the inquest of her best customer who had dropped dead in the middle of a charity luncheon. The meal had been catered by 'Coriander's Cuisine' and the customer had suffered violent stomach pains, casting an inevitable if unjustified slur on the caterer. No smoke without fire, people said. No stomach pains without food poisoning.

By the time she had dealt with the fall-out, Corrie was in serious need of her belated honeymoon. She didn't care where they went as long as it

5

was peaceful, relaxing and as far away from crime and catering as possible. A place where Jack's phone couldn't ring and people didn't suddenly keel over clutching their stomachs.

Jack chose the location and it seemed ideal – a tiny Greek island, like a pebble dropped in the sparkling Ionian Sea. Afterwards, Corrie felt that the name of the island – Katastrophos – should have sounded a few alarm bells in the ear of a sensitive person like herself, but at the time all she could think about was the prospect of two blissful weeks with Jack knowing that she wouldn't have to cook and he was at last off duty. Or was he?

THE CLERK AND THE NANNY

A few miles away, sitting round the kitchen table in the bride's home, another couple, some twenty years younger than Jack and Corrie, were also looking forward to their honeymoon. In a few days Tim and Ellie would become Mr and Mrs Watkins. They were so painfully young and so patently happy, sitting close together, holding hands, smiling round at their families as they discussed the final wedding details.

Everyone had known Tim and Ellie would marry. They had been inseparable since primary school. Ellie had been timid and delicate and Tim had immediately taken it upon himself to look after her. As teenagers they didn't go clubbing like their friends, preferring to stay at home, making plans and saving. The longest they spent apart was when he went to his cashier's job at the bank and she went to the nursery fifty yards down the road, where she worked as a nanny.

They were young lovers, desperate to be alone, so when they spotted tiny Katastrophos on a zoomed-in web map of the Ionian islands, they booked their honeymoon straight away. It was perfect, they said, secluded, unspoiled and completely cut off from the outside world. Ingenuous and quixotic, Tim and Ellie had no way of knowing that total isolation, whilst romantic in abstract, would prove terrifying in reality.

THE INSURANCE MAN AND THE WIFE

The last time Marjorie Dobson had had a holiday was on her honeymoon in Bournemouth, thirty years ago. She supposed she wouldn't be having one now if she hadn't come into a little money of her own. It had been very daring of her to go ahead and book it without asking Ambrose first, and of course he had been furious when he found out. Shouted a lot about how she was throwing 'his' money down the drain because they didn't need a holiday. He might not but she did.

Marjorie had never been abroad and it had been quite difficult finding a resort that would suit. Ambrose had a weak heart and disliked most things associated with holidays. Tourists, children, noise, beaches, shops, foreign food, sunbathing, sightseeing – he seemed to object to anything where there was a risk of people enjoying themselves. Ambrose said people weren't put on this earth to enjoy themselves.

With the help of a very nice young man in the travel agency, she had eventually chosen Katastrophos. It was unbelievably quiet, he assured her; no nightclubs or tourist attractions – no tourists, come to that. Just the occasional independent traveller. On Katastrophos, Ambrose could be as difficult as he liked without offending anyone. Of course, she could always go on her own, but that wouldn't suit her purpose – which was to celebrate their thirtieth anniversary. Of course it was.

THE PROFESSOR AND THE PLAYGIRL

Professor Cuthbert Delauncey Gordon, respected botanist and author of several books on the subject, was feeling a tad miffed. Things had not been going according to plan of late and, as always, *tempus fugit*. He opened his sample case and began to pack the equipment he would need for the trip to Katastrophos. Wonderful little island. The most amazing flora in the world. There were plants growing in the olive groves that nobody but he had ever seen and soon his research and his remarkable discoveries would make him world famous.

He had been visiting Katastrophos to study the plants for some years, but this next trip was to be the most important – so much depended on it. On this occasion, he had persuaded his beautiful young American wife, Diana, to accompany him. She was never keen, finding his remote little paradise too dull for her exuberant, cosmopolitan lifestyle and, to be fair, he neglected her shamefully once his passion for plants took hold. This time, however, he proposed to pay her much more attention.

THE PLUMBER

Sidney Foskett leapt to his feet and yelled: 'Up the Gunners' along with 50,000 other fans. His beloved Arsenal had scored their first goal of the season. Cheering himself hoarse down the home supporters' end, he realized he would miss their next match because he'd be on holiday. It had been a busy year for plumbers. Burst pipes all winter, blocked drains and floods most of the summer and people wanting new, luxury bathrooms all the year round. Good for business but, come August, he was knackered. All the same, he had been in two minds about a Greek island. Greece was full of crumbling old ruins and as far as Sid was concerned, when you've seen *one* pile of bricks …

But his favourite hotel in Benidorm was full up and he'd left it too late to book anywhere decent in Majorca, so he had settled for a last-minute bargain break on an island called Katastrophos. He'd never heard of it and the girl in the bucket shop didn't know a lot but she reckoned it had been around since 2000 BC. That should get the holiday adrenaline going, he thought wryly. Bloody funny name, Katastrophos, but as long as there was plenty of sun, beer and crumpet, he guessed it would do.

THE NEW AGE TRAVELLER

She would use the name Sky for the duration of her visit. Even among third- and fourth-generation travellers there were still too many Rainbows and Moonbeams, and such names did not reflect her wounded spirit. She was glad to be going home to Katastrophos where she knew she would find healing and comfort, but this was not how it was meant to be – not how they had planned it.

And now it seemed that Nemesis, that implacable executrix of justice, had taken a hand, urging her to wreak vengeance on the hubris of those who think that by abusing others, they make their own superiority the greater. She did not yet know what she must do or when. Once she reached Katastrophos, Nemesis would tell her.

CHAPTER ONE

It was a drab day for a smart funeral. Overcast with a drizzle of rain and a whippy north-westerly that lifted skirts and tugged at umbrellas. The priest read the prayers in a sonorous monotone as the coffin was lowered into the cold, damp grave and mourners began to file past, tossing in handfuls of earth and long-stemmed roses.

'Good turn-out,' whispered DI Jack Dawes, counting the Armani suits standing three-deep around the grave. 'They're not short of a few bob, this lot. Some of them have even brought chauffeurs. But then the deceased was well-minted herself, wasn't she?'

His wife shot him a reproving look. 'Lavinia was a warm, gracious person, never mind her money. And I wish you wouldn't call her "the deceased" as though she were one of your suspicious deaths.' Coriander Dawes pulled off her glove and stepped forward to throw a bunch of fragrant herbs on to the coffin. It was a last gastronomic goodbye to the lady who had been her favourite customer. She had also been by far the most lucrative. Corrie flung the bouquet garni and watched as it sailed into the grave rapidly followed by her glove, which landed on the coffin with an embarrassing plop.

Jack suppressed the appalling urge to laugh that always afflicted him at funerals. The smallest thing would set him off, which was particularly inconvenient for a Detective Inspector on Scotland Yard's murder squad as funerals were a fairly inevitable part of his job. Struggling to control an erupting chortle, he peered down at Corrie's brand-new leather glove disappearing beneath a growing pile of earth and roses.

'Shall I jump in and get it?'

'Certainly not.' Red-faced, Corrie grasped Jack's arm and hurried him away to her battered white van which was cowering in a corner of the cemetery away from the Porsches and Bentleys. They climbed in and belted up, thankful to be out of the rain.

'Why do they always have funerals on such ruddy awful days? Let's go home.' Jack fiddled with the collar of his raincoat, trying to stop the accumulated rivulets of water from running down his neck.

'I'm surprised you wanted to come in the first place.' Corrie started the engine after several turns and a lot of cursing and nosed the van out of the cemetery gates and on to the roundabout. 'It's not as if you knew Lavinia that well. I shall really miss her.' She glanced at Jack and read his expression. 'No, not just because she spent a lot of money on dinner parties. She was a kind, considerate customer. Not like the ones who book you to cater for a party of twelve and when you get there, you find twenty have turned up.' A nasty suspicion sneaked into her head. 'Jack, why *did* you come? You're not investigating one of the mourners, are you? Promise me you're not still on duty. If we have to cancel another honeymoon ...'

Detective Inspector Jack Dawes assumed his innocent '*Who, me?*' face and held up blameless hands in mock submission. It was a ploy that worked quite well in tricky matrimonial situations. And this, if he didn't handle it carefully, had all the makings of a *very* tricky matrimonial situation.

'Sweetheart, trust me.' It was true that DI Dawes had gone to Lavinia Braithwaite's funeral to have a good look at the mourners but it wasn't so much the ones who were there who interested him, it was the ones who were not. 'I promise you we shan't have to postpone our honeymoon a second time. We're going to Katastrophos on Saturday, come hell or high water.'

Bold words, guaranteed to tempt the mischief of the gods.

On the other side of town in an unremarkable house on an unremarkable estate, Ellie Brown – soon to be Mrs Eleanor Watkins – stood in her mother's bedroom, looking at herself in the old-fashioned mahogany cheval mirror that had belonged to her grandmother. Ellie had been a strict vegetarian since the age of five, when she discovered that piglets eventually turned into sausages. Now, at nineteen, she was thin and pale with short ginger hair and freckles. She never wore make-up and hated dressing up, preferring clothes that were practical rather than feminine. Her wedding dress, a plain satin affair with a short veil, hung on her sparse frame like a shroud. Like most brides, she was nervous about her

wedding day on Saturday. It was the thought of being the centre of attention, having all those people staring at her. There had been times when
she had longed just to marry Tim quietly, wearing jeans and a T-shirt,
then sneak away without anyone knowing. But she knew she could never
do that – it would break her mum's heart.

She was to be given away by her uncle. Her mother had never
married, having become pregnant in the middle of her college course in
the days when it was still considered irresponsible. Loyal Ellie neither
knew nor asked about the identity of her father, feeling instinctively that
it had been a period in her mother's life that she preferred not to discuss.
Since she had grown up, Ellie rarely thought about her father, but family
events such as her marriage inevitably caused her to wonder. She imagined him to be tall and handsome with twinkling eyes and a nice smile.
She couldn't think that her mother would have had anything to do with
an unkind person. Briefly, she pictured herself walking down the aisle on
his arm, then she shrugged off her dress and hung it back on its padded
hanger. Uncle Bernard would do just as good a job of giving her away
and soon she would be miles from all the fuss and attention, alone with
Tim on Katastrophos – her dear little honeymoon island. She ran downstairs and was soon sitting cross-legged on the rug, playing happily with
Poppy the Puppy, the spaniel Tim had given her as an early wedding
present.

In a way, Marjorie Dobson could understand why her husband was
permanently disagreeable. It couldn't be much fun living with a
dangerous heart condition, having to take tablets to stay alive – the exact
amount at the same time every day. Ambrose continually reminded her
that he must never tax himself, get excited or overdo it and often shouted
at her for making him angry. He was very accommodating when it came
to taking things easy, though. He never once complained about her doing
all the heavy work at home and he always stayed overnight at a hotel
when he went to his Lodge meetings so he wouldn't overtire himself with
travelling. He went to rather a lot of Lodge meetings.

This holiday was to celebrate their anniversary and would, she hoped,
resolve a lot of the conflict in their marriage. Originally, she had fancied
a cruise. There was no end of advantages to being out in the middle of
the ocean among hundreds of holidaymakers but Ambrose would never
have agreed to it. It had been hard enough persuading him to spend two
weeks on a quiet island and even then he insisted that, if he disliked it,

they would come straight back home to Hampshire. She finished ironing the last of her husband's shirts – a fresh one for every day they would be away – then folded them carefully before placing them neatly in his suitcase.

Ambrose Dobson did not approve of casual holiday clothes. He could see no good reason, he said firmly, why spending two weeks abroad should constitute an excuse for sloppy dress standards. He would wear a collar and tie under his suit, regardless of the heat and no, Marjorie might not buy a bathing suit as he had no intention of permitting her to cavort half-naked in front of foreigners. As a concession to the climate, however, he had bought himself a new panama hat, mainly to protect his very expensive gentleman's hair replacement system from the hot sun. The attractive young lady assistant in the shop had told him the hat looked very dashing on a gentleman with such a good head of hair. He wished there had been more time to cultivate her acquaintance.

Sidney Foskett was nudging forty and although he said it himself, he was in pretty good shape. He had broad shoulders, slim hips and biceps that bulged like a sock full of conkers. He had bought himself a pair of very brief speedos for the beach and reckoned he didn't look half bad in them. Apart from these and some photochromic sunglasses, Sid had worn the same holiday gear for the last ten years, regardless of his destination. This consisted of a selection of off-white T-shirts printed with obscene lager slogans (free gifts from grateful breweries), army-surplus combat shorts that had seen action on beaches from Blackpool to Benidorm, market-stall trainers, the treads still clogged with hallowed Emirates Stadium turf and, unbelievably, a floor-length Arsenal scarf that went everywhere with him. Now all he needed was something to protect his head from the sun. The temperatures in the Greek islands that summer had soared to record levels. He grabbed last year's sombrero with a Union Jack on it from the top of his wardrobe and crammed it into his holdall.

Sidney wondered idly what the plumbing was like on Katastrophos. If it was still the ancient Greek variety, it must be pretty grim by anyone's standards. While he grappled routinely with ceramic disc technology and the hazards of differential pressures, he balked at the thought of a 4000-year-old khazi. But he wasn't going there to work, he reminded himself, he was going to have a good time. He was a free spirit. No wife or girlfriend to worry about. Not for want of trying though. Unfortunately it was one of life's vicissitudes that the ladies he fancied never seemed to fancy him, especially on holiday. Perhaps he'd meet a real stunner this time. No harm in dreaming.

In a stylish townhouse on the Upper East Side in the borough of Manhattan, New York City, between Central Park and the East River, Professor Gordon looked impatiently out of his dressing-room window at the humid afternoon. The five-square-kilometre neighbourhood, with its elegant rows of landmark mansions, once known as the 'Silk Stocking District' constituted some of the most expensive real estate in the United States. Some believed it to be the greatest concentration of individual wealth in the nation. Cuthbert Gordon was glad to be back in the States. He had wasted far too much time in England and to little advantage.

Behind him, his English valet was packing his clothes for the trip to Katastrophos. Whatever was the man doing packing silk shirts and his white tuxedo? He wouldn't be needing anything of that nature. This was a working trip and a vital one in terms of the success of his ongoing research. Shorts, anoraks and plenty of surgical gloves, that was what was required. He sighed. No doubt his beautiful wife Diana had a hand in this. She rarely accompanied him on his trips to the island, finding it interminably boring. Having agreed to go with him this time, it seemed she proposed to liven things up, at least in the evenings, and was doubtless packing low-cut evening gowns at that very moment. Well, he had no problem with that. She was a party animal and no doubt she would soon find someone to party with. She usually did. Men flocked around Diana like scavenging flies around an *Amorphophallus*, although in fairness, she didn't stink of rotting flesh like a carrion flower. Just the opposite, given the enormous sums she spent on perfume. He left his valet to finish packing. What harm would it do if he had to dress up a bit and spend some time with his wife? As long as he achieved his objective, nothing else mattered.

Corrie Dawes had been packing since seven in the morning. She peered into her wardrobe and chewed her lip. What kind of clothes do you take to a Greek island so small it isn't even in the tourist guide? She took out her one posh frock – then put it back again. She and Jack were hardly likely to go clubbing. What did it matter what she wore, anyway? It would be enough just to have her husband to herself for two whole weeks without the blasted phone ringing and Jack grabbing his coat and shooting off to another crime scene. She wondered if she should have bought a new suitcase. She was still using the one she had taken on honeymoon with her first husband, twenty years ago. It was a bit the worse for wear now but still perfectly serviceable – like its owner. Would she ever forget that ghastly ill-fated honeymoon? She had spent the whole turbulent two weeks in a bathroom in Provence. It was her first and only encounter with escargots. Confined to the primitive facilities of a rustic *gîte*, she learned that snails moved very much faster after you'd eaten them than they did when they were alive. It wasn't a good start to the marriage and a year later, Tom left her for a robust Scandinavian fitness instructor with her own sauna and a digestion like an incinerator.

Like many abandoned wives with bottle, Corrie dealt with the blow to her self-esteem by committing herself totally to work. Her catering business, Coriander's Cuisine, became her top priority. She worked seven days a week and if the customer required it, late into the night as well. Her aim was to build up a stable of clientele who would support a gastronomically excellent but financially sound catering business. By the time she considered herself a success, she was more or less resigned to staying single.

But life can always be relied upon to chuck in something unexpected. Corrie had been serving drinks and savouries at the cocktail party of a wealthy and influential turf accountant when the then Detective Sergeant Jack Dawes and his squad had burst in like something out of *The Sweeney* and nicked everyone. By the time Corrie had persuaded him she wasn't part of the bookie's money-laundering racket, just an innocent creator of canapés and an impaler of things on sticks, they were on first-name terms and she was cooking him intimate gourmet dinners.

Afterwards, Corrie claimed that without her masterly intuition and tireless assistance throughout the investigation, DS Dawes would never have cracked the case and rounded up several of the nastier members of the underworld. She was equally convinced that it was thanks to her that he had been promoted to DI and transferred to the murder squad. At the time, he had been churlishly ungrateful, declaring that she mostly got in the way and even put herself at risk. She was lucky, he said, that her interference with dangerous criminals hadn't landed her at the bottom of the Thames wearing a concrete apron.

Then, to Corrie's complete and utter amazement, he proposed. It was for her own protection, he said. She wasn't safe out on her own and as a copper, he couldn't take responsibility for releasing her on her own cognizance. Either she married him or he would nick her for interfering with a policeman in the course of his duty.

The wedding, whilst eye-catching, would never have graced the pages of a celebrity magazine. Jack in uniform, six-foot-three and balding, with a big nose, jug-ears and an off-centre grin, his features having undergone considerable repositioning during his rugby-playing days. Corrie in ivory silk, five-feet-nothing, perilously short-sighted and on the wrong side of a size sixteen. Not Romeo and Juliet in any orthodox sense, but a loving, symbiotic partnership nevertheless.

DI Dawes had never been a confirmed bachelor. Indeed, he had been a very reluctant one. Work had always sabotaged budding relationships, and girlfriends would get fed up with him not turning up for dates or, worse, rushing off just at the climax of something crucial. Eventually they left him for blokes in less demanding jobs. In Corrie, he had found a kindred, feisty spirit where work and partnership lived mostly in peaceful co-existence – as long as he could curb her compulsion to interfere.

This second time around, Corrie had looked forward to a perfect spring honeymoon in Paris – with no snails. But the honeymoon gremlin struck again and they had scarcely popped a champagne cork when Jack was called back to duty to head a murder enquiry, all leave cancelled. It had developed into a long and gruelling investigation with Jack more than usually affected by the circumstances. During the worst of it, he and Corrie had promised each other a relaxed, romantic honeymoon as soon as the case was over. The destination was negotiable, they would pick somewhere at the last minute. But wherever they chose, it must be as far away from crime and cooking as possible.

'It says here ...' said Jack, wandering into the bedroom waving a computer print-out, '... that Katastrophos is a tiny Greek island, like a pebble dropped in the sparkling Ionian Sea.'

Later, Corrie reckoned that her masterly intuition should have kicked in then. What sort of a name is Katastrophos if not full of portent and omen?

'Sounds perfect.' She held her swimsuit against her, a miracle of cantilever engineering with a clever skirted bit designed to conceal fat thighs. She grimaced at herself in the mirror. 'Tell me more about Katastrophos. It's hard to picture it without glossy brochures.'

'There isn't much to tell.' Jack lay back on the bed and swung his feet up. 'It's the smallest of the Ionian Islands, which run down the western coast of mainland Greece. It's also one of the few islands not shown on any tourist map. Only eight kilometres long and three kilometres wide. Must be a kind of sausage-shape, I guess. It's called Katastrophos because of a catastrophic earthquake a couple of centuries ago that destroyed most of its Venetian buildings and a lot of the inhabitants.'

'I see. It's a seismic sausage. Doesn't it say anything nice?'

''Course. Listen to this blurb. "*Katastrophos has an intimate charm that has escaped the blight of tourism. Apart from a very small annual influx of tourists ...*" – that'll be you and me –"*... there is little to disturb the soporific atmosphere. If you crave peace and quiet or need to retreat from the stress of modern-day living, Katastrophos is the ideal 'get away from it all' holiday destination*".'

'Wonderful. Just what we need.'

'And what about this bit? "*According to Greek legend, Katastrophos was created by Poseidon who struck the Ionian Sea with his trident to create a secret island paradise to share with his wife Amphitrite.*" What better place for a honeymoon than a secret island paradise?'

Corrie climbed on the bed, hauled up her glasses dangling on a chain around her neck and began reading over his shoulder.

'I don't like the sound of that.' She pointed. 'It says Antony and Cleopatra are reputed to have had a dinner party at Katastrophos on the eve of the Battle of Actium.'

'So what?' Jack grinned. 'Are you cross you weren't around to tender for the catering?'

Corrie gave him a withering look. 'You know what happened at Actium?'

'No. Should I?'

'The combined forces of Antony and Cleopatra were defeated by Octavian. It completely destroyed their plans for the future. It was a turning point in the history of Egypt and Rome.'

Jack stared at her. 'You know, I worry about you sometimes. What sort of sad person remembers stuff like that? You need a holiday, Corrie. Two weeks in a luxury hotel overlooking a stunning horseshoe bay, flanked by silver-green olive groves and majestic rows of cypress. Nothing to do but swim and sunbathe. And plenty of wine and Greek food that you haven't had to cook yourself.'

'OK. You've convinced me. How do we get there?'

Jack produced his meticulously planned itinerary.

'Flight from Gatwick to Kalamata Airport on the Peloponnese peninsula. Coach transfer from the airport to the ferry port south of Methóni.
Then ferry across the Ionian Sea to Katastrophos. It's the only route. The
island's too small for its own airport. There's just the one main resort,
Agia Sofia – St Sophia. I reckon if we get the eight o'clock flight from
Gatwick, we should reach Hotel Stasinopoulos in time to freshen up,
have a glass of wine and enjoy a romantic dinner outdoors, under the
vine-covered pergola, watching the sun set over Katastrophos Bay.'

Corrie stopped folding clothes and imagined herself there already.

'Heavenly. You know, you're right, Jack. We both need a holiday.
Especially you. That last murder case really got under your skin. I could
tell.'

Jack shrugged. The young man had undoubtedly been guilty, had
admitted his guilt, but the custodial sentence was unexpectedly severe,
mainly because drugs were involved. The look of utter devastation on his
parents' faces as he had been taken down was something Jack found
hard to forget.

'And I'm still sad about Lavinia,' said Corrie. 'It isn't just that I miss
her as a friend, it's the effect it's having on the business. Lots of those
wealthy people at the funeral had become good customers, thanks to
Lavinia's recommendation. Then she goes and dies of a mysterious
stomach complaint at a luncheon party catered by Coriander's Cuisine.'

'That wasn't your fault.'

'I know, but it doesn't look good, does it? One minute she's chomping
down my confit of duck Béarnaise. Next thing, she's writhing in agony
with stomach cramps and drops dead before the ambulance arrives.'

'Nobody blamed you.' Jack put an arm around her. 'It was made
perfectly clear at the inquest. The post mortem didn't find any evidence
of food poisoning – or any other kind of poisoning, come to that. She
was an elderly lady and she died of heart failure brought on by some sort
of stomach virus. If there'd been any doubt, the coroner would have
given an open verdict instead of natural causes.'

'What makes me feel really awful is the money she left me in her will,
bless her. She wanted me to use it to buy a posh new van with Coriander's
Cuisine painted on the side. She must have noticed my old one was knackered from the clouds of blue smoke outside her window when I turned up
with the party food. She was such a kind, generous person.'

Jack looked thoughtful. 'According to the newspapers, she left the
bulk of a very considerable fortune to charity.'

'Mm. There were just one or two small legacies to people like me who worked for her and some others who raised funds for her charities.'

'What about relatives?'

Corrie shook her head. 'She'd been a widow for years and I don't think she had any children. At least, if she did, she never talked about them. Sad, really. I think she might have mentioned a sister once, or was it a brother? I can't remember. Anyway, they couldn't have been very close because I didn't see any relatives at the funeral.'

'No,' said Jack. 'Neither did I.'

CHAPTER TWO

Corrie was not a morning person. She barely spoke before nine and never until she had absorbed a great deal of caffeine. It was now 6.30 on Saturday morning and she and Jack were in a queue for the long-stay car park at Gatwick. It was moving reasonably quickly but ground to a halt when the old buffer at the head of the queue reached the ticket machine. He sat for some time gazing out of his car window at it. Then his wife passed him his glasses and he peered even closer.

'It's a ticket machine,' snapped Corrie. 'Press the button and take the ticket, you dithering old pillock.'

Jack grinned. 'He can't hear you, grumpy-knickers.'

'I know, but it makes me feel better. If he took off that silly panama hat he could stick his head out of the window and see what he's doing.'

Corrie hated flying but she had no intention of admitting it to Jack. She had psyched herself up for this trip and, fighting back the rising nausea, she marched bravely into the terminal building only to find that the flight from Gatwick to Kalamata Airport had been delayed by two and a half hours. By the time they boarded, Corrie had been in the Knicker Shop eight times, bought five pots of high-factor anti-wrinkle cream, eaten at least ten chocolate bars and read all the diet magazines. Now, at last, they were on the plane and settled in their seats. Jack leaned back and stretched his long legs into the aisle.

'Belt up, sweetheart.'

'Pardon?'

'Fasten your seatbelt. The cabin crew will be round to check in a minute. Once we're in the air I'll order some drinks. How do you fancy champagne?'

Corrie swallowed hard. Only the whitening of her knuckles on the armrests betrayed the terror of the inner woman as she contemplated flying at 35,000 feet with nothing more substantial than clouds between her and the ground. Or the sea. She had never understood why they didn't give you a parachute.

'Champagne at half past ten in the morning? Isn't that a bit flash?'

'This is our honeymoon. My first and your last. Sod the expense.'

After the second glass Corrie felt much better.

The August temperatures were in the mid-nineties as the tourist-packed Boeing nudged the melting tarmac of Kalamata Airport. Drowsy taxi drivers woke reluctantly from their afternoon naps and braced themselves for the onslaught of eager holidaymakers. In the *tavernas*, cooks slammed quick-frozen *moussaká* into microwaves and whipped the clingfilm off the Greek salad. Local wine that had wintered in Esso cans was deftly decanted into summer carafes and at the flick of a switch, *bouzoúki* twanged from loud speakers suspended in the olive trees. Greece was ready to work its ageless charm on another batch of foreign *touristas*.

Corrie paused at the top of the aircraft steps as the heat from the simmering concrete blasted her in the face. After the air-conditioned cabin, it felt stifling and airless, like walking into a furnace. She wished now that she had dressed for Greece instead of Gatwick but she was glad to get off the plane despite the heat. She peeled off a couple of sweaters and resolved not to start dreading the return flight until it was absolutely imminent.

Half an hour later, Jack had wrestled their luggage off the carousel and, sweaty and uncomfortable, they were outside the building, shielding their eyes from the phosphorescent sunlight. Immediately in front of them was a fleet of shiny new air-conditioned coaches, parked in a neat herringbone along the kerb. Beside each coach, a smart, uniformed courier hovered with a clipboard and a fixed smile.

'Which one's ours?' Corrie asked.

'I think it must be that one.' Jack pointed to a battered old bus painted in drab camouflage colours that looked as though it had once seen service as an army transport vehicle. It was parked right at the end, almost out of sight behind the swanky coaches, like a poor relative at a posh wedding. There was no courier but the driver, a swarthy man in a greasy cap with a formidable collection of St Christophers around his neck, was holding up a square of cardboard with '*Ferry Methóni*' scribbled on it in black felt tip.

'It can't be.' As they came closer, Corrie could see bald tyres and quite a lot of rust. 'It doesn't look roadworthy to me.'

'Don't worry, sweetheart,' said Jack, subconsciously totting up the number of regulations the vehicle violated. 'It isn't far to the ferry port and the roads are good by Greek standards. It should only take a couple of hours and then we'll be on the ferry drifting lazily across the Ionian Sea to Katastrophos and two weeks of idleness and luxury.' He wondered if it were possible to carry the luggage and cross his fingers at the same time.

'You want ferry – Methóni?' The driver's cigarette, stuck firmly to his bottom lip, bobbed up and down as he spoke.

'That's right.' Jack rummaged in his travel bag for the documents but the driver had already picked up the suitcases and was hurling them into the almost empty luggage compartment in the side of the bus. The rusty floor juddered ominously beneath the weight and Corrie had a worrying vision of her clothes strewn all along the road to the ferry port. The thought of a pair of her big knickers adorning one of the roadside shrines was not a reverent one.

'Everybody here. We go now.' The driver motioned them aboard and climbed into his creaky driver's seat where rosary beads and pictures of saints dangled from the rear-view mirror. Sadly, the saints had not seen fit to bless the bus with air-conditioning so the inside was unbearably hot.

There were only four other people on board which surprised Jack. His information had led him to expect more. He glanced around, attempting to match his fellow-travellers to the hastily compiled briefing in his pocket. A couple in their fifties, obviously English, had already claimed the front seat behind the driver. The woman, pleasant-looking in a floral frock and comfortable wide-fitting sandals, nodded and smiled as Jack and Corrie passed. Her husband, clearly miffed about the standard of transport, leaned forward and began berating the driver, who ignored him.

The other couple, locked in each other's arms on the back seat, looked about sixteen. They were so engrossed, it was doubtful they even knew they were on a bus, let alone aware of the other passengers. Jack and Corrie, upholding the deep-rooted British tradition of not fraternizing with strangers on public transport, settled themselves somewhere near the middle. The driver started the engine and after much grinding of gears and stamping on the floppy clutch, he steered the bus out of the terminal car park and on to the main highway to Methóni.

Soon they were bumping along the coast road that skirted the dazzling Gulf of Messinia. The sea flashed below, blue as a kingfisher's wing. Jack stood up and wrenched open the window to let in a welcome breeze. It smelled of the open sea. He leaned close to Corrie and spoke into her ear so she could hear him above the noise of the engine and the rattle of loose bits of bus.

'That bloke must be baking in those clothes. Makes me sweat just to look at him.' He indicated the man in the front seat who was ignoring both his wife and the stunning scenery and reading an English newspaper.

Corrie looked and smiled. The man was a caricature of the old-fashioned, British, middle-aged man abroad – short and portly with dull brown hair and bland, rimless spectacles. Despite the soaring temperatures, he was wearing a collar and striped tie under a brown worsted suit. Corrie knew even before she glanced down that the socks in his leather brogues would be of the hairy woollen variety. He looked vaguely familiar but it was only when she spotted the panama hat placed carefully on top of his wife's neatly folded cardigan that she remembered, with a pang of guilt, where she had seen him. He was the 'dithering old pillock' who had held up the queue at the car-park ticket machine. He had a very red face and kept taking out a khaki handkerchief to mop his brow. His wife, cool and bare-legged under her sleeveless dress, sat quietly by his side looking out of the window.

'D'you reckon they're going to Katastrophos?' Corrie asked Jack.

'Probably. She looks pleasant enough but I bet he's a real pain in the arse.' Jack's recollection of his briefing more or less confirmed it.

'You never know,' said Corrie. 'They might be stopping off at one of those other islands. The ferry passes between them before it puts out to sea.' She glanced back at the young couple who were sharing a cheese torpedo, nibbling at it lovingly from either end. She nudged Jack. 'I hope they're coming with us. Aren't they sweet?'

Jack put a finger down his throat in a mock vomiting gesture and Corrie smacked him on the arm.

The bus veered west, away from the coast, as the road curled inland, cutting across the south-west promontory of the Peloponnese peninsula. Now they drove through tiny villages with narrow streets snaking between flower-decked, whitewashed houses. Washing was strung out to dry from every balcony, bright as bunting. In the gardens, walnut-skinned crones in black headscarves dozed in the shade of magenta bougainvillea as the afternoon sun gonged down out of a brazen sky.

Jack wondered what the traffic cops back home would make of the driver's road safety. Occasionally he drove on the right, but more often than not he steered straight down the middle, hooting and shouting Greek obscenities at the drivers coming the other way. Since they were also driving down the middle, they responded in a similar manner with much gesturing and cursing but there was no real malice, as far as Jack could tell. To them, it was perfectly normal. The rationale seemed to be that you drove on whichever part of the road was shady and had the fewest potholes.

The atmosphere freshened as the bus began to drop back down to the coast on the west side of the peninsula. The road looped around the headland and Corrie had a fine view of a pretty bay and the closer group of islets. According to the short and vague directions that Jack had managed to pull off the Internet, the ferry port that served Katastrophos was roughly five miles south of Methóni.

The bus driver pulled up next to the harbour of a tiny fishing town alongside a dilapidated wooden jetty and everyone clambered out, hot and sticky. Still with pendulous cigarette, the driver heaved everyone's suitcases out of the luggage compartment and dumped them on the quay-side. Jack and the young man each put coins in his outstretched hand but 'short-and-portly' blatantly ignored him, and started fussing with his bags and his panama hat. His wife looked embarrassed.

The driver trousered the cash, smiling happily. 'Which island you go? Sapientza – see lighthouse? Schiza? Venetiko? Very nice – very secluded.' He winked at the young couple, still joined at the hip.

'Katastrophos.' The reply was unanimous.

It might have been Corrie's imagination but she thought the driver's smile faded fractionally. He fingered the bunch of St Christophers at his throat. 'Good luck!' he called ambiguously and climbed back into his bus. 'Ferry leave in one hour. Maybe.' Soon he was jolting back down the bumpy road to Kalamata.

The six travellers stood in an awkward circle around their bags like girls at a nightclub waiting for the music to start.

'Well,' said Jack, affably. 'I suppose we should introduce ourselves since we're all headed for the same island.'

'I don't see why,' said 'short-and-portly' pompously. 'My wife and I dislike holiday friendships. They impinge on one's privacy.'

Now they were up close and she had her glasses on, Corrie could see that his dull brown hair was actually a hairpiece and a not very convincing one. How pretentious. She smothered a giggle. The Greek sun would play havoc with the glue.

'I wasn't suggesting friendship.' Jack gave Corrie a look that said: *I told you this bloke was a pain in the arse.* 'I just thought that as Katastrophos is so small, with just the one hotel, we're likely to keep bumping into each other.'

'Absolutely,' said the young man. He withdrew an arm reluctantly from around the waist of his beloved and held out his hand. 'I'm Tim Watkins, and this ...' he looked at her adoringly, as if he could not believe his luck, '... this is my wife, Ellie.'

The two were wearing identical shorts, T-shirts and trainers and were physically intertwined to such an extent that it was hard to see where one started and the other finished. They had short matching haircuts and scrubbed freckled faces. For modern youngsters, they were quaintly wholesome and distinctly uncool, thought Corrie. Like presenters from a very old Blue Peter programme.

Ellie smiled at Tim, blushed and lowered her eyes to look at her wedding ring.

'We're on honeymoon.'

Looking at the agonizingly young newly-weds, Corrie suddenly felt embarrassed. She and Jack were on honeymoon, too, but they were in their forties and it seemed slightly indecent somehow. She relaxed, knowing instinctively that Jack would keep it secret. He had already asked her not to tell anyone he was a policeman. It was a profession, he said, second only to undertaking for making people feel uncomfortable on holiday. She and Jack were incredibly close when it came to under-standing each other's feelings. Almost telepathic. He would sense immediately that their honeymoon status was not something she would want to advertise.

'That's a coincidence,' he blurted. 'My wife and I are on honey ... ouch!' Sometimes, thought Corrie, telepathy needs a helping hand – or foot.

'I'm Coriander Dawes,' she said amiably, 'and this is my husband, Jack. Congratulations to you both. You look very happy.'

Tim and Ellie smiled shyly and re-entwined.

'Dobson,' muttered 'short-and-portly' gruffly. 'Ambrose Dobson.' Then he added, almost as an afterthought, 'This is the wife, Marjorie.'

'Pleased to meet you.' Marjorie smiled as if she might like to chat further but her husband took her arm.

'Come along, Marjorie. We'll sit over there and wait for the ferry.' He steered her towards a rickety wooden seat further down the jetty.

At seven o'clock they were still waiting. Corrie had always been fascinated by Greek mythology but now, watching the sun begin to set over Homer's wine-dark sea, she began to feel a compelling affinity with the gods of ancient Greece that was totally unexpected and a bit spooky. It was almost as if she could feel their presence, watching and waiting to amuse themselves with mere mortals, like cats toying with mice. More substantially, her stomach began to rumble. So much, she thought, for their romantic dinner under a vine-covered pergola at Hotel Stasinopoulos.

The quayside was practically deserted. It was that time of the evening when holidaymakers are indoors getting dressed up for the clubs or a meal at their favourite *taverna*. Apart from the Katastrophos group, there was just one young woman, sitting cross-legged on the sea wall reading a Greek magazine propped up on her backpack. She was dressed in the old hippy style with braided, purple-streaked hair, black lips and eyes and an awesome array of tattoos.

'I suppose we're in the right place,' said Corrie, drowsily. 'I can't see anything remotely like a ferry – only that tatty old fishing-boat.'

Just below them, a salt-encrusted vessel with six inches of dirty water sloshing around in the bilge, bobbed gently up and down on its moorings. Jack checked the travel documents again.

'This is the place all right. I expected more people to be waiting here, though.'

'But didn't you say very few tourists visit Katastrophos?'

'Yeah. Apparently the ferry can only carry a handful of passengers and the service is sporadic, which seems to mean "when the ferryman feels like it". I guess the island *is* very remote. People who go there, go mainly for a specific reason. It isn't the kind of place travel agents normally recommend. Obviously you and I and Tim and Ellie are here for a private, romantic honeymoon. I suspect the Dobsons are here because he's a miserable old sod and doesn't want to socialize with anybody.'

'You don't know that. He might just be shy,' said Corrie charitably.

25

The prospect of being alone with Jack had seemed like bliss when Corrie was at home. Now, she was slightly uneasy about being cut off completely from civilization for two weeks with not even a mobile phone for comfort. They would never find a signal on an island in the middle of the Ionian Sea. Mindful of her honeymoon hex, she was starting to wonder whether it might not be safer to stay where they were on the mainland. These mental meanderings were cut short when a taxi pulled up and a tall, stooping, spindly-legged man in shorts and a fluorescent orange anorak jumped out. He ran round to the boot and dragged out several pieces of expensive-looking Louis Vuitton luggage with huge bony hands. Then he ran back round to the front and dragged an equally expensive-looking blonde away from the drooling taxi driver. He gathered everything up, including the blonde, and struggled across to the jetty.

'Well, here we all are then!' He beamed at everyone as though he were greeting old friends. He had a thin, blotchy face with a hawklike nose, slightly bulging eyes and tufts of ginger hair sprouting from everywhere except his bald head.

'Gordon's the name. Professor Cuthbert Gordon. I'm a botanist. You may have read my books.'

'For Chrissakes, Cuthbert, of course they haven't. Normal guys read thrillers and spy novels and porn. They sure as hell aren't interested in books about boring old plants.' The nasal drawl, Corrie reckoned, was definitely New York, probably Manhattan. The designer shirt and skin-tight jeans might have been Madison Avenue, or Paris, or Rome. The blonde, drop-dead gorgeous and oozing sex, homed in on Jack like a testosterone-seeking missile and offered him a slim hand with a huge diamond on the scarlet-tipped middle finger. A cloud of musky perfume settled over them like acid rain.

'Hi there, honey. I'm Diana Gordon.' She tossed back a thick curtain of golden hair and smiled seductively at him from beneath impossibly long eyelashes. 'I hope you're coming to Katastrophos. We'll have a real good time.'

Over my dead body, fumed Corrie. She glanced at Jack. He was holding Diana's hand and his mouth was open but no sound was coming out, so Corrie decided she had better take charge of the introductions.

'Hello, dear. I'm Corrie Dawes and that hand you're holding belongs to my husband, Jack.' She smiled sweetly.

'Corridors?' repeated Diana, amused. 'Your name is Corridors?'

'Yes, I know. Awful, isn't it? It's short for Coriander.'

'Not at all awful.' The professor's face lit up. '*Coriander sativum* is an excellent herb. Solid ridged stems and sensible bipinnate leaves. Relieves flatulence and aids the digestion.'

Thanks a bunch, thought Corrie.

Diana teetered off on four-inch Blahnik heels to repeat the vamping routine with Tim Watkins, but her husky voice was drowned out by a deafening racket like a huge, defective lawn mower starting up. Clouds of smelly blue smoke billowed up from the old fishing-boat moored below.

Professor Gordon rubbed his hands together enthusiastically. 'Splendid!' he bellowed over the din. 'Old Charon's woken up at last. On board, everyone, he won't wait for dawdlers.'

Jack and Corrie exchanged glances.

'That's never the ferry,' said Corrie, horrified.

'Charon?' Ellie giggled nervously. 'Wasn't that someone nasty in Greek mythology?'

'The ferryman of the dead,' said Professor Gordon. 'Just a macabre nickname, my dear. They have a droll sense of humour, the Katastrophans.'

They watched as a wizened old man in a filthy peaked cap clambered, wheezing, on to the jetty. He hawked and spat a couple of times, then began throwing everyone's luggage down into the bilge water in the bottom of the boat. Glowing embers fell from his stinking cigarette and etched themselves into Diana Gordon's Vuitton vanity case.

The prospect of putting out to sea in a decaying old rust bucket with a wheezing pensioner at the helm was not an appealing one. Nobody seemed keen except Professor Gordon, who was clearly eager to be off.

'Damned outrage!' blustered Ambrose Dobson, predictably. 'Call that a ferry? It's a blasted disgrace. So is the captain. I'm going nowhere in that wreck. I shall write a strong letter to the travel company, sue the blighters. Come away, Marjorie.'

Tim and Ellie simply clutched each other even tighter and waited to see what everyone else was going to do.

'I take it you've been on this ferry before, Professor?' said Jack.

'Oh yes – many times. Safe as houses. Been coming here for years. It's the flora, you see. There are plants on Katastrophos that you won't find growing anywhere else in the world. Fascinating, don't you think? Of course, my lovely wife doesn't always come. She's very much younger than me, as you can see. Prefers a bit of excitement, don't you, old girl?'

'You bet,' drawled Diana, winking at Jack.

Old Charon began gesturing wildly at them to get on board. '*Ghríghora!*' he screeched. 'Hurry!'

Corrie looked uncertainly at Jack. If she wanted to spend her long-awaited honeymoon on Katastrophos, she had little choice.

'Come on.' Jack took her arm. 'I'll look after you if you look after me.'

Bracing themselves, they followed the Gordons down into the boat which rocked precariously. Tim and Ellie separated just long enough to climb in, then re-entwined anxiously. The Dobsons appeared to be having a heated debate on the quay during which she could be heard pleading, 'Please, Ambrose.' Then they too picked their way down the weed-slimy steps and into the boat.

The young Greek hippy who had been sitting, staring out to sea, stood up and walked briskly down the jetty. She threw her backpack into the boat, jumped nimbly down and settled herself on some cases of wine stacked up in the stern – as far away from everyone else as possible.

The old ferryman opened the throttle and the engine changed up an octave from a moaning wail to a high-pitched scream.

'Oi! Wait for me!' Another passenger came tearing along the jetty and flung himself and his bags headlong into the boat just as it was moving away. He staggered unsteadily to his feet, swayed a bit, then wriggled his behind into a gap between the Dobsons.

'Evening all,' he said cheerfully. 'That was a close one.'

He had a smile that lit up not only his face, but a goodish part of the world around him, like a lighthouse.

'Are you all right, dear?' asked Marjorie, concerned. 'You landed with a terrible wallop. You haven't broken anything, have you?'

The newcomer peered anxiously into an airport carrier bag and checked the bottles. 'No, it's all right, love. Nothing's broken.' He rummaged in his pocket, pulled out a deck of business cards and handed them round. 'Sidney Arthur Foskett. Master plumber. Anything from a dripping tap to a rat up your downpipe. Pleased to meet you.'

The engine belched a plume of oily smoke high up into the sky and next minute they were bucketing out of the harbour in an erratic zigzag, mainly because half the rudder was missing and Charon had let go of the wheel to light another fag. The old fishing-boat wobbled and dawdled across the dark-blue crescent of the harbour, through the narrow strait between the Oinousai islands and out into the open sea beyond. Somewhere out there, Corrie remembered, were the far lagoons where the Battle of Actium was fought and lost. The thud and swing of the open sea began to make itself felt.

'Well, this is very jolly, I must say. We don't normally have such good company, do we, Diana?'

Professor Gordon beamed at everyone over his half-moon spectacles like a benevolent scoutmaster rallying his troop. They were several miles out to sea and the swell was tossing the boat up and down like a roller-coaster. The professor turned to Sidney, who was an unfetching shade of green.

'Have you been to Katastrophos before, old chap?'

'No, squire, and I'm starting to wish I wasn't going now.' He put a hand over his mouth and gulped.

Corrie didn't dare look at Jack. He got seasick just listening to the shipping forecast. Even the glamorous Diana looked a tad ruffled. Tim and Ellie were leaning over the side, still welded together, even while throwing up. Only Marjorie seemed calm, passing tissues to Ambrose who alternated between vicious defamation of the travel company and saying goodbye to his breakfast, lunch and tea. The young woman in the stern, whilst not physically sick, was clutching the rails and looking grimly at the horizon. Blithely oblivious to the angst going on around him, Professor Gordon took a paper bag out of his backpack and peered inside.

'Anyone hungry? I seem to have far too many garlic-sausage sand-wiches here.'

That did it. The combined odours of garlic and diesel kept them bent grimly over the gunwales for the remainder of the trip, while the old boat pitched and rolled its way across the Ionian Sea to Katastrophos.

CHAPTER THREE

It was late into the night. Darkness had fallen slowly over the cobalt sea, veil upon veil, turning it first to lead and then silver under the full moon. Corrie had begun to believe her honeymoon hex had struck again and they were doomed to drift *'for two nights and two days ... wandering in the swell of the sea ... hearts boded of death'* like Homer's luckless Odysseus. Suddenly Charon shouted *'Ayoo'* and pointed a finger, its nail black beyond scrubbing, at a row of lights, twinkling in the far distance.

Fifteen minutes later they dropped anchor at Katastrophos Island and tied up at the tiny landing stage belonging to the Hotel Stasinopoulos. Exhausted, the small band of ten disembarked on wobbly legs, pathetically grateful to be on dry land. Old Charon hovered at the end of the gangplank, his grin a dentist's nightmare. As the group tottered past, he held out his hand optimistically. Sid put a business card in it.

Hotel Stasinopoulos was the only hotel on the island and with just eight bedrooms; the guests and staff now filled it to capacity for the first time in living memory. Yanni and Maria Stasinopoulos, the owners, greeted everyone with typically polite Greek island hospitality, despite the late hour. Then they fell upon Professor Gordon as though he were an old uncle with vigorous handshakes and cries of *'Kalós írthate!'* Welcome! He hugged them both in return and showing little sign of weariness, he introduced the rest of the bedraggled travellers.

Despite Yanni and Maria's insistence, nobody but the professor could face anything to eat, and without even signing the register, which could wait until morning, everyone trooped up to their rooms with hot drinks before falling gratefully into bed.

Jack's face fell when he saw the twin beds. It was clearly not what he had in mind for a romantic honeymoon.

'Don't worry.' He flexed his muscles and spat on his hands. 'I'll push them together.'

'No, I don't think so—' Corrie began.

'It's all right. It won't take a minute.'

At first, Corrie was too tired to argue, then, fearing he would do himself an injury that would blight the rest of their honeymoon, maybe even the rest of their married life, she pointed out that the beds were set into concrete and cemented to the floor.

Although they were both exhausted, neither could sleep. They tossed and turned in the oppressive heat, listening to the relentlessly cheerful chirping of the cicadas outside the window. Jack lay on his back, his arms behind his head. Suddenly, apropos of absolutely nothing, he said into the darkness:

'Why do people do it, Corrie? Why kill someone just for money? I mean, how much money does one person need to be happy? And how can they ever be happy knowing that they've taken a life to get it? I'm pretty hard-nosed after twenty years in the Force, but I still don't understand it. Probably never will, no matter how long I stay in the murder squad.'

Corrie sat up and put on the light. She assumed that exhaustion and sleeplessness had conjured up demons from Jack's last murder case. A young man from a decent, loving family, engaged to be married and with a promising career as a doctor, had foolishly got into massive debt through gambling. His debtors had threatened both him and his fiancée and pressured him into supplying drugs to pay off his debts. Eventually, under the intolerable strain of getting deeper into crime and with discovery imminent, he had lost control and stabbed the drug dealer. He died instantly. Good riddance people had said at the time, but even a first-class mitigation plea had not saved the young man from being sentenced to a long stretch in prison, his career in ruins. Jack had been the DI in charge of the case and as always, had been scrupulous in his investigations. But, pragmatic as he was, he could not forget the despair of the parents and fiancée when sentence was passed.

In the hollow hours of the night, that deceiving time when every problem seems larger than life and impossible to solve, Corrie could find no comforting or credible answers to Jack's questions. She climbed out of her bed, slid into his, and put her arms around him.

'I don't know, sweetheart. But if we're honest, I guess we're all capable of one murder. It's just that most of us are fortunate enough never to be forced into a situation where we're tested.'

They were silent for a while. Despite her original anxiety, Corrie was glad they were effectively incommunicado for a fortnight. Jack needed a complete rest. She changed the subject.

'The Gordons are a strange couple aren't they? She's young and glamorous and he's a crusty old boffin, and he's got to be at least twenty years older than her. Mind you, it isn't hard to see why she married him, is it? Did you see the size of that diamond on her finger?'

Jack nodded pensively. 'Money would certainly seem to have been the incentive for the marriage. And Diana's clearly used to spending it.'

Corrie sighed, envious, but only for a nanosecond.

'What do you make of Ambrose and Marjorie?'

'He's an obnoxious, bad-mannered little twerp in a badly fitting wig and she lets him bully her.'

'I know! I keep wanting her to stand up for herself. She's like the stereotypical "little woman" from the fifties. I asked her if she'd had a job since she was married and she said no, Ambrose would never allow it. Apparently, he makes enough fuss about her bit of charity work. Wives like her set the rest of us back decades in terms of the equality we're all supposed to have earned. I bet she doesn't even vote.'

'And men like him make the rest of us blokes feel uncomfortable. I suppose they're both a couple of dinosaurs in terms of modern marriage.'

Corrie frowned. 'Funny though, I'm sure I've seen her before, somewhere.'

Jack yawned. 'You have. She was sitting next to him when he was holding up the queue at Gatwick.'

Corrie frowned. 'No, I mean before that. And not with her husband – on her own. Her face is familiar. I know I've seen her before.'

'Doubt it. He'd never let her go anywhere on her own. I expect you're confusing her with someone else. She's got one of those ordinary, commonplace faces.' He grinned. 'I really like Sid, don't you? I reckon he could be a good laugh. He'd better watch out though, I think Diana's got her predatory eye on him.'

'Diana's got her eye on all the men. Be careful her Medusa gaze doesn't turn you all to stone. This is a Greek island, after all. Not Tim though, he's adorable. So much in love he probably hasn't even noticed Diana's rather obvious charms. I hope he and Ellie have a super honeymoon.'

'Me too. If only they weren't so flipping young. They keep looking at us like we should be in a home.'

Corrie stifled a yawn. 'All the same, it's nice to think that although we're twice their age, we're still young enough to be on honeymoon, doing the same thing they are.'

'Yes, darling,' said Jack, yawning again, 'but I expect they do it more often and much faster.' He turned over and began to snore.

Nine o'clock next morning: the sun, already fierce, scorched down out of a cloudless sky. Corrie got up first, leaving Jack still in the shower, and went outside to have her first glimpse of Katastrophos in daylight.

Hills dominated the landscape, rising the length of the island from east to west, craggy but slight, like the bumpy vertebrae of a dinosaur. Because they rose so sharply and the island was small, they assumed a dominance far greater than their modest altitude warranted. Corrie reckoned they were probably limestone as the peaks had that bare and eroded look. Around the foothills were low-lying olive groves, rich and very old with huge-trunked trees, some of them marvellously twisted.

The Hotel Stasinopoulos was not the ugliest building Corrie had ever seen but it came pretty close. It was built into the side of a slope so that it had three storeys at the front but only one at the back. She and Jack were at the back with a balcony view of the hills and olive groves. The balconies at the front looked out across the turquoise crescent of Katastrophos Bay.

The crumpled information leaflet for *touristas* that Corrie had found on the reception desk was in peculiar English and badly misspelled but she worked out that the hotel used to be an old merchant's house in the days when pirates regularly raided the sea villages on the Greek mainland. They hid the booty (and themselves) in the hills and sea caves of obscure, hard-to-access islands like Katastrophos.

Corrie wandered around to the front and glanced up at the flaking façade of the ugly house. There were three large and hideous stone sculptures gazing down from the flat roof. She recognized them from her school days as the Gorgons – three female monsters with wings, claws, and repulsive human heads. The middle one was Medusa, which was a spooky coincidence after what she had said to Jack the previous night about Diana eyeing all the men and turning them to stone. Mischievously, Corrie recalled a particular myth in which Medusa was originally a beautiful maiden with long golden tresses, but she made the mistake of desecrating Athena's temple by lying there with Poseidon, god of the sea. Hardly a big deal, thought Corrie, because randy Poseidon exerted his power over women whenever he could. He had it off with virtually everyone in the mythological world, including his own sister. Not surprisingly, his many love affairs resulted in some strange children, including one by a sea nymph that was half-human, half-fish, and Pegasus, the flying horse, a product of his hanky-panky with Medusa. Athena, however, was outraged and turned Medusa's beautiful golden hair into living snakes.

Poseidon, thought Corrie dreamily, was a maddening personification of male bigotry and chauvinism. If you looked hard enough, you could find a parallel for everyone in Greek mythology. If Diana's roving eye made her Medusa then Ambrose, sexist and domineering, was clearly Poseidon. Corrie shielded her eyes with her hand and gazed out at the aching glitter of the sea, unaware that the ancient myth and mystery of Katastrophos were already working their powerful magic on her.

Breakfast was served outdoors, under the vine-covered pergola where Jack had promised Corrie a romantic meal alone. However, the Greek tradition of conviviality meant that everyone dipped into the same dish, so they were seated together around a big oval table made of gnarled olive wood. Not totally together, because the young Greek woman sat a little away from them, eating her breakfast under a tree. The meal consisted of orange juice, slices of seed-cake, Greek yogurt and honey. Maria fussed round them with slices of juicy melon and tiny cups of thick, sweet coffee.

Ambrose Dobson, still wearing a collar and tie and braces but with his jacket hung carefully over the back of his chair, made a huge fuss about how he couldn't drink coffee, especially strong coffee. He had a serious congestive heart complaint, he said importantly, that needed constant medication to control its pumping rate. He took tablets at exactly the same time every day and Marjorie saw to it that he had the accurate dose. Caffeine, he said, and anything else that might interfere with it, was out of the question. He turned on Maria unpleasantly.

'What do you mean, there's no decaffeinated coffee? What sort of a hotel is this?' He sighed. 'Oh very well. I'll have some camomile tea.'

Maria looked anxious and fished a dog-eared phrase book out of her apron pocket. She turned the pages nervously while Ambrose continued to grunt and grumble.

'Sorry. No camomile,' she said inevitably.

Ambrose turned scarlet. 'All right, bring me some water then,' he retorted. 'I take it you've got some of that, or do we have to get our own from a well?' He turned angrily on his wife. 'I told you we should have gone to Bournemouth again but oh no, you wanted to go abroad. Well, look where it's got you. An eighteen-hour journey under appalling conditions followed by two weeks in a primitive foreign boarding house without even the most basic requirements. I hope you're satisfied.'

Marjorie, as usual, said nothing but looked apologetic and everyone felt sorry for her except Corrie, who was willing her to stand up and give Ambrose a good clip round the ear.

Professor Gordon filled the embarrassed silence that followed by giving them a potted lecture on Katastrophos, to the undisguised boredom of his wife who had clearly heard it many times before. But to those who had not, his obvious affinity with the island and everything on it was compelling.

'Katastrophos is a sleepy, rocky, some might even say a dull little island where time, if not standing still, is at best wandering about rather aimlessly. The best Homer could say about it was that it was "good for goats".' He leaned forward and his expression became more intense. 'But don't be misled. This island has a strange, hypnotic quality – a disengagement from reality. The air around you becomes slowly more intoxicating, more magical.' His pop-eyes took on a slightly fanatical gleam as he spoke. 'You will become dreamers, bewitched and subject to indiscretions outside the boundaries of your narrow domestic lives. On Katastrophos, anything is possible.'

Tim and Ellie, already bewitched, were feeding each other chunks of melon. They wore fresh but still identical T-shirts and shorts, this time with the addition of matching canvas bucket hats and walking-boots. They reminded Jack of the Flowerpot Men. Sidney, in his customary holiday gear, had a distant, yearning look that had less to do with the magical properties of Katastrophos than the eggs, bacon, sausage, kidney, tomato, baked beans, mushrooms and fried bread that he would now be enjoying had he gone to Majorca. He was also acutely aware of a naked foot under the table that had been creeping up and down his bare thigh for the last ten minutes. If it went up the leg of his shorts, he decided, he would have to leave the table a bit rapid. He looked across at Diana, mouth-watering in a Donatella Versace sundress and he didn't need specs to see that she had nothing on underneath it. She winked at him.

'I feel no magic.' The young Greek woman who had signed the register simply as 'Sky', spoke for the first time since they arrived. She got up from her stony seat under the oleanders and came across to the table. 'I feel the synergy of vengeance and retribution,' she whispered, her eyes half-closed. 'Nemesis, winged balancer of life, dark-faced goddess and daughter of justice rules here.'

Because she hadn't spoken before, Corrie had assumed that the girl didn't speak English. In fact, her Greek accent was a barely perceptible lisp. She looked even more bizarre in the morning light, her face a caricature of black make-up above a plain black tunic with tattoos on her shoulders and arms. There was an awkward silence with everybody looking at each other but nobody knowing what to say.

'Load of blasted mumbo-jumbo,' said Ambrose eventually. 'The girl isn't all there.'

'Yes, well …' Jack stood up, 'if you'll excuse us, Corrie and I have some sightseeing to do.' He took his wife's elbow and steered her away towards the lobby. 'Hypnosis? Bewitched indiscretions? Vengeance and retribution?' he muttered out of the corner of his mouth. 'Are they barmy or is it me?'

At only twenty square kilometres, Katastrophos was easily walkable but in fact, there were very few sights to see beyond the main town of Agia Sofia, named after the saint who brought Christianity to the island. Tiny, compact and photo-snappingly pretty, the town, which was in the south of the island, had a small square, edged with such of the Venetian buildings as had survived the earthquake. A maze of whitewashed alleys led off the square with clusters of geranium-decked houses overlooking a small fishing harbour. Given the remote location of the island, it was surprising that there were no large sea-going boats. This was because most Katastrophans had little desire to sample the delights of mainland Greece, where evidence was stark of the Greek love affair with the concrete mixer and a willingness to bulldoze beautiful beaches to make a fast euro. Indeed, many of the older inhabitants had never left the island. The only building of any size was the church of St Sophia with its red dome and scarred old clock face. It housed the mummy of the island's patron saint circled by brass oil-candle holders but little else. According to the sparse tourist information, the church's revered religious icons, including St Sophia's precious relics, were kept elsewhere on the island for safety. Corrie was not surprised. The theft of icons and other valuables from Greek churches and monasteries was on the increase, with a growing market in rich collectors.

'It says here, St Sophia has special responsibilities for fecundity and childbirth.'

'She's doing a sterling job,' observed Jack.

It was true, there were children all over the place – running, swimming, playing – totally unaffected by the heat. As they came out of the dark church the sunlight was blinding, bouncing off the white walls like a magnesium flare.

'Picturesque seclusion. That's what sells this place.' Jack pointed. 'Look. Two mini markets, a bakery and a *kafeneíon* but nothing much in the way of tourist shops and no nightclubs, thankfully.'

They stopped at the *kafeneíon* where old men sat with worry beads, drinking *ouzo* and spitting at lizards in the dust. Naturally gregarious, Sidney sat amongst them enjoying a cold beer. He kept taking off his photo-sensitive sunglasses to check that they had gone dark, in case he'd paid nine-pounds-fifty for nothing.

'Morning, Jack ... Corrie.' He raised his sombrero, wincing as the noonday sun pounced on his thinning scalp. 'Bit quiet, here, isn't it? I fancy a bit of adventure, me. I wish now that I'd done one of those activity holidays where you go down potholes or crawl inside volcanoes.' He took a long swig of his beer. 'Tell you what, though. I wouldn't mind having a look up there.'

Sidney pointed to a spectacular rock rising some seventy metres out of the sea just off the island's south-east coast. On the summit they could see a ruined building with hundreds of steps leading up to it, hewn out of the stone.

'These blokes reckon it was an old monastery,' said Sid, indicating the men drowsily clicking their *komboloi*. 'It looks like it's in the sea but when you get close, it's actually on a little island connected to Katastrophos by a causeway of stepping-stones. It wouldn't take long to nip across and have a butcher's.'

Jack peered at it, shielding his eyes. 'It doesn't look like anyone's been up there for years; the steps are all overgrown.'

'Oh, there's definitely someone up there,' asserted Sid. 'I couldn't sleep last night for the heat and those bloomin' chirpy things, so I went outside to get some air. There was a light flashing inside the monastery. You don't reckon the monks still live in it, do you? Hell of a journey to fetch a newspaper in the mornings.'

He fell about at his own wit and upset two old men's backgammon board. They gabbled at him in furious Greek. He apologized in Spanish and went off to get them a couple of *ouzos* by way of compensation.

CHAPTER FOUR

On their way back to the hotel, Corrie and Jack passed Marjorie Dobson sitting quietly outside a café, sipping a small glass of lemonade.

'Hello, Marjorie. Are you enjoying Katastrophos?' said Jack genially.

She smiled politely. 'Very much, thank you, but I'm afraid Mr Dobson isn't liking it at all.' She pointed inside the dark café where Ambrose was arguing with the owner about the cost of her lemonade. He was fanning his beefy red face with his panama hat.

'He looks very hot,' said Corrie, secretly appalled that Marjorie referred to her husband as 'Mr Dobson'. 'Maybe he'd feel more relaxed sitting on the beach or having a gentle swim. I know he has to be careful, with his heart trouble, but the sea here is lovely and warm and there's a slight breeze this morning.'

'Thanks but I don't think so. He says the sea is polluted with filthy Continental effluent and what good is a beach without any deckchairs.'

'We did hear him mention this morning that he would have preferred a holiday in Bournemouth. Is that where you usually go?'

'We went once, on our honeymoon.'

'Don't tell me you haven't had a holiday since your honeymoon?' Corrie tried to keep the incredulity out of her voice.

Marjorie shook her head. 'We live in Hampshire, you see. My hubby says you don't need a holiday if you live in Hampshire.'

Tight sod, thought Jack.

'So what brought you to Katastrophos?'

'It's our anniversary next week. Thirty years. I recently came into a little money and I thought it would be nice to spend it on a holiday. I've never been abroad before. The nice young man in the travel shop said

Katastrophos was the quietest, most isolated place he could find. He said it wasn't in the package-tour brochures, being more of a location for private travellers. Not so much a place to see as to remain unseen. Ideal, I thought.'

'You didn't fancy somewhere with a bit more life, then?'

'Oh no.' She said it in a way that didn't sound wholly convincing. 'Mr Dobson dislikes mixing with other tourists – especially Germans. And Italians and Spaniards and Scandinavians and Americans. Come to think of it,' she said, a mite tartly, 'there are quite a lot of things he dislikes – nightclubs, music, dancing, foreign food, mobile phones, smokers, alcohol, rich people, poor people, gay people, old people, young people – it was a little tricky finding somewhere he *would* like.'

'But if you were paying for it, surely you were entitled to an equal say, at the very least?' Corrie felt Jack's restraining hand on her arm. She knew she was crossing the boundary between polite interest and interference but couldn't stop herself. This was the sisterhood – she was a member!

Marjorie gave her a tepid smile. 'Men always want you to put them first though, don't they?'

'No!' said Corrie with vigour, 'and even if they do, you don't have to go along with it.' Has this woman no balls at all? she wondered.

Ambrose emerged from the café, his face beetroot.

'That lemonade, Marjorie, has just cost the equivalent of fifty p. Make sure you drink it all …' Then he noticed Jack and Corrie. 'Oh. Good morning,' he mumbled almost grudgingly. 'Come along, Marjorie. I can't stand here gossiping. I need to buy some repellent for these blasted mosquitoes.'

He removed his panama, delicately so as not to dislodge his hairpiece, and slapped himself hard on the back of the neck. Corrie's hand ached to swat the next one for him.

'Naturally, we shan't be staying here,' he said self-importantly. 'I propose to return to Hampshire first thing in the morning.'

'I don't think we can, dear,' said Marjorie, timidly.

He snorted. 'Don't talk rubbish. Of course we can. I shall instruct—'

'Actually,' interrupted Jack, 'Marjorie's right. As I understand it, once the ferry has dropped off any visitors, it doesn't return until it's time to take them back. There's no other transport to the mainland.'

'What?' Ambrose was flaming. 'You mean we're stranded on this abominable island for two weeks whether we like it or not?'

Jack nodded. ''Fraid so.'

Dobson turned on his wife. 'Now see what you've done, you stupid woman!'

They watched him strut angrily away, carrying his suit jacket carefully over one arm with Marjorie hurrying obediently along beside him. Corrie opened her mouth to vent her barely contained spleen but before she could speak Jack said calmly, 'Corrie, it's none of our business.'

They went for a swim and a long laze on the beach, then meandered back to the Hotel Stasinopoulos in time for a drink and a shower before dinner. Outside, among the olive trees, a tiny hobgoblin of an old woman was dozing on a camp bed. She was no bigger than a ten-year-old and wore a thick black dress and a black head-scarf. The skin of her face was soft and brown and thick-looking with deep pink wrinkles. Witchlike, her long chin curved firmly upwards towards her nose.

Outside the hotel kitchen, Yanni Stasinopoulos was chasing rats away from a flat, broad tree-stump that served as a chopping block and a place to bash an octopus tender. Morsels of meat and fish still adhered to the rough surface, rotting gently in the heat. Corrie thought of food regulations and her scrupulous attention to hygiene when preparing meals for Coriander's Cuisine and shuddered. It would be a miracle if they didn't all get food poisoning.

Yanni spoke a little English but not nearly as much as his wife Maria, who handled most of the communications with the guests. Seeing Jack and Corrie, he shouted 'Ya sas' and a few other greetings in loud, effusive Greek. Seeing them glance at the old woman snoring in the shady olive grove, he obviously felt some introduction was called for. He jabbed a thumb in her direction.

'That – Ariadne,' he explained. 'She – Maria's *mitéra* – er – mother. She cook.'

The expression that accompanied this last statement implied that he would not recommend the house menu. Ariadne, they discovered, was also the island's midwife, clairvoyant and general hot line to St Sophia. She was also passionately fond of Professor Gordon, considering him a king among men. He could often be found in her kitchen, gossiping to her in Greek and stirring things in her black, satanic cooking pots.

In response, Jack pointed at Corrie. 'This – Corrie. She – my wife. She also cook. Ow!' Corrie had slid her hand down to Jack's buttock and pinched it hard. When they had agreed to keep quiet about Jack's job and their honeymoon status, they had also agreed not to reveal that Corrie was a professional caterer. Experience had shown that in any kind of food emergency, people would expect her to pop on a pinny and slap up a meal. But it was too late: a look of hunger and envy had flitted briefly across Yanni's lugubrious features.

'Oi, Yanni mate.' It was Sidney, calling from his balcony. 'What are those lights I keep seeing up the old monastery?'

Yanni shook his head. 'No lights, *kyríe* Foskett.'

'You sure? They flash on and off in the middle of the night.'

'No lights. Nobody there.' Yanni looked uncomfortable.

'Can I go up there tomorrow and have a bit of a poke round?'

'Sorry, not possible,' said Yanni. 'Is forbidden. Holy place of St Sophia. Nobody go there except on pilgrimage.' He turned and disappeared into the kitchen.

As they went inside the hotel Corrie glanced up again at the hideous Medusa sneering down at them from the roof. She was evil personified. Little wonder that Perseus performed a ritual murder on her, a revenge killing committed with the full complicity of the Olympians who provided him with most of the equipment he needed. A sudden movement at one of the second-storey windows attracted her attention. Sky, the young Greek woman, was staring down at them. She had a look that Corrie could only describe as malevolent. It was chilling and unexpected and despite the heat, Corrie shivered slightly.

'Did you see that?' she asked Jack.

'See what?'

'Sky. She was watching us from her room. Her face was full of ... well, hatred almost. What's she got against us, do you think?'

'Nothing,' said Jack. 'How could she? She only met us yesterday. We might not be the most loveable couple in the world but we don't usually repulse people within twenty-four hours. Don't worry about it. She's one of those tortured souls who hate everybody, including themselves. You heard all that metaphysical hippy nonsense at breakfast about Nemesis and retribution.'

'I wanted to be a hippy when I was a teenager,' said Corrie nostalgically. 'I even went to Glastonbury once, to "feel the vibes".'

'So did I,' said Jack. 'Only I went to feel the collars. You didn't try to get in under the fence or smoke anything dodgy, did you?'

'Who, me?' said Corrie, crossing her fingers behind her back.

*

In the cool, violet-grey twilight of the approaching evening, people gravitated slowly back from various places on the island to the big olive table under the vines for dinner.

'*Mezédes*,' said Maria, indicating appetizers in lots of dishes. They were undoubtedly the work of Ariadne because they were, for the most part, distinctly unappetizing. Some of the ingredients had been so mutilated that even Corrie had trouble identifying them but she recognized cold stuffed vine leaves, aubergine soaked in olive oil until slimy, fried squid tentacles and a bowl of mud-coloured taramasaláta garnished with olives. In fact, everything was garnished with olives, which were obviously in glut. The only thing that looked remotely edible was a colourful Greek salad. The big wooden bowl contained thick slices of juicy red tomatoes, chunks of peeled cucumber, red onion, lettuce, green peppers, *feta* cheese and the ubiquitous olives. Oregano and olive oil were sprinkled liberally on top.

'What are they?' Sid whispered to Corrie, pointing to a bowl of small brown shrivelled things. He was ravenous but wary.

'They're called *marídes tiganítes*,' she whispered back. 'Small fish. They take them straight from the sea, dip them in flour and fry them.'

'What – you mean they don't take the innards out first?'

'No.'

'What about that?' He pointed to the muddy taramasaláta.

'Fish roe beaten smooth and mixed with olive oil. It's normally pink, though.'

He grimaced. 'And those?'

'Octopus balls.'

'I didn't know an octopus had ...' He was interrupted by Ambrose.

'This food is disgusting,' he declared officiously. 'I propose to draft a strong letter to the travel company demanding my money back, which I shall pass round for everyone to sign.'

'Blooming nerve,' said Corrie to Jack. 'It wasn't even his money – it was Marjorie's.'

People began sampling morsels of the *mezédes* with caution. By a happy quirk of fate, Ellie was left-handed and Tim was right-handed. They had discovered that as long as Ellie sat on Tim's left, they could fork up their food and still keep an arm around each other. The communal dishes of food meant people tended to move around the table, Greek style, rather than pass the dishes, so Tim and Ellie often had to change seats several times during a meal in order to keep hold of each other, but they didn't seem to mind at all. Now, Tim stood up and walked round to the end of the table to hijack the Greek salad.

'Excuse me.' His voice, rather louder than his usual apologetic *sotto voce*, cut through the preprandial hum. 'It's for Ellie,' he explained, defensively. 'She's vegetarian. She can't eat this other food. She only likes lettuce and things like that.'

Professor Gordon, who had been happily chewing on gobbets of raw, marinated squid and chatting earnestly to Yanni, suddenly rose to his feet and leaned across the table. He thrust his whiskery face, belligerent and intimidating, into Ellie's until his nose was just inches away and his ginger hair and hers were barely separable in the twilight.

'I suppose you know,' he barked, eyes bulging, 'that a lettuce emits a virtual scream when you tear it from the ground. Plants are living things to be studied, nurtured and conserved, not stuffed in your mouth like chocolate. They have a genesis, a fundamental life process that a silly girl like you can only wonder at.'

The professor, now well into his stride, dismissed poor, cringing Ellie with overt contempt and turned to lecture the wider audience.

'Plants are the single most important part of our lives. They generate the oxygen, fuel and medicine that allow so-called higher life forms to exist. Plants absorb carbon dioxide, a greenhouse gas that in large amounts affects global climate. What more evidence do you need to treat them with respect instead of mindlessly ripping them from the ground and ramming them down your ignorant throats?'

There was a stunned silence, then Ambrose sneered: 'Poppycock! Everything we eat comes from plants, either directly or indirectly. They're at the bottom of the food chain. If you're implying we should leave them alone and eat only meat, you're an idiot. Animals eat plants and we eat animals.'

Professor Gordon turned and stared at Ambrose for a long time. Then he spoke in a cold, menacing tone.

'You have a heart complaint, Mr Dobson. What medication keeps you alive?'

'Digoxin, if it's any of your business.'

'And digoxin, now synthesized, is a drug originally derived from the foxglove plant, *Digitalis lanata*. I wonder, Mr Dobson, how many plants gave their lives in order to ensure yours, and if, indeed, it was an equitable exchange. Personally, I think not.'

Ambrose jumped to his feet, fists clenched, temper blackening his puffy features. 'How dare you!'

Several voices joined the protest.

'That was a bit much, Professor ...'

'Take it easy ...'

'Cuthbert, don't be a jerk ...'

Corrie was startled to see Jack on his feet, ready to get between the two men. It wasn't like him to overreact and only hours before, he had been warning her not to interfere in other people's business. Maybe there was something particular about this conflict that Jack wanted to avert. In the event, the potentially explosive situation was defused by Sidney emerging, clench-faced, from the gents.

'The prof's right,' he said. 'Don't eat the stuffed tomatoes.'

The band arrived shortly after. Three solemn old men from the town of St Sophia carrying *bouzoúki*. They seated themselves on the edge of the terrace, now twinkling with candle lanterns, and soon they were twanging away. It might have been a jolly dinner but the unpleasantness of the disagreement still hung over them.

Yanni, who had not understood the cause of the angry exchange but sensed an atmosphere, served copious quantities of wine from proper wine bottles, which was an improvement on the anonymous carafes, even though the bottles had no labels. Everyone agreed that for wine made locally on such a tiny island, it was astonishingly good. Sky took some food and went straight up to her room. She had come to Katastrophos, she said, to bathe her wounded spirit, not party with peasants.

'What's up with her?' asked Sidney, refilling his glass. 'Bit surly, isn't she?' He smiled his cheeky, lighthouse smile. 'Sounds like a weather forecast.' He pursed his lips and spoke in a camp voice. 'Tomorrow the Sky will be Surly.'

The professor, in that conveniently absent-minded way that eccentrics cultivate, instantly forgot his angry outburst and was smiling lovingly at his young wife, radiant in emerald-green silk, her golden hair tied up with a matching scarf. By the time Maria arrived with the main course, a kind of glutinous stew with lumps of gristly meat floating in it, they were all merry enough to eat some without shuddering.

When the band stopped for a break, Maria took off her apron and stepped diffidently into the centre of the floor.

'Tomorrow,' she announced, 'it is the Feast of St Sophia, the patron saint of our island, and my mother, she will prepare the special meal to celebrate.'

'Oh good,' muttered Sid, picking something stringy out of his teeth.

Maria's eyes sparkled with hope and anticipation and she clasped her hands together excitedly. 'This is a very special time for the women of Katastrophos. Before the feast, all the childless women will be given a lamp, then we make the pilgrimage up the many steps to the monastery where St Sophia's precious relics are kept.'

She turned and pointed to the massive rock rising out of the amethyst sea, the monastery ruins now standing stark and forbidding against the moonlight.

'There, we must first eat a small piece of the wick, then we light our lamps and make the journey back down. Those women whose lamps still burn after they reach the ground have consumed the blessing of our saint and will be ...' she tweaked the well-thumbed phrase book from her apron pocket and searched desperately for the English, '... they will be fruitful,' she finished, triumphantly.

'What does she mean – hic – fruitful?' asked Sid, a bit drunk.

'In the club, mate,' translated Jack.

'You mean they get pregnant just by going up there?' said Sid, whose spiritual edge was somewhat blunted. After twenty years of unblocking other people's lavatories, he saw the world for what it was. 'But don't they have to ... you know ...' he gestured vaguely with his hands, '... first?'

Jack was spared from trying to explain the island's mystic interaction between sex and superstition, because the *bouzoúki* players had started up again and Diana, in a cloud of Chanel, scooped Sidney up and swept him on to the tiny square of paved dance floor. With scant respect for ethnic accuracy, they began performing a spirited Spanish flamenco to the Greek music. Sid had tied Diana's silk scarf around his head, bandit-style, and she wore his sombrero.

Diana was spectacular. She stamped her heels and twirled sinuously around Sidney, swishing her skirts in a way that gave the audience a sporadic but dazzling view of her minuscule knickers. Everybody clapped and laughed, enjoying the impromptu cabaret apart from Ambrose, who sat at the far end of the table wearing an expression that was part disapproval, and part something decidedly more visceral.

'Would you like to dance?' Yanni held out his hand to Marjorie. For an older lady, he felt she looked unnaturally subdued and downcast. He had, after all, been brought up on an island whose culture decreed that matriarchs automatically enjoyed respect and authority.

Immediately, Ambrose snapped, 'Marjorie, I forbid you to get up on that floor and make a fool of yourself. Stay where you are.'

Marjorie shook her head regretfully at Yanni and said, 'Óchi. No. Thank you, Yanni.' Then, as if she felt her husband needed defending, she turned to Corrie sitting beside her. 'Ambrose doesn't like dancing. It's not that he doesn't like me to enjoy myself. I shouldn't want people to think that. It's just that he mustn't dance himself because of his bad heart and it upsets him to watch other people doing it. He's never really got over being deprived of his career, you see. He had to take early retirement on the grounds of ill-health.'

'What work did he do?' asked Corrie, wondering who would employ a man with such intolerant, outdated views.

'He sold insurance. Life policies, mostly.' She smiled. 'Handy, really, because I was able to get him well insured before his heart complaint was diagnosed.'

The flamenco had developed into a Paso Doble. Diana held out her skirt like a matador's cape and Sid, holding two forks against his head for the bull's horns, bent down, pawed the ground and charged at it. His aim, impaired by several glasses of wine, was well off and he missed the target by miles. Head down, he carried on galloping and, as he shot past the end of the table, one of the forks caught in Ambrose's toupee and whipped it clean off.

Diana collapsed in hysterics, as did most people including the dour *bouzoúki* players. Sheepishly, Sid held out the fork to Ambrose with the wig hanging upside down from the prongs like a hairy brown bat.

'Sorry, mate. It must have been loose. I expect the heat melted the glue.'

Furious, Ambrose snatched it and stomped off inside the hotel and up to his room, presumably to gum it back on. Marjorie followed him.

It was one o'clock before the party broke up and people began drifting off to bed. Corrie was still giggling as they climbed the winding stairs.

'Did you see Ambrose? He was livid.'

'I know,' said Jack. 'I kept wanting to shout "keep your hair on".'

'No sense of humour at all,' chortled Corrie. 'He had a face like a smacked ...' she stopped and put a finger to her lips, pulling Jack back into a darkened recess in the stairs, out of sight.

The sounds of heavy breathing and urgent whispers were coming from the landing above and intuition told her this was not a good time to barge through.

'Come on, love, I know you want it. You've been asking for it ever since you got here – going around half-naked, flaunting everything you've got. Well, how about it, then?'

Jack and Corrie looked at each other, shocked. The man had lowered his voice to a hoarse whisper, but it was unmistakable nevertheless.

The now familiar Manhattan drawl came back, cool and unperturbed, with an edge of contempt. 'If you don't take your hand off my tit, you sad old creep, I'll deck you.'

They heard a scuffle and Jack made a move to climb the stairs and intervene but Corrie stopped him. She suspected a woman like Diana would have handled similar situations many times before and with consummate ease, so it would be less embarrassing all round if she sorted it on her own without witnesses. The man whispered again, this time louder and with more insistence.

'You know you don't mean that, sweetheart. Women are all the same – saying "no" when they really mean "yes". You're gagging for it really. Just let me feel under that skirt and I'll soon show you what I can—'

There was the sound of a slap and the wheedling whisper turned into angry abuse. The voice was panting with pent-up sexual excitement.

'Don't come the virtuous wife with me, you gold-digging little tart. I've watched you, teasing and flirting and playing hard to get. Well, you've asked for it and now you're going to get it ...'

There was a scream of pain. Seconds later, Ambrose Dobson limped past them down the stairs in a half-crouch, his hands between his legs.

'If that was his best chat-up line,' whispered Jack laconically, 'it didn't work.'

Then Diana appeared from the shadows, calmly smoothing down her skirt. She rubbed her knee briefly, then sashayed elegantly along the landing, hips swaying, and disappeared into the room she shared with the professor.

'I don't *believe* that man!' exploded Corrie. 'This isn't even his floor. He must have been purposely lying in wait for her. Not only is he an insufferable, hypocritical pig, he's a dirty old man as well. Treating his wife like a servant then trying it on with Diana behind her back.'

'He has to be the world's biggest optimist,' said Jack. 'I've never under-stood what makes blokes like that think they're even in with a chance.'

'Sheer arrogance, that's what. To Ambrose, all women are fair game, like pieces of meat. He belongs in the Stone Age, shambling about carrying a club with his knuckles dragging on the ground.'

'Why does Marjorie put up with him?'

'Don't ask me. I'd have shoved him off the ferry on the way over.'

Corrie suddenly stopped and bit her lip. She was thinking about life insurance, Medusa and Poseidon and what the professor had said about indiscretions outside the boundaries of their narrow domestic lives. This was indeed a strange, hypnotic island.

When they reached their room, Corrie opened the windows and went out on to the balcony. The air was hot and very still. Even the cicadas had stopped chirping. Katastrophos seemed to be holding its breath, sensing a storm. From the back of the hotel she had a clear view of the hills and, to the south, the monastery ruins soaring high above the dark, brooding sea. She stood for some time, not moving, then she called out suddenly to Jack.

'Quick, come here and look at this!'

Jack ambled out on to the balcony wearing his pyjama bottoms and with a foaming toothbrush in his mouth. 'What?'

'Look.' She gestured up at the summit of the towering rock. 'Sidney was right. There *is* someone in the monastery. There's a light flashing up there.'

Jack took the toothbrush out of his mouth and pointed with it. 'Yes, and look there.'

Far out on the silent indigo sea, another light signalled back in response.

CHAPTER FIVE

The next day dawned humid and heavy. The threat of a storm had become a promise. Jack had seen Greek island storms – they were dramatic and dangerous. It was a spectacle you never forgot and more important, it was distracting, so it was crucial that he stayed alert and ready to act.

He had known from the start that this assignment carried more than an acceptable degree of risk. Under normal conditions, he would have found a safer way to handle it but as the chief super had pointed out, the conditions were far from normal and there really was no other way.

'You'll be flying by the seat of your pants on this one, Jack.' You could always rely on the DCS to dredge up a weary platitude to boost your confidence. There had been no time to plan properly or do sufficient groundwork and knee-jerk policing was not Jack's style. Detection based on hunches and intuition had a nasty habit of going balls-up when you got to court. But he acknowledged that this was an exceptional case, requiring exceptional measures and the price of getting it wrong was high. What he had not foreseen was that he would be trying to operate whilst impeded by a bunch of muppets. What the hell was wrong with everybody? If he didn't know better, he would say they were doing all they could to foul things up on purpose. According to his sparse background information, most of these individuals were reasonably rational, well-balanced people when in their natural habitat. But from the moment they arrived on the island, Katastrophos seemed to have loosened everyone's screws.

There was that pompous old idiot Ambrose trying, impossibly, to jump Diana, whilst Diana was quite obviously planning to get into Sid's shorts at the earliest possible opportunity. Ostensibly, that was none of Jack's business except it could be a real complication if she managed it, and he had no doubt that she would. It was impossible to get any sense out of Tim and Ellie who were going about like a couple of tits in a trance. He had no clear idea of what, if anything, he should to do about them but the situation needed watching. As for Sky, the unhinged hippy – God alone knew what planet Sky was on. Nobody had briefed him about her.

The professor's loony rant against murderous salad-eaters had come as no surprise, it was predictable and in character, but what with Maria and her mother summoning up saintly impregnation, Yanni looking shifty most of the time and ghostly lights flashing in the middle of the night, Jack was starting to wish he had access to some back-up. Even his lovely, wacky Corrie was weirder than usual – banging on about Greek gods and Marjorie's life insurance. But that was nothing compared to the strop she'd go into if she knew he was still on duty on their honeymoon. Thank heavens for Sidney. What you saw was what you got. Nothing remotely inscrutable about good old Sid.

He just hoped that when push came to shove – as he was now certain it must – they wouldn't get in his way. Or, even more important, that they wouldn't get hurt in the cross-fire.

The storm was closing in. On the balcony, Corrie watched the sea churning, dark and restless, spawning tales of Poseidon riding the mistral and shipwrecking fleets. Diana was lying down, the atmospheric pressure, she said, had triggered one of her migraines. Tim and Ellie, the human book ends, had gone into town to see if they could buy matching rain-hoods. Ambrose was in the lobby, complaining to Yanni that his room had not been cleaned properly, while Marjorie stood patiently by, looking at her watch to ensure she gave him his tablets at the exact moment they were due. Nobody knew where Sky was. She had muttered something obscure about going out to look for a systemic ambience in which to balance her chakras.

'Where's the professor?' asked Jack.

Corrie came in from the balcony. 'Maria said he's been out since dawn with his sample case, looking for specimens.'

'I think I'll just go and see if he's all right,' said Jack. 'Will you be OK on your own?'

''Course. Since when have you been interested in botany?'

Jack grinned. 'Just because I'm a big, hairy copper doesn't mean I can't appreciate a pretty flower.'

Sidney was in the bar, looking bored. Good, thought Jack. His suspicion that Diana might not be lying down on her own was unfounded – at least for the moment.

'Going somewhere interesting, squire?'

Jack shrugged. 'Depends what you mean by interesting. I'm going to watch Professor Gordon nurturing his little friends.'

'I'll have some of that,' said Sid, putting on his sombrero.

They spotted the professor's orange anorak in the olive grove, flitting from flower to flower like a restless butterfly. Jack could see that he was totally engrossed and expected him to be annoyed at the intrusion, but he seemed genuinely delighted to see them and more than willing to give them a guided tour of the island's flora.

'It's so gratifying that ordinary men like yourselves, from quite mundane walks of life, should nevertheless have sufficient intelligence to appreciate the fascinating botanical world that we are privileged to share with plants.'

The professor said this in wide-eyed innocence, simply stating a fact and quite oblivious to the condescension.

It would be interesting, thought Sid, to see how useful his plants were next time his pipes burst. He'd be blooming glad of a mundane plumber, then. He bent down to examine a small bristly cucumber growing out of the stony ground.

'I wouldn't touch …' warned the professor. 'Oh dear. Too late.'

The fruit exploded violently, squirting out a sticky liquid all over Sid's hand.

'That's an *Ecballium elaterium*,' said the professor affectionately. 'The squirting cucumber. Active right through to September. Magnificently virile. See how far he spreads his seed in just one ejaculation.'

'Very impressive,' said Sid, wiping it on his shorts. 'I went scuba-diving in Majorca to look at a cucumber but it wasn't like that.'

'What was it like?' asked Jack.

'Dunno. I couldn't get me specs on under the face mask.'

'I'd keep an eye on your hand, old boy. That mucilaginous liquid can cause mild irritation, even inflammation, if you're susceptible. That's why I wear these.' The professor stroked the spent fruit with hands protected by surgical gloves. 'He's most efficient, this little chap. His juice is a very potent purgative.'

'Nice for him,' said Sid.

They watched the professor taking specimens expertly with a scalpel so as not to harm the host plants.

'What a whopping great onion!' Sid lifted a huge bulb out of the sample case. It must have weighed six pounds. 'Don't tell me you're taking it back for Ariadne to cook for the feast tonight?'

'Goodness me, no.' Professor Gordon reclaimed it carefully from Sid and bent to put it back in the case. 'That's an *Urginea maritima* – the sea squill – and you're right, it belongs to the same family as onions and garlic. But its uses are pharmaceutical, not culinary. This one is the white variety – used as a diuretic, stimulant, and expectorant, but frankly, I wouldn't recommend it for medicinal purposes unless you know exactly what you are doing.' He straightened up. 'There's also a red variety. Slightly toxic but nothing severe. Peasants on Katastrophos make rat poison from it.'

'Does it work?' asked Jack.

The professor shrugged. 'Sometimes the rats die and sometimes they don't.'

Professor Gordon meandered on slowly, his bulging eyes swivelling from right to left like a chameleon's, on the look-out for more samples for his experiments. Jack reckoned he must have worked this part of the island for years, because he knew every inch. He and Sidney ambled alongside, watching with interest.

'You certainly know your subject, Professor,' said Jack. 'I suppose you teach it to others through your books and lectures. It must be very rewarding to be able to share your knowledge with another generation of botanists.'

Professor Gordon stopped and took on the evangelical, almost fanatical gleam that he always acquired when speaking about his research.

'My specialism, as you know, is in plant-based medicines. Did you know that more than eighty per cent of the world's population uses plant remedies either in part or entirely?'

'No, but I'm not surprised,' said Sid. 'My old gran was forever dosing us with jollop she'd boiled up on the stove. Senna pods were the worst. Didn't half make you—'

'Much work,' continued the professor, swiftly, 'has already been done based upon the traditions of the Chinese, Egyptians and American Indians. Information on plant medicines has been handed down over the centuries. Even as we speak, scientists are investigating newly discovered cultures and this has resulted in the introduction of a number of new plant compounds into pharmaceutical research.'

He paused and his face took on a fervent flush. 'But I can assure you, gentlemen, those people have barely scratched the surface. They cannot begin to imagine the amazing discoveries I have made, the incredible power that I can unleash from my plants.' He waved a scornful, dismissive hand. 'A tuppenny-ha'penny botanist announces the discovery of a "wonder herbal medicine" responsible for miracle cures and suddenly everyone is using it. Well, very soon, I shall be more famous than any of them and my genius will at last be recognized world wide. I shall be numbered among the greatest botanists of our time.' His staring eyes glazed over, dreaming of the adulation.

'Really? And how's that, Professor?'

'Oh yes indeed. I'm honoured to say that I have been offered the position of master at a prestigious Swiss university. When I take up the post, which will be very soon, I plan to endow the Gordon Botany Research Scholarships. Botanists will flock there from all over the world to marvel at my revolutionary research and study at my feet.'

Jack's eyebrows went up and he whistled. 'Scholarships in Switzerland, eh? That'll cost a few quid, won't it?'

'Naturally, funding any scholarship is expensive and these particularly so.' He spread his hands modestly. 'But happily, money isn't a problem. It's my work that's important.'

'Your missus is lying down with a migraine,' said Sid. 'Haven't you got anything in your revolutionary research to cure it?'

'My dear Foskett, I just wish Diana shared your confidence in me. She needs good old feverfew, *Tanacetum parthenium*. It contains a serotonin antagonist – very effective at lowering the frequency and severity of the headaches. It can even abort early attacks. If I could persuade her to chew a few fresh leaves she would find it most effective but she won't try any of what she calls my "quack cures". Insists on tablets from the doctor.'

While they were talking, Sidney had been ambling slowly backwards with his hands in his pockets. Suddenly, he tripped on a root and sat down hard in a large bush with purple flowers.

'Oh, bad luck, old chap!' exclaimed the professor. 'You've found a *Vitex agnus-castus*. It's called the chaste tree. Ancient Greeks and Crusaders believed that the scent of its flowers was an anti-aphrodisiac.'

'That's just what I need,' muttered Sid, struggling to get up. Somehow, though, he didn't think sniffing a flower would protect him from the irresistible and persistent attentions of the delicious Diana.

The professor laughed. 'Don't worry. We'll find you some saffron. That has the opposite effect, they say.' He winked. 'Its aphrodisiac properties are believed to be so powerful, you have to consult a doctor to obtain it on some Greek islands.' He chuckled at their scepticism. 'Oh yes. Like many others, this ancient belief has somehow managed to climb into the prescription book of the modern chemist. But of course, a prescription would be impossible here.'

'Why?' Sid wanted to know.

'Because sadly, Katastrophos has no doctor or chemist.'

'So what happens if you're ill?' asked Jack.

'If you need any kind of medical attention other than from Ariadne, who delivers all the island's babies, you have to go to the mainland for it, I'm afraid, and that means getting old Charon to ferry you across.' He looked philosophical. 'Unfortunately, he's a bit elusive – something of an entrepreneur. In the past, when there's been a serious accident or emergency, by the time they've found him and he's come over and ferried the patient back to hospital, it's usually been too late. I suppose that's the price we pay for the isolation and seclusion we enjoy on this splendid little island.'

They continued in silence for a while, assimilating this rather uncomfortable piece of information. Then Professor Gordon stopped and bent to admire some exotic blooms with crimson centres and long yellow stamens, thick and swollen with pollen. He fondled one lovingly, almost sensually, then sniffed his fingers.

'Look gentlemen. *Hibiscus syriacus*. The most beautiful, tenacious and feminine plant there is. What a joy to see her in high summer, thrusting her musky pudenda at us from beneath her flowing skirts.'

He straightened up to put an arm around Sid's shoulders and spoke discreetly in his ear, man to man.

'You know, in my erotic dreams, women and hibiscus are often interchangeable.'

Sid caught Jack's eye but resisted the urge to tap his forehead.

They left Professor Gordon chatting up his hibiscus and sauntered back to the hotel for a cold beer.

'Brilliant man, the professor,' said Sid.

'Brilliant,' agreed Jack.

'Loaded too. Did you see that Rolex on his wrist? Not much change out of twenty grand there.'

'Nope.'

'He must have a blinding brain to remember all that plant malarkey, never mind writing books and stuff.'

'Blinding.'

'And now he's going to be Master of a University with scholarships named after him. Amazing bloke.'

'Amazing.'

Sid strolled on in silence for a while, thinking about squirting cucumbers and chastity bushes and the pudenda of a hibiscus. Then he said:

'You don't think the prof could be ever so slightly barmy, do you?'

'No "could be" about it,' replied Jack.

Back at the Hotel Stasinopoulos, Corrie had wandered down to the kitchen to satisfy her caterer's morbid curiosity regarding the special menu for the Feast of St Sophia. People would need something fairly substantial after their pilgrimage up to the monastery and in her view, a menu consisting of the superfluous parts of cephalopods swimming in olive oil would not be sufficient.

Ariadne, still heavily garbed in black, was sweating over a brace of bubbling cauldrons. She looked like one of the witches in Macbeth only smaller and with more warts. Maria said her *mitéra* – mama – had been up since dawn, preparing the food. It clearly took a great deal of time and effort, thought Corrie, to make decent ingredients taste disgusting. Apparently, the only English words Ariadne knew were Winston and Churchill which made conversation rather limited. Any communication had therefore to be in mime.

'*Ya soo*, Ariadne. What are we having for dinner tonight?' Corrie mimed eating with a knife and fork.

Ariadne pointed her meat cleaver at the olive grove outside the kitchen door where a goat bell jangled. The goat, unaware of its *table d'hôte* status, was chewing contentedly on some left-over lumps of meat from the previous night's stew. Probably the remains of his old nanny, shuddered Corrie, blanching slightly. She left Ariadne to her stifling kitchen and escaped gratefully outside into the fresh air. As she passed the tree stump that served as a chopping block, she noticed the bodies of several dead rats around its roots. At least someone had seen fit to exercise some rodent control at last. Either that or the rats had eaten some of Ariadne's *mezédes*, she thought wryly. It was too much to expect Katastrophos to have a public health inspector but she fervently hoped Ariadne would at least remove the corpses before she dealt with the goat.

On the terrace, she found Jack and Sidney drinking beer and teasing Maria who was already wound up to a state of barely suppressed religious fervour. She and Yanni had longed for a child from the day they married, parenthood seemingly being the acknowledged pinnacle of happiness and success to which most Katastrophans aspired. Yanni and Maria had been trying for years and to be blunt, they were not getting any younger. Each year, the Feast of St Sophia and her promise of fruitfulness rekindled their hopes.

'You will come, too, *kiría* Dawes?' Maria begged Corrie. 'The more women who undertake the pilgrimage, the happier it will make St Sophia. Perhaps then, she will bless me.'

Corrie hesitated. 'Well, I don't know …'

Back home in south London, if anyone had suggested to Corrie that it was possible to induce pregnancy by climbing up to an old ruin, swallowing a bit of lampwick, and climbing down again, she would have advised them to seek help. But now, on this strange island, ominous with myth and superstition she no longer felt wholly positive about anything.

'Go on, Corrie,' urged Jack, grinning. 'It's only a "girls' night out". What harm can it do?'

What indeed.

Maria must have applied similar emotional blackmail to the other guests, because at dusk Corrie and Jack were surprised to see Diana, Ellie and even Sky lining up with various other childless women from around the island to make the pilgrimage up to the monastery. Marjorie Dobson had come to provide moral support and to enjoy the unaccustomed luxury of an evening without Ambrose, who had dismissed the whole thing as pagan balderdash. Besides, it looked like rain and he had no intention of getting his hairpiece wet. He remained alone in his room, reading. Reading and brooding.

Like most self-opinionated, overbearing men, Ambrose Dobson was also very vain. He therefore remained incandescent with rage at Diana's humiliating and ill-considered rejection of his advances. He was in no doubt that before that ridiculous Gordon fellow picked her up, she had been a hooker in some seedy Brooklyn bar or stripping in a club similar to the ones he frequented in Soho when the mood took him. He'd met her sort before. Far from attacking him, she should have considered herself highly flattered that he, Ambrose Dobson, Freemason and respected senior Rotarian, had even looked at her.

Slappers like her needed putting in their place, teaching a lesson they would not forget.

The Feast of St Sophia was something of a party night as well as a saintly pilgrimage and small crowds of islanders had assembled outside the Hotel Stasinopoulos. While the childless women prepared themselves spiritually for the climb, the men did the same, knocking back large quantities of the excellent local wine, singing rowdily and, when they remembered, tossing the occasional small libation to St Sophia.

At the propitious hour the throng began to wind in a long crocodile from the hotel to the short causeway of stepping-stones that linked Katastrophos to the tiny islet where the ruined monastery towered high above the rocks. The sea surrounding the causeway was vividly phosphorescent. Streams of metallic green sparks swirled past, mesmerizing and dazzling.

It was, according to the professor, a phenomenon that occurs in Greek waters during the summer months and is at its brightest when a thunderstorm is imminent. 'The cause of this display,' he said, 'is *Noctiluca miliaris*, a minute, unicellular animal only just visible to the naked eye.'

No one doubted his scientific explanation, but the effect of the phosphorescence was strangely transcendental and added to the trancelike piety of the pilgrimage.

Once they reached the foot of the steps the men began to shout encouragement.

'You going up, Marjie?' called Sid. 'I notice Old Misery Guts isn't here to cheer you on.'

Marjorie Dobson laughed. 'Me? Oh no dear. I think it's a bit late for me, don't you? And anyway, I believe only childless women are allowed to take part in the actual climb.'

'I didn't realize you and Ambrose had children,' said Corrie. In her experience, most women mentioned their children within ten seconds of meeting you.

Marjorie's eyes misted over. 'Oh yes. Daniel, our son, a fine, clever boy. Well, he's a man now, of course. He's a systems analyst in London. Very successful. He has a beautiful apartment overlooking the Thames.'

'Do you see much of him?'

Marjorie's happy smile faded for the first time that evening.

'No, I'm afraid not. He and Ambrose don't get on.'

Corrie wasn't in the least surprised. She couldn't imagine an intelligent, free-thinking systems analyst seeing eye to eye with an old-fashioned bigot like Ambrose, even if he was his son.

'That's a pity, but surely that doesn't stop *you* from seeing him?'

She looked guilty. 'I visit Dan and his partner secretly sometimes, when Ambrose is at one of his Lodge meetings. He'd be very angry if he knew.'

'Is she nice, your son's girlfriend?'

'That's the root of the problem, actually. It isn't a girlfriend, it's a boyfriend. And yes, he's very nice.'

That explained it. Corrie wished she hadn't probed. Sometimes, she thought crossly, I'm like a dog with a flipping bone. Wind your neck in, Coriander, and mind your own business.

Surprisingly, since no plants were instrumental in St Sophia's miracle, Professor Gordon was wildly overexcited and rushed about, eyes popping, handing out the lamps and wishing the women luck in vociferous Greek.

Scrambling up and down hundreds of filthy steps encrusted with seabird droppings – probably in the rain – did not strike Corrie as an occasion requiring designer chic. Diana, however, looked stunning in a white silk shirt, very brief shorts and a tangerine, cashmere pashmina tied loosely around her shoulders. Only her customary four-inch heels were missing, replaced by a pair of Jimmy Choo flats. Corrie had opted for one of Jack's old polo shirts, a pair of Tesco trainers and maroon leggings that made her bum look like a massive plum. She determined not to stand anywhere near Diana.

'You don't really think we'll all get pregnant, do you?' simpered Ellie, giggling. Tim was kissing her goodbye at some length, as if she were about to climb Everest.

'No way, honey!' Diana laughed. She nodded at her husband, full of wine and bluster. 'In my case, it would take a miracle bigger than anything St Sophia could rustle up.'

'Missing you already,' trilled Ellie to Tim.

'Missing you too,' he replied, kissing her again.

Sky, as usual, stood apart looking distant and troubled. Corrie called to her. It didn't hurt to try and be friendly.

'I see Maria twisted your arm, as well.'

'Not at all,' she replied in her cold, formal English. 'I should very much like to have my partner's baby in nine months, but unlike the others …' she indicated the excited women, 'I know that cannot happen.'

Corrie was desperate to ask why but her new resolve not to pry and the forbidding look on Sky's face stopped her.

Jack came across to whisper in her ear. If she was expecting sweet nothings, she was disappointed.

'Have a good look round while you're up there, love. I reckon there's something fishy going on in that monastery.'

Corrie sighed. Once a detective, always a detective, even on honeymoon.

It was a deceptively long slog and some of the plumper women found it hard-going in the airless, stormy heat. Diana, of course, was depressingly fit, and virtually sprinted up. She even found the breath to chat to Maria as they climbed, asking her what she would call the baby if that was the happy outcome of the pilgrimage.

When at last they reached the top the remains of the monastery proved unremarkable. The outside view gave the illusion that the building was still more or less intact, with its ornate arches and carvings, but inside it was much less substantial. Despite that, Corrie reckoned the ruins were probably more interesting than the original monastery had ever been. But the view was stupendous. Far below, the Ionian Sea was inky-purple and murmuring ominously as thunder rumbled around the island.

Chattering nervously, the women prepared to make their invocation to St Sophia. Corrie was amused at their strangely ambivalent attitude towards their patron saint. It seemed to be a compound of the personal and sceptical but with no hint of irreverence. Also, they were not averse to scolding her if things went wrong, or they felt she was not pulling her weight. Far from beseeching, these women sought to coax her into the right frame of mind to grant their desire for fruitfulness. At no time did Corrie sense any disbelief in St Sophia's powers but unlike conventional prayers, the superstition was that to utter extravagant praise aloud would be to risk igniting the devil.

The invocation over, everybody silently nibbled a piece of their wick in the hope of consuming the blessing of the saint, then the lamps were lit and they started back down. It was easier than the journey up, but this time, the younger women went on ahead except for Sky, who stayed close behind Corrie.

They were halfway down when the storm hit. Lightning forked across the blackened sky and the parched rocks steamed and hissed as torrential rain drenched them. The women were soaked to the skin in seconds and trying desperately to protect the flames in their flickering lamps. Corrie watched, fascinated, as the squall picked up fishing boats moored in the harbour and hurled them on to the beach like empty walnut shells. With thunder crashing all around, it was easy to imagine Poseidon rising from the waves, brandishing his trident. Katastrophos seemed to raise itself from the ocean floor with spray exploding all over it.

The steps became treacherous and the slippery handrail – where there was one – hard to grip. When she heard the scream, Corrie thought someone had fallen. But it came again – agonized and drawn out, like an animal caught in a trap. She squinted down through the driving rain. There was some kind of scuffle going on below. She could see a woman in something orange – oh my God, Diana! – thrashing about, dangerously, while another figure tried to restrain her. The women behind Corrie started to panic and surge forward. She felt a sudden hard shove between her shoulder blades and almost lost her footing on the greasy steps but she flung her lamp into the void and managed to hang on with wet, shaking hands. She scrambled on down and reached the two struggling women just as the scream came again.

The woman in the sodden, tangerine pashmina, clinging like a fly from the splintering handrail, was not Diana.

It was Maria.

CHAPTER SIX

Corrie reached out and grabbed Maria around the waist, just as Diana grasped her legs. Between them, they managed to get her arms around their shoulders, still with Diana's soggy pashmina clinging to her. The driving rain continued to lash them, leaving no breath to speak as they slithered and slid the rest of the way down the treacherous steps. Other women put out hands, trying to help support Maria from above and below, as best they could. She had stopped screaming and struggling, but only, Corrie realized, because she was now almost unconscious.

The men, who had been watching helplessly from below, rushed forward to take Maria from them as soon as they reached safety. Yanni picked her up in his arms and carried her to the temporary shelter of a rocky outcrop, crooning to her and begging her to speak to him. Tim ran forward and scooped a weeping Ellie into his arms.

'Corrie, what the hell happened up there?' Jack took off his jacket and wrapped it around her trembling shoulders. Marjorie, visibly shaken by what she had witnessed, offered her cardigan.

Corrie took a long, shuddering breath. 'I don't know. Is Maria OK? Where's Diana?'

Drenched to the skin, Diana was sitting on the ground, gasping and dazed. The professor, who had been buzzing about like a mad bluebottle throughout the preliminaries, was now nowhere to be seen. Sidney, minus his usual lighthouse grin, produced a flask of fiery Metaxa from his pocket and held it to her lips. Then, in the absence of anything more chic, he took off his Arsenal scarf and wrapped it around her, several times.

A low chanting of 'St Sophia' began among the crowd as centuries of superstition took hold and people began making up their own explanations for the near tragedy. Jack took charge.

'Come on. Everybody back to the hotel out of this rain. We can find out what happened then.'

The storm continued to rant and rage as they made their way back, Poseidon having perversely chosen this occasion to summon all his Tritons from the deep to stir up the waves. Yanni politely refused any help to carry Maria. She was semi-conscious and moaning pitifully. When they reached the hotel, he set her down on a lounger in the shelter of the vine-covered pergola and put his arms around her, trying to comfort her.

Old Ariadne, who had been laying the table for the feast, took one look at her prostrate daughter, undoubtedly cursed rather than blessed by St Sophia, and pulled her apron up over her head. She sat in the corner and rocked backwards and forwards wailing '*Ayoo! Ayoo!*'. This response from their trusted visionary and hot line to St Sophia did nothing to inspire confidence in the already disturbed crowd.

'Can you tell me exactly what happened, Diana?' Jack sat down beside her at the table. 'It's important.'

'I don't know. It all happened so fast.' She rubbed her dripping hair with the end of Sid's scarf. 'I was coming down the steps behind Maria. She was feeling great because her lamp was still burning, in spite of the rain. She said that this time she was sure St Sophia would bless her and she'd get pregnant. Then suddenly she felt dizzy and said she was sick. I figured she was just cold, so I took off my pashmina and wrapped it round her shoulders.'

'Then what?' Jack asked.

'Then she dropped her lamp, clutched at her stomach and started screaming. She was jerking all over so I guessed she was having some kind of seizure.' Diana trembled slightly, remembering. 'She started acting crazy, like she was going to jump, so I grabbed her and hung on like hell. Then you came, Corrie, and together we carried her down.'

'That's right,' confirmed Corrie. 'She seemed to be in a lot of pain. Then she virtually passed out and—'

'Diana! Oh, my darling Diana!'

It was Professor Gordon roaring in anguish as he raced from inside the hotel to where the crowd had gathered under the vines.

'What's happened? Where is she? Diana!'

He shoved his way through the stunned villagers and fell blindly to his knees beside the body on the sunbed, partly obscured by an anxious Yanni but still wrapped in Diana's distinctive pashmina.

'I'm over here, Cuthbert.' Diana called from the table. 'I'm fine. Don't make such a fuss.'

He looked up in surprise, hearing his wife's calm Manhattan drawl, then turned around and breathed a deep sigh.

'Oh my dear, thank goodness you're safe. I thought ...' It seemed he couldn't finish.

Jack looked hard at the professor for a moment, then went across to Maria and knelt beside her, listening to her laboured breathing. His basic police training in first aid was certainly not adequate for this. He spoke to Yanni.

'I don't like the look of her, Yanni. I think we should contact the mainland immediately – get them to send an emergency launch or something. She needs a doctor at the very least, probably even hospital.'

Yanni looked up, his face contorted. 'Not possible. *To tiléfono* – no wires!'

Poseidon, it seemed, had scored a direct hit with his trident on the primitive island telecommunications, never robust at the best of times. The electric storm had completely burnt out the wiring and it would be some days before it could be restored. Because this happened quite often, many Katastrophans still used old German field telephones, acquired during the last war.

'What about Charon? Where is he?'

Yanni shrugged eloquently. 'Charon not come here for several days.' He pointed at the thrashing sea. 'His ferry not safe in this storm.'

'Isn't there *anyone* on this bloody island with some medical experience?' asked Jack, running desperate fingers through his hair.

'May I see?'

The clipped English with a soft Greek lisp was unmistakable. Sky, her spiky hair now plastered to her head, had rivulets of black eye make-up running down her face. She crouched beside Maria, lifting her eyelids and looking at her lips and inside her mouth.

'Her pulse is very erratic,' she said at last. 'And her vision is disturbed. I believe it is some kind of poison but I cannot tell what.'

Corrie felt Jack stiffen.

Sky looked up at them 'We must empty her stomach. I need salt to make her sick.'

Nobody moved.

'Now! Quickly!'

Spurred into action, Corrie grabbed an empty glass and began to fill it with water from a carafe on the table. She looked around for help. Ellie was crying quietly in Tim's arms. It was useless asking Ariadne, who was still under her apron, wailing.

'Quick! Marjorie!' she shouted. 'Get some salt from the kitchen. Hurry!'

Marjorie, startled out of her shock, shot off at an impressive turn of speed and was back with the salt in seconds. Sky mixed up a strong saline solution, while Jack eased Maria to a sitting position. Yanni stood aside helplessly, while they forced Maria to drink. For several tense seconds, it seemed it wouldn't work. Then Maria began to heave. In a gesture of supreme sacrifice, Sidney closed his eyes and held out his sombrero.

Some minutes later, Sky felt Maria's pulse again. Then she said something in rapid Greek to Yanni. He lifted Maria tenderly in his arms and carried her inside and up to their room with Sky following close behind.

The villagers gradually drifted back to their homes in shocked silence. Never had there been such a violent disturbance on the Feast of St Sophia. Their saint was affronted by something – or someone – and appeasement must surely follow.

At Hotel Stasinopoulos, the bedraggled group sat around the big olive-wood table, not knowing what else to do and reluctant to go to bed knowing they would not sleep. Wet and confused, they listened to the rain hammering down on the vine leaves. Nobody spoke. Soon, Yanni reappeared looking strained but a little happier. He carried armfuls of towels and a huge jug of *avgolémono* – a kind of egg and lemon broth with rice.

'Sky say she think Maria will be OK,' he said with obvious relief. 'When storm is over, maybe Charon come and I can get doctor.' Yanni smiled weakly and hurried back to Maria's side. He didn't care if she never got pregnant as long as she was alive and well.

'Well, it's not all bad,' observed Sidney, brightening. 'At least we don't have to eat the goat now.'

He poured some hot broth into the bowls on the table and handed them round with chunks of crusty bread.

'Bloomin' funny thing to happen, though, wasn't it? I mean ... I thought my old mum was a bad cook but she never actually poisoned any of us.' Sid looked accusingly at poor old Ariadne in the corner, who had wailed herself to sleep and was snoring loudly under her apron.

'Oh, I say ...' ventured Tim, 'you surely don't think it was something in the food?'

Sid shrugged. 'What else could it be? They eat some very funny grub here, don't they? It's all snails' legs and rubbery bits.'

'And what about all the dead rats and the scavenging cats that you see around the kitchen?' said Marjorie. 'Mr Dobson says the island's a health hazard.'

Sid grimaced. 'Don't tell Old Misery Guts about it, Marjie, for gawd's sake. We'll never hear the last of it.'

Jack looked at Corrie. 'You know all about food hygiene,' he said, too far down the table for a kick. 'Is it likely Maria has got food poisoning?'

'Very likely,' said Corrie. 'The standard of cleanliness in the kitchen's a nightmare.'

'But surely even small hotels have to comply with some sort of regulations?'

Corrie nodded. 'Well, the EC Food Hygiene Regulations are supposed to apply to everybody except people just cooking for their family. But I don't suppose Ariadne has even heard of them, much less complied with them. This is Katastrophos, remember. The Brigadoon of the Greek islands. Few people know it even exists and I can't see anyone traipsing out to the middle of the Ionian Sea to carry out an inspection. And we don't actually see what Maria eats, do we?'

'How do you know all that stuff about food regulations, Corrie?' asked Sid curious. 'I thought you said you worked in a shoe shop.'

'Oh – er – I learn a lot of things from the Internet.' A smarter woman, thought Corrie, would beat a hasty retreat now that both cooks – Maria and Ariadne – were out of action.

'The food sure is bad this time,' said Diana. 'Worse than usual. I wonder we haven't all been poisoned. What do you say, Cuthbert?'

The professor had been deep in thought for a long time. The question was clearly exercising his scientific mind, since silence was a rare condition for him. He pronounced judgement.

'From Maria's symptoms, I think it was almost certainly a contaminated egg – probably salmonella at its most virulent. Those hens of Ariadne's scratch around and pick up all kinds of filth. Bad luck for Maria of course, but no reason to panic.'

Tim held Ellie closer. 'All the same, I think I'd better taste the soup first, Ellikins,' he said.

On their way to bed, Jack and Corrie passed the Dobsons' room. When Marjorie went anywhere without Ambrose, even for a few hours, she faced the third degree when she returned. Shock and fatigue meant her guard was down or she would never have made the mistake of telling him about Maria's food poisoning. The sound of his discontented badgering carried right down the landing and promised to be protracted.

'Blasted scandal! God knows what we've eaten since we've been here. Filthy Continental muck. It's a miracle nobody's died. Well, that settles it, I'll certainly sue. You can't trust foreigners to do anything properly. It's your own fault, Marjorie. I take no responsibility for this at all. We should have gone to Bournemouth. It would serve you right if my heart packed up right now and you had to spend the rest of your life managing on your own. See how you'd like that!'

Lying side by side in their concrete cots, Jack remained silent, deep in thought, while Corrie prattled, unable to wind down.

'Poor Maria. What a ghastly thing to happen and all because of a bad egg. Thank goodness she's going to be all right. She really would have jumped off those steps if we hadn't grabbed her, you know. I understand the basic facts about salmonella, obviously, but I never realized it could affect you like that. It was almost as if she were having a terrifying hallucination.'

'Diana was impressive,' said Jack.

'Yes she was,' conceded Corrie, grudgingly. 'Who knows, there may be a very deep, compassionate person under that shallow, mercenary exterior – but I wouldn't put money on it.' She sighed. 'And did you see how distraught the poor old professor was when he thought it was Diana who was hurt. He obviously adores her. Sad really because he must know she only married him for his money.'

'Mmm. You don't think he overdid the concern a bit?'

'Certainly not! Some men can't help showing their feelings. They don't all have an upper lip with scaffolding round it like you.'

Corrie glanced sideways at Jack. She recognized that vacant look – he wasn't listening. His detective's mind was a beehive of buzzing thoughts that flew too quickly for him to catch them. She gossiped a tad louder to regain his attention.

'What about Sky, though? Who'd have thought she'd take control like that? For all we know, she might well have saved Maria's life. I guess she must have done a first aid course or something. It just goes to show you shouldn't judge people by appearances.'

'Mmm,' said Jack again. 'Corrie, what did you see when you were up in the ruined monastery?'

She looked suspicious. 'Why? You're not up to something, are you?'

''Course not. I'm on honeymoon. I was just curious about those lights we saw.'

'There wasn't much to see, really. It's just a load of crumbling walls. The abbey church still has some of the roof on it – they keep St Sophia's precious relics in a kind of vestry down the sheltered end. There's a fancy chair, Byzantine allegedly. The women kept insisting St Sophia, herself, sat on it.'

'How do you know she didn't?'

'Well, it's on castors with an adjustable back rest for a start. I don't recall anyone mentioning she was a typist before she became a saint. Oh yes, there was a medieval winch contraption on the east wall overlooking the sea – probably where the old refectory used to be. I imagine the monks used to winch up their food from boats to save running up and down all those steps.'

'Was there anywhere you could hide something dodgy?'

'Like what?'

'Oh, I dunno – portable laboratory equipment, chemicals, stuff like that.'

'Why? You don't think somebody's making a bomb up there, do you?' Corrie sat up, her face suddenly illuminated. 'Actually, Jack, it would make a brilliant hiding place for stolen goods.'

She hopped out of bed and sat on the end of his.

He groaned. 'Corrie, you're doing it again ...'

She carried on, undaunted. 'D'you remember what it said in that leaflet I found in reception? When Hotel Katastrophos was first built, smugglers used to raid the mainland and hide the loot in the islands.' She looked at him expectantly, as if he ought to know what she was getting at. 'What if it's still going on?'

'Eh?'

'It could be stolen icons or Greek bronzes – there's a big market for that kind of thing, especially in the States. Rich American collectors would pay a fortune. And with more than fourteen hundred Greek

Islands to choose from, who'd come to Katastrophos to look for them? I've never seen so much as a village policeman here, have you? I doubt there's any kind of structured law and order at all, apart from the old priest and he must be at least ninety.' She began to pace the room, piecing together the scam. 'All you'd have to do is make the hit, nick the stuff, have it away fast and stash it in the monastery. Then you lie low and when the heat's off, you fence it to the highest bidder.'

'Corrie, don't be so lurid. Try to remember you're a caterer. You're starting to sound like a seventies TV villain. Nobody talks like that in real life.'

She ignored him, warming to her crime. 'It would explain those lights we saw. The boat bringing the loot across from the mainland signals to his accomplice up in the monastery, who flashes back to let him know he's up there, ready to receive the icons. The boat ties up on the cliff side of the islet, out of sight, and they use the medieval winch to haul up the stuff. The accomplice hides it in the abbey church until it's safe to contact the buyer, then they flog it and split the cash. How's that?' She folded her arms with a triumphant flourish.

'Sounds risky to me.' Jack grunted. 'What if somebody else spots the signals, gets curious, and goes up there to investigate?'

'They wouldn't. You heard what Yanni said when Sid asked about it. Except for pilgrimages, nobody slogs up all those steps and even if they did, they wouldn't poke about among St Sophia's precious relics. This is a profoundly superstitious rural community. They live under their saint's protection and they sincerely believe something bad will happen to anyone who displeases her.'

'Any danger of you going to sleep tonight,' asked Jack, wearily.

Corrie grinned. 'Not much. Pity I didn't have time to case the joint properly while I was up there, but the storm was brewing and we had to come down.' She went back to her own bed and lay down. 'I don't feel like climbing back up for another look, though, do you?'

'Nope,' said Jack. His eyes closed and he went straight off to sleep.

CHAPTER SEVEN

Next day, the storm had cleared. At dawn, Helios, in his sun-chariot, emerged from his golden palace in the east and leapt up into the brazen sky where he would rest until evening.

Corrie stood on the terrace, shielding her eyes and staring out to sea, intoxicated by the candescence of sun on water with boundless blue sky pouring into it. She was not aware of Professor Gordon standing behind her until he spoke in his deep, educated voice.

'You are not, of course, the first visitor to Katastrophos to be mesmerized by "*To Phos*" – the light. The Greeks believe it is the naked eyeball of God that blinds the wicked and the unwary.'

She turned and smiled self-consciously. 'It's easy to believe almost anything on this spellbinding little island. Even the Greek myths take on a kind of relevance to human nature.'

After witnessing their sexual contretemps that night on the landing, Corrie was even more seduced by her notion of sultry-eyed Diana as Medusa and Ambrose as the lecherous, cheating Poseidon.

As if reading her thoughts, the professor nodded. 'The Greek gods were the first gods to resemble humans. Not just look like them, but act like them too. They each had his or her own personality and shortcomings. Some were beautiful, some were lustful, some were ruthless and so on. The entire mythological world is based on humans.'

'You make them sound very ungodlike and fallible,' said Corrie.

'By no means. The myths were full of heroes, men of genius who destroyed their enemies by their superior intelligence and wit. For example, Oedipus beating the Sphinx at the riddle and murdering his father when he crossed his path. Ancient Greeks had an unquenchable curiosity about creation and, more to the point, destruction. Death to them was nothing more than a means to an end and they didn't hesitate to kill in order to achieve a higher objective.'

'But did the Ancient Greeks have a healthy respect for plants, Professor?'

He smiled, sensing she was teasing him. 'I'll give you an example, Coriander. Athena and her uncle, the sea god Poseidon, were in competition for the affections of the Greeks. It was decided that the divinity who created the most useful object would win the right to have the capital city named after them. Poseidon provided a magnificent horse, but Athena created the olive tree, giving shade, oil and olives. Naturally, the Greeks preferred her gift and so the capital of Greece is Athens, not Poseidonia.'

Smiling, he touched her shoulder in a friendly farewell and strode away in the direction of the olive groves, carrying his sample case.

Jack appeared from inside the hotel, eating a slice of seed-cake he had pinched from the kitchen, since nobody seemed to be doing anything about breakfast.

'What did the professor want?'

'Nothing really. We were just having a chat.'

'Do you know where he's gone?'

'Yes, he's off to collect more plants.' She looked thoughtful. 'He really is a fascinating man, Jack. Compelling, even. Most of the time, he's all bluff, cranky and absent-minded, but then you get a glimpse of a determined, almost obsessive personality underneath. I mean, look at the way he worships Diana despite the way she behaves. Stereotypical professor, I suppose. But you have to admire his absolute dedication to his work. You can see why he's so highly respected and wealthy.'

Jack shot her a sudden glance, then shrugged dismissively. 'Yanni's looking for you. I don't know what he wants.'

I bet I bloody do! thought Corrie.

Maria was fully conscious now and much better, but the prolonged bouts of vomiting and diarrhoea had left her too weak to get out of bed. Corrie sympathized, recalling her encounter with the deadly Provençal snails. Food bugs could quite literally lay you out. Ariadne was still deeply disturbed by her daughter's sudden illness but even more so by her apparent fall from St Sophia's grace. Thankfully, she had stopped wailing, but refused to leave Maria's bedside except to put out the traditional battery of charms and offerings needed to flatter the saint and coax her into lifting her curse.

In the meantime, there was no one but Yanni in Hotel Stasinopoulos to prepare and cook the food.

Corrie knew what was coming as soon as she saw him approaching, wringing his hands in humble supplication, like a Greek Uriah Heep.

'*Kiría* Dawes,' he began in a wheedling tone. '*Kírie* Jack says you are very good cook – excellent cook – *ipérocho*!' He threw his hands up as if overwhelmed by the sheer brilliance of her catering skills.

'Yes, all right,' said Corrie, bowing to the inevitable. 'Cut the flattery and spit it out, Yanni.'

'*Kírie* Jack say to ask if you could … if you will …' his English was running out and he ended up pointing towards the kitchen, hopefully.

Corrie made a mental note to have a quiet word with '*Kírie* Jack' who, she suspected, had acted more in the interests of his own stomach than for altruistic reasons.

It was only later, when she was up to her elbows in goat's entrails that it dawned on her. She and Jack were supposed to be on honeymoon – a relaxed, romantic holiday that was a 'retreat from the stress of modern-day living' and, most of all, as far away from crime and catering as possible. Now here she was, slaving away in a primitive foreign kitchen while Jack was skulking around like Inspector Clouseau, questioning people about flashing lights and contaminated eggs. She was cooking and he was detecting. The two things they had both promised each other they wouldn't do! And as for a retreat from stress – they had only been there four days and so far, she had narrowly escaped falling to certain death off a cliff, been soaked to the skin and almost struck by lightning, witnessed the near expiry of the hotel owner from salmonella poisoning and been given the evil eye by a demented hippy.

'If this is paradise island,' she grumbled aloud, 'give me demonic south London any day.'

Hearing Corrie muttering imprecations to herself in the kitchen indicated to Jack that a little masterly disappearance might be in order, so he took himself off to the *kafeneíon* in St Sophia for a beer. Sid was there, chatting and laughing with the old men, an interaction achieved solely through his irrepressible charm since he spoke no Greek and they spoke no English. When he saw Jack he motioned to the bar owner, already a bosom pal, to bring him a beer.

'Wotcher, Jack, mate! Where's your good lady?'

Jack grinned. 'Back at the hotel. I think she's volunteered to cook some food for supper.'

Sid's face lit up. 'Smashing! For someone who sells shoes, she certainly knows a lot about food, your missus.' He picked up a deck of cards from the table. 'Fancy a game?'

It was then that Jack noticed an angry, blistery rash on Sid's left hand. He pointed.

'That looks nasty. Is it a burn?'

Sid rubbed at it. 'No. I think it must be some sort of allergy. Don't know what, though.'

Jack remembered their botany lesson in the olive groves with the professor in his surgical gloves.

'I bet it was that squirty cucumber thing. The professor said watch your hand for any reaction because the liquid can cause irritation.'

'Yeah, that's what I thought to start with. But then I remembered – it was the other hand that got squirted.' Sid held out his right hand which was unblemished. 'Queer, eh?' He shuffled the cards and started to deal. 'You want to watch these old geezers, Jack, they cheat worse than me.' He beamed his lighthouse smile at the old men, who chuckled wheezily over their dangling cigarettes and slapped him on the back.

Jack took a long slug of beer and picked up his cards, but his mind was on something quite different.

Once she got organized, Corrie discovered that the quality of the local produce was actually extremely good – it was what Ariadne did to it that made it disgusting. Two of the blackened cooking pots had their bottoms burnt right out as if she'd been boiling something up for days.

Ariadne cooked mostly in an outdoor oven, a humpy whitewashed dome with a blackened mouth, nearly as big as Ariadne herself. As far as Corrie could make out, you lit the fire inside the oven and smoke escaped from time to time when you unplugged a small hole. When the heat was intense, you raked out the fire and put in the food which baked in the hot air. Not particularly responsive but not a health hazard either, although the ancient clay storage jars that she still used might well be. There was a whole row of them, holding all kinds of staple foods including the infamous eggs. Corrie couldn't believe that any provisions would keep well under such conditions. One of the jars contained a number of what appeared to be small medicine bottles with old-fashioned stoppers. She uncorked one, sniffed it, turned slightly green and had to lean against the sink for a bit. Herbs, definitely, probably preserved by Ariadne for flavouring her noisome stews. It was, Corrie thought, food poisoning simply lying in wait for its next victim.

By dinner time Corrie had prepared baked red mullet, a huge moussaka, Greek salad with herbs and feta cheese, sausages and chips for Sidney and *tirópitakia* – small pastry triangles filled with goat's cheese – for Ellie. For dessert, there was fruit salad and a honey cake which she had knocked up using nuts and spices from the clay storage jars, that she had considered safe to eat.

She looked at everything spread out on the big, olive-wood table and felt ridiculously pleased with herself. She even considered putting Greek food on the menu of 'Coriander's Cuisine'. She could introduce 'Greek Dinner-Party Nights' and let the guests smash the plates afterwards. She would need something to revive the business when she got home. Profits had plummeted since poor Lavinia died. Corrie frowned. The mysterious stomach upset that had caused her fatal heart attack had struck very suddenly, just like Maria's, but unlike Maria, there was definitely no question of food poisoning, the post mortem had been unequivocal. Nevertheless people tended to be cautious. Perceptions had been more persuasive than reality and catering bookings had dropped almost overnight.

With the exception of Sky, who came down to dinner very late and only ever picked at the food anyway, everyone tucked in with gusto. Even Ambrose admitted grudgingly to Marjorie that while the food was still 'Continental muck' it was much improved muck. At the end of the meal, they gave Corrie a round of applause.

'That's the best meal I've had since I left Stoke Newington,' said Sidney. 'You know, Corrie, you're wasted in a shoe shop. You ought to take up cooking professionally. I bet you'd do really well.'

Jack choked on a laugh and Corrie gave him a look cold enough to stun a polar bear.

'Thanks, Sid. I'll give it some thought.'

He winked. 'Any chance of a bit of egg and bacon in the morning?'

But Corrie knew she'd really cracked the authentic Greek menu when Yanni asked if he could take some food up to Maria as the smell of the cooking had rekindled her appetite.

Much later, basking in the glow of approbation and far too many glasses of Yanni's excellent wine, Corrie found herself sitting next to Diana under the vine-covered pergola. Her new resolve not to poke her nose into other people's business had vanished along with her prim misgivings about the young American woman's obvious lack of moral rectitude and her unforgivably gorgeous figure. All this forgotten, she chatted amiably.

'So how do you think you'll like living in Switzerland?'

'Pardon me?' Diana looked at her, puzzled.

'You know ...' Corrie, rather tipsy, nudged her in the ribs with her elbow, '... the Gordon Research Scholarships. It isn't a secret, is it? The professor was telling Jack and Sidney about how he's soon going to be Master of a Swiss University. It must be such a great honour for him. I bet you're really looking forward to it.'

'The hell I am.' Diana's green eyes flashed briefly. 'There's no way I'm going to be buried alive in some crummy college just so Cuthbert can play the great benefactor to a bunch of plant nerds.' She drained her glass of wine in one go.

Corrie was beginning to wish she hadn't started this conversation but she was in the proverbial hole and too much wine had deprived her of the sense to stop digging.

'But it need not be crummy *all* the time, surely. There are lots of really super things in Switzerland.'

'Like what?'

Corrie racked her wine-fuddled brains, trying to think of some. 'Well, there's skiing and wrist watches and ... er ...' she could hear herself talking drivel but couldn't shut up, '... those little army knives and ... er ... Swiss roll.'

'I've already told Cuthbert, I'm not going.' Diana was adamant.

'But Diana, he was very excited about it. Jack said he regards it as the culmination of a lifetime's work in botany – the international recognition of his genius. If you refuse to go with him, aren't you afraid he might go anyway? Without you?'

Diana laughed and put a confidential hand on Corrie's arm.

'Oh no, honey. Cuthbert can't go anywhere without me.'

She stood up in a storm cloud of perfume and sashayed across to

Sidney, who refilled her glass. A few minutes later they were attempting a really awful rendition of 'I Got You, Babe'.

It was three in the morning. The initial sedative effect of the wine had worn off and Corrie was wide awake. The euphoria of her triumph with the food and her odd conversation with Diana spun round in her mind, preventing her from going back to sleep. She peered through the deep-purple shadows at the motionless body in the other bed.

'Jack ...'

There was no answer, just peaceful snores.

She raised her voice slightly.

'Jack, darling.'

Still nothing.

'Jack, are you awake?' she yelled, tetchily.

'I am now.' Jack's sleepy voice drifted back through the darkness.

'Good. Are you listening, sweetheart? I had a really weird conversation with Diana tonight.'

'I know – I saw you. And it was *last* night. It's tomorrow, now, in case you hadn't noticed.'

'What? Oh never mind that. The thing is – I asked her if she was looking forward to being a master's wife at the Swiss university and she said ...'

'... she wouldn't go,' finished Jack.

'That's right. So I said, "*but what if he goes without you?*" and she said—'

'... he couldn't go without her.'

Corrie sat up in bed and snapped the light on.

'Jack, I really hate it when you do that! It's so irritating. Why can't he go without her? I don't understand. Is there something I don't know? Your copper's nose has been twitching like Bugs Bunny ever since we got here. What are you up to?'

Jack sat up then, yawning and scratching his head.

'Nothing you need worry about, my love. There's just something I need to keep a bit of an eye on, that's all.'

'Why? We're on holiday and you're hundreds of miles from the squad. What do you need to keep an eye on? Tell me.'

'There's nothing to tell, yet. Nothing's making any sense at the moment.'

'It's got something to do with Maria's food poisoning, hasn't it?'

'It might have. But what I can't work out,' murmured Jack, mainly to himself, 'is where the lights in the monastery fit in, why Sky's tattoos washed off in the rain and how come Sid's rash is on the wrong hand.'

'Jack, none of that has anything to do with you – you're on leave and even if there is something dodgy going on, Katastrophos is not your patch – it's not your responsibility.'

He looked sheepish. 'Well ... a bit of it is.'

'How can it be? There isn't any local police for you to liaise with and you're not on the end of a phone so they can't possibly have called you with something urgent. Unless ...' Corrie got out of bed and eyeballed him now. 'Unless, you knew about it before we came.' His open face gave him away and Corrie pounced, angrily. 'You did, didn't you? You're on a job. Jack how could you? You promised this honeymoon would be—'

He put his arms around her. 'Now don't go into one, love. It's just a simple little matter I said I'd investigate if I had time. It need not interrupt our honeymoon in the slightest. You'll hardly know I'm working.'

'All right then,' she challenged, 'what do you need to investigate? Is it something about Diana? Tell me and I'll find out for you.'

'Oh no,' said Jack decisively. 'This time you stay right out of it, sweetheart. No interfering – I mean it.'

He put the light out and lay down, the discussion clearly at an end.

Corrie went back to bed and lay there fuming. How could she interfere when she didn't know what was going on? Huh! A fine honeymoon this was turning into.

CHAPTER EIGHT

Despite her initial resistance, Corrie continued to prepare the meals in Ariadne's absence. In truth, it was not too much of an imposition since most of the dishes were cold except for the main course at dinner and she found she enjoyed experimenting with the fresh local ingredients. So far, nobody else had keeled over clutching their stomachs, so she assumed her conscientious attention to hygiene and the rigorous scrubbing she had given all the surfaces had paid off.

She had also ditched several pots that were beyond cleaning. Some looked as though they had been used for long and fiendish alchemic experiments. The massive black cauldrons with the bottoms burnt out were obviously too big and heavy for tiny Ariadne to lift, so Corrie guessed she had probably just kept boiling one lot of stew on top of another and doling it out with a ladle. They smelled foul, like decaying meat and very old cabbage water.

If she was honest, she was quite glad to be cooking. It gave her something to do when Jack was preoccupied with whatever it was he was keeping his eye on. If nothing else, she thought charitably, it had at least taken his mind off that last harrowing murder investigation. Sometimes, when he was satisfied that his eye could take a rest, they went into town, or lazed on the beach or simply sat on their balcony, sipping wine, but even when he was dozing Corrie had the uncanny feeling he still had one eye open.

Argus the All-Seeing, came into her head unbidden, as had so many of the Greek gods she thought she had forgotten until the mystic influence of Katastrophos conjured them up again. Argus got his soubriquet from his unorthodox number of eyes. Some said he had four – two in the usual place and two in the back of his head. Other accounts claimed he had up to a hundred, all over his body. This excess of ocular equipment made Argus an excellent private eye, able to watch around the clock since he could always keep a lid or two peeled while the rest caught a little shut-eye. Yes, Jack was definitely Argus, mused Corrie fancifully. She recalled that Zeus's wife had hired Argus to keep watch on her husband, who was king of the gods, ruler of Mount Olympus and a serial miscreant. So if Jack is Argus, who is the all-powerful Zeus? Her whimsical imagination would come up with only one possible answer – Professor Gordon. But why would Jack be keeping an eye on Professor Gordon?

The days of the Greek gods were passed in endless pleasure – much like a group of tourists on holiday. They enjoyed an everlasting dinner party seated round golden tables on which there were served limitless supplies of untaxed nectar and ambrosia. They never wore out physically, having an elixir of life flowing in their veins instead of blood. They lived from impulse to impulse – keeping their lives exciting and unpredictable. Their passions were not always laudable – anger, jealousy, lust, greed – but despite this they remained supremely free of any self-reproach or guilt. In fact, Olympus was simply a glorified *taverna* with celestial call-girls. Oh yes, there was a good deal of pretty hot skirmishing for maidens up on Zeus's Olympus.

The sun blistered down on Sidney's pallid kneecaps, endowing each with a fiery glow. Sweating profusely, he stripped down to just speedos and trainers and climbed gingerly into the old rowing boat. He leaned forward, dipping his oars, missed the water entirely and toppled on to his back. Gulls rose, shrieking. Sid struggled back to a sitting position and sculled again, this time making a few pitiful ripples on the surface of the silver sea. This rowing lark wasn't as easy as it looked. At this rate, by the time he found the cove the sun would have set and Diana would be on her way back. And he was far from sure that he ought to be going after her in the first place.

He had met her just as she was pulling away from the hotel landing stage in one of the two small rowing boats that Hotel Stasinopoulos put at the disposal of its guests. She looked ball-achingly sexy in a skimpy red bikini and a huge floppy sunhat. He knew he was staring and forced himself to blink before the sun shrivelled his eyeballs.

'I'm going to sunbathe down the other end of the island where it's more private,' she had whispered. 'I need to tan my white bits. Why don't you get the other boat and follow me? We'll have lunch together in one of the caves.' She patted the picnic basket that Ariadne had been prevailed upon to provide. 'You bring the wine, honey. See ya!' And she'd pulled expertly on her oars and skimmed away like an Olympian athlete going for gold. Sid watched the fluid movement of her arms and legs, bronzed and sinuous, as she disappeared around the curve of the bay and out of sight. Then, consumed with a lust that totally annihilated his better judgement, he went to fetch a bottle of Yanni's wine and the other boat.

Now, he bent to his oars again and at last got some sort of rhythm going. All he had to do was follow the coast until he spotted Diana's boat beached on one of the little coves at the north-west end of the island. After that, he wasn't sure what he'd see but he had a pretty good idea and it made his mouth dry.

Marjorie was in the lobby of the hotel, furtively sticking a stamp on a postcard to Dan. She had bought it secretly in St Sophia and had hoped to post it, equally secretly. Ambrose was sitting outside on the terrace, ostentatiously drafting letters of complaint to the travel company and his solicitor, both of which were currently running into six pages. It would keep him occupied for some time, she thought. He seemed to be enjoying himself for the first time since they arrived. She even heard him laugh a couple of times, anticipating the distress and alarm he was sure his threatening rhetoric would evoke. He had an unpleasant, mirthless laugh, more of a neigh really. She could hear him now. Hner, Hner, Hner.

Ellie appeared, fresh and scrubbed in one of Tim's check shirts and over-large, cropped cargo pants from which her thin white legs protruded like a couple of pieces of string. She was clutching a postcard, too.

Marjorie was surprised to see her alone. It was rare to see one half of the heavenly twins without the other.

'Hello, dear. Where's Tim?'

Ellie smiled, her dim blue eyes peeping out from under her ginger fringe. Like a startled fawn, she never seemed to look anybody straight in the eye.

'He's still in the shower. If I hurry, I'll be back before he realizes I'm missing. I just popped down to post this card.' She dropped it in a cardboard box on the desk, which had POST written on it in red felt tip.

'Is it to your mother, dear? Only it's just occurred to me that the post must have to go to the mainland and I expect that means Charon will collect it when he comes to pick us all up again in his ferry on Saturday week. We'll probably be home long before our postcards arrive.'

Ellie giggled. 'I never thought of that. Oh well, never mind. This card is for Poppy, my puppy. I can read it to her when I get home.' She skipped off, straight back upstairs to her besotted husband.

If anything, thought Marjorie, smiling fondly after her, that girl is even drippier than when she arrived. But the mutual bond between her and Tim was there for all to see, shining and solid, like golden chains binding them together. Marjorie wondered if Ellie knew how lucky she was. She posted her card through the slot in the box and made her way outside, this time through the front door, preferring the angry gaze of the Gorgons to the even angrier gaze of Ambrose. She shielded her eyes and stared out to sea, bathing in the dreamy, soothing blueness of Katastrophos Bay. Has it all been my fault for allowing it? she wondered. She sensed that that was what Corrie thought. But when you've suffered years of bullying and humiliation, in whatever relationship and however deserved or undeserved, it isn't just your self-esteem that goes, it's your faith in the future, your ability to believe that anything you might do could make the slightest difference. Life seems pointless when you can't see an end to the misery. What do you do when there aren't any bits of happiness left to cling to?

'I'll tell you what you do,' she said aloud, into the sea breeze. 'You pull yourself together and you put a stop to it.'

Sidney spotted Diana's boat halfway up a pebble beach in a very pretty cove with sparkling white sand. The sun gonged down on the burning shingle but there was shade from some olive trees that grew right down to the shoreline. He couldn't see Diana but as he dragged his boat up the beach next to hers, he noticed the cave – one of the sea grottos Yanni had told him about, only found on the exposed north-west coast. It had a big hole in the roof and a clump of cypress at the entrance. He fetched the wine from the boat, and crunched up the beach into the cave, calling her name so she would know he was coming.

Diana was lying on a blanket in the shaft of sunlight that streamed in through the hole in the roof. She was smiling. He knew that because he was focused firmly on her teeth to stop himself ogling her bare breasts like some sad yob. It was with considerable relief that he noticed she was still wearing the bottom half of her bikini – a tiny red triangle held in place by a couple of strings. She rose languidly to give him a welcoming kiss. At the same time, he bent awkwardly to receive it and found his face winging in at bust level. One glorious breast actually brushed his cheek. A faintly unsettling experience, but nothing to the one into which he was plunged a terrible moment later. Handing over the bottle of wine, he somehow contrived to trap her nipple between his fingers. He recoiled with a small gasp and apologized.

She laughed, a delicious gurgle. 'Sidney, relax.' She produced a corkscrew from the picnic basket and, with the bottle gripped firmly between her thighs, she uncorked the wine, the impact jiggling her super-structure just enough to make Sid's hot head sing.

It wasn't as if Sidney was unaccustomed to toplessness. In Benidorm, acres of boobs in various shades of brown stretched supine to the sea, trembling the air above them with shimmering oil. There, though, they were impersonal. They could be anything – cakes with cherries on, skull-caps, stranded jellyfish – anything. But these boobs were Diana's: firm, delectable and quite clearly available to him.

He coped reasonably well at first, managing not to look when she began stroking sun-oil into one of them. It was when she handed him the bottle and asked him to do the other one that the rudder of his self-control was shot away. He jumped up with a light laugh, concealing the straining bulge in his speedos with a carefree hand, then ran down the shingle and hurled himself trembling into the sea.

When he came back, cooler and with a grip on himself, she had poured the wine and set out the food. He picked up one of Ariadne's anonymous kebabs and nibbled at it, his appetite eclipsed by another more urgent need.

'The sea's very clean here, isn't it? I could see me trainers through it. Course, if you believe Corrie Dawes, there's monsters out there.' He scanned the horizon, shading his eyes against the Ionian glint. 'Sirens, Tritons, you name it. To hear her talk, you'd think half of flipping Loch Ness comes down here in the summer.'

Diana laughed. 'They say Lord Byron thought Katastrophos so beau-tiful he wanted to buy it, but Homer describes it as "overrun with barren rocks and cliffs and only good for goats" – that's assuming Katastrophos was the island they were referring to. Nobody can be sure.' She looked around her, sipping her wine. 'Don't you just love it in here, Sidney? This is the Cave of Nymphs where Odysseus is supposed to have hidden some treasure on his return from the Trojan War. I lie here sometimes, imagining how incredibly randy Penelope must have felt, seeing her husband again after ten long years.'

Sidney looked at her in surprise. 'Fancy you knowing all that academic stuff.'

She sighed. 'You disappoint me, darling. Don't tell me you see me as a blonde bimbo, too?'

'No, course not,' he said earnestly. 'It's just that I was temporarily blinded by your amazing body. Be fair, Di. It's the first thing to hit a bloke and it stuns him before he has time to investigate the brain department.' He drank some wine, feeling his self-control gradually ebbing away. 'I suppose I don't really know anything about you, do I?'

'There isn't much to know. My mother's Swedish, my dad's American and I was born in Cairo. I can speak five languages, drive a truck, hit a mean home run and I'm after your body. What more do you need to know?'

Sid grinned. 'I guess a clever man like the prof would have spotted your brain a mile off. How did you meet him?'

Diana refilled their glasses. 'At college. I was a student and he was my faculty head. He was interested in me then. Now I think he'd only notice me if I grew leaves.' She laughed but not happily.

'Oh Di, if you were mine, I'd ...' Sid broke off because she wasn't and he couldn't.

'Sidney, you are so cute.' Without warning, Diana threw her arms around him and pressed soft lips on his.

Sid struggled – but only slightly – and concealed his feelings, as he always did, by joking.

'Madam, please. Put me down. You're crushing my *souvláki*!' He picked blobs of greasy kebab off his chest, thinking that if he were one of those Sunday newspaper journalists, this would be the time to make his excuses and leave.

Diana smiled seductively, stood up and slowly untied the strings on the bottom half of her bikini. Then she parted her legs slightly and let it fall to the ground.

Had he found himself dropped into a whole cave full of naked girls, the situation might have taken a sexual turn, certainly, but Sid felt he would have coped. A bit of raunchy banter, winking and so forth, but he pictured himself remaining cool, poised, nonchalant, even occasionally stifling a sophisticated yawn and examining his fingernails. Not sitting, as he was now, mesmerized and helpless, his eyes rolling around in his head like marbles in a soup plate.

'Strewth!' he heard himself croak. He'd been able to have a half-decent conversation with her until she stripped off and dried his throat. 'Look, Di, I want you like hell, but I don't think we should be doing this. I mean, you're married and there's the prof to consider and …'

She sank to her knees beside him and breathed a throaty sigh that sent tremors through the only thing she was wearing – her diamond necklace. Then she kissed him again, slipping her tongue slowly into his mouth. This came as a surprise to Sid, whose main experience of women's tongues was hearing them nag him about how slowly he worked and how expensive he was. Before he could recover, Diana grasped his head and pulled his face against her bare breasts, bouncing his lips from nipple to nipple.

'You don't give up, do you?' he said, muffled.

'No, Sidney, baby. You're the one who's going to give up.' She pushed him gently backwards until he was lying on the blanket, then slowly straddled him, looking deep into his eyes. He heard himself jabbering inanely, anything to take his mind off what he knew was about to happen so he might keep a vestige of control over the rampant bulge which was threatening to burst through his speedos.

''Course, the beaches where I come from – you know, Southend and Margate, the councils spend their money on deckchairs and bandstands and lifebelts and coloured lights on the lampposts and stopping the piers from rotting and going round with spikes, picking up rubbish off the sand and …' he gulped as she slid her fingers into the top of his speedos and eased them down.

Sidney felt a brief – a very brief – pang of guilt. It wasn't his style to have it off with another man's wife. On the other hand, the prof didn't seem to care or even notice. He was more turned on by the pudenda of a hibiscus – whatever that was. It was such a terrible neglect of a passionate, beautiful woman. Too late now, anyway. Diana was already well on top of the situation. So he lay back and thought of England. They must have been playing unusually well because pretty soon he heard himself shouting out loud with sheer joy.

With Corrie occupied in the kitchen, Jack the All-Seeing was lounging outside the hotel on Ariadne's camp bed, admiring the crescent of turquoise glass that was Katastrophos Bay. One half-open but vigilant eye had spotted Diana, rowing swiftly away in the direction of the deserted, north-west end of the coast. He was surprised, briefly, knowing Diana to be a gregarious, fun-loving woman who became bored very quickly with her own company. As far as he knew, that part of the island had only historic or mythological interest. There were sea grottos where pirates had once hidden their loot and, according to Corrie, a couple of monsters whose names he couldn't remember had lived in one of the caves, eating passing sailors alive and making deadly whirlpools by sucking in and spitting out seawater. Charming. A few minutes later he saw Sidney come out of the hotel with a bottle of wine and climb into the other boat. After a shaky start, he had set off in the same direction. Jack shrugged. So that was it. Well, whatever they were about to get up to, he didn't think it had much to do with pirates or sea monsters – and anyway, it was none of his business. At least it meant he could relax for a bit. He closed his all-seeing eyes.

'Jack, I've just remembered!' Corrie came hurrying out of the kitchen and into the shady olive grove where she plumped down hard on the foot of his camp bed. The head end rose several inches into the air, bouncing Jack upright.

'What have you remembered, my little suet dumpling?'

'I've remembered where I last saw Marjorie.'

'I hadn't realized we'd mislaid her.'

'For goodness' sake, Jack, try to concentrate. This is important – or at least, I think it is. Do you remember when we first arrived, I said I thought I'd seen her before, without Ambrose, but I couldn't remember where?'

'Yes.'

'Well, now I've remembered.'

'Good for you.' He tipped her gently off the end of the bed on to the scrubby grass and lay down again.

'Don't you want to know?'

'Not especially.'

Corrie sat down again, harder this time, and Jack had to grip the sides to avoid being catapulted off. 'I know why you're doing this.' She pulled a cross face. 'It's to put me off the scent, isn't it? Stop me from helping you.'

He grinned. 'Helping me with what?'

'The case – the person you're keeping an eye on. It's Marjorie, isn't it?'

'Why do you say that?'

'Because I've remembered where I last saw her.'

'I think this is where I came in.' He struggled to sit up. 'Shall we have a cup of tea or would you prefer a glass of wine?'

Corrie pushed him back down. 'Neither, thank you. Marjorie was at Lavinia Braithwaite's funeral.'

This made Jack sit up. 'Are you sure?'

'Quite sure. She was standing on the other side of the grave when I accidentally threw my glove in.'

'Why would she be at Lavinia's funeral?'

'She must have been one of her fund-raisers. It all fits if you think about it. She told me Ambrose won't allow her to get a job. She said he makes enough fuss about her charity work. And she recently came into a little money which she used to pay for this holiday on Katastrophos. It was a legacy from Lavinia, like the one she left me to buy a new van. I've got it all worked out. You never did explain why *you* were at Lavinia's funeral when you barely knew her. I asked you at the time if you were investigating one of the mourners. It was Marjorie Dobson, wasn't it?'

Jack looked convincingly nonplussed. 'Why would I want to investigate Marjorie?'

'Because she's married to Ambrose, who's been a bastard to her for thirty years. He has a bad heart and she has him insured for a very large amount. And because you think she's brought him to Katastrophos to bump him off.'

CHAPTER NINE

The following Saturday morning at breakfast, everyone gathered around the olive-wood table chatting cheerfully and tucking into scrambled eggs with tomatoes and smoked Greek sausages, fragrant with nutmeg and cinnamon. Everyone, that is, except Ambrose Dobson.

'Where's Old Misery Guts this morning?' asked Sid, mopping his plate with Corrie's home-made bread. 'Doesn't he want any grub?'

'He's having a lie-in,' replied Marjorie. 'He wants me to take him some up on a tray.' She carried on eating without showing any sign of the anxious haste to carry out his orders that had been so apparent when they first arrived.

'And are you going to?' asked Corrie.

'Eventually.' She helped herself to more sausages from the communal dish of food in the middle.

'Better hurry up, Marjie, or there won't be any left,' said Sid, blithely unconcerned.

'Well, he'll have to go without, then, won't he?'

Whilst Corrie delighted in Marjorie's new-found spirit, she was nevertheless uneasy. Ambrose struck her as, like Poseidon, his mythological *alter ego*, an insidious kind of bully, exerting his power over weak women and glorifying masculine brutality. He was of the kind who would not hesitate to use violence when he lost his temper and, like Poseidon, would consider it his right to inflict fear and punishment. Enough to provoke even the most timid woman into bumping him off. She spoke quietly so the others wouldn't hear.

'You will be careful, won't you, Marjorie?'

Marjorie put a hand on her arm and smiled. 'Don't worry, dear. I'll be careful. I'm really good at it. I have a diploma in careful.'

Maria appeared at the end of the meal, hollow-eyed and noticeably thinner, but back on her feet and smiling.

'Thanks to St Sophia, I am now well again,' she announced.

To be fair, thought Corrie, a few others of us had quite a lot to do with it, Sky in particular, but she said nothing.

'My mother is now able to take over the cooking again, *kiría* Dawes, and we are most grateful for your kindness in helping out. It is after all your holiday and you are our guest.'

Corrie nodded graciously.

'Tonight,' continued Maria, 'there will be another, very special feast.'

Sid and his stomach groaned inwardly at the news of Ariadne's reinstatement. He looked glumly at Maria. 'Don't tell me – let me guess. This time the feast is to celebrate the accidental martyrdom of St Crematorios, patron saint of barbecues. They're going to carry his chargrilled remains through the village on a ceremonial bap.'

Diana giggled and prodded him. 'Sidney, don't be a dork.'

'No,' said Maria politely, not understanding any of it. 'Yanni and I simply wish to give thanks to St Sophia and everyone here for their part in my safe recovery.' She lowered her eyes, shyly, and the guests had the good grace to applaud and even cheer a bit.

That evening, there was a real party atmosphere. Yanni hung every candle lamp he could find in the olive trees and hired the best band in the village. This meant there were now four wrinkly geriatrics with *bouzoúki* instead of the usual three, but their playing was superb. Their gnarled old fingers flew across the strings like mad brown moths round a flame.

Everyone had made a special effort to dress up. Diana looked particularly breathtaking in a long white evening gown, low-cut and split daringly to the thigh. It fell in soft folds from a huge gold brooch, obviously wildly expensive, clasped to one shoulder. Tonight, she wore her hair piled high on her head in a mass of shining curls held by two gold combs. Undulating around the tiny dance-floor, she was teaching a helplessly captivated Sidney how to rumba. He had abandoned his T-shirt and army surplus shorts and borrowed a Gianni Manzoni dinner jacket from somewhere. The slightly too-long sleeves suggested it might be one of the professor's, but he looked surprisingly suave and they made a striking couple.

Watching them, Jack felt sure from the satisfied gleam in Diana's eye and their unmistakable body language, that she had, as he suspected, devoured poor defenceless Sidney in one of the sea caves to the north of the island. Jack wasn't in the least surprised. Goodness knows, most blokes would succumb to Diana's charms if she were really determined, especially on Katastrophos where everybody seemed to be out of their tree anyway. And as Jack expected, the professor was now so deeply engrossed with his plant experiments that he wouldn't even have noticed that Diana was missing, let alone care what she was doing. Although it was none of his business, Jack reckoned it could really make his job difficult if it meant that Sidney and Diana would spend the remainder of the fortnight welded to each other and sneaking off out of sight, like Tim and Ellie. So much so that Jack thought he might have to take one or both of them into his confidence.

He put an arm around Corrie's shoulders and leaned across to murmur in her ear. She snuggled close, waiting for him to say something romantic.

'Doesn't Diana look smashing in that dress? Like a Greek goddess.'

'Diana was a Roman goddess, actually,' Corrie replied, stonily, wishing she had brought her posh frock after all, 'but I suppose the name does suit her.'

Jack raised a quizzical eyebrow.

'The goddess, Diana, was a huntress,' she snapped. 'On the other hand, she was also a virgin goddess and an emblem of chastity, so maybe it isn't so appropriate after all.' She looked at Jack's dopey expression and gave him a sharp dig. 'Stop drooling or I'll stamp on your tongue!'

'Timsy' and 'Elliekins', as everyone now called them, drifted down from their room wearing the invariable matching shorts and shirts. Looking deep into each other's eyes, they strolled dreamily on to the dance floor, where they meshed as silently and smoothly as Bentley clutch-plates. They had a definite glow, thought Corrie fondly, the kind that is turned up to full wattage when people are in love. She wondered if she and Jack glowed – probably not. At their age, they probably just flickered, like a candle just before it sputters out.

Jack had also noticed Tim and Ellie arrive but he was satisfied that he no longer needed to keep such close surveillance. He conceded that he may have been over-zealous there, much of the information in his briefing being based on hypothesis rather than evidence. Besides, he had enough on his plate watching the rest of them.

Professor Gordon's eyes glittered with excitement. He seemed totally oblivious to the fact that his wife now had one long, shapely leg wrapped around Sid's thigh and was gyrating sinuously up and down it like a pole-dancer. The professor pointed to the wine, said something in Greek to Yanni and slapped him on the back. They both burst out laughing. Jack, the All-Seeing, watched them.

'We shan't be staying long, Marjorie,' said Ambrose, his shifty little eyes darting this way and that, hoping for surreptitious glimpses of Diana's bare thigh. 'This alleged religious feast has all the signs of turning into a disgusting pagan orgy. An excuse for bawdy and vulgar behaviour. We shall eat our dinner, since we have paid for it, then we shall go straight up to our room.'

'Shall we, dear?' said Marjorie, calmly. She was wearing a touch of lipstick and eye-shadow, another small rebellion.

Ambrose looked hard at her. 'I'm not sure I understand your tone, Marjorie. And I hope I don't need to remind you that I haven't yet taken my nine o'clock medication, so we must be back in our room by five minutes to nine at the very latest.'

'Must we, dear?' repeated Marjorie, absently.

He gestured at the *bouzoúki* players, twanging like mad.

'Mind you, I doubt we shall get a wink of sleep with that infernal racket going on half the night.'

'I rather like it, dear.'

Maria appeared, staggering beneath the weight of a huge earthenware platter – the main dish of the feast. She placed it in the centre of the table with some ceremony, as though it were a rare delicacy to be appropriately admired before eating.

'What are they, Maria?' enquired Sidney, peering at the long skewers of unidentifiable meat with what looked like fat brown worms wrapped around them.

'*Kokorétsi*,' she announced, proudly. Then seeing the blank faces, she fetched out the dog-eared phrase book. 'Spitted entrails. It is the goat's *sikotária* – er – spleen, liver, heart and lungs tied with intestines and spitted. My mother's spit is the best in all Katastrophos.'

It went ominously quiet.

'Let's all have some wine.' The professor broke the silence, filling everyone's glass with an encouraging flourish. 'Yanni has opened a case of something really special to celebrate. Superior vintage, eh Yanni? As good as anything you'd find on the mainland.' They winked at each other.

Sidney noticed that everyone, including Old Misery Guts, appeared to be enjoying the dark, ruby-coloured wine. Even Tim and Ellie, who mostly drank water, were sipping it with relish. Only Sky abstained, taking a plateful of *kokorétsi* and disappearing up to her room as usual. Sid was a life-long lager-drinker but if wine was on the menu, then wine was what he drank and he intended to taste it properly, like the experts on the telly. To everyone's amusement, he stood up and went through the motions of swirling it in his glass, sniffing it ostentatiously then swilling it round his mouth with a noise like bath water going down the plughole. Finally, he swallowed and rolled his eyes.

'Oh yes, definitely a rugged, versatile little wine, cheeky but not impudent. First used – if I'm not mistaken – by Hannibal the Great to dispatch his elephant after it broke a leg in battle.' He took another mouthful. 'I'm getting paint-stripper on the nose ...' he gulped again, '... and on the palate, turpentine strained through a bus driver's sock.'

That set the tone for the evening and it was all downhill after that. In terms of a religious feast giving thanks to St Sophia, it had more in common with an eighteen-to-thirty reps' night out. Dionysus would be proud of us, giggled Corrie, drawn irresistibly into her parallel world of myth. Of course! That was who Sidney reminded her of – Dionysus, god of wine, whose mission was to end care and worry and promote peace and happiness. He represented all the benefits of wine as well as its intoxicating power to liberate mortals from their mundane selves. So it was under the influence of Dionysus that everyone drank too much, laughed too much and ate too little – except for Ambrose and Marjorie, who went up to their room at 8.50 precisely. Corrie watched them go. Poseidon and his insignificant wife Amphitrite, considered too inconsequential for myth to link her with her tyrannical husband on equal terms and further diminished by poets to a mere metaphor for the sea. But then, thought Corrie, Amphitrite didn't have Poseidon's life insured for a very large amount of cash.

August is the month for folk dancing in the Greek islands and Katastrophos was no exception. When the *bouzoúki* began to play a throbbing *syrtáki* – Yanni had to dance. The music started slow and heavy. He stood in the centre of the floor, arms outstretched and eyes half-closed, bending his knees and swaying as if in a trance. As the tempo increased, he danced a sudden sharp twist or leap in the air before returning to the pulsating rhythm. Sidney, who considered himself a snappy little mover especially when he'd had a few, reckoned it looked just like 'Zorba's Dance' and he'd done a bit of that in the clubs. He joined Yanni on the floor, one arm around his shoulders. It was a bloke's dance, this, so he motioned to the others and soon Tim and the professor had joined in, circling the floor in a line holding each other's shoulders.

'Go on, Jack,' Corrie urged.

'Not on your life. I don't …'

Corrie pulled him to his feet and shoved him on to the floor. She owed him one for putting her on the spot with the cooking. Sid and Tim grabbed him as they danced past and he joined the line winding its way round the floor, stumbling self-consciously while he tried to sort out his feet.

The music was faster now and the ladies were cheering them on, including Marjorie, who had given Ambrose his nine o'clock medication and left him to sulk while she came back down to enjoy the rest of the evening. An even larger rebellion, Corrie noted. It was just as the professor described. Katastrophos really did encourage behaviour outside people's normal, domestic lives. Corrie leaned across, raising her voice to be heard above the music.

'We've met before, briefly, haven't we?'

Marjorie smiled. 'I didn't think you'd recognize me, dear. It was at poor Mrs Braithwaite's funeral, wasn't it? We were on opposite sides of the grave. What an amazing coincidence we should both choose the same island for a holiday.'

'Mm. Wasn't it.' Corrie was starting to believe that nothing about Katatsrophos was coincidence. It was all part of a mystical, cat-and-mouse game designed by the gods to manipulate the lives of mere mortals.

'Terrible thing to happen, her dying like that in the middle of lunch,' continued Marjorie. 'Such a kind, generous lady. I expect you've already worked out that it was her legacy that paid for this trip. I used to help raise funds for her charities.' Marjorie leaned closer. 'Of course, I didn't believe for a single moment that it was anything from Coriander's Cuisine that poisoned her.'

'Thanks,' said Corrie grimly, 'but I expect you're the only one.'

The dancing was starting to hot up. Yanni took one step forward then one step back. The others followed suit. Sometimes his movements were sultry and athletic, other times they were were simply joyful. Yanni took two steps to the left then two to the right. All the line moved in unison. Then Yanni whirled away in front of them, arms raised sideways, taking fast and tricky steps. Suddenly he leapt – waist high it seemed – his body inclining sideways in the air as he fetched his right hand down to slap both his flying heels. Sid crossed his legs, leapt in the air, flicked up his heels and fell over, bringing the whole chorus line down with him.

The shrieks of raucous laughter were so loud that for some time, nobody noticed a different shriek – piercing and tortured. Then the musicians stopped abruptly and everyone turned to see where the screaming was coming from.

Ellie was writhing on the ground, clutching her stomach.

'Oh no, not Ellie,' Corrie heard Jack whisper under his breath. 'Please God, not Ellie. This is all my fault.'

Corrie wanted to ask what he meant but everything became frantic, with people rushing about trying to help but not helping.

Tim scrambled up from the jumble of arms and legs on the dance floor and dashed to his wife's side. He tried to hold her in his arms but she fought him off, raving and delirious.

'Whatever's wrong with her?' he begged. 'Help her, please, somebody help her.'

Corrie and Jack were on their knees, trying to calm Ellie down, but nothing seemed to work. It was as if she couldn't hear them and now she was wheezing, fighting for breath.

'She's really bad, Corrie,' said Jack, desperate. 'This should never have happened and I don't know what to do for her.'

Corrie shook her head helplessly. 'Neither do I.'

'Why are there no bloody doctors on this island and where the hell is Sky?' yelled Jack in frustration. 'Somebody fetch Sky!'

Marjorie was nearest and shot off up the stairs. It seemed like an age but it was only moments before she reappeared with Sky, who wasted no time when she saw Ellie's condition. It was significant, Corrie thought afterwards, that in an emergency nobody questions the qualifications of the person who strides confidently past the anxious crowd saying, 'Stand back – let me through.' They're just relieved that somebody, who appears to know what they're doing, has taken charge of the situation and relieved them of responsibility. So it was when Sky appeared.

'There are too many people crowding her. Please stay back,' she ordered. She knelt and examined Ellie in the same cool, dispassionate way in which she had tended Maria. It was while she was taking her pulse that

Ellie began to jerk and twitch violently, as if having a fit, then she shivered once and went limp. Sky leaned over her, listening, then she sat up abruptly.

'Her heart has stopped.'

Tim's cry of anguish was animal-like in its intensity – like a bull elephant trumpeting its grief. He grabbed Sky's hand.

'Don't let her die, please! She mustn't die. I couldn't bear it.'

In that instant, Corrie was terribly reminded of Orpheus and Eurydice, married and so happy until Eurydice died from a poisonous snake-bite. Orpheus was distraught and pleaded for her life with Hades, God of the Underworld, just as Tim was pleading now.

Sky shook him off and struggled out of her sweater to give herself freedom to move. Then she bent quickly to her task. Placing the heel of her hand in the centre of Ellie's chest, she put her other hand on top and locked her fingers. Arms straight, she began pressing and releasing fast, counting each compression out loud in Greek. Then she stopped, tilted Ellie's head back, pinched her nose and, taking a deep breath, blew into Ellie's mouth. She took another breath and blew again.

Nobody spoke. The only sounds were Tim's desperate choking sobs and the irrepressible cicadas. Biting her lip with tension, Corrie glanced up at Diana and was surprised to see silent tears running slowly down her cheeks.

Sky returned to the compressions, then more breaths – again and again. Time seemed to stand still with everyone praying to their god, to the saints, to anyone they thought might listen – pleading for some sign of life. Ellie was so painfully, heart-breakingly young, not yet out of her teens. It was inconceivable that she should die here on this bewitched and bewitching island, the victim of some mysterious food bug.

Sweat began to drip down Sky's forehead into her eyes and Marjorie leaned carefully across and mopped it gently with her handkerchief. Sky paused almost imperceptibly, trying to judge whether there was any point in carrying on but Tim, tears streaming down his face unchecked, sensed her hesitation and begged her to keep going. Just when everyone had silently given up hope, Ellie trembled, very slightly, then she drew in a long shuddering breath on her own. They must have heard the cheers of relief on the mainland.

Unsmiling but perfectly composed, Sky dismissed their praise but she did allow Tim to hug her briefly.

'Thank you, oh thank you. I'm so grateful. What's wrong with her? Will she be all right?'

Sky looked solemn. 'I believe your wife has ingested the same toxin as Maria. Her symptoms are the same – erratic pulse, vision disturbance, seizures and stomach cramps – but in this case much more severe, resulting in heart stoppage. This indicates that she has probably had a larger amount.'

'Well, that knocks your salmonella egg theory on the head, Cuthbert,' drawled Diana. 'The kid didn't eat any eggs.'

'I'll ring for an ambulance and get her to hospital at once,' said Tim, taking out his mobile phone without thinking.

'Ambulance?' croaked Sid. He was ashamed to find himself choked up and shaking, much more affected by events than he cared to admit. He pulled himself together and put a hand on Tim's shoulder.

'This is Katastrophos, son – not the Isle of Wight. The closest they get to emergency services here is an old monk on a donkey who comes and tells you which saint to speak to. Isn't that right, Prof?'

'I fear so,' said the professor. 'The sea has no timetable, no sense of urgency. You can be trapped on this island for days at a time when the weather has turned sour and destroyed all communications. And, of course ...' he steepled his fingers philosophically, '... your mobile phones are of no use whatsoever.'

Tim helped Ellie gently into a sitting position and almost immediately, she began to vomit violently, with hardly a gasp between spasms, as though she would never stop. This time no emetic had been necessary. Tim kept insisting Ellie should be taken to the mainland and hospital.

'What about the hotel phone? Aren't the wires mended yet?'

Yanni shook his head, his face bleak. 'Still no *tiléfono* to get help,' he said, struggling with the words. 'It was very bad storm. And no ferry will come until next Saturday.'

Tim was frantic. 'But there must be fishing boats, surely. Couldn't we take Ellie across in one of those?' he pleaded.

Jack put an arm around his shoulders. 'I don't think so, Tim. You've seen the boats in the harbour. Most of the larger ones were badly damaged in the storm and as for what's left – I wouldn't risk an owl and a pussy cat, let alone a sick girl. What if there was another storm when you were halfway across? There just isn't anything reliably seaworthy.'

Jack's face was lined with worry. Corrie watched him take Sky to one side and put a hand on her arm. She shrugged it off and turned her face away. Jack stood with his back to Tim and spoke quietly so he couldn't hear.

'Sky, I don't know the extent of your medical experience, but the way you did that CPR makes me think you have considerably more than the average person. In your judgement, will Ellie make it? If we can't move her to hospital until next Saturday, will she survive? Could you look after her here in the meantime? What are her chances, do you think?'

She glared. 'How should I know? I am not God.' Her expression was cold and obdurate, like a hostile witness, refusing to answer his questions. 'You appear to have taken charge here, Inspector Dawes. You are the one giving the orders. *You* decide what to do.' She walked abruptly away from him then turned and spoke over her shoulder. 'You could start by finding out what poisoned her. Then maybe you could obtain an antidote instead of wasting time on pointless speculation.' She returned to Ellie, who was still vomiting painfully but at least she was alive.

Jack watched Sky go. Apart from her strange and unprovoked hostility, there was something odd about what she had just said. He tried to remember her exact words but already they had slipped away from him.

Two hours later they persuaded an exhausted Tim to leave Ellie's bedside where she was sleeping fitfully, watched over by Sky, wordless, unsmiling and vigilant. They sat him down at the big olive-wood table and closed around him, as if trying to provide some sort of comfort. Sid gave him a shot of Metaxa and watched to make sure he drank it. The poor bloke was shattered.

'We were on honeymoon – I promised to love and cherish her, but I didn't, did I? I almost let her die. She *would* have died if it hadn't been for Sky. I should never have brought her to this terrible island. She's too precious and fragile. It's all my fault.'

Tim had reached that final stage of despair where he had begun to blame himself, looking for ways he could have protected Ellie better and prevented this whole, ghastly nightmare from happening.

'What on earth made her so ill?' he kept asking, over and over. 'I know the goat's innards were awful and smelly but she's vegetarian and she didn't touch them. Wouldn't even sit near the plate. She got up and changed her seat twice. And she certainly didn't eat any contaminated eggs like Maria. All she had was salad and half a glass of wine. I don't understand it.' He looked around at them for an explanation.

Corrie frowned. 'I know foreign water can sometimes give you a dodgy tummy but I can't believe there was anything in that Greek salad poisonous enough to nearly kill someone.'

'She's a fit enough young woman,' agreed Marjorie. 'Not what you'd call strapping, perhaps, but it's hard to imagine anything could have affected her so drastically that it stopped her heart.'

'Bloody funny that when Corrie stopped preparing the food, someone else gets poisoned,' said Sid, darkly.

'What do you think, Professor?' asked Jack, pointedly. 'I'm sure you must have some ideas about what it was a young, healthy vegetarian swallowed that nearly killed her.'

'Yeah, you're the great plant expert, Cuthbert,' taunted Diana. 'Give us the benefit of your genius.'

Professor Gordon, who had remained, throughout, a quiet observer on the periphery of the crisis, now became interested and he launched into what threatened to become one of his more technical lectures.

'Well, naturally, I could provide you with an educated guess or two. There *are* plants on Katastrophos that contain toxins – quite potent ones, if you know where to look – but I'm positive Ellie didn't eat any accidentally in her salad. A few rogue leaves picked by mistake by Ariadne would never have that violent effect. No, for an organic poison to be that powerful, you'd first need expert knowledge to identify the appropriate plant – possibly even cross-pollinate using another plant of the same species to modify the genes and increase its potency. Then you'd need to know how to extract the toxin without impairing it and finally distil it into a concentrate. But all that, of course, could not occur accidentally. It would require exceptional skill and expertise and some suitable equipment.' He looked openly at Jack. 'And in any case, why would anyone want to do it?'

'And even if someone did go to all that trouble,' reasoned Corrie, 'how would it find its way into Ellie's salad?'

It was a question that would continue to vex everyone except Jack, who was sure he knew the answer and the reason why – insane though it seemed.

'I've read about foreign plant poisons,' said Sidney, knowledgeably. 'There's a fungus that gradually eats away your gristle. It starts by—'

'Sidney!' they chorused. 'Shut up!'

After a while Tim started to fret, wanting to get back to Ellie, so there was little more anyone else could usefully do that night. They trudged wearily to bed although it was doubtful whether anybody slept much. It had been such a sudden and shocking experience and one not easily forgotten. Never mind a hex, thought Corrie, this is turning into the honeymoon from hell. There were 1,400 Greek islands to choose from and Jack had to pick Katastrophos. She yawned and started to get undressed. Jack was quiet and distracted and Corrie was puzzled. She had recognized the beetle-brows and jutting jaw when he was asking Professor Gordon what he thought caused the sudden illnesses. It was Jack's 'interrogation' face.

'Why were you giving Cuthbert the third degree?' she said accusingly. 'You're not on duty now, you know, and it's very rude to grill people like that, especially when they're on holiday.'

Jack shrugged. 'I wasn't "grilling" him as you delicately put it, I was just accessing his expertise like I would any specialist witness. It's the only way to get information.'

'Oh no you weren't. I know that look. You think he's responsible in some way, don't you? You think he left one of his plant experiments lying around in Ariadne's kitchen and it somehow contaminated Maria's food and then got into Ellie's salad.'

He looked at her but didn't answer.

'Jack, that's absolutely barmy. He's meticulous about keeping his experiments secure – he even wears those surgical gloves to avoid any possible contamination. He'd never be careless enough to allow anything poisonous to get into the food by mistake.'

'What if it wasn't a mistake?' muttered Jack.

Corrie pulled a face. 'What? You think he poisoned Maria and Ellie on purpose? Deliberately used them as guinea-pigs to test something? Now you really are being ridiculous. He's eccentric and a bit arrogant, I admit, but not sadistic. He might poison a few rats but he wouldn't harm human beings. And he'd certainly never hurt Maria. He's been coming to Katastrophos for years. You saw how they welcomed him – like a favourite old relative! In any case, he was down on the ground with you and the other men when she was taken ill.'

'What about the way he went for Ellie when Tim said she was vege-tarian? And then Ambrose because of his plant-based medication. Corrie, the man's clever but he's also a fanatic. You heard him earlier on. He was virtually bragging that he was skilful enough to do it.'

Corrie sighed. 'Jack, you're being melodramatic. He's a professor of botany with a brilliant mind, not a psychopath. He's committed to preserving living things, not killing them. His life's work is based on finding new medicines to cure people.'

'It's plants he's passionate about. I don't believe he's overly concerned about people.'

'OK,' agreed Corrie, humouring him. 'Let's suppose you're right – although I don't believe it for a moment. Suppose he has some crackpot notion that if people eat plants, they deserve to be poisoned by plants. We'd all be potential victims, not just Maria and Ellie. He'd be planning to bump us all off, one by one, and I think somebody would notice eventually, don't you? There'd only be Diana left. He wouldn't experiment on her; he simply adores her.' She became thoughtful for a bit. 'I'm surprised he doesn't pay her more attention, though. Did you see her dancing with Sid? That slimy old creep Ambrose was leering at her. Cuthbert must be very trusting. He doesn't seem to notice other men fancying his wife. It's funny how the assumption of dominance implied by paying for everything is quite obvious in Ambrose and Marjorie's marriage but totally absent in the professor and Diana's. Don't you find that odd?'

'Mmm,' said Jack. Being unable to tell Corrie everything was difficult for him but he knew what would happen if he did. She would interfere. She wouldn't be able to help herself and he didn't want her involved. It was dangerous and the likely outcome was still too unpredictable for him to call. He'd already got it badly wrong in poor little Ellie's case. He must watch more closely, follow up the smallest suspicion. But to move too soon would scupper the whole operation. He stood up, went across to the window, and stared out for some minutes. Then he suddenly hurried back and started to pull on his trousers.

'Now, what's the matter?' asked Corrie, exasperated.

'That light's flashing in the monastery again – I'm going up there to find out what's going on.'

'Not without me, you're not,' said Corrie, hopping about with one leg already in her knickers.

CHAPTER TEN

They had been climbing fast and the steps, hewn from bare rock by the hands of medieval monks, were getting steeper and more irregular.

'What did I tell you?' Corrie's breath rasped painfully from burning lungs. 'Someone's up there, signalling to the crooks that it's safe to bring the loot across and stash it in the monastery!'

Jack, still ascending rapidly, glanced back to make sure he wasn't leaving her behind. She took a deep breath and increased her pace. It had been hard enough on St Sophia's pilgrimage when the steps were wet and slippery in the storm. Now it was pitch-dark except for a dim glow from Jack's torch and, even though she couldn't see it, she was acutely aware of the sheer drop if she lost her footing. They had been halfway up before she realized she was still wearing her slippers. Fortunately they were a Christmas present from her mother so if you ignored the pom-poms, they were fairly sturdy jobs with non-slip rubber soles. Jack stopped for a moment so she could catch her breath. He switched off his torch, plunging them into blackness. There was no moon and the night was so still, the smallest sounds carried. Somewhere in the hills, a far-off kri-kri coughed. They clung to the flimsy handrail, breathing hard.

'Sweetheart, I wish you'd go back.' Jack leaned close and spoke softly in her ear. 'I've no idea what we're going to find up there.'

'I have,' she panted. 'We'll find the thieves' accomplices waiting to winch up the stolen icons and loads of other stuff. We'll hide in the ruins till they've fetched it all up, then you can leap out and pounce on them and I'll grab the—'

Jack sighed. 'Corrie, slow down. You don't know that it's anything of the sort.'

'Yes, I do,' she wheezed, stubbornly. 'Look there.' She pointed out to sea where a light was flashing at regular intervals from a boat not too far away and getting ever closer. 'The crooks are on their way over now. The sea has been too rough for a boat to risk the crossing till tonight. I bet they're desperate to stash the loot somewhere – it must be red-hot by now.'

'Suppose you're right. They aren't going to welcome us turning up and poking our noses into their scam, are they? Please go down. Things could get rough.'

'Don't worry, squire,' came a hoarse whisper from below. 'I'm tooled up.' There was the sound of someone ring-pulling a lager.

Jack and Corrie nearly fell off the steps. They clutched each other, hearts pounding.

'Bloody hell, Sidney! What are *you* doing up here? You nearly gave us a heart attack, you silly sod.'

'Sorry, mate.' Sid advanced a few steps in the darkness, his lighthouse grin instantly recognizable in the light of Jack's waning torch. 'I couldn't sleep for thinking about that poor kid nearly dying tonight. I was out on my balcony when I saw you and your missus legging it towards the monastery, so I thought I'd tag along in case you needed some help. What *are* we doing up here, anyway?'

'We're on the track of a gang of international Greek icon smugglers,' whispered Corrie, excited. 'They're up there, now. Probably a dozen of them.'

'Blimey,' Sid whispered back. 'You going to arrest 'em single-handed, Jack, or do you want me to zap a few as well?'

'Will you listen to yourselves?' hissed Jack, exasperated. 'You're like Batman and Robin. Let's just get to the top before we all break our necks, shall we?'

They carried on climbing in silence, hoarse from all the whispering. Then Jack stopped, suddenly registering what Sid had said.

'What did you mean, you're "tooled up"? You haven't got a gun, have you?'

''Course not. I've brought Ariadne's goat crook.' He waved it about recklessly.

'What good's a goat crook going to be?' Corrie wanted to know.

'Dunno really. I suppose I thought there might be wild animals.'

'Halfway up a Greek mountain?'

'This is a bloody funny island, Corrie. You never know what you'll meet. A mad rat attacked me in the olive grove. Bit right through me sock.'

'I'm starting to understand how it felt,' hissed Jack. 'For God's sake, belt up you two. We're nearly there.'

They crept into the darkened ruins in single file – Jack in the lead, Corrie padding along in her slippers and Sid bringing up the rear with his crook, like a psychotic Bo Peep. We must look ridiculous, thought Jack. If there *were* any smugglers, maybe he could take them by surprise while they were weak from laughing.

The first thing Jack noticed was a pungent smell. It was very familiar but he still couldn't quite place it. The second thing was the grinding noise. It was coming from the far corner of what Corrie had identified as the monastery refectory, overlooking the sea. She grabbed his sleeve and put her mouth close to his ear to whisper.

'That'll be the winch. They must be pulling up something really heavy. Statues maybe.'

The noise was harsh, metal grating on metal, drowning any footfall as they sneaked silently down the nave of the abbey church, one behind the other, then along the east wing until they reached a crumbling archway at one end of the cloisters. It was a good place to hide, crouched down behind the remains of an ornate column. Jack put a finger to his lips and they strained their ears to listen. The grating noise was jerkier now, indicating that a heavy load was nearing the top. Christ Almighty, he thought, irreverently. What if Corrie was right? He hadn't seriously considered it for a single moment. Written it off as one of her barmier brainwaves. Despite what he'd said, he had a pretty clear idea of what he expected they would find in the monastery and it had nothing at all to do with smugglers and stolen icons. Now he wasn't so sure.

He turned and motioned firmly to Corrie and Sid to stay exactly where they were, out of sight behind the column. They were on no account to follow him. They nodded that they understood; Sid confirmed it with a thumbs up. Jack began to edge his way slowly and silently towards the disintegrating portico that was once the elegant entrance to the refectory. Sid and Corrie gave him a couple of yards' lead, exchanged glances and followed him. Jack inched round the last bit of decaying wall and peered into the gloom, dimly lit by the lamp that had been used for signalling which now hung from a rusty iron curlicue on the crumbling wall. A shadowy figure, dressed in a long black cloak with a hood covering his head, was hunched over the winch, cranking the handle.

Had someone conducted a survey of who were actually in their beds that Saturday night in the Hotel Stasinopoulos, they would have discovered that all the men had gone missing. Shortly after Jack, and then Sidney, had crept out of the hotel to investigate the mystery in the monastery, Tim Watkins, still fully dressed, had left his room, unable to rest without his precious Ellie. They had moved her to the other twin bed in Sky's room two floors above, so Sky could watch for any changes in her condition. Sky said that while Ellie had not deteriorated further, she was still in urgent need of proper hospital treatment. Tim sat cross-legged on the floor outside Sky's door, desperate with worry. It was five whole days since the storm and the telephone system was still far from being restored, needing vital parts from the mainland. And although the sea was now calmer, there were no boats on Katastrophos in a sufficiently seaworthy condition to risk a crossing. Tim lowered his head on to his arms. There was still a whole week – seven more endless, nerve-racking days before the ferry would come.

Ambrose Dobson slipped his Paisley silk dressing-gown over his striped pyjamas and quietly eased open the bedroom door. He glanced at Marjorie, lying on her back with her mouth open, snoring gently. He had begun to think the woman would never shut up and go to sleep, going on and on about the silly Watkins girl and what a miracle it was that she had not died. As far as he was concerned, the miracle was that the rest of them had not been poisoned along with her. One thing he was sure about, he would be very careful indeed what he ate from now on, especially with his dicky heart. God alone knew what filth that old foreign witch was putting in their food.

He had heard the quick, light footsteps of Cuthbert Gordon going downstairs some time ago. A light sleeper, he had heard the professor do this on a number of nights and on those occasions he had been gone some time. Tonight, Ambrose planned to take advantage of his absence but he'd had to wait until after Marjorie dozed off before he could creep down to confirm the old fool would be occupied for a while. He moved slowly towards the light that shone in the shambolic kitchen. The professor was chopping something on one of Ariadne's slabs – he couldn't see what. Obviously he was taking precautions by preparing his own food, thought Dobson. The man must be making himself a sand-wich. The professor strolled across and stirred something simmering in one of Ariadne's black pots on the still-hot embers of the stove. From the smell, Ambrose reckoned the idiot was making soup or something similar. In any event, he reckoned it would keep him busy for a while longer. Long enough, anyway.

He nipped smartly back up the stairs towards the room the professor shared with Diana. His heart beat a little faster – not from exertion but from excitement about what he planned to do next. He smiled to himself. His heart wasn't quite as weak as he led Marjorie to believe. As long as he took his medication and avoided anything that might interfere with it, he kept pretty fit. But it suited his purpose to have her running about after him, fussing over him, making sure he didn't overdo it.

His heart had coped well enough a couple of weeks ago on his regular trip to London. He had given that young tart a good going over, no problem. She'd pretended she didn't want to do what he'd paid her for. Women were all the same – they only resisted because they enjoyed being roughed up. He'd shown her he was still a strong, virile man – loosened a couple of her teeth in the process. Well, she could hardly complain, could she? Not in her line of business.

Now he was going to give that brash American bitch a seeing-to she wouldn't forget. Any nonsense and he'd threaten to tell her rich husband she was shagging the plumber. That should change her attitude a bit. Wouldn't want to risk losing all that lovely money, would she? He knew what she was up to. He'd seen her going off in the rowing boat to sunbathe – nude most likely. Then Foskett had sneaked off after her in the other boat. The thought made his mouth go dry and he began to perspire. The stuck-up little Yankee scrubber wouldn't call him names and knee him in the groin this time. He would make her pay for that. Oh yes, he knew how to make her pay all right. He was outside her door now, reaching for the handle, breathing heavily with anticipation. He wondered if she slept naked. He hoped so. He gripped the doorknob with clammy fingers and gave it half a turn. Then he heard the professor's footsteps coming back up the stairs. Damn Marjorie! Why hadn't she gone to sleep sooner? Never mind. It would keep. He slunk quickly back to his own room and climbed into bed, this time making no effort to be quiet. Marjorie sat up.

'What's the matter, Ambrose? Are you ill?'

He thumped his pillow in frustration. 'Go to sleep, woman!'

*

When Maria roused from a half-sleep and reached out a hand to touch Yanni, it met a cold, empty depression in the mattress instead of his lanky, comforting warmth. She woke properly then and swung her legs out of bed. If her husband was where she thought he was and doing what she suspected, he would be hungry and thirsty when he returned. She put on her dressing-gown and tied the frayed cord around her still too-slender waist. She doubted now if it would ever swell and throb with new life. The pilgrimage had been a disaster. St Sophia had not blessed but cursed her, putting terrible pain in her belly instead of a baby. And now the young English girl who also longed for a child and had gone with them to the monastery had been cursed also. What could it mean? What had they done to offend their saint? She believed that it was due only to the generous offerings of amulets and charms that her mother had bestowed on St Sophia that the saint had allowed Ellie and herself to survive. Downstairs in the kitchen she tidied away the customary debris left behind by Professor Gordon, who often came down to use the kitchen during the night. Then she opened a bottle of wine and put out goat's cheese, bread and pickled onions for Yanni when he came home. She hoped he had trodden carefully that night and done nothing further to offend St Sophia.

The hooded figure cranking the winch had its back to them, and because of the grinding noise did not hear them approach. Jack tiptoed forward in a half-crouch, ready to spring at him from behind, unaware that the other two had ignored his instructions and were close on his heels. As Corrie rounded the last bit of crumbling wall, she spotted the sinister figure and clapped a hand over her mouth to stifle a gasp of surprise. Sidney, bringing up the rear, was the last to see him and, unversed in the art of subterfuge, reacted totally spontaneously.

'Blimey, it's a monk!'

The figure whipped round, letting go the handle which spun madly backwards. The rope was unwinding fast with sparks flying from the screaming reel of the ancient winch. Whatever was suspended from the end crashed back down on to the rocks below. Gulls rose shrieking from their roosts and flew into each other, panicking. Like a cornered animal, the hooded figure summed up his situation in seconds and looked frantically for a means of escape. Finally, he made a desperate dash for the crumbling portico and the steps beyond.

Having lost the element of surprise, Jack leapt forward, blocking his path but although he was only feet away, the figure jinked nimbly round him. The chase was on and the monk did three laps of the shadowy refectory, dodging and side-stepping like a ballet-dancer, while Jack made rugby-type lunges at him and Corrie hopped about shrieking and getting in the way. Sidney watched them for a bit, then as the monk came sprinting past with what looked like a clear run to the exit, Sid shouted, 'Oh no you don't, sunshine!' and hooked him neatly round the ankle with Ariadne's goat crook. The monk pitched headlong on to his face.

Jack was on him in a flash. He dragged him to his feet, pulled back the hood and shone the torch in his face.

'Well, I'm blowed!' exclaimed Sid. 'It's old Charon.'

Almost instantly the agile smuggler who, seconds before, had been ducking and diving so nimbly to escape capture reverted to the poor old Greek ferryman with total amnesia. He knew nothing, he gestured. He had little English. He didn't understand what they were saying. They should leave him alone. He had done nothing. He was a sick man. He coughed and spat spectacularly to prove it. It was then that Jack recognized the pungent smell – cheap Greek roll-ups. The sinister garb which in the half-light had looked so like a monk's habit turned out to be a long, hooded fisherman's coat.

'So if Charon's up here with us,' reasoned Corrie, now calm and trying to make sense of it, 'who's down below unloading the stolen icons from his ferry and tying them to the rope?' Her hand flew to her mouth as she realized the full meaning of what they had done. 'Oh my God, Jack! We've just smashed umpteen priceless Greek artefacts on the rocks. They'll probably deport us. We'll be public enemies of the Greek Culture Department, like Lord Elgin after he had it away with their marbles. What on earth are we going to do?'

Sidney, pragmatic as ever, was over by the winch, looking down at the sea.

'Jack, come and have a butcher's at this. What a terrible waste.'

Jack went over to the window, still gripping Charon by the collar of his coat. Corrie followed and they peered down. Dawn was breaking and in the early morning mist Corrie thought it was dark-red blood she could see all over the rocks. Then she spotted the dozens of shattered wine bottles. While they stared down, appalled at the scale of the Dionysian disaster, a figure appeared dressed in dark-coloured trousers and donkey jacket with a cap pulled down over his eyes. Only when he stepped back and looked up to see what had gone wrong with the winch did they recognize the gaunt, swarthy features. It was Yanni.

Further investigation of the abbey vestry revealed case upon case of top quality Greek wine, hidden among St Sophia's precious relics. Jack had no interest in a wine scam. The cursory search he had made of the monastery had not revealed what he was looking for, what he had hoped to find. He frowned, disappointed that yet another hunch had led to nothing and he had only five days left. It confirmed his misgivings about police work based on intuition. He was about to let Charon go when he had one of his better ideas.

'I take it your ferry is anchored down there somewhere?'

The old man nodded and began gabbling again. 'But I am innocent. I know nothing.'

Back, fleetingly, in her parallel universe, Corrie decided Charon was the perfect nickname for this dreadful old reprobate, as the mythological ferryman of the dead was invariably depicted as a sulky, bad-tempered old man. The classical prototype of an undertaker.

'Right,' said Jack firmly. 'We've got a very sick girl on the island. What you're going to do is take her across to the mainland and get her to hospital pronto. Do you understand? Erm … *subito* … *vite* …'

'*Amésos*,' offered Sid, who hadn't wasted *all* his time in the *kafeneíon* drinking and playing cards.

Corrie viewed him afresh and liked him even better. There was much more to this Dionysus than a sombrero with a Union Jack on it.

The old ferryman, aware that he had form as long as his grimy arm for theft and receiving stolen goods, reckoned this was one rap he might avoid if he complied.

'Yes, sir. I go now. I bring ferry round to hotel, sir.' He wriggled free and scuttled off, mumbling Greek oaths and gesturing obscenely at Jack behind his back.

Dawn had barely broken when they eventually got back down to safe ground again. Rather than disturb the other guests, they trooped wearily into the hotel via the kitchen door, which stood conveniently open.

Sidney spotted the bread, cheese and pickled onions on the table.

'Oh good – grub. I'm starving.'

'So am I,' said Corrie. 'I suspect Maria left the food for Yanni but I doubt if he'll show up for a while. We may as well eat it.'

They sat round the kitchen table and Sid poured them each a glass of the illicit wine, wondering if that made them accessories to the crime. With hindsight, he reckoned the Prof must have known about it – all that winking and joking in Greek with Yanni every time he opened a bottle – so that made him an accessory too. He smiled at the thought. It was impossible to imagine the old Prof being involved in any kind of crime. He bet he'd never even had a parking ticket.

Jack grinned at Corrie. 'Looks like you were wrong, Sherlock. Not valuable Greek artefacts – just hookey wine.'

'I was very nearly right.' Corrie bridled. 'I just got some of the finer detail wrong. I said thieves were stashing stolen goods from the mainland up here in the monastery and so they were.' She held up the bottle with no label. 'This wine's obviously nicked or they wouldn't be sneaking it across in the middle of the night. If I'm not much mistaken, what we've been glugging in gargantuan quantities every night is a single variety *Agiorgitíko*. Wine experts have compared it to a good Merlot. It's much too good to be cheap local plonk. Haven't I've said so all along?'

'Yes, dear.' Jack continued to grin infuriatingly.

'*Agio* – what?' Sid asked.

'It's a red grape grown in the Nemea region of the Peloponnese since ancient times and I bet that's where they pinched the wine from.'

'She's good, isn't she?' Sid winked. 'I still think you're wasted in that shoe shop, Corrie. Why don't you pack it in and have a go at catering?'

She winked back. 'Old Charon receives the wine from whoever nicks it in Greece, then ferries it across to Katastrophos where he sells it to Yanni at a profit. Yanni steams off all the labels so nobody recognizes it and sells it to his guests at a bit more profit.'

'Nice little earner all round.' Sid helped himself to more goat's cheese. 'Nice little Greek earner, in fact.' He nudged Jack and winked. 'Geddit? Nice little Greek URN-er?'

'Yes, Sid, very funny,' said Jack wearily. 'I understand the process all right. What I don't see is why they went to all the trouble of smuggling it in at night. And why hide it in the monastery? It's a hell of a business getting it up there. Why didn't they just put it in Yanni's cellar and have done with it? I doubt whether anyone would have noticed, much less cared. It's not as if there's any vigilant law and order on the island.'

'That's right,' said Sid, cheerfully. 'You could get away with murder, here.'

'Come to think of it,' said Corrie, 'when we came across on Charon's ferry, he had some cases of wine in the stern then. Sky sat on them. He brought those across in broad daylight and unloaded them on the quay. Why all the cloak and dagger stuff now?'

'Obvious, isn't it?' Sid mis-speared an onion and it shot across the table and snookered itself behind the wine bottle. 'They had to change their *modus operandi* when they found out Jack was a copper. Must have given them a very nasty turn. I expect they thought you'd been sent to investigate 'em. 'Course, it all went a bit pear-shaped when the storm knocked out the phones because Charon wouldn't have been able to tip off Yanni he was bringing another consignment across. They had to rely on the flashing lights.'

'Wait a minute.' Jack was concerned. 'How did they find out I was a policeman? We didn't tell a soul. Made a point of it, actually.' It had been considered imperative to the success of his assignment that nobody on the island knew.

'Do me a favour, mate,' laughed Sid. 'You've got Old Bill written all over you. Smartly ironed shirts, sharp haircut, nice shiny Plod boots – dead give-away.'

'Oh,' said Jack, sheepishly. He glanced down at his lovingly polished black brogues, wondering why he had not had the gumption to look more like a scruffy holidaymaker. Too little time to plan properly. Always a mistake.

'Anyway, it wouldn't have mattered what you looked like really,' finished Sid, 'because Sky told everyone you were a copper when we first arrived.'

The penny dropped then. Sky had said something odd during their hostile exchange over Ellie but he hadn't been able to put his finger on it at the time. Now he remembered what it was. She had addressed him as Inspector Dawes. How the blue blazes would a Greek hippy he'd never seen before in his life know he was a copper? Not just a copper, but an inspector. It was worrying because it had the potential to foul things up completely if everyone knew. Still, too late to do anything about it now. He would just have to stay alert but look relaxed. He broke off a chunk of bread.

'They needn't have worried. Katastrophos is well outside my jurisdiction. Anyway, I'm off duty. It's for the Greek police to sort out their little fiddle, if they ever manage to track it down to a minuscule island miles from anywhere.'

Sidney uncorked their third bottle of wine. He liked old Yanni so he reckoned it was only right to help dispose of as much of the evidence as possible. He filled Jack's empty glass. 'Is your name really Jack Dawes?' he asked, curious.

'No, it's Rupert actually. I got the daft nickname when I joined the force.'

Sid grinned at Corrie, blearily. 'I bet you're not really called Coriander either.'

'Oh yes I am,' said Corrie. 'It was my mum's fault. She was a cook, too, and she was stuffing a noisette of lamb with herbs when she went into labour with me and my twin brother. She must have been light-headed from the gas and air because she called me Coriander and my brother Basil.'

Sid whistled. 'Lucky she wasn't stuffing a chicken. She might have called you Sage and Onion.'

'Or Parsley and Thyme.' Corrie giggled tipsily. 'Sid, you do make me laugh and you have a lovely smile. How come you're not married? I'd have thought some nice girl would have snapped you up years ago.'

Sid fiddled with the tassels on his scarf. 'I've never had much luck with nice girls. Most of 'em are looking for someone suave and sophisticated, like James Bond, not a plumber who works twenty-four-seven, lives on takeaways and supports Arsenal. I don't understand what makes women tick a lot of the time.'

'Join the club,' mumbled Jack.

Sid peered into the depths of his glass, as if expecting to find the answer there. 'They seem to prefer the bastards who treat them like dirt to a genuine bloke who wants to take care of them. Look at that nice Marjorie Dobson. Thirty years she's been married to Old Misery Guts. Why does she put up with it?'

Corrie shrugged. 'No good asking me. The feminine tendency to self-sacrifice has always been entirely absent in my disposition. Maybe you have to have a child before it kicks in.' Corrie emptied her glass and poured another. 'But I think you underestimate your pulling power, Sid. Diana Gordon finds you very attractive, anyone can see that.' She ignored the cautionary glare from Jack, telling her she was drinking too much and trampling blithely about on sensitive territory.

Sid laughed dismissively. 'She's a cut above the sorts that get down the Stoke Newington Arms on karaoke night, that's for sure. Diana's a lovely lady but it's only a bit of a lark. She's just bored because the Prof's too busy working to spend time with her and like you say, I make her laugh.'

'I think you're very fond of her.' Corrie, more than a little drunk, leaned precariously sideways to whisper confidentially in his ear and lurched almost off her chair. She grabbed the table to steady herself. 'Why don't you say something – hic – instead of pretending it's just a holiday fling? You never know what might happen.'

Sidney fidgeted, uncomfortably. 'Leave off, Corrie. You sound like one of those god-awful women's magazines – all heart-warming and syrupy where everyone lives happily ever after. Real life's nothing like that. Diana's used to the best. She's used to a seriously rich husband, which I'm never going to be. It just couldn't work, could it? I've nothing to offer her.' He'd been absently unpicking the fringe of his Arsenal scarf and now it began to unravel. 'Shit!' he said. 'Sorry.'

'Well, one good thing's come out of last night's fiasco,' said Jack, brightly, sensing Sid and Corrie were in danger of getting maudlin, having consumed awe-inspiring quantities of wine. 'In a couple of hours Ellie will be on her way to hospital.'

'Yeah, that's good. Really good,' slurred Sid. 'Been a heck of a long day, hasn't it? I'm knackered.' He picked up another bottle and staggered towards the stairs for a couple of hours' kip before morning. 'G'night all.'

For once, Jack and Corrie fell into their beds and just lay there, too exhausted for their usual post mortem on the day. Their minds, however, remained determinedly restless. Jack planned to speak to Tim as soon as it was properly daylight and then go down to the landing stage to see them both safely on to Charon's ferry and off to the mainland and hospital. It would be an uncomfortable journey for Ellie but she would have Tim with her and he was confident it was the best thing to do. Jack made a mental note to find out what hospital they took her to. Eventually, they might be able to shed some light on what had poisoned her although it would be too late to help him in the short term. At least she would be safe once he got her away from Katastrophos. This blasted island! It had a way of sidetracking you, upsetting your concentration. He had known Ellie was at risk; all the background information had pointed to it, yet he had still stood by and allowed it to happen. Well, he wouldn't be caught off guard next time – and he knew there would be a next time. He was beginning to gain some insight now, although there were still some aspects that defied logic. What had been the motive for poisoning Maria, or could it simply have been just a rotten egg? Why hadn't his briefing on Marjorie Dobson picked up on her connection to

Lavinia Braithwaite? Where did the weird and stroppy Sky fit into all this and how did she find out his name? And the business of Sid's rash on the wrong hand still niggled at the back of his mind. But the thing that exercised his brain the most, the crux of the whole operation that he had come to Katastrophos to find, still eluded him. He had been so confident the answer was up in the ruined monastery, but he was wrong. He'd wasted a week already and he was running out of places to look. Only seven days left.

Corrie was adrift in no man's land – that nebulous state between sleeping and waking where dreams meet reality and mingle until they become indistinguishable. She had watched Katastrophos work its subtle magic on all of them – not to change them but to liberate their innermost feelings. This weird, hypnotic island had empowered them in some way, intensified the hopes and ambitions that had lain hidden when they arrived. A fanciful notion anywhere else, thought Corrie, but true here. Look at Marjorie, gaining more self-assurance than Amphitrite ever dared to assume. Sidney, cheery Dionysus, falling helplessly in thrall to a mesmerizing but married Medusa, completely beyond his reach. Tim and Ellie, so very nearly Orpheus and Eurydice, the tragic lovers, with timid Tim, made strong by the need to coax his wife back from Hades and Ellie, ever the nervous nymph, who nevertheless made the bold pilgrimage to the monastery in the hopes of a honeymoon baby. On the darker side, there was Sky, vengeful Nemesis, struggling beneath the weight of some huge, bitter injustice she had not yet managed to lift; Ambrose, strutting like Poseidon, believing himself capable of subjugating any woman he chose, and Zeus, the God King – the professor, obsessed with his plants, maybe to forget the bitter reality that his young wife had married him for money and power rather than for love.

Had Katastrophos bewitched Jack? she wondered. Probably not. It was true he was behaving like Argus the All-Seeing, twitchy and watchful. He was always like that when he was working on a case. But he wasn't supposed to be on a case, was he? He was off duty – on honeymoon. So she, Corrie, was the only one to remain unaffected, unbewitched. She was the same as ever, sensible and down to earth. Katastrophos hadn't persuaded her to do anything out of the ordinary. Except for continually feeling herself drawn into a compelling parallel world of ancient Greek gods, cooking for ten people when she was supposed to be on holiday from catering, imagining an international smuggling ring that didn't exist and climbing a mountain in a violent thunderstorm in order to eat a bit of lamp wick. No, she wasn't bewitched at all.

CHAPTER ELEVEN

Sunday morning. Unaware of the nefarious high jinks of the previous night, some of the guests at Hotel Stasinopoulos were surprised to see Charon's ferry moored at the landing stage when they came down early for breakfast. At Jack's instigation, Maria and Sky had prepared Ellie, swaddling her in blankets for her voyage, as the morning sea mist was damp and chilly. Yanni constructed a makeshift stretcher and Tim and Jack carried her to the boat. Jack was privately dismayed that she looked so ill and weighed so little. Even her bright ginger hair seemed dull and lifeless. Jack prayed that with hospital treatment, she would make a complete recovery.

Everybody came down to the quay to see her off except Professor Gordon, who had gone out at dawn to forage in the olive groves on the far side of the hotel, so would not have seen the ferry. Charon and Yanni looked edgy and avoided Jack's eye. In fact, thought Jack, they had done him a favour although they did not yet realize it. Had it not been for their wine fiddle, Ellie would have waited seven more days for hospital care and he tried not to speculate on what that might have meant.

'Take care, dear. I hope you'll be well again soon.' Marjorie Dobson leaned over the stretcher and kissed Ellie lightly on the cheek, then she kissed Tim, tense and anxious to be off. 'Such a shame their honeymoon has to end in this awful way,' she remarked to Corrie.

Corrie glanced at Ambrose, standing a few yards back, shivering irritably in the cool morning air and looking disagreeable. No change there. She was surprised he had made the effort at all, then she had a sudden thought.

'I wondered, Marjorie, since the ferry is making an unscheduled trip back to the mainland, whether you and Ambrose might have taken advantage of the opportunity and gone home early. I remember Ambrose saying he wanted to leave last week.'

Marjorie's expression was hard to read. 'Mm. I was expecting him to start playing up, insisting we went home, too, but he said there was something he still needed to do on the island. We'd paid for two weeks and he was staying until he'd had his money's worth. Well, my money's worth to be accurate. "There are still some debts outstanding" was the way he put it. And naturally, I don't want to go yet. I rather like it here and I don't know about Ambrose but there are certainly some things I promised myself I'd do before I went home.' She smiled enigmatically, pulled her cardigan closer and walked back to Ambrose.

'Good luck, kid.' Diana stepped forward. Her blonde hair was tousled as if she'd just got out of bed and she wore an ivory silk peignoir trimmed with maribou. Even without make-up she still looked gorgeous, Corrie observed ruefully. She was surprised to see her discreetly shove a fistful of notes into Tim's hand. 'Get something to make her feel good – roses, perfume, you know the kind of thing she likes.' Easy to be generous with your husband's money, thought Corrie uncharitably.

Sidney had climbed aboard the ferry with Jack and was helping to make Ellie as comfortable and stable as possible for the trip. The sea promised to be calm – at least for the next twenty-four hours. Satisfied, they came ashore and joined everyone else on the jetty, waiting for Charon to start the engine. The last person to leave Ellie was Sky. She had spoken at length to Tim and provided such medical advice as she could with regard to the journey. He hugged her and she was visibly moved. Then she stepped nimbly up the gangplank on to the quay and disappeared back to the hotel without speaking or looking at anyone.

'I thought Sky might have gone with Ellie,' Corrie said to Jack.

He shrugged. 'So did I. But she said there was nothing more she could do for her and she needed to stay on Katastrophos for a while longer. Something she needed to do.'

'I don't suppose you feel like going home, do you?' said Corrie, wistfully. Her honeymoon hex had kicked in with a vengeance this time and she was homesick for her squashy, king-size bed and a deep, hot bath full of bubbles. She was also keen to find out if she still had a business or whether the answerphone was bristling with cancellations following poor Lavinia's unfortunate death.

'Not really, sweetheart. I admit it's tempting but there's something I have to finish here before I can leave.'

What *were* all these things that people felt they absolutely had to do before they could leave Katastrophos? There was nothing Corrie wanted to do. As far as she was concerned, she could cheerfully leave right now, without a backward glance!

'Besides,' said Jack, giving her a squeeze, 'we still have the rest of our honeymoon to enjoy.'

She stared at him. 'I can't believe you just said that. It's been sheer unadulterated hell so far. Why should it suddenly become enjoyable?'

'What's happening? What's going on?' Professor Gordon approached at a trot, his spindly legs twinkling towards them. He still carried his bulging sample case. 'Why is Charon's ferry here? It's not due until Saturday.' His tufts of bright ginger whiskers bristled with alarm 'You're not leaving, are you, Diana? You're not going home without me?' His face was filled with concern.

Bless, thought Corrie. It was heart-rending the way he adored his wife in spite of her being a mercenary, duplicitous little tart.

Diana strolled over to him. 'Does it look like I'm going home, Cuthbert?' She held out the silk skirts of her négligé, revealing glorious naked thighs. 'I don't regularly travel in my night clothes.'

He calmed down. 'No, of course you don't, my darling. Silly of me.'

Charon started the engine and they stood clear of the clouds of stinking blue smoke.

'The ferry is taking Ellie to hospital, Professor,' explained Corrie.

'Already?' He seemed agitated. 'But I thought she wasn't going until next Saturday.'

'Slight change of plan.' Jack spoke to the professor but was looking at Yanni. 'Charon turned up unexpectedly on another matter entirely and was kind enough to agree to take Tim and Ellie back with him.'

'Oh. I see. Well, that's splendid – er – splendid.' The professor appeared distracted. He consulted his Rolex, which was when Jack noticed the blistery rash on the back of his hand.

'That looks nasty, Professor. How did it happen?'

He glanced at it, vaguely. 'What? Oh, that. I nicked one of my surgical gloves with the scalpel when I was taking specimens. Must have let some sap through.' He rubbed at it absently.

'I had a rash just like that,' said Sid, holding out the back of his hand. 'Mine's nearly gone now, though.'

The professor beamed. 'Yes, I remember, old chap. It would have been the mucilaginous liquid from the *Ecballium elaterium*, the squirting cucumber. Magnificently potent! I did warn you it might cause a reaction.'

'No, I don't think it was that,' began Sid, 'because the squirty cucumber was on the other ...' He stopped abruptly as Jack grasped his arm with iron fingers. 'Er – yes, I guess you're right, Professor.' He raised puzzled eyebrows at Jack.

'Well thank goodness that's all sorted.' Corrie took Jack's arm briskly and led him back up the path to the hotel and breakfast, such as it was. 'You've solved the riddle of the flashing monastery, Ellie's safely on her way to hospital where they'll do tests and find out what made her ill, and Maria's fully recovered from her bad egg or whatever it was she ate. And so far, Marjorie hasn't shown any obvious signs of bumping off Ambrose. Even if we can't go home yet, maybe we shall get a few days' peace and quiet with no more crises. Maybe, too, you'll relax at last and stop treating Professor Gordon like some latter day Dr Crippen.'

'What did you say?' Jack was miles away.

'I said maybe we'll get a bit of peace and—'

'No – I mean the bit about Dr Crippen. He was a poisoner, wasn't he? He poisoned his wife. I wonder what he—'

'Jack! Don't start! Just do not start!'

They were lying in the ripples, where baking sand met the silvered calm of the Ionian. The sun beat down on the arid rocks where lizards squinted and shed their skins. They had oiled their supine bodies so that they should not shed theirs. For the first time since their arrival, Corrie felt Katastrophos seemed like something approaching Poseidon's island paradise instead of the holiday resort from Hades. But even so, her mind would not relax totally. So much had happened that was still unexplained and the answers shimmered, like smoke and mirrors, just out of her reach. It was that blasted disengagement from reality that the professor had talked about. She squinted sideways at Jack, lying apparently dozing but with that 'coiled spring' look that implied he could leap into action at a moment's notice.

'Haven't you got small feet,' he observed, drowsily nudging her toes with his.

'Small feet run in my family.'

'Big noses run in mine.'

They giggled at their feeble jokes then Corrie asked:

'How d'you suppose Sky found out you were a copper?'

'Dunno,' he said without opening his eyes. 'Maybe she saw my hand-cuffs.'

'What?' Corrie sat up, horrified. 'Jack, you didn't bring your hand-cuffs on honeymoon! Whatever will people think? I expect Sky has told everyone about them as well. They'll have us down as one of those weird couples who do kinky things to each other.'

'I didn't bring them on purpose, sweetheart,' he lied. 'I just forgot to take them out of my jacket. Stop getting wound up about nothing. Like you said, all the crises are over now. Let's just relax and enjoy the sun.'

Unconvinced, she lay down again and put her sunhat over her face. If I were a betting person, she thought, I'd put next month's profits on Jack the All-Seeing being up to his multiple eyes in something dodgy that he still isn't telling me about.

It was early evening and the sun had lost much of its fire as they strolled back to Hotel Stasinopoulos to see what was for dinner. They heard the wailing and moaning even before they reached the paved forecourt. Jack broke into a run and together they raced to the kitchen where everyone was crowding around Ariadne. She was flapping her apron and screeching '*Ayoo! Ayoo!*' Her distress was obvious and very noisy. Maria tried to comfort her but she would have none of it and continued afresh, her cries rising and falling in ear-splitting crescendos.

'What's the matter with her?' Jack asked Diana.

Diana shrugged. 'Search me. She was taking her usual nap in the olive grove, when she woke up suddenly and started that god-awful howling. I'll fetch Cuthbert. She's crazy about him. He'll calm her down.'

'For Gawd's sake, Ariadne, give it a rest, love,' Sid bellowed. 'You're giving us all GBH of the ear'ole. What's up? Are you in pain?' He looked round at them bemused. 'Who'd have thought a racket like that could come out of such a little old lady? We could do with her in the crowd up the Stadium.'

'Damned woman's probably poisoned herself instead of us, for a change,' said Ambrose, cynically. 'Serves her right. Someone give her a good slap.'

'Dear me,' said Marjorie to Corrie. 'You don't think she really is victim number three, do you?'

'I doubt it. She isn't clutching her stomach or writhing in pain – just sitting there shrieking.'

Diana returned then with the professor. He went straight to Ariadne and spoke gently to her in Greek. She gabbled back, plucking at his arm and gesticulating. Jack feared it might indeed be another case of poisoning until he caught the words: 'Agia Sofia' a couple of times and guessed it was something superstitious that was making her bawl. He relaxed – but only slightly.

'Ariadne has had a dream,' announced the professor with heavy portent.

'Is that all!' Sid sat down. 'I have nightmares most nights. Usually about Arsenal losing at home to—'

'Yes, thanks, Sid,' interrupted Jack. 'What sort of dream, Professor?'

'She says St Sophia appeared to her. The saint is very angry because women – foreign women – who are not from the island were permitted to take part in her pilgrimage.'

'Oh *Mitéra*!' Maria was horrified. 'But we thought she would be pleased. Is that why she sent the sickness of the stomach to poor Mrs Watkins and me?'

Ariadne gabbled some more, then buried her face in the professor's jacket and would speak no more.

'It appears,' he said, patting her small head, 'that St Sophia has cursed Katastrophos and that one by one, all the women will take the sickness and die.'

'Oh nice,' said Sid. 'With a saint like that you don't really need the devil, do you?'

Corrie glanced at Jack to see what he thought of Ariadne's revelation, but he wasn't looking at her, he was watching Cuthbert Gordon.

'I'm not standing here wasting my time listening to this absurd clap-trap!' Ambrose grasped Marjorie's elbow. 'The woman's clearly unhinged. Living in the Dark Ages. She'd have been burned as a witch not so long ago. Come along, Marjorie, I need you to cut my toenails.'

'In a minute, dear.' She gently but firmly unhooked her arm from his grasp. 'I want to hear what the professor thinks. You go on up – I'll be there in a minute.'

For a moment it looked as though Ambrose was about to protest, make a humiliating scene and order Marjorie to do as she was told. Indeed, he opened his mouth to do just that, then he saw her firm, unwavering expression – one he had never seen before – and thought better of it. He would speak to her later about her persistent and unacceptable rebelliousness. He folded his jacket carefully over his arm and walked with small petulant steps towards the stairs.

'My mother has the powers,' explained Maria. 'She is what you call ...' out came the ancient phrase book, '... soothsayer.'

'That's all we're short of,' mumbled Sid. 'A flippin' prophet of doom.'

'Last week,' continued the professor, 'just before the pilgrimage to the monastery, Ariadne came to me and told me she had been walking on the great white cliff above Katastrophos Bay. Suddenly, she saw the sea curdle and become very still. Far out, a dim form rose up, hovered there pointing a finger, then disappeared again beneath the waves. She believes the figure was St Sophia. Ariadne says it was a warning which went unheeded.'

'Ariadne's nuts,' said Diana shortly.

'It's all very well to scoff, my darling,' admonished the professor, 'but there is a special kind of presence here on this island. It's not at all uncommon for visitors of sensibility to have an almost uncomfortable feeling that evil is close by, at their elbow, just out of sight. Ariadne is a Katastrophan of some twenty generations. In her, this sensibility is magnified many times into a gift that can translate mere instinct into premonition.'

'All right,' said Sid, 'ask her who's going to cop it next. At least we'll get a bit of warning this time.'

But Ariadne would say nothing more. As it turned out, her soothsaying was about as reliable as her cooking because the next victim of St Sophia's imagined wrath wasn't a woman at all – it was a man.

The days that followed felt surreal to Corrie – like living in a time warp where nothing moves on because everyone is waiting for something to happen. What she couldn't understand was why they hadn't all legged it back to the mainland double quick when they had the chance. She would have gone like a shot. They were all masochists in her view. The professor didn't want to leave until Saturday because there were still some specimens he needed, Diana had promised she would stay with him and Sid didn't want to leave as long as Diana was there. Everybody else, including Jack, apparently had 'things they needed to do' before they could go home. Barmy, the lot of them.

Professor Gordon continued to spend his days in the olive groves and his nights in Ariadne's kitchen. Diana sunbathed down the other end of the island, making love and drinking wine with Sid who had decided it was his moral duty to dispose of as much of the evidence from the smuggling fiddle as physically possible. Sky spent her daylight hours bathing her spirit in *To Phos* – the Incredible Light. Not that her spirit showed any noticeable signs of improvement. She was just as surly and withdrawn as when she arrived. Marjorie went into town on her own and bought a pair of rather nice terracotta vases for her son and his partner without any reference to Ambrose whatsoever. Ambrose lurked in corners, spying on Sid and Diana, his piggy little eyes glittering hungrily. All he needed was a dirty raincoat.

'Come here, Marjorie, I wish to speak to you.' Ambrose was waiting for her in their room when she returned from shopping for souvenirs. She regarded him for a moment, sitting stiffly upright on the edge of his bed, a sour expression on his puffy face. It was as if she was seeing him through the security peephole of a door – turnip head, bulbous nose, bulging eyes, spherical body and short, fat little legs. She smiled to herself at the analogy then put down her bags and turned to confront his scowl.

'If it's one of your pompous lectures, Ambrose, make it snappy because I've promised to meet the others in the bar for a glass of wine and you know what an old windbag you are, once you get going.'

Ambrose turned a very unhealthy mauve. 'How dare you speak to me like that! I have to say, Marjorie, I've noticed a most unpleasant truculence creeping into your behaviour since we've been on this infernal island and I'm telling you now – I don't like it. And as for meeting the others, you will do nothing of the sort. I will not have my wife drinking in bars like a common trollop.'

Marjorie looked him straight in the eye, her gaze steady. 'Yes, well you'd know all about common trollops, wouldn't you, Ambrose? You spend quite a lot of your time and money on them.'

Ambrose was furious but at the same time cautious, sensing that he was losing some of the moral high ground. How had the wretched woman found out about his trips to Soho? Had she been snooping – going through his pockets, checking his bank statements? No, she wouldn't dare. Wouldn't have the wits. All the same, this needed careful handling. He took a deep breath, thinking fast.

'I shall ignore that somewhat hysterical remark because you are clearly unwell. I suggest you lie down and keep quiet for the rest of the day and we'll say no more about it.'

'I've never felt better in my life and I've no intention of lying down.'

She opened the wardrobe, took out a fresh blouse and began to change. 'Ambrose, you really must try to drag yourself into the twenty-first century, you're like some pathetic old Victorian patriarch – all piss and wind.'

'Marjorie!'

'Because you're so totally self-absorbed, you probably haven't noticed, but wives aren't slaves and chattels any more. We don't warm slippers, have dinner waiting on the table and speak when we're spoken to. We have careers and lives of our own. Speaking of which, I've decided to get a job when I get back to Hampshire. Fund-raising for charities, most probably. I'm good at that.'

Incensed, Ambrose jumped up and grasped her firmly by the shoulders. 'You will do exactly what I tell you! I think you may have forgotten, Marjorie, the little chastisements I was forced to inflict upon you when we were first married and you needed discipline. Don't imagine for a moment that I'm incapable of punishing you now if you persist with this insolence.'

'Is that what you do to your trollops? Punish them? Is that why there's blood on your pants when you come home?' She shook herself free and her lip curled with disgust. 'You're sick, Ambrose. Sick, pathetic and ridiculous.'

He struck her, a back-hander across the face with all his strength. She staggered backwards but did not fall. Slowly, she raised her head and lifted a hand to her lips, tasting the blood from the cut made by his Masonic signet ring. He had expected her to be contrite, her flash of rebellion crushed, but her face was defiant, full of contempt.

'That's the last time you will ever do that. And that's a promise.'

CHAPTER TWELVE

The endless ranks of dense olive trees meant that walks on the inland hillsides of Katastrophos were scenic but monotonous, unless, of course, you were a botanist. The trees were ancient and each family had its own grove; the result being a golden oil that Corrie believed would probably snaffle a clutch of international medals if it ever became public. She intended to take some home for Coriander's Cuisine. It was a gloriously sunny day so she persuaded Jack the All-Seeing that a blink was not out of the question and he could accompany her to St Sophia to buy some oil and possibly some of the island pottery and wood-carving to take home. As they made their way down the stony path that led from the front of the hotel to the road, Jack paused, staring up at the peeling façade and the three hideous Gorgons glaring down from the roof.

Although he considered himself a tough copper, Jack was not insensitive to myth embodied in sculpture. As he met Medusa's gaze, he began to feel the sinister, ethereal nature of the island. The insane grin, the goggling eyes, the hissing ringlets of snakelike hair, the spatulate tongue stuck out as far as it would go between sharp protruding fangs. No wonder she turned blokes to stone. He looked hurriedly away, and went to catch up with Corrie who had stopped to admire the hibiscus, although not with quite the same intimate intensity as the professor.

'Blast!' Jack felt in his pockets. 'I've left my wallet in our room. Wait here a minute and I'll nip back and get it.' He turned back towards the front entrance, leaving Corrie rehearsing some choice remarks about security and the poor example set by policemen who don't look after their valuables, in return for the lecture he'd given her when she'd inadvertently microwaved her credit cards.

She was watching Jack loping easily across the hotel forecourt when out of the corner of her eye, on the very periphery of her vision, she thought she saw Medusa move. She looked away, then looked back. No, it was just shimmering in the sun – an optical illusion, like Tarmac in a heat wave. Her sunglasses must have distorted her distance vision. She took them off, polished them, then squinted again. This time there was no doubt about it. The heavy stone sculpture, central and most terrifying sister of the ghastly trio of Gorgons, was rocking silently on her plinth. Only a sprinkling of dust heralded her imminent descent. Oblivious, Jack was almost beneath her when she started to topple.

It was useless to yell. He would simply have stopped right where he was and turned to see why she was shouting. It had to be a split-second, knee-jerk decision and Corrie made it. She had seen plenty of flying tackles at police rugby matches but never dreamed she would need to attempt one herself. She flung down her handbag – an unnecessary preliminary for most half-backs – sprinted the distance between them and dived at Jack's knees, bringing him down just feet from where Medusa crashed thunderously and spectacularly to pieces in a cloud of dust and stone. The Gorgon's last act of malice was to split Jack's head open with a flying snake, shattered from her hair.

They lay in the debris, gasping, bits of plaster raining down on them from the crumbling façade – but they both heard it. Footsteps running away across the roof. This was no accident. Medusa had been poised steadfastly on her perch for at least 200 years – she had not fallen off without considerable help. Blood was pouring down Jack's face from a nasty gash across his forehead and he was clearly dazed. Both Corrie's knees were badly grazed and one elbow was throbbing but she scrambled up and ran for the hotel entrance.

'Stay there!' she shouted, somewhat gratuitously. 'I'm going after him.'

Jack struggled to his knees, blood in his eyes. 'Corrie, no! Come back! You don't understand ...'

Yanni and Maria came running out, alarmed at what sounded to them like the beginnings of an earthquake. Corrie did not stop to explain. Inside the hotel, a quick glance confirmed that the lobby was empty. Good. He was still up there. She would search the roof and all the rooms if necessary. What she would do when she found him, God alone knew, but she would want to know why he was trying to kill Jack, because that was undoubtedly what would have happened if Medusa had fallen on him. She took the low stairs two at a time, wheezing now and wishing she were slimmer and fitter. When she reached the top floor, she flung open the double doors at the end of the landing, leapt out on to the balcony and scrambled up the little ladder on to the roof.

Corrie was too late. Someone had been there and left in a big hurry. The ubiquitous pots of geraniums that adorned most houses on Katastrophos, had been knocked from the iron railings and upturned, spilling earth and crushed red blossoms. Here at the back, the hotel was deeply embedded in the side of a steep slope. This meant only one storey, making it easy for someone to climb on to the flat roof and from there, up into the hills, to disappear among the dense olive groves and thick banks of cypress. Rough footprints in the spilled earth confirmed the direction of the culprit's escape. Corrie swore. She had assumed she would meet whoever it was running down the stairs, or at least corner him in one of the rooms. At no point had it occurred to her that he would get away across the roof. He could be anywhere by now.

She scratched about for a bit, looking for clues as Jack would have done, but she couldn't find anything unusual – just some old earthenware pots and a rusty old crowbar that looked as though it had been up there for years. As Jack said, in real police investigations they very rarely found incriminating buttons or convenient pieces of material caught on a nail, which instantly identify the villain. Of course, there was always DNA, assuming Jack could ever get it analysed out here. The bloke must have sweated a bit pushing the statue off the roof but even if he had, any dampness would probably have evaporated by now in this blazing sun. Maybe he had left some skin behind. She crossed to the front of the roof and looked to see if anything had snagged on the two remaining Gorgons. A few hairs would be good – one hair, even. What she found exceeded her wildest expectations.

Jack was in the kitchen, where Maria was bathing his head and gabbling apologies, clearly under the impression that the near fatal accident was caused by the instability of the hotel's external fabric. He was clearly relieved to see Corrie safely in one piece, albeit with bumps and grazes and didn't even give her the usual row about interfering. She had retrieved her handbag and prudently concealed in it the evidence she had found. She didn't need DNA to know who it implicated but to her, it didn't make any sense. Why would he want to harm Jack? Jack was still shocked and would have a formidable headache for a while. She decided it might be wise not to mention what she'd found until she had done a bit of investigating of her own, so when Jack gave her a questioning look, she shook her head. One sniff of her evidence and he would be in there with his handcuffs, reading the man his rights. That was, if an English copper could do that on a Greek island. One thing was certain, you couldn't call a local policeman on Katastrophos. Better to let people think it was the result of structural subsidence for the time being – just an unfortunate accident. A case of being in the wrong place at the wrong time.

Jack winced as Maria swabbed his gash with antiseptic. There was no chance of getting it stitched – not for a week anyway. He grinned ruefully.

'Essentials everyone should pack for a carefree honeymoon on Katastrophos – sun cream, a swimsuit, your own supply of blood plasma and a couple of syringes of anti-toxin. I'm sorry Corrie. This hasn't turned out the way I expected at all.'

Jack wasn't entirely sure what he *had* expected. The operation had never been properly thought out. He'd been flying by the seat of his pants, as the Chief Super put it, since day one. But he was ninety-nine per cent certain he knew who was responsible for the attempt on his life and he was annoyed with himself. He should have been on his guard for something of the sort once he knew his cover had been blown. Now that his quarry was on to him it would be nigh on impossible to nail him.

That evening at dinner Ambrose appeared minus his hairpiece. He looked so completely different without it, like Humpty Dumpty in a suit, it was impossible that it would pass without a comment from somebody.

'What's happened to your wig, mate?' asked Sidney without preamble.

Ambrose was clearly seething, having spent several hours confined to his room arguing with his wife. He had no intention, he told her, of appearing in public without his hair. It was a matter of personal pride and his dignity was at stake. They would therefore both remain in their room except for when they went into town and then he would go down wearing his panama. This meant they would have all their meals sent up. Marjorie, her derision barely concealed, informed him she would do nothing of the sort. She was going down to dinner with or without him. She also said that in her opinion, he looked quite ridiculous with a lump of dead hair glued to his scalp and his baldness was, if anything, a slight improvement. She privately suspected that, in addition to his hairless-ness, he did not wish any of them to see her cut lip, now badly bruised and swollen.

Ambrose answered Sidney with cold disdain. 'My hair enhancement was stolen this morning while I was in the shower. Quite outrageous. This place is nothing but a seething sewer of thieves, half-wits and the criminally insane. I'd report the theft to the police if there were any on this god-forsaken island. The sooner I get back to Hampshire and civilization the better.'

'It's a bit queer, though, isn't it?' said Sid. 'Who'd want to nick your rug? You sure you haven't just lost it somewhere?'

'Of course not!' Ambrose bristled with anger and embarrassment. 'I know perfectly well where I left it and when I came out of the shower, it had gone.'

'He hangs it on the door handle over night,' said Marjorie, conversationally. 'At home, he puts it on one of those wig stands on the dressing-table. Used to give me quite a turn when I woke up in the night and saw it reflected in the mirror. Like a dismembered head.'

'Can you please stop discussing my private affairs in public, Marjorie? It really is extremely bad taste and you should know better. Goodness knows I've tried to teach you some refinement over the years but you're clearly too crass to learn anything.'

'Marjie, that's a very nasty cut on your lip,' said Sid, concerned. 'I couldn't help noticing. Looks real painful. How did you do it?'

'She fell and hit her mouth on the corner of the bedside table,' answered Ambrose, immediately. 'Probably too much to drink, she always was clumsy. And my wife's name is Marjorie, if you don't mind. Diminutive names are the prerogative of the working class.'

Diana, furious at this put-down, both on behalf of Sidney and Marjorie, picked up a napkin and began to polish Ambrose's bald head vigorously, making squeaking noises. 'Never mind, Amby, honey,' she cooed, mockingly. 'I think you look real cute without your hair. Like a bad-tempered baby.'

He fended her off with a look of sheer menace. She laughed at him.

The food arrived then – rough lumps of meat stewed in a kind of brown slurry and served on a large metal dish.

'Oh, good,' said Sid gloomily. 'Looks like braised armadillo on the half-shell again.'

They helped themselves, picking at it warily. The insubstantial but niggling possibility of food poisoning hung inexorably over them each time food was served. It was not the cheeriest of meals but when Sky appeared, the storm clouds really gathered. She looked as though she had seen a ghost. The tan acquired from bathing in the Incredible Light drained from her skin, and her deep-set, red-rimmed eyes burned with almost spectral intensity. Then, without a word, she turned and went back upstairs to her room.

Under cover of the general buzz about how ill Sky looked, probably due to lack of sleep while she was nursing Maria and Ellie, Corrie opened her handbag under the table and nudged Jack to look inside. He glanced down casually then his eyes widened in disbelief.

'Would you excuse, us, please?' He stood up, grabbing Corrie's throbbing elbow making her wince. 'There's something I need to discuss urgently with my wife. We'll be back shortly.'

He frogmarched her inside the hotel, across the lobby, and out through the front door where the shattered remains of Medusa still lay in a murderous heap.

'Why the hell did you pinch Dobson's wig, you daft bat?' Jack was totally dumbfounded. It was a completely incomprehensible thing to do, even for Corrie.

'I didn't pinch it and keep your voice down.'

'Well, who did then?'

'No one. I found it – up there.' She pointed to the two remaining Gorgons on the roof and the empty space between them, like a gap in a row of decaying teeth.

'What? Why on earth didn't you tell me before?'

Corrie was unrepentant. 'You were wounded and dazed. I didn't want to worry you. Besides, I needed to do some snooping first. Obviously I deduced immediately that it was Ambrose Dobson who heaved Medusa off the roof and lost his wig in the process. The glue melts in the heat and it slides about pretty easily – we saw that when Sid accidentally hooked it on his fork last week.' She was animated now, warming to her theory. 'Once I knew it was him, I wanted to march up and smack him hard in the mouth but I couldn't because first I had to find out his motive. Why does he want to kill you? That's the important question. Well, I reckon I've worked it out. He's a wanted criminal on the run and he escaped to Katastrophos where he thought nobody would find him. All that talk about wanting to go home was a smokescreen. After all, he didn't go when he had the chance, did he? And I remembered Marjorie saying he still had "some unfinished business", meaning finishing you off. When he found out you were a copper, he thought you might recognize him from his mugshots, so he had to silence you before you got home to England and had him brought back to face justice. He's a nasty piece of work – form as long as your arm, I shouldn't wonder. Robbery with violence, blackmail, drug-running, money-laundering, you name it. I bet he's travelling under an assumed name with a false passport. Anyway, I thought I'd wait till he and Marjorie went out, then I'd go up and have a bit of a snoop around. See if I could find out his real identity. Trouble is, he hasn't left his room all day because he didn't want anyone to see his bald head. I expect the wig's part of his disguise and—'

'Corrie, for pity's sake!' Jack passed a weary hand over his eyes. 'Ambrose Dobson is a retired insurance man with a weak heart. Not a convicted criminal, not an escaped gangster and not the person who pushed Medusa off the roof. The effort would probably have killed him rather than me. He's just a harmless, rather unpleasant little man who—'

'... hits his wife,' finished Corrie defiantly. 'How do you know he's not a wanted criminal?'

'I just do, that's all. You'll have to take my word for it.'

'So *he* isn't the one you've been keeping an eye on since you got here, either?'

'No. Now please give him back his hair and try not to interfere any more, my darling. Especially don't go snooping about in people's rooms. It's breaking and entering.'

'What if I pinch the key?'

'Corrie, promise me!'

'Oh, all right,' Corrie said grudgingly. 'I'll hang it on his door handle in the morning. But if it wasn't him, how did his wig get on the roof?'

'I've no idea. Maybe someone wanted me to think it was Dobson.'

'I see what you mean.' Her imagination went into overdrive again. 'Someone nicked it this morning while Ambrose was in the shower, then planted it at the scene of the crime to make him chief suspect in a murder. But who dislikes him enough to put him in the frame like that? He's only been here a week.' She had a sudden thought. 'Oh Jack, you don't think it was Marjorie, do you? I mean, she's an obvious suspect and she had motive and opportunity. She must loathe the miserable little bugger after thirty years of being bullied. It would be the perfect way to get shot of him. What's the prison sentence for attempted murder?'

'Don't be daft. Marjorie isn't strong enough to heave a statue off the roof and in any case, I don't think she'd be prepared to kill someone just to get her old man put away.'

'No, course not. And she wouldn't be able to claim on his life insurance, either. She needs him to be dead, not just in the nick. I wasn't thinking it through properly. OK, so what we have to do now is—'

'Corrie, you're not going to do anything. This isn't a game of Cluedo, it's serious and people have been hurt already, including you. Look at your knees.'

She looked down. They were raw and inflamed and very sore.

'So please, do me a favour and stay out of it. I'll tell you everything when it's all over.'

'Promise?'

'Promise.'

CHAPTER THIRTEEN

The following morning, Jack and Sidney went fishing in Katastrophos Bay. One of the local fishermen made a bit of cash from the occasional independent traveller by offering trips in his boat, rods and bait provided. He had optimistically come by the hotel to see if anyone was interested. Sid was keen and Jack agreed to go with him, which surprised Corrie. For a start he got seasick just watching the sponge floating in the bath and she didn't think he'd want to be out at sea after what he'd said about keeping a close eye on things on the island. She wondered how he was still able to do it from a fishing boat. Or could it be that Sidney was the one he was keeping an eye on? In any event, Corrie decided it was the perfect opportunity to do a bit of fishing of her own, now she had discovered Jack was on some kind of mission. She knew she'd promised not to interfere, but then hadn't he promised he was off duty? It was a diabolical liberty, working when he was meant to be on honeymoon. Anyway, where was the harm in a bit of snooping? If she found something useful, it would be a bonus and if she didn't, no one would be any the wiser. She'd been thinking about it during a hot, sleepless night and there were lots of questions milling around in her head. Vague recollections of a shove in the back during the storm, towels stained with dark-blue dye, and the undisguised malice of Nemesis. She was especially intrigued by Nemesis. It was time to find some answers.

By mid-morning the hotel was deserted of guests. Corrie went down to the reception desk and pretended to write postcards until Maria bustled off to the kitchen to help Ariadne with lunch. The Medusa incident had been passed off as just an accident waiting to happen in a building as old as Hotel Stasinopoulos and Yanni had climbed up on to the roof to check the stability of the two remaining Gorgons. He was pleased because he had found his missing crowbar up there. Only Ariadne suspected foul play. She was sure St Sophia had been responsible and that it was Corrie she had intended to kill, not Jack. She still swore by her premonition that the saint had cursed the women involved in the pilgrimage and gradually they would all die. As far as Ariadne was concerned, the saint had simply been having an off-day and missed her target.

Corrie slipped behind the desk and took one of the keys from its hook. Good old-fashioned iron keys – not those electronic cards they used in modern hotels that only worked when they felt like it and usually on the wrong door. She crept cautiously up the stairs. There was one particular room where Corrie wanted to have a good poke around. She hesitated briefly outside the door, wondering if this was a good idea after all and whether it still constituted breaking and entering if you had obtained the key by stealth. Then she decided the end justified the means, turned the key quietly and stepped inside. To start with, she just stood and looked. It was impersonal, practically bare of the considerable holiday clutter that had accumulated in Jack and Corrie's own room. The bed was made with clinical precision and the only personal items on show were a make-up bag on the wash stand and a pair of black flip-flops under the chair. It almost looked as if the person whose room it was only occupied it intermittently and stayed elsewhere on the island the rest of the time. Corrie moved across the room to the chest of drawers, taking care not to disturb anything. She found what she was looking for in the very first drawer she opened.

'Look what I've got!' Jack was in the deserted hotel kitchen, proudly holding up three plump red mullet.

'And look what I've got!' Corrie had seen him coming from the balcony and ran down to meet him, keen to impress him with her detective work. She was holding up a passport.

Jack dropped the fish in the sink for Ariadne to clean for supper and approached Corrie with a scowl of deep suspicion. 'What have you been up to? Whose passport is that? I've only been gone a couple of hours and you promised—'

'Listen to what I've found out before you go into one of your lectures. While Sky was out seeking the Incredible Light, I was in her room seeking her incredible identity. I suspected all along there was something not quite right about that young woman. Why should she hate and despise mankind generally and us in particular, when she's never even met us before?' She opened the passport. 'According to this, she's a Greek citizen, born on Katastrophos, and her real name is Katina Stephanides.'

Jack looked blank. 'So…? I've never heard of her.'

'No, but what about Tina Stephens? Doesn't that name ring a bell?'

Jack smote his gashed forehead with his palm and flinched. 'Of course it does. She was the fiancée of the young man I put away for knifing that drug dealer. He was studying to be a doctor and got engaged to a Greek nurse in the same teaching hospital.'

'How come you didn't recognize her?'

'During the investigation I only ever saw her in a nurse's uniform – I genuinely didn't know her with purple hair, tattoos and all that black stuff on her eyes.'

'It explains her medical know-how, though.'

Jack ran cautious fingers through his hair. 'God, no wonder she hates me. She must blame me for the long prison sentence.'

'And me too, by association.'

'What made you suspicious?'

'It was that night of St Sophia's pilgrimage, when we were coming down those ghastly steps in the storm. Someone tried to shove me off. At the time, everyone was panicking and I put it down as an accident. But later I noticed Sky's tattoos had come off on the towels Yanni brought us, and she had purple streaks running down her face from her coloured hair. And did you see her nails? Clean, short and manicured. She was no genuine hippy and I started to think she was hiding something. I couldn't understand why she was so bitter and hostile all the time. Then yesterday, when Medusa nearly flattened you and you were so sure it wasn't Ambrose Dobson, I decided Sky could bear a bit of investigation.'

'Of course, we can't be sure it was her.' Jack sighed, watching yet another of his cast-iron theories disintegrate. He'd been ninety-nine per cent sure he knew who'd done it but he certainly hadn't suspected Sky, not for a moment. 'She's very slight – I wouldn't have thought she had the strength to push half a ton of stone off the roof.'

'She levered it off. There was a rusty old crowbar of Yanni's up there, I didn't pay much attention at the time because I was convinced a man had been responsible. I don't think there's any doubt it was her, now we know who she is. And she was born and brought up here, so she probably knows the olive groves like the back of her hand. No trouble escaping across the roof and losing herself in the hills.'

'But surely she didn't follow us all the way over from England just to get some kind of revenge.' The Squad had checked the travel bookings and given Jack a briefing on all the people going to Katastrophos on this trip, including the one he was interested in, but there hadn't been much time and they had warned him it wasn't comprehensive. They could find no background at all on a wandering traveller called Sky.

'I doubt it. More likely she was hurt and unhappy after her fiancé went to prison so she was going home for a while to find some peace and comfort. Then she discovered that by some incredible quirk of fate, you and I were going to Katastrophos at the same time. I expect she recognized you straight away, probably at the airport, but she didn't want you to recognize her, hence the hippy disguise. It worked very well.'

'But why try to kill me? What good would that have done?'

'You can't apply logic to this, Jack. Don't forget she was brought up on this grisly, superstitious island. She may have been a practical, disciplined nurse in London but it's my guess that as soon as she returned here the whole grotesque influence kicked in. You remember all that stuff she spouted about vengeance and retribution the morning after we arrived?'

'Yes, it was something about the daughter of justice ruling here.'

Corrie nodded. 'Nemesis. I think Sky believed that the dark-faced goddess had purposely engineered our simultaneous journeys to Katastrophos so that she could settle a score.'

'Or it could just be that the poor girl was so depressed at seeing me again, it temporarily unhinged her. You have to admit, it was a terrible coincidence.'

'No, Inspector Dawes,' said a voice in clipped, formal English with a soft Greek lisp. 'Terrible I agree – but coincidence has nothing to do with it.' Sky stood in the doorway. She had picked up Ariadne's meat cleaver and was holding it tightly in both hands. The black lipstick and kohl had gone and her pale face was red and swollen with crying. Her misery was so raw, it was almost tangible.

'Your wife is right. I have Nemesis to thank for this encounter. Such a cruel, tormenting paradox, don't you think? You are here on your honeymoon, happy together and enjoying yourselves.' Her voice shook and tears began to trickle down her cheeks. 'It's so unfair! Mark and I should also have been here on honeymoon but we are not, because you have locked him away in a cell for years and years. He was sick. Gambling is an illness. Why could you not leave him alone? The man he killed was filth, getting rich and fat by preying on other people's misery. Mark was simply exterminating vermin. Even you must see that.'

Sky was hysterical now and advancing on them unsteadily, holding the meat cleaver aloft in both hands like an avenging angel. Corrie knew from using it to cut through joints of stringy goat that it was razor sharp, lethal in careless hands.

'I'm going to kill you – both of you. You deserve to die for what you have done. Then I shall kill myself, because I have nothing to live for!' She began sobbing violently, completely out of control. Her mind had finally cracked under the weight of relentless grief and animosity. She brandished the cleaver wildly, close enough now to strike.

'Tina,' said Corrie quietly. 'Tina, listen to me. Jack did what he had to do, what he's trained to do, just as you did when you nursed Maria and Ellie. You did it automatically, without hesitating, because it's your job and you knew it was right. You saved Ellie's life. That's an amazing thing to have done. How can you think of taking lives, now?'

Tina hesitated, unsure just for a second, and Jack would have rushed her, made a grab at the cleaver. Sensing it, Corrie put out a restraining arm. Getting his head split open twice in as many days wouldn't improve his mental dexterity. She carried on speaking, surprised to hear her voice calm and persuasive, despite the turmoil going on inside her.

'If you kill us and yourself, who will be there for Mark when he comes out of prison? Who will help him to rebuild his life? Don't do it, Tina. Don't abandon Mark when he needs you most.'

Tina looked frantically from one to the other, desperately uncertain now. She shrieked, a single sharp howl of pain and anguish, and Corrie felt sure she was going to run at them, slicing and slashing. Then the cleaver dropped slowly from her grasp and she sank to her knees, weeping as though her world had finally ended. Nothing left to lose and nothing more to gain.

'Blimey, that was close.' Jack and Corrie were sitting on their balcony sipping their third medicinal Metaxa. Maria and Marjorie had helped Corrie put Tina to bed. It was symptomatic of the bizarre atmosphere that had developed in Hotel Stasinopoulos over the last week that neither felt the need to ask any questions. Despite the late-afternoon sunshine, Jack shivered slightly. 'For a minute, there, I really thought she was going to bury the hatchet – in my head.'

Corrie sipped pensively. 'Did you see her face when she finally let it go? It was if all the hatred and bitterness drained out of her in that single moment. She must be completely exhausted with the strain of bearing her anguish all these weeks. I felt so sorry for her.'

'It *was* Tina who levered Medusa off the roof intending to smash my skull, remember.' Jack felt just a tad aggrieved.

'Yes. And when that didn't work, she tried a more direct approach. But don't be too hard on her; it wasn't the real Tina Stephens – the trained, caring professional. This was Tina as Nemesis. I believe her mind was unbalanced by this horrible, malevolent island. Too much solitude to dwell on her resentment and her need for revenge, fuelled by the bitter irony of coming home to Katastrophos only to find that the policeman who put her lover in prison is here too, under her very nose, and as a final insult – on his honeymoon. Imagine what affect that must have had on her state of mind. Instead of going to her family in St Sophia for comfort, she decided to take a room here in Hotel Stasinopoulos, where she could stay close to us, waiting for her chance of retribution. Of course, she knows what she did was wrong and she certainly shouldn't have compounded the felony by pinching Ambrose Dobson's wig and trying to frame him.'

'Yes, that was odd, wasn't it? Why did she do that?'

'Nemesis again. She said he was another cruel, heartless pig who needed teaching a lesson.'

'Very perceptive. She wasn't totally unhinged, then?'

'No, just full of a fierce, self-destructive kind of poison, poor girl.'

'Talking of poison ...' Jack began.

'Don't start!'

It was late evening. Out in the west, beyond the furthest Katastrophan hills, Helios was sinking beneath the darkening world and black night Nyx let friendly shadows veil the light. At least, that's what Corrie had said before she went to bed. She was asleep now, no doubt dreaming of her Greek gods and goddesses. Jack sat alone on the balcony with a nightcap, assessing his progress – or rather, the lack of it. This was a bloody funny island. It made simple, ordinary people do wild, impulsive things. Standard criminal profiling was useless here, he needed a degree in flipping psychoanalysis if he was going keep ahead of them.

He had only a few days left and in terms of crime-stopping, all he had done so far was stumble across a local wine fiddle that was none of his business. It had been Corrie who solved the Medusa thing and stopped

Tina from braining him with an axe – she'd been brilliant actually, although he dared not tell her. It was hard enough as it was preventing her from leaping in every five minutes with her sensational and totally unlikely crime scenarios. The worst part was that sometimes her barmy intuition was actually right. All *he* had done was stand by like a spare part at a wedding while two women were poisoned – one nearly fatally.

Well, time was running out and he was still no nearer to finding what he was looking for than when he arrived. He had to get the evidence he needed while he could still nail his villain and that meant in the next two days, three at most. Plan A – a watching brief – had not worked out as it should have. Time to deploy Plan B, and for that he needed a bit of assistance and a lot of co-operation.

It was always risky, involving members of the public. They were, for the most part, undisciplined and unpredictable but he couldn't see any other way. One small ray of hope – his quarry might not yet be on to him as he had feared. The attempts on his life had turned out to be nothing at all to do with the current case, so maybe he still had that element of surprise. He guessed he would soon find out.

It was Wednesday morning when Ambrose Dobson spotted his golden opportunity. He had left Marjorie having a lie in and gone down to sit under the vine-covered pergola to write more letters, this time claiming excessive compensation from the insurance company for the theft of his hairpiece. Even though it had mysteriously reappeared, hanging from the door handle, it had clearly been manhandled by the unprincipled scoundrel who had stolen it and it was, of course, ruined and quite unwearable. His bald head sweated badly in his panama and it was good to sit in the shade without it. He smiled greedily. With the sort of sum he had in mind, he could order one of the really expensive wigs, custom-designed and hand-made from superior quality hair for a perfect fit. He had no intention of repeating the embarrassment of the last couple of days and he was entitled to recompense for the stress and trauma he had suffered. A lifetime in the insurance business enabled him to word his claim in terms guaranteed to screw the maximum settlement out of them. It was with this objective uppermost in his mind – making someone pay – that he glanced down to the seashore and saw, in that instant, a golden opportunity for settlement, of a different and much more vindictive nature.

CHAPTER FOURTEEN

Diana pulled hard on the oars and felt the sea breeze ruffle her hair as the boat slid swiftly through the sparkling water. She was heading for her favourite Cave of Nymphs to sunbathe and look forward to what she would do to Sidney when he arrived. He was a great guy and she guessed he was pretty stuck on her. That felt real good. OK, so plenty of guys back home were stuck on her but with Sid, it was genuine and uncomplicated. Most of all, she knew he wasn't influenced by her background; he couldn't be because he hadn't a clue what her background was. She thought briefly of Cuthbert. He knew only too well, none better. She guessed the time was rapidly approaching when he would demand a serious discussion with her. It would be about money. It was always about money. Sometimes she thought money was nearly as important to him as his damned plant experiments.

By the time Diana disappeared out of sight around the rocky headland that provided Hotel Stasinopoulos with natural protection from the sea, Ambrose had crammed his panama on his bald head and scurried down to the landing stage where the second boat was moored. His heart was pounding pretty rapidly but nothing he couldn't control – nothing to worry about. He took some deep breaths. He had to hurry because Foskett would be there any minute with his bottle of wine and his pathetic tongue hanging out, like a lovesick puppy. Ambrose sneered smugly to himself as he untied the boat and prepared to climb aboard. The sordid little plumber would not be getting his hanky-panky today. Because he, Ambrose, was going to beat him to it. He had promised himself he would get the little tart and it had to be before Saturday, when they all went their separate ways. But even in his wildest, most sadistic fantasies, he hadn't dreamed a chance like this would present itself. All

alone with her, miles away from possible interruptions or some interfering idiot hearing her screams and rushing to her aid. And the beauty
of it was, she couldn't say a word about it afterwards, because he held
all the aces. He had the power to put a stop to her extravagant lifestyle
overnight and he'd make sure she knew it. If she didn't co-operate, he
wouldn't hesitate to tell Gordon how she was putting it about behind his
back like a bitch on heat. He would even maintain that Diana had made
disgusting advances to him and probably all the other men in the hotel.
And if he wasn't much mistaken, the old fool was not the kind of man
who would tolerate being made a public laughing-stock. With his money,
thought Ambrose enviously, he could simply ditch the bitch and buy
himself another younger, more exclusive model.

'I say, Dobson, old chap.'

Ambrose jumped violently at the sudden voice of the 'old fool' in
question who had emerged from a clump of cypress and was standing on
the jetty behind him. His heart thumped even harder and he had to gasp
to catch his breath. His head began to spin, dizzily.

The professor was holding a picnic basket. 'Sorry if I startled you, but
I wondered if you wouldn't mind doing me a favour. Thing is, Diana has
gone off down the coast to sunbathe.' He winked. 'Likes to do it in the
nude, so she goes where people can't spy on her. Silly girl went without
her lunch.' He indicated the basket of food. 'Ariadne just gave it to me
and wants me to go after her with it. I thought, since you're going out
yourself, you wouldn't mind just dropping off Diana's lunch on your
way. Can't miss her, her boat will be beached outside the cave she likes
to use.' He grinned. 'Might have to shut your eyes and whistle when you
get there, though. What about it? D'you mind? I'd go myself but you've
got the only other boat and anyway, I've got quite a bit of work on at the
moment.'

'Er ... yes, I suppose so. Give it here,' growled Ambrose ungraciously.
He had recovered from the shock and was thinking fast. His first instinct
had been to tell the absurd old moron to bugger off, especially after the
appalling way he had insulted him regarding his digoxin, which Gordon
seemed to have conveniently forgotten. But on second thoughts, there
was no need for this to upset his plans. Gave him a legitimate reason to
go looking for the woman, in fact. He just had to hurry before blasted
Foskett arrived and offered to take the food himself.

'Many thanks, old man. Jolly decent of you.' The professor handed the
basket into the boat and loped off, his spindly legs lurching in ungainly

strides across the quayside in the direction of his *dulce domum* in the olive groves.

Ambrose Dobson grabbed the oars and without a backward glance began to pull on them vigorously. He was excited now at the prospect of what he would soon be doing to the delectable Diana, the nice little tricks he had planned for that beautiful body, and the sweat began to trickle down his neck from beneath his panama hat. So vivid were his imaginings that he rowed several strokes before he realized he wasn't moving. He swung round to see what had happened and saw that someone had retied the rope to its mooring.

'Where are you going Ambrose?' Marjorie stood above him on the jetty, her arms folded and her lips in a grim line. She knew exactly where he was going. He wasn't the only one to have witnessed Diana's and Sidney's regular excursions to their love tryst. She liked Sidney and her only thoughts on the matter were that she hoped he wouldn't end up badly hurt. Then she had seen Ambrose from her window, scuttling down to beat Sid to the boat and chase after Diana like the bloated, rutting, farmyard hog she knew him to be. His regular trips to the knocking-shop were one thing. This was altogether different and very much nastier and she was not about to let it happen.

Ambrose was furious. Damn and blast the woman! She must have crept up while he was fiddling with the bloody picnic basket. Well, he wasn't going to let this stop him. He might not get another chance.

'I thought you were asleep! Go back to your room.'

'Ambrose, I don't think you should be taking out a rowing boat on your own. Your heart isn't up to it.'

'I shall do exactly as I choose. Go away when I tell you!' The cocktail of pent-up sexual excitement and the frustration of being continually thwarted made him reckless. He reached out to free the rope and as he did so, Marjorie hopped nimbly into the boat and sat down.

'Well, if you insist on this foolishness, Ambrose, I have no choice but to come with you. Someone has to keep an eye on you. What if you embark upon some physical activity that is too much for you and you have a heart attack?' She looked him full in the face and her unyielding gaze left him in no doubt that she knew exactly what physical activity he was planning. Her glare defied him to argue – challenged him to invent a reason why she couldn't accompany him. He looked at her swollen lip and wanted desperately to hit her again. He would seriously have to consider getting rid of her when they were back in Hampshire if she was going to adopt this rebellious attitude every time he gave her a simple order. She could go and live with her pansy son. Let him keep her. In the meantime, there was little he could do short of throwing her bodily out of the boat into the water. He stood up.

'Now where are you going, dear?' she asked sweetly.

'Back to the hotel. I've decided I don't want to go out in the boat after all.'

'Well, that's a shame, Ambrose, because I quite fancy a trip round the bay now and you obviously feel fit enough to row. The doctor said a little gentle exercise was good for you.' She lifted the lid of the basket. 'Oh, how nice. A picnic. Are we to eat it or are we taking it to someone else, dear?'

He realized then how she had found out what he was up to. She had overheard his conversation with Gordon. There was nothing for it but to go along with the charade or he would look guilty and ridiculous and there was no way he was going to do that.

'You'll regret this, Marjorie.' He began to row.

Sidney was frustrated, too. He had gone to fetch a bottle of wine from Yanni and to ask if it was all right for him to borrow the boat again, when Maria had collared him. He was obviously keen on exploring the coast, she said, so she would give him some tips on the best places to visit. For the next twenty minutes, she had regaled him with a comprehensive tourist guide to all the beauty spots along the shores of Katastrophos. The white sand and pebbles made very clear, turquoise sea, she said, and some of the best swimming and snorkelling was to be had at the north of the island where there were many quiet coves. She even went and hunted out an old mask and snorkel left behind by a previous traveller. She was such a nice lady and Sid's sensitivities were such that he couldn't bring himself to be impatient with her, so by the time he'd thanked her, collected his wine from Yanni and sprinted down to the jetty, not only was he running late but the boat had gone. His face fell. Somebody had beaten him to it, although he couldn't imagine who, because as far as he knew, he and Di were the only people who had used the boats since they arrived on the island. He looked at his watch. By now, she'd be wondering where he was. Very likely she had the right hump at being stood up and wouldn't want to see him again. He tried to look on the bright side. Maybe whoever had borrowed the boat wouldn't keep it long and there would still be time for him to go and meet her. Forlorn, he sat down on the jetty and waited.

After a couple of hours, Diana had to concede that Sidney wasn't coming. At first she was peeved, then she realized something must have happened and she knew it would need to be pretty important to keep him away. She couldn't even ring his mobile to see if he was all right. Life on this goddam island was worse than being suspended in space – at least astronauts had some decent communications. It was all very fine for Cuthbert. He was so hung up on his plants, he didn't notice that every time there was a storm they were virtually cut off from civilization for days on end. It could be downright dangerous, especially when someone got sick. She still couldn't forget how that poor kid, Ellie, had nearly died. It had really shaken her up. There had been something about Ellie that connected with her – the vacuous, empty-headed smile, peeping like a frightened animal from beneath that sparse ginger fringe and her funny, pinched face peppered with freckles. It was spooky, indefinable, as if they'd met before someplace – almost as if she had known her for years. She went for a brief skinny dip then put her bikini back on. No point in hanging around without Sid and she was getting hungry. She must have left her picnic lunch in Ariadne's kitchen.

When Diana Gordon sculled lazily into the landing stage, her arms and legs bronzed and gleaming, Sid was still waiting. As soon as he spotted her, his glum face lit up with his lighthouse smile and she had the usual urge to hug him, press her body against him and feel him respond, but she guessed it wouldn't be smart right there, in full view of the hotel.

'What the hell happened to you?' she said instead.

Sid grabbed the rope she threw him and tied it to the mooring bollard. 'I'm really sorry, Di. Everything went wrong. Maria kept me talking and it was difficult to get away without being rude to her. You know what she's like once she gets going. Anyway, by the time I got down here, someone else had pinched the boat.' He reached out a hand to help her. She took it and jumped nimbly up on to the jetty, brushing his cheek briefly with her lips and fondling his behind as she passed him.

'That's real strange. All the vacations I've spent here, hardly anyone has taken the boats out except me.'

'Doesn't the Prof ever keep you company in your Cave of Nymphs? It crossed my mind that he might have got bored in the olive grove and decided to come and find you. I haven't seen him around all day.'

Diana laughed. 'No way. Cuthbert would never waste good plant-hunting time on me. The only other person who might have taken the boat is Yanni.'

'Yanni?'

'Sure. Sometimes he rows Ariadne down to the Sacred Grotto of St Sophia.'

'I didn't know St Sophia had a sacred grotto. I've never noticed it when I've been rowing round the coast.'

Diana dug him in the ribs affectionately. 'It isn't all lit up with flashing lights like Vegas, you dummy. It's well hidden. You wouldn't see it from a boat. Ariadne likes to go there with flowers and charms and all that stuff. According to her, St Sophia can handle every emergency from plagues to earthquakes and every human ailment from warts to sterility.'

'Sterility, eh?'

A brief shadow fell across Diana's face and then was gone. 'Yeah. That old thing. She believes her gifts to the saint will help Maria get pregnant.'

'Well, it wasn't Yanni who took the other boat out. He was there while I was talking to Maria. He gave me this wine.' Sid held up the bottle, only a third full now.

Diana grinned. 'I get it. Drowning your sorrows. What about mine?'

'I'm sorry, Di. I'd been really looking forward to our ... well, you know ... our picnic. Been thinking about it all day.'

'Me too.' She linked her arm through his. 'Come on, tiger. I'll get changed and we'll finish the wine on the terrace.'

He stuck out his bottom lip like a sulky toddler. 'OK. But it won't be the same, will it?'

She giggled, amused at his obvious disappointment. 'Never mind, baby, there's always tomorrow. And guess what I have planned for you then ...' She leaned across and whispered something graphically obscene in his ear. Sid cheered up immediately.

On their way across to the hotel, Diana glanced back at the jetty. 'So where's the other boat now?'

'Dunno. Whoever took it hasn't come back, yet.'

It was evening before they realized something was wrong.

'Anybody seen Marjie and Old Misery Guts? Not like them to miss dinner.' Sidney was ravenous. He and Diana had snatched a dangerous but irresistible half-hour in his room and it had stimulated every part of him, including his appetite. He helped himself to a plateful of rice and some chicken that had been festering all day in one of Ariadne's black cauldrons. It was swimming in olive oil with slices of lemon floating on top, but Sid decided it didn't taste half bad washed down with plenty of the hookey wine.

There were just four of them for dinner. Nurse Tina Stephens had taken food to her room as usual, seeming to find it even more painful to be near DI Dawes and now uncertain of her fate following her deliberate attempt to brain him with a statue. The professor was out in the dusky olive groves in his illuminated miner's helmet, darting about like a demented firefly.

'I saw Ambrose this morning,' said Corrie. 'He was sitting here at the table, writing more of his threatening letters. Haven't seen him since, though.'

'He wasn't here when I came back from town this afternoon and I haven't seen Marjorie all day.' Jack's face creased with concern as it did most of the time now. He hadn't been in St Sophia, he'd been deploying his all-seeing eyes somewhere quite different for most of the day but whilst he'd seen a number of interesting things, he still hadn't found what he was looking for and none of his all-seeing eyes had spotted the Dobsons.

'I expect they went for a hill walk and lost track of the time,' offered Diana. 'Or maybe he's taken Marjorie out for a special anniversary meal at the taverna in St Sophia.'

'That's right,' agreed Corrie. 'I remember Marjorie telling me. Today is their thirtieth anniversary. They could be out celebrating.'

'Leave off,' said Sid scathingly. 'Old Misery Guts celebrating? Can you see him spending money on a meal when dinner's already paid for here? And he's far too tubby to go hill walking. Besides, he never stays out after it starts to get dark. No, I reckon they were having a nap in their room and lost track of the time.' He stood up, dabbing his oily chin with his napkin. 'Excuse me, folks, I'll just go up and knock on their door. Let Marjie know grub's up.'

Maria came in at the end of this conversation, carrying a dish of fresh fruit and a bowl of yogurt. She shook her head. 'Mr and Mrs Dobson are not in their room, they are still out,' she declared firmly. 'Their key is on its hook behind the desk. I checked before I served dinner.'

'There you go, Sid.' Diana prodded him in the ribs. 'What did I tell ya? The old creep has taken Marjorie out to dinner, like I said.'

In the olive grove nearest to the hotel Professor Gordon turned off the lamp on his helmet and crept stealthily across the stony approach to the pergola. For a while he lurked in the gathering shadows, unable to identify exactly who was seated down at the end of the table hidden by the encroaching vines. He was surprised to see anyone there at all and he certainly hadn't expected them to be sitting, calmly eating dinner. He edged closer until he could see more clearly, then cursed silently to himself. Eventually he emerged from the shadows and blustered across to the table, removing his helmet.

'Good evening, everyone.' The professor sat down, helped himself to food and began to tear off pieces of bread, dipping them in the oily lemon sauce. He looked at Diana, lovingly. 'Which old creep were you talking about, my darling?'

'Ambrose Dobson,' she replied, shortly. 'Nobody's seen him since this morning.'

He looked at her, puzzled. 'But surely you saw him at lunchtime, angel? He agreed to row out to your cave with the picnic basket you left behind.'

Sid and Diana exchanged glances, realizing now who had taken the other boat and sabotaged their date.

'Well, he never turned up.' Diana pulled a face. 'The old guy didn't like me much so he probably ate my lunch himself out of spite. How petty can a man get?'

Jack turned to the professor. 'Was Marjorie with him?'

'Not when I spoke to him, old boy. He was on his own when I left.'

Yanni, who had come out to corkscrew more wine, overheard the gist of the discussion and attempted to assist. 'I see Mrs Dobson from the ... er ...' He pointed upwards, struggling for the English, then, deciding it would be quicker, he spoke rapidly in Greek to Maria. She translated.

'Yanni says he was up on the roof, cementing the statues to make them safe, and he saw Mr Dobson already in the boat and Mrs Dobson on the quay, talking to him. Yanni thinks they may have been arguing. Then she too climbed in the boat and Mr Dobson rowed away.'

'What time was this?' Jack was in full-on interrogation mode.

Yanni thought for a bit. 'Eleven o'clock – I think, *kírie*.'

Corrie looked at her watch. 'That was over nine hours ago. Oh, my God, Jack, they can't still be out there, can they?'

'Something's up,' said Sid. 'I don't reckon Old Misery Guts should have been rowing a boat in the first place with his dicky ticker.'

'Has anyone checked to see if their boat's back yet?' asked Corrie, squinting down to the shore. Tendrils of mist were drifting in from the sea, obscuring the view of the landing stage.

Jack stood up, wondering why he hadn't thought of that. 'Come on, Sid. I'll fetch my torch and we'll go and look. You three stay here in case one or other of them turns up.' As he passed her chair, he bent and put his mouth close to Corrie's cheek as if to kiss her goodbye but instead, whispered in her ear. 'Keep your eye on Diana.'

'Why?' mouthed Corrie, but she didn't get an answer.

As Jack feared, only one boat was tied up at the tiny landing stage belonging to Hotel Stasinopoulos and that was the one in which Diana had returned. As Sid pointed out, she had left her straw hat and sun cream in it.

'OK, DI Dawes. What do we do now?'

Jack smiled grimly. 'For one barmy moment, I was about to say we call out the coastguard.' He looked at the deep-purple sky. 'It'll be dark soon and it gets black as hell here at night. I'm not sure there's much we *can* do until morning.'

'We can't just do nothing,' said Sid. 'Poor old Marjie could be out there, drifting, with Old Misery Guts too ill to row or something. There's still a bit of light left and ...' he coughed, awkwardly, '... I know the route to Di's cave pretty well. That's where they were headed. What say we have a bit of a row about, see if we can see their boat?'

Jack hesitated briefly, trying to see how this latest crisis fitted in with what he already knew. It didn't. 'Yes, all right, Sid. The sea's calm and we can hug the coast. You row and I'll flash my torch all along the beaches and caves. Maybe they'll see it if they're stranded somewhere.'

They were three-quarters of the way to the Cave of Nymphs and Sid was pulling smoothly but purposefully on the oars. He'd never tried this rowing lark before he came to Katastrophos and now he was getting really good at it. Amazing what you can do, he thought, with the right incentive.

'Look, there!' Jack shone his torch. In the failing, misty light, they both spotted the dim outline of the second boat. Someone had dragged it part-way up the steep beach, apparently with some difficulty as it was just barely clear of the water. Sidney stopped rowing and manoeuvred his craft around and into the shore. They both jumped out into the water and towed it up on to dry land. Then they raced over to the other boat, unsure of what they would find but nursing some vague, idiotic hope that Ambrose and Marjorie would still be sitting in it. Of course, they weren't. It was completely empty and there was a gaping hole in the bottom of the hull.

Jack looked at it with growing anxiety. 'Christ, they've holed it. Where the hell are they?' Irrationally, he turned and looked back out to sea as if expecting to see their bodies floating there.

Sid tugged his arm. 'They must be here on dry land somewhere, mate. You don't drown having first conscientiously pulled your sinking boat out of the drink.'

Sid and Jack began to explore the cove, calling the Dobsons' names. Then they beat about in the coastal scrubland and delved amongst the olive trees, but with no success. The encroaching sea mist did not help. Surely the couple hadn't tried to *walk* back home across the island, after their boat was holed. It was perfectly feasible if you were young and fit but not if you were middle-aged and portly with a heart condition.

'Over here!' Jack had disappeared behind a clump of dense cypress, the dark-green foliage made black by the approaching night. Sid raced after him. There was a cave, a spacious one, its mouth concealed behind the trees. He followed Jack inside. It smelled of the sea, dank and fetid from rotting seaweed and the decay of stranded marine creatures, and cutting across that was the sickly stench of oil. Jack shone his flashlight in a wide arc around the cave. In the far corner, a long, flat, altar-shaped rock had stubs of dead candles ranged along its length. A picture of a saint was festooned with charms and rosaries and beside it was an over-turned lamp, explaining the taint of oil on the air. This, thought Sidney, must be the sacred grotto of St Sophia, alleviator of all ills from erupting volcanoes to athlete's foot.

Jack trained the torch beam wider and the dim circle of light picked up the bloated figure of Ambrose Dobson, sitting on the sandy floor with his back propped against the cave wall and his fat little legs sticking out in front of him. He was soaked to the skin, very pale and his mouth was tinged with blue. Sid knelt down beside him.

'What's up, mate? Are you ill?'

'No, he isn't ill.' Marjorie's voice, calm and controlled, came from somewhere behind them. They swung around, the torchlight dancing wildly on the walls of the cave. She was sitting on a rock, her hair wet and tangled, her soggy cardigan clinging to her shoulders. There was an angry red weal down the left side of her face as if she had been hit with something solid. She looked at them, quite composed, and for long moments, nobody spoke. Then she said, 'Ambrose isn't ill – he's dead.'

CHAPTER FIFTEEN

I t was an awkward silence. Diana and Corrie sat at one end of the big
oval table with Professor Gordon down at the other. Jack and Sid had
not returned, so Corrie assumed they had gone off to search further for
Ambrose and Marjorie. She would have preferred to wait for Jack down
on the landing stage but he had told her to keep an eye on Diana and
that's what she was doing. It was a pity he hadn't told her why – she
might have made a better job of it. He really was irritating sometimes.
He never tired of telling her how he was unable to discuss any details of
his murder cases with her. They were always hush-hush and could only
be disclosed to special individuals on a need-to-know basis because
leaked information jeopardized convictions blah, blah, blah. It was the
usual load of policeman's balls. But it didn't stop him from using her to
keep an eye on people and listen for information when it suited him and
without giving her the smallest clue why she was doing it. It was hardly
surprising that she ended up having to work things out for herself, and
naturally the law of averages decreed that occasionally – just occasionally, mind you – she got it a bit wrong.

They sat for a very long time, not speaking. The professor had finished
eating and was scribbling notes on the back of his napkin with a gold,
diamond-studded Caran d'Ache pen he had bought on his last trip to
Geneva. Corrie sipped her wine and peered through the gathering gloom
at the jetty. It was too dark to see whether Jack and Sid had taken the
other boat out but she thought she had heard the slip-slap of the oars in
the stillness.

Diana was bored without Sid. She yawned. 'It doesn't look like the
guys are coming back for a bit. I think I'll hit the sack. Wake me if there's
any news.'

'Oh, is that a good idea?' asked Corrie quickly. 'Don't you think we should all stay here until they come back?'

'Why?' Professor Gordon looked up from the arcane doodlings on his napkin.

'Well – er – in case they need help.'

'What kind of help?'

'Erm – well, I don't know.' Corrie thought fast. 'Maybe they'll need us to form an official search party.'

'I hardly think so, Coriander, my dear. For a start, I doubt very much whether even that imbecile Dobson is capable of losing himself just paddling quietly around the coast – unless of course he's attempting to row back to the mainland. He's quite stupid enough to try it, I suppose. But even if he has, there's little we can do before morning.' He stood up. 'Come along, Diana, my darling. I'll turn in with you. I've had a long – and I might add – most unsatisfactory day.'

Corrie breathed a private sigh of relief. Whatever it was that Jack was worried about when he'd told her to watch Diana, she was hardly likely to get up to any mischief in bed with her husband. She picked up her glass and the wine bottle and went down to the quay to sit and wait for Jack.

Jack performed a cursory examination on Ambrose, looking for vital signs but with little hope. Marjorie was right, he was quite dead, and had been for some hours in Jack's opinion.

'Oh Marjie, love, what a terrible thing to happen. And on your anniversary, too. He should never have tried to row a boat, not with his dodgy heart. It was asking for trouble.' Sidney squatted down next to her and put his arm around her shoulders. 'You're soaking wet, Marjie, and that's a really nasty swelling on your face. What happened? Did the boat hit a rock and sink or something?'

She didn't answer. Jack left Ambrose's body and came across with his torch. Although she had sounded normal, Marjorie was unnaturally still and didn't seem to be feeling or hearing anything. Jack recognized the fairly classic symptoms of trauma. In his experience, people reacted differently to a distressing experience. Some panicked and had hysterics, others became emotionally detached, dissociating themselves from the painful memory. Marjorie was preoccupied and distant. This 'numbing out' was frequently followed by confusion and memory problems, so he suspected she might never be able to tell them exactly what happened. It hardly mattered. Dobson had been under strict medication for a congested heart and he had brought on a fatal attack by over exerting himself. Natural causes in anybody's book. Spending several hours alone in a stinking cave with the body of your dead husband was horrific enough without having to answer a barrage of questions. He edged Sid away so he could speak privately out of her hearing – if indeed she was hearing anything.

'Don't ask her any more questions just now, Sid. She'll tell us what she can when she's got over the shock. What we have to decide now is how we're going to get her and – er ...' he jabbed a thumb over his shoulder at the corpse, 'back to the hotel.'

'Couldn't we leave his nibs here till the morning? I mean, he isn't going anywhere, is he?'

Jack was doubtful. 'I don't think so. Crabs and things might have a go at him during the night. I don't expect Marjorie would be happy about it when she found out.'

'Yeah, you're right.' Sid scratched his head. 'Well, we've only got the one good boat. Frankly, mate, I don't think I'd want to risk the four of us in it. Especially at night when you can't see the rocks. And besides, we can't ask Marjie to sit in a rowing boat with her dead husband propped up against her.'

'Exactly what I was thinking. How do you feel about taking Marjorie back on your own? I'll stay here with the body until you come back, then we can lay him down in the bottom of the boat with a blanket over him and sit one up each end with our legs round him. That should balance us safely and is a reasonably respectful form of transport for the deceased. What d'you say?'

''Course. No problem. As long as you don't mind being left here on your own in the dark with a stiff.' Sid shuddered. 'Don't think I'd fancy it. Still, with you being a copper, I guess you're used to it. You don't see many dead bodies in the plumbing trade – mind you, there was one occasion when I was called in to find out what was blocking this bloke's soak-away, and it turned out he'd—'

'Sid,' said Jack hastily. 'Could we just get on with the job in hand, please?'

'Sure, Jack. Sorry, mate.'

They went back to Marjorie, who hadn't moved. She sat looking straight ahead, her eyes blank. Jack and Sid each took an arm and eased her gently to her feet. Sid peeled away her damp cardigan then took off his jacket and threaded her limp arms through the sleeves.

'Better put this on, Marjie, love. Might be chilly out there. Now, I'm going to row you back to the hotel in my boat, then I'm coming back for Jack and Old Misery ... er ... Mr Dobson. Is that all right?'

She said nothing, allowing them to lead her out of the cave without any resistance or reluctance to leave her husband's body. Sid settled her as comfortably as possible in the boat.

'I'll see if I can get hold of a blanket and another torch,' he shouted to Jack, then disappeared into the darkness, leaving just a wake of ebony ripples.

Jack went back inside the cave to wait. If Ambrose had been unprepossessing in life, he was considerably more so in death. Jack sat on the rock where they had found Marjorie, and regarded the body. His face was ghostly white and his lower lip protruded, round and thirsty-looking. His piggy eyes were staring and afraid as if he had seen death coming. There were a couple of speckled patches on the sand close by him, so he'd obviously thrown up prior to death. Jack noticed when he examined him that rigor mortis had already begun to set in. In a warm climate like this, it usually started three to four hours after death so he had probably died between lunchtime and late afternoon. It tended to set in faster in people who were active immediately prior to death, such as rowing a boat as Ambrose had been. Full rigor would take effect after about twelve hours which meant that by the time Sid came back, Dobson would be impossible to manipulate, having died in a sitting position. They might have to prop him upright in the boat after all.

Jack stretched out his long legs and his foot kicked against something. He looked down. It was the fateful picnic basket with Diana's lunch in it – the apparent reason Ambrose and Marjorie had gone out in the boat in the first place. It was unlike the man to offer to do anyone a good turn, thought Jack wryly, and it was ironic that the first time he did, he ended up dead. Automatically, he took out his handkerchief and covered the handle before he opened it. Now why did I do that? he asked himself. This isn't the scene of a crime. In fact, this is probably the least suspicious death I've attended in years. He looked inside the basket. Most of the food and half the fruit juice had gone. They probably ate it at lunchtime before Ambrose had his heart attack. Not surprising, since they didn't know how long it would be before they were missed and someone came looking for them. There were a couple of sandwiches left and Jack had missed most of his dinner. He was about to reach in and take one when he thought better of it. Somehow it didn't seem right, munching away in the presence of a cadaver, although the blokes back in the pathology lab didn't seemed to have any problems with it. The place always reeked of formaldehyde and pepperoni pizza.

He wished Corrie was with him but was glad she wasn't. She'd be nattering on about Ambrose really being Poseidon's *alter ego* and attempting to rape a nymph that didn't belong to him or some such nonsense, and now he had been punished for it by Zeus. Even so, it was a pretty macabre situation, keeping a corpse company in a sacred grotto in the middle of the night. It could only happen on Katastrophos. The whole trappings of feasts, saints, vengeance and superstition had taken possession of the bloody island. Sometimes Jack found himself nearly believing all this rubbish. There was something about the atmosphere on Katastrophos that made it very easy to get drawn into the quagmire of auto-suggestion and self-delusion that seemed to infect everyone. It was vital that he resisted it and stayed focused on what he had come to do, and with all due respect to the Dobsons, this was just another distraction he could have done without. Only two more days and his chance would be gone.

He shone his torch on his watch. Another half-hour and Sid should be back. Unperturbed by his gruesome companion, he rested his back against the wall and closed his eyes. The susurration of fabric against rock as Ambrose's dead body toppled slowly sideways in the throes of rigor made Jack leap suddenly to his feet. But it was the long-drawn-out moan as Dobson's last breath was expelled from his lungs that caused DI Dawes to stride smartly outside to wait for Sid in the fresh night air.

It was nearly eleven o'clock when Sid helped Marjorie out of the rowing boat and on to the landing stage – almost twelve hours since she had left it. Corrie, still waiting patiently, leaped up and put her arms around her.

'Marjorie, thank goodness you're safe. Where's Ambrose?'

Sid shook his head vigorously behind Marjorie's back and made a chopping motion across his throat.

'Not ... dead?' mouthed Corrie, incredulously.

Sid nodded. 'There you go, Marjie, my old duck. Corrie will look after you now. You'll soon be out of those wet clothes and tucked up in bed, nice and warm. Try and get some sleep, love. We can sort everything out in the morning.' He turned to Corrie. 'Get her to have a brandy – she needs it.'

'What on earth has happened?' whispered Corrie.

'Can't stop now,' said Sid. 'Tell you later. I just need to fetch a blanket and a torch then I'm going back for Jack and ... er ...' he winked and jerked his head a couple of times. Five minutes later he was back in the boat and rowing hard. He wondered if all this exercise would give him a six-pack.

Everyone had gone to bed and the hotel was silent. Corrie helped Marjorie up the stairs to her room and helped her to undress. Her clothes were still damp and clung to her. Corrie hung them outside on the balcony. She found a nightie and while Marjorie put it on, she went downstairs to pour a large Metaxa. The poor soul was shivering violently, probably a combination of shock and cold, and her face was badly swollen and bruised down one side. Sid was right – she needed a good shot of brandy. When she got back with it, Marjorie was sitting up in bed looking a little better. She took the glass, smiled gratefully at Corrie and drank a good slug. It seemed to thaw out her numbness.

'Thank you, dear. You're all very kind – you and Jack and Sidney. I'm so sorry I'm being such a nuisance.'

'You're nothing of the kind.' Corrie was aching to ask what had happened but even with her pathological curiosity, she realized this was not the time for an inquest. In the event, Marjorie came right out with it.

'He's dead, you know. Ambrose, I mean.'

'Oh dear,' said Corrie, lamely. 'I'm so sorry. What a terrible thing to happen and on your anniversary, too. I suppose it was his bad heart.' From the state of Marjorie's clothes and hair and her injured cheek, Corrie thought perhaps she had fallen overboard and Ambrose had died trying to save her. 'Was there some kind of accident?'

Marjorie took another gulp of brandy and looked Corrie straight in the eye.

'Oh no, it wasn't an accident. Not at all. You see – I killed him.'

For once, Corrie was lost for words. She collapsed on the edge of Marjorie's bed, open-mouthed.

Marjorie lay down. 'Naturally, I shall confess everything to your husband in the morning but I think I'd like to go to sleep now, dear, if you don't mind. I suddenly feel terribly tired.'

'Of course,' stammered Corrie. 'I'll – er – see you in the morning, then. Goodnight.' She put out the light and closed the door quietly behind her. Then she went down to the bar, poured another large brandy and knocked it back in one.

*

It hadn't been easy getting Ambrose into the boat. He was a dead weight – obviously – and thanks to the advanced rigor mortis, his legs were sticking resolutely out at ninety degrees to his body. Their first task was to get him out of the cave and down to where Sid had beached the boat, having already dismissed the alternative notion of dragging the boat up the steep slope to the corpse and then hauling it back down the shingle to the water's edge with the body bouncing about inside. As Sid pointed out, 'his bum'll be like a bag of rotten plums by the time we get him home'. A fireman's lift seemed the best option considering the shape Dobson was in, but after several abortive attempts, Jack said he didn't think his back was up to it. Eventually they devised a makeshift 'bosun's chair', each sliding a hand beneath and behind the corpse and gripping one another's wrists. In this way they struggled down the beach with him in a sitting position. Even so, he was a heavy man and they had to put him down every few yards for a breather.

'I don't suppose we could *roll* him down to the boat?' Jack wondered.

'What – and deliver him back to Marjorie covered in bits of dead crab and seaweed? I don't think so. Come on, grab your end, we're nearly there.'

The original idea of lying him flat in the bottom of the boat covered decorously with a blanket was clearly a non-starter. On the other hand, if they sat him upright he could topple sideways and capsize the boat.

'We could turn him over and slide him, bum first, under the thwart board,' suggested Jack, stroking his chin thoughtfully.

'That's no way to transport the dear departed – all trussed up like a Tesco's turkey,' said Sid shocked. 'No, he'll have to sit next to you in the stern.'

After a good deal of manoeuvring, they finally propped him up on the seat and Sid draped the blanket over his rigid legs.

'What did you do that for?' asked Jack. 'He's hardly likely to feel the cold, is he?'

'I know – I know.' Sid felt awkward. 'It just seems more respectful, that's all. Now put your arm around him and hold him steady and I'll row us back to the hotel.'

The boat slid silently over the dark indigo sea like the nocturnal cortège of a sombre Viking funeral until Sid observed, 'Apart from being a funny colour and not blinking, no one would ever clock him for a stiff.'

It was after two in the morning when they sculled wearily into the landing stage. Jack's back was throbbing and Sid's arms felt as though they were being torn from their sockets. They decided they would need some extra muscle to get Dobson's body out of the boat and up to the hotel. As Sid remarked, in their weakened state they could easily lose their grip on him and drop him in the drink, which was unthinkable. The professor would hardly be much use, he was more brains than brawn, so they would wake Yanni. Apart from anything else, they needed to find somewhere in the hotel to lay Ambrose out. Sid went to knock on his bedroom door.

Jack found Corrie asleep on the bar. She was sitting on a stool with her head resting on her arms. It was unlike her to fall asleep before he came home, but then he saw the bottle of brandy at her elbow. Someone had given it a bit of a hammering. He jogged her arm, gently.

'Corrie – I'm back. Where's Diana?'

Corrie surfaced reluctantly from the depths of a deep, alcohol-induced sleep. She struggled to get her bearings and tried to shake off the idiot who was disturbing her.

'Go way. Tired.' She dropped her head back on her arms. Then memory of the night's terrible revelations returned with a start and she sat up abruptly, her eyes wide, her speech slurred. 'Jack! Something ghastly! Got to tell you!'

'What?' He became agitated then. 'Is it Diana?'

Corrie frowned, puzzled. 'No. Diana's in bed with Cuthbert. *She* hasn't killed anybody.' She grabbed his arm, her eyes crossing with the effort of focusing on his face. 'Try to keep up, Jack. It's important.' She picked up a jug of water from the bar and took a long drink from it, dribbling some down her chin. She wiped it away with the back of her hand, then she grabbed two handfuls of his shirt-front, pulled his face very close to hers and spoke in an exaggerated stage whisper. 'Ambrose is dead!'

'Yes, I know.' Jack reeled slightly from the blast of brandy fumes. 'Sid and I have just brought him back in the boat. Is Marjorie all right?'

''Course not!' Corrie gave him a pitying look.

'No, I suppose not,' conceded Jack. 'I guess it was always on the cards that Dobson might pop his clogs suddenly with a heart as dodgy as his, but all the same, it must have been a nasty shock for her.'

Corrie continued to be very agitated and kept shaking her head, maintaining her vicelike grip on his shirt and much of the hair beneath it. Jack reckoned he might soon have to uncurl her fingers.

'Wasn't a heart attack.' Her face was so close to his their noses were touching.

'What do you mean? Of course it was. Ambrose was rowing them around the coast in a boat and his heart gave out.'

'No.' She paused theatrically, looked right and left to ensure she was not being overheard, then whispered again, hoarsely. 'Marjorie murdered him.'

Jack sighed. 'Corrie, if this is another of your lurid deductions pulled together from scraps of spurious information, I shall—'

'She did it. She killed him. Told me so herself. Going to confess in the morning.'

'Are you sure, sweetheart?'

She nodded vigorously. 'Positive.'

'Oh wonderful! Bloody wonderful!' Jack closed his eyes wearily. 'A murder confession from the wrong person. That's all I'm short of.'

'You're not going to arrest her, are you? I mean, he was a beastly little bully with a fat gut and beady eyes. Felt like topping him myself. We all did. She won't go to prison, will she Jack? She isn't …' Corrie eyes glazed over and her grip on his shirt slackened. Then she slid slowly and gracefully down off the bar stool into a tidy heap on the floor. Passed out – probably for some hours, thought Jack. He covered her up then went to help Sid with what now looked like the victim of a suspicious death.

CHAPTER SIXTEEN

Jack tossed and turned until dawn, kept awake by Corrie's stentorian snores and the vexed issue of whether Marjorie had, in fact, murdered her husband. His gut instinct was that she was incapable of such a crime. A decent lady, who had, by all accounts, loved and cared for her husband for thirty years despite the appalling way he treated her, was unlikely to bump him off on their anniversary. But then his dispassionate, analytical policeman's brain kicked in and told him that here was a woman, pushed beyond endurance, who had finally cracked, encouraged by the hypnotic, compelling effect of Katastrophos which might well have 'made her subject to an indiscretion outside the boundaries of her narrow domestic life'. Could be she had brought him here, their first trip away from home since their honeymoon, with the express purpose of getting shot of him. What better location than a remote island with no emergency services and all formal law and order miles away on the mainland? She wasn't to know there would be a DI from the murder squad present, and when she did find out, she might have judged it worth the risk anyway.

She was in the perfect position to kill him, of course, and she had both motive and opportunity. She understood exactly the vulnerability of her husband's heart and was in sole charge of his medication. How simple it would be to give him too much – or too little. No one would question his death after all that rowing, not even his doctor, and not only would she be rid of her tormentor for ever, she would have a nice big pay-out on his life insurance to help her enjoy the rest of her life. But if that was the case, why would she then confess to his murder? That fouled up the whole theory. No lump sum from the insurance company and maybe a long stretch behind bars. It made no sense at all.

He got out of bed and padded to the bathroom to splash cold water on his face. It didn't make things any clearer and he decided it was pointless to speculate further. He would wait until he had heard Marjorie's version of events but he couldn't help remembering what Corrie had said the first night they arrived – everybody is capable of one murder.

Predictably, Ariadne's explanation was that the fat, rude Englishman had died because he had violated St Sophia's sacred grotto. She could not be shifted from this view, however much sensible evidence there was to the contrary. The only point she was not clear about was why his wife had not died too. Eventually, she decided that the saint had spared Mrs Dobson because she had suffered enough already after thirty years in a cruel, loveless marriage and, unlike the others, she hadn't already offended St Sophia by desecrating the pilgrimage to the monastery. It was a pity, she thought, that all husbands could not be like Professor Gordon – a god among men. Always, on his visits, he brought her expensive presents, wonderful charms and amulets for St Sophia from holy shops in the big cities. She had been privileged to help him with his work for many years in her own, modest way, and she was proud that he trusted her. Everyone else, even Maria, treated her as if she were simple and senile, no longer able to understand important things – but not the professor. They shared many jokes – many secrets. She would do anything for him.

Thursday morning. Breakfast, not surprisingly, was a solemn affair. Jack, Sidney, Diana, and unusually, Tina, sat silently around the big olive-wood table, toying half-heartedly with melon and yogurt. Mostly they just sipped coffee. Marjorie had not yet come down and the professor, as was his custom, had gone out at dawn in search of samples. Corrie was still in bed nursing a monumental hangover.

Sinister news travelled fast on Katastrophos and by nine o'clock few people were unaware that the blustering, red-faced Englishman in the straw hat was dead. The island's hypotheses regarding the manner of his demise were many and varied – always imaginative, often grisly, rarely close to the truth. For the time being, Jack, Sid and Yanni had put the deceased in the cellar – the coolest part of the house – sitting with his back against the south-facing wall.

'Should we leave him like that?' Sid had asked. 'Might give someone a nasty turn if they wander in looking for a bottle of wine and see him sitting there. Maybe we ought to hammer him straight.'

'No need,' Jack had replied. 'He'll start to ease off after a few more hours then we can lay him flat and cover him up.'

Now, in the warm, golden beginnings of what promised to be another scorching Katastrophan day, Jack had many things on his mind, not least the irreversible disturbance of what might now turn out to be a crime scene and what to do with a rapidly decomposing corpse down in the cellar. He seriously doubted whether there were any facilities for refrigeration of bodies on Katastrophos. Yanni certainly didn't know of any and displayed a typically Katastrophan reluctance to speak about dying and its implications. Maria had been a little more forthcoming regarding how death was managed on the island.

'When someone in the family dies,' she said quietly, 'we stay with them for twenty-four hours. Everybody sits around and tells religious stories. The body must face the east, towards the sun. To prepare it, we first wash it with wine and wrap it in white material. Then we dress the dead person in normal clothes, tie the jaw shut, cross their hands and tie them together, and fasten the feet with a white ribbon. Finally, an icon and flowers are placed on top of the body inside the coffin. When people come to pay their respects, they give money to light a candle. They ask the deceased to pass on messages to their dead loved ones. Then burial takes place in the churchyard of St Sophia. Before they are buried, the deceased's hands, feet and jaw are untied so they are free to go to their new life. All this is done respectfully but with necessary haste. The hot climate … you understand?'

That, mused Jack, was in cases where death had been from natural causes. After he had spoken to Marjorie, it might well turn into a murder enquiry, in which case he would have to find some way of preserving the body until it could be taken to the mainland and then back to England for an autopsy and an inquest and all the other paraphernalia of a suspicious death. The last thing he needed, now that his operation was approaching crisis point, was the distraction of another case. It was at this point in his deliberations that Corrie crept gingerly down the stairs, holding her head in her hands. She went outside to the pergola and sat, carefully.

'Marjorie is on her way down.'

'How is the poor old duck?' asked Sidney.

'Surprisingly calm under the circumstances.' Corrie poured herself some of the thick, black Greek coffee. 'She wants to talk to you, Jack.'

When Marjorie came out and sat next to Jack under the sun-dappled vine leaves, the others stood up awkwardly, intending to leave, but she stopped them.

'No, please, don't go. I'd like you all to hear this, as you knew Ambrose.'

Diana reached across the table to grip Marjorie's hand. 'I'm real sorry, Marjorie.' Now the man was dead, she would never mention the number of times Dobson had whispered filthy obscenities in her ear whenever he could corner her, alone. 'I didn't know your husband had passed over until this morning.'

'Thank you, dear. But he didn't pass over unaided – his death was my fault.'

Jack interrupted hastily. 'Marjorie, before you say anything else, I really think you should wait until we get back to England and you can have your solicitor present ...'

'Bless you, Jack, but I want to get it off my chest. Tell you exactly what happened while it's fresh in my mind. Then I'll leave it to you to decide what's best.' She sipped some of the coffee Sid had poured her, then began, diffidently: 'You see, Ambrose wasn't quite the respectable English gentleman that you all believed him to be.' They exchanged furtive glances but didn't contradict her. 'He liked to spy on people, women especially. Yesterday morning, he saw you, Diana, rowing away to the other end of the island to sunbathe in the nude and he ran down to get the other boat and follow you.' She paused. 'I'm sorry, dear. It's horrible, I know, the thought of an ageing peeping Tom hiding in the olive trees to ogle you. Well, I saw him from my window and I knew what he was up to, and I decided to put a stop to it. Just as I got close, the professor appeared with a picnic basket, so I stayed back behind the oleanders and did a little spying of my own. I heard him say to Ambrose that since he was going out in the boat anyway, would he kindly drop off your lunch as you'd forgotten it. Of course, this gave him the perfect excuse to make a nuisance of himself, so I came out of my hiding place and jumped into the boat. I told him I had decided to go with him. Of course that didn't suit his purpose at all and he was very unkind – told me to go away. When I wouldn't, he stood up and went to climb back on to the jetty. Said he didn't feel like a boat trip any longer. If I had let him go, he would still be alive today.' Marjorie's voice broke a little and she pulled out a handkerchief and dabbed at her eyes. 'But I was so cross with him, I said that I quite fancied a trip round the coast.' She turned to Jack. 'I goaded him, you see, I asked if there was a reason why he didn't want to take me with him, knowing full well he wouldn't admit what he was really up to. I forced him to row when I knew his heart was weak.'

Corrie interrupted. 'But that isn't murder, Marjorie. He didn't have to do it, did he?'

Marjorie smiled wanly. 'Maybe not, but that isn't the worst of it. While we were rowing along in the sunshine, I asked him if he realized that day was our thirtieth anniversary. I told him thirty years meant "Pearl" and how I'd really like a pearl necklace I had seen. I was happy to buy it myself. He snarled at me then – told me to save my little bit of money because I was going to need it. He had decided to throw me out when we got back to Hampshire. He'd had enough of me and my quarrelsome attitude – answering him back all the time. He said I could take just what I stood up in, nothing more. He was furious, really red in the face. Everything was in his name, he said, the house, the car, everything and I wasn't getting any of it. He told me to go and live with Dan.'

She stopped again and sipped coffee, clearly finding it harrowing to recall the cruel insults. Sid put an arm around her.

'You don't need to tell us any more, Marjie. It must have been awful for you.'

'Yes, I do, Sidney. I have to tell you how Ambrose died. I stood up for myself, you see. I shouldn't have argued, but I did. I said divorce wasn't like that these days. Wives had rights. I would get myself a good solicitor and sue him for every penny that I was entitled to. He started to rant and rage and I told him not to get so worked up – to think of his heart. He sneered at me, then. Said his heart wasn't as bad as I thought. Never had been. He had exaggerated, so I would wait on him like a servant. He said he had every intention of getting very worked up – especially when we got to your cove, Diana. He said some hideous things – things I couldn't repeat – about what he was going to do to you. It made me feel sick and ashamed. He even suggested I should stay and watch – I might learn something. It was then that I lost control of myself. The worst of it was his blithe assumption that I had to go along with his wickedness – that years of bullying had made me too feeble and pathetic to do anything about it. I told him he was a disgusting, filthy old man and I was going to put a stop to him. It was then he hit me with the oar.'

She fingered the angry red weal running down the length of her face. 'We were quite a distance from the shore and I was frightened he intended to knock me out of the boat – leave me to drown. I grabbed the end of the oar and we struggled, then the blade struck a patch of rotten wood in the bottom of the boat and went right through it. Water came pouring in through the hole. I don't swim very well and I was terrified. Ambrose jumped over the side and left me – just splashed ashore without a backward glance. I climbed out and managed to cling on to the boat until my feet touched the sand, then I dragged it ashore, as far as I could.'

'Why?' Jack asked. 'Why didn't you just leave it to sink?'

'Well, for a start it was hotel property. Loaned to us in good faith. I couldn't just abandon it. Besides, I thought if I left it out there on the beach, you'd spot it when you came to look for us.'

'Good thinking, Marjie,' said Sid.

'The picnic basket was still in it, so I rescued that too, seeing as I didn't know how long it would be before we were missed and someone came to find us. I hadn't a clue where we were but I knew we were a long way from the hotel. Then I went to look for Ambrose. He was sitting on the floor in the cave where you eventually found us. I thought he'd be feeling terribly ill but he seemed fine for a man with a badly congested heart – just a bit out of breath. Straight away he started shouting at me, telling me I was a stupid, useless, dried-up old woman and how this whole disaster was my fault. He said he'd never loved me and now he couldn't even bear to be anywhere near me. As soon as we got home, he had every intention of replacing me with a young prostitute he had met who knew how to please him, how to satisfy him. Then he spotted the basket and he said, "Give that to me. I've had nothing since breakfast and it could be hours before those idiots find us." He snatched it and started to help himself to Diana's lunch. After that, he completely ignored me and just sat there cramming food into his mouth and slurping orange juice.'

'Didn't the bastard share it with you?' Diana asked, appalled.

'No dear. That wasn't his way. I wasn't hungry anyhow.' She hesitated, then braced herself and looked steadily at Jack. 'It was then that I did something really terrible. Something I must confess to you, Jack, and a crime I shall have to pay for – not just in this world but probably in the next.'

It went deathly silent – not a breath of breeze or birdsong. Even the cicadas stopped chirping.

'I went across to the shrine of St Sophia, knelt down, and I prayed to her to punish him. Right then and there, in her sacred grotto. I asked her, on behalf of all wretched and oppressed women, to destroy him. A few minutes later, he started to gasp for breath and moan. I went across to him and felt his chest. His heart was beating wildly, erratically, much faster than it was supposed to. Naturally, I didn't have any of his medication with me – his digoxin. He wasn't due a dose until evening and he wasn't supposed to take extra ones in between. I tried to loosen his collar so he could breathe better but he beat me off, yelling and screaming, as if he was having some kind of hallucination. He vomited violently a couple of times – then he shuddered and slumped back against the wall, still and quiet. I felt his pulse but I knew straight away that he was dead. That I'd killed him.'

'No, you didn't, Marjorie,' said Corrie vehemently. 'Dear God, if every time we wished somebody would drop dead they actually did, the world would be littered with corpses. Tell her Jack! Tell her she isn't responsible.'

''Course you're not Marjie,' added Sid.

Jack looked sombre. For a while he said nothing, summing up the evidence associated with Dobson's death, or rather the lack of it. Marjorie Dobson was either an unusually ingenuous woman – or a very clever one. He decided to give her the benefit of the doubt. There was no point in doing anything else. If she had somehow murdered her husband, there was no way in the world that here, on illusive, treacherous Katastrophos, he could find enough evidence to prove it. And even if he could, a good brief would plead all kinds of mitigating circumstances and no jury in the land would convict her.

'Nothing you have told me inclines me to suspect that Ambrose died from anything other than natural causes. It may be that he underestimated the severity of his heart condition. Clearly, the unaccustomed exertion – rowing some distance – the shock of falling in the sea and his bouts of uncontrollable temper and excitement proved too much for him. They might well have proved too much for any man his age so I suggest you try to forget what you did in the cave, Marjorie. You were driven beyond endurance and even at the end, you tried to help him.'

Marjorie seemed to shrink back into her chair – become smaller and lighter with the lifting of her burden. 'Thank you, Jack.'

'What we have to do now, if you're up to it, is decide how to proceed with regard to Ambrose's remains. To be frank, I'm not at all sure what the options are. I'm sorry to face you with it so soon, but in a hot climate ...' Jack left the sentence unfinished. He knew the score with regard to standard procedures when a British national dies abroad but he was damned if he could see how they applied to a sparsely populated island like Katastrophos where none of the usual support structures was in place.

'Maybe I can assist.' Tina Stephanides spoke quietly and with much less venom than had been her custom. 'I was born and brought up on Katastrophos and local procedures are, of necessity, more relaxed here than on other Greek Islands. A foreigner dying on the island is a rare occurrence – I can only recall one such instance in my lifetime – and the course of action is much more complicated. The next of kin must decide whether to take the deceased home or carry out a local burial, here in the churchyard of St Sophia. Naturally, the permission of the priest must be obtained for that.'

'What about cremation?' asked Marjorie.

'Cremation is not permitted. For that, you would need to take Mr Dobson back to the UK. And if he is to be repatriated, his remains must be embalmed as soon as possible and placed in a zinc-lined coffin. This may cause delay and distress, since many certificates – civil registry of death, embalming certificate, doctor's death certificate and another giving permission to transfer the remains to the UK are all required in order to ship the body. These can only be obtained on the mainland and will take time. Mr Dobson has already been dead for over eighteen hours. It will be another two days before his body can be transported to the mainland and we still have no means of communication to speed this up.'

'Oh dear,' said Marjorie. 'I was really hoping to be able to go straight home when the ferry comes on Saturday.' She looked down at her hands from which she had removed the wedding ring. 'I'm sure you'll understand when I say that I have no desire to take Ambrose's body home with me and I certainly don't want him embalmed. Our son, Dan, would not wish to attend his father's funeral. I should much prefer to bury him here as quickly as possible.' She looked at Tina. 'What must I do to achieve that?'

'Permission to sign the necessary documents for an island burial is devolved to the Mayor of Katastrophos in situations such as this. He could assist you, providing Inspector Dawes, as the only representative of UK law, has no objection to going ahead.'

Jack nodded.

'I didn't know there was a mayor of Katastrophos,' said Sid, surprised.

Tina smiled at him. Everyone smiled at Sidney. 'I think you have met him. He owns the *kafeneíon* in St Sophia.'

Sidney had met him all right – got to know him well over the last couple of weeks. He was a man in his early forties with a droopy moustache and lugubrious jowls whose ruling characteristic was his good nature – certainly unlike the pompous, self-important civic dignitaries down at the council offices whose sanitary ware Sid had installed.

'Well, I'm blowed. Small island, innit? How soon can we get the documents for Marjie?'

'We could really do with the help of someone who speaks Greek to ask the priest for permission to bury Ambrose in the churchyard here,' added Corrie, looking pointedly at Tina.

'May I suggest,' boomed a voice from the perimeter of the pergola, 'that in disposing of Dobson's remains, Mrs Dobson could choose to help the environment?' Professor Gordon, taking brief respite from his studies, was pouring himself orange juice. 'Bury him in a cardboard box under an olive tree, madam. His decomposing body will provide the tree with nutrients and the tree will convert carbon dioxide into life-giving oxygen for decades.' He smiled wryly. 'Probably the only useful function your husband will have ever served in his futile existence.'

Blunt as ever, the professor was no respecter of a widow's sensitivities.

'Cuthbert, have a thought for Marjorie,' said Diana, frowning at him.

'No, really,' said Marjorie, 'I'm not in the least bit offended. Professor Gordon is right. I can think of nothing that Ambrose ever did in his lifetime that was kind, considerate or altruistic. I like the idea of ensuring he does this one thing in death.' She turned to Tina. 'Would I be allowed to bury him as the professor suggests?'

Tina looked blank. 'There is no precedent here for such a thing but I don't see why not, if we can obtain the necessary permissions.'

It was early evening, still and balmy. A small group of mourners – if they could be considered as such – gathered around the grave in the olive grove. At first the religious islanders had greeted the idea of an environmentally friendly funeral with consternation and the promise of long-term benefits with utter scepticism. But since it was the wish of the widow and nobody could come up with any sound reasons why it should not take place, permissions were granted. Marjorie Dobson, dry-eyed and dignified, watched as the local funeral director and his swarthy son carried out the formalities and her husband of thirty years – all of them miserable – was lowered into the ground in his cardboard box. Foreign Greek soil from the island he had so openly disliked was chucked unceremoniously on top of him. Only Ariadne boycotted the proceedings. Tiny Ariadne, with her crow's singing voice and her sloppy slippers. With much crossing herself backwards, she invoked her saint not to take this devil's burial as an insult.

Corrie looked down at the last remains of Ambrose Dobson. She had known him barely a fortnight but had been strongly affected by his gratuitous unpleasantness and meanness of spirit. Unlike those virtuous souls who feel the need to find some good in everyone, Corrie felt no such obligation. The man would not be missed or mourned. His grave would not be marked. Drowsing in the sunshine, watching the coffin disappearing beneath a pile of Katastrophan dirt, the myth of Diana and Acteon popped into her head unbidden. Diana had been the patroness of hunting and there was an incident, uncomfortably analogous to yesterday's events, when Acteon spied upon Diana and watched her bathing, naked. Incensed, Diana had transformed him into a stag and his own hunting dogs had turned on him and killed him. Dogs that hitherto had been subservient to his bidding, obedient without question – like Marjorie. Corrie snapped out of her reverie, forcing herself back to reality. She had to stop these macabre meanderings – they were not helpful.

Marjorie stood on the other side of the grave. Her face was enigmatic, her thoughts impossible to divine. Corrie was transported back to Lavinia Braithwaite's funeral. Then, Marjorie had been standing opposite her, much sadder and considerably more bereft at the loss than she appeared now. She looked up, suddenly aware she was being watched, and their eyes met. Marjorie smiled.

CHAPTER SEVENTEEN

Friday, the travellers' last day on Katastrophos, dawned sultry and oppressive. For Corrie, Saturday and the ferry could not come soon enough and she had started packing already. Throughout the last two weeks, the atmosphere on the island had become increasingly claustrophobic and hostile and now she couldn't wait to go home where things were normal. Normal, that was, if you excluded Lavinia suddenly keeling over with mysterious stomach pains so severe that her heart stopped. But wasn't that exactly what had been happening here? Coincidence? Probably. Almost certainly. But what if there was a connection? What if that was why Jack had brought her to Katastrophos? Meeting Marjorie Dobson's eyes across her husband's grave, just as she had at Lavinia's funeral, had been a chilling moment from another dimension. What if...? Stop right there, Corrie, she ordered herself. Stop looking for trouble – you're imagining things. Just go home and don't interfere. It's none of your business.

Marjorie was also looking forward to going home and spoke enthusiastically about what she planned to do now she was free and would soon be considerably better off. She fancied a cruise, she said, possibly in the Caribbean. She would ask Dan and his partner if they would like to come; they both worked very hard and needed a holiday. Then she would get on with her charity fund-raising and take driving lessons, so she could use the car. Was this confident, assertive widow, Corrie wondered, the same downtrodden, dispirited 'little woman' of a fortnight ago, systematically deprived of independent thought or ambition, who had trotted obediently behind her cruel, despotic husband? For Marjorie, the journey to Katastrophos had been every bit as life-changing as the road to Damascus.

But not everyone was keen to leave the island. The professor was becoming increasingly agitated that *tempus fugit* and he had not yet completed the single, most important piece of work he had come to do, even though he now had all the resources he needed to achieve it. Tina, who had come home to her island intending to stay for a while, now expected she would be obliged to return to the mainland and possibly even the UK in order to answer serious charges of attempting to murder a senior police officer. For Sidney and Diana, star-crossed lovers by anyone's standards, tomorrow must see the end of their unlikely but deepening relationship. Katastrophos had given them a glimpse of another, more fulfilling life and it was one they were both reluctant to let go.

Jack, like the professor, was acutely aware that time was running out and he could no longer risk a watching brief. He must act before it was too late. It was imperative that he spoke to Diana but, as he had feared, it was increasingly difficult to prise her away from Sidney. This morning he was lucky. He had woken at dawn, hot and thirsty, and had taken his glass of water out on to the balcony, so as not to wake Corrie. He spotted Diana, jogging alone on the beach. Jack pulled on some clothes and hurried down to join her.

'Anyone seen Di?' Sidney came down to breakfast early, anxious not to waste a second of his last day on Katastrophos. His last day with a woman so beautiful and clever and funny, he would never have believed she would even look at him, much less make love to him. But he had no illusions. She was used to the kind of life a rich professor could give her, and a plumber could never compete. To Diana, he had simply been an amusing diversion. Tomorrow it would end and he would never see her again. They wouldn't promise to keep in touch, write letters, nothing tacky like that. It had been a holiday fling – heady and exhilarating – no point in spoiling it by pretending otherwise. She would forget him the second she kissed him goodbye. And once he was back home in Stoke Newington mending leaky pipes and cheering on the Arsenal, he would forget all about her. Of course he would.

Maria looked up from serving slices of yellow seed-cake with thin apricot jam. 'Mrs Gordon was walking on the beach with Inspector Dawes earlier. I do not believe they have returned yet.'

Sid reached the shore just as Jack and Diana were returning. Jack looked sombre and Diana had obviously been crying. Sid lengthened his stride, and as he got nearer he caught the tail end of their conversation.

'Thanks for that, Diana. It was the last place I thought to look but it makes sense after what you've just told me.'

'And you'll be there at the end, Inspector, with your handcuffs?'

'Yes, Diana. I'm so sorry. I had hoped it wouldn't come to this but I really don't have any choice, now. You do see that?'

'Yeah, sure. I understand.' She pulled out a tissue and blew her nose.

'You don't have to go through with this, you know.'

Diana braced herself and looked at him, steely and resolute. 'Oh yes I do. Even if it turns out to be the very last thing I do.'

'What's the matter, Di?' By the time Sidney reached them, his lighthouse smile was completely extinguished. 'What's upset you?' His concern eclipsed any discretion he might have felt and he put his arms around her. She hugged him fiercely but did not answer.

'Come on, Sid.' Jack took his arm and began to draw him away. 'You and I are going fishing.'

'What? Why? I don't want to go fishing.' He tried to shrug Jack off. 'I want to know what's going on. What is it Diana has to do? Can't I do it for her?'

'Please, honey.' Diana kissed his mouth in the way that always made his knees buckle. 'Just do what Jack says. I'll see you later.'

'But why can't I—?'

'Sid, listen to me. I'm going to need your help, mate.' Jack's face was so grim that Sidney stopped arguing and allowed himself to be led away.

As they approached the landing stage the first thing they saw was Charon's ferry. Jack was immediately on the alert. The ferry wasn't due until tomorrow morning and it wasn't like the old ferryman to change his habits. As they approached, Charon shambled ashore carrying a large box. He was even scruffier than usual and grumbled over his shoulder at someone still in the boat. Clearly he had made the trip under duress. When he saw Jack, he scuttled guiltily away to Hotel Stasinopoulos for an early ouzo with Yanni. Jack waited, keen to see who else had come across on the ferry. A familiar figure climbed carefully out of the grimy fishing smack and tottered unsteadily down the gangplank towards them.

'Tim Watkins!' Jack greeted him with a warm handshake and Sid gave him a manly hug. 'What are you doing back here? I should have thought this is the last place you'd want to be.' He looked back at the ferry. 'Surely Ellie isn't with you?'

Tim shook his head. It had been a terrible night crossing with lurching waves and the stink of Charon's cheap cigarettes and he was feeling far from well. 'No, I left her back in the hospital.'

Jack had a sudden, terrible thought. 'She's all right, isn't she?'

'Yes, thanks. The doctors say she's doing very well and I'll be able to take her home soon. It's because of Ellie I'm here. I didn't want to leave her, obviously, but she insisted. Said it was important that you knew straight away. She got really worked up about it so in the end, I gave in and paid Charon to bring me over. Could we talk somewhere private?'

'Don't mind me,' said Sid. 'I'll walk back with Di and see you later, when you're ready to tell me about that other business, Jack.'

Jack took Tim to the now familiar gathering place where so much had happened already – the pergola under the vines. They sat at the olive-wood table and Jack poured him some of the coffee that was still lingering there. He didn't fancy anything to eat.

'I don't understand any of what I have to tell you. Neither does Ellie, but she was sure you would want to know before something horrible happens to someone else on this evil island.'

Jack decided this was not a good time to tell Tim about Ambrose Dobson. He was distressed enough as it was. 'Go on.'

'When we got Ellie to the hospital last Sunday, the first thing they did was to carry out lots of tests to try to find out what the substance was in her system that had given her such awful pain and then stopped her heart. The toxicologist told us he had found traces of a very potent organic poison probably of plant origin. It wasn't one he had encountered before so the doctors were at a loss to know what to give her as an antidote.'

Jack nodded grimly. Sometimes hunches turned out to be right. He was pretty sure he knew what was coming next.

'But here's the really strange bit,' said Tim. 'When they did some more blood tests two hours later, it had gone. Completely disappeared. Not a trace of it left in her body. They had never seen anything like it. They think whatever it was must have broken down incredibly rapidly after she ingested it – a sort of instantly biodegradable toxin.' Tim hesitated, obviously uncomfortable with what he had to say next. 'Ellie thinks … that is, she asked me to tell you … well, she believes that Professor Gordon poisoned her. Now, I'm not accusing him of doing it on purpose

– although Ellie thinks he did. She believes he had a grudge against her because she's vegetarian. But it could have been an accident, couldn't it? I mean, he was always experimenting, leaving bits and pieces of onion bulbs and leaves lying around in Ariadne's kitchen. Something might have got into Ellie's salad by mistake. I can't believe a great botanist like the professor would deliberately try to kill a young woman for such a fanatical reason. He'd have to be insane.'

Undoubtedly, thought Jack, but there was another, much more fundamental reason why Professor Gordon would want Ellie dead, although she had no way of knowing that. Sooner or later she would have to be told, but he didn't feel it was his call and now certainly wasn't the right time.

Tim picked up his coffee cup, looked at the thick, black sludge, then thought better of it and put it down again. 'Ellie made me come and tell you because she was worried, you see. She said that it would be so easy to murder someone using such a poison and never get found out because by the time they got the victim on the slab for a post mortem, there wouldn't be any proof. They would think the person died of natural causes because this toxin, whatever it is, apparently induces heart failure. I don't know what you make of all that, Inspector Dawes, or even if it's relevant, but at least I've told you, like Ellie wanted.'

Jack revised his opinion of Ellie Watkins. There was more to that young woman than the dopey scatterbrain she had at first appeared. And it had been brave of her to send Tim to let him know, because he was sure she would have preferred her husband to stay by her side.

'Thanks, Tim. I'm grateful for the information and I know what it must have cost you to leave Ellie and come back here. What a rotten honeymoon you've both had. What will you do now?'

'I thought I'd stay in our room tonight as it's still technically ours, then go back to the mainland with you all tomorrow morning. Oh, and I nearly forgot. Charon brought over a box of spare parts in the ferry to repair the telephone system so the island shouldn't be cut off for much longer. I thought I'd try to phone the hospital and speak to Ellie later, after I've had some sleep.'

That was the best news Jack had heard for ages. He would be making a few calls to the mainland himself as soon as it was possible.

Tim frowned. 'I guess the hospital would have filled you in about Ellie's peculiar toxin tomorrow and personally, I couldn't see what difference a delay of one day would make, but Ellie seemed convinced it would be too late.'

Jack nodded but did not comment, because Ellie was absolutely right.

A flotilla of fishing boats dawdled across the turquoise crescent of Katastrophos Bay. Jack and Sidney were on one of them. They were going after swordfish this time and would not be back until early evening. Before he left, Jack had engaged in a rather arduous discussion with Corrie.

'Now listen to me, darling.' Jack turned her to face him so he could be sure she was paying attention. You could never tell with Corrie. Since they had been on Katastrophos, half her mind had been up on Olympus with Greek gods and heroes and the other half had been trying to second guess what he was working on and as usual, getting it disastrously wrong. He put on his 'this is serious' expression. 'While I'm gone, I want you to go into St Sophia for the day and stay there. Get some souvenirs and have lunch out at the taverna. Have another look around the church. After all, we're going home tomorrow, so you may as well make the most of our last day and there must be things you want to buy.'

'I'm not sure there are,' said Corrie perversely. Left to herself, she probably would have gone shopping but she never liked being told what to do.

'Where *are* you going then?' Jack seemed unusually keen to keep tabs on her.

'I thought I'd finish packing, ask Ariadne to make me a salad for lunch, then sit out on the balcony drinking wine and watching the boats out in the bay where Sid will be fishing and you'll be feeling seasick. A nice lazy day. God knows we haven't had many of those since we've been here.'

'Please, sweetheart. Go into town.'

'Why?'

'Because – well, because it may not be safe for you here.'

'Jack, what are you talking about? Of course it will be safe. What could possibly happen to me? I'll even make my own salad if you're worried about bits of dodgy leaves getting into it.' She had a suspicious thought. 'Anyway, if something dangerous is likely to happen, why are you going fishing with Sid? Why aren't you staying here to keep your "all-seeing eye" on things?'

Jack had sighed, wearily. He would be so bloody glad when this case was over and he was back with the squad. Working single-handed was like juggling jelly – and he still needed to brief Sidney. 'Just for once, Corrie, won't you please just do as I ask without asking questions?'

'If you told me what was going on, I shouldn't have to. I might even be able to help.'

'Corrie, you can't help. You just have to trust me. I need you to be out of the way.'

'Oh all right, if it's that important to you.'

'Thank you, darling. I love you to bits, you tetchy old bat!' He had kissed her gratefully and set off with Sid for the harbour, appearing suddenly very relaxed and whistling.

Corrie came down from her room half an hour later, carrying her sunhat and a voluminous bag containing, amongst all the other touristy para- phernalia, her swimsuit and sun oil. It was very hot and she thought that after her shopping she might spend some time on the beach, since Jack had made it clear she was to stay out until evening. She looked around her – the place was deserted. Quite what catastrophe Jack anticipated in the drowsy, peaceful hotel she couldn't imagine, short of a tsunami or an earthquake. She was beginning to think she would never find out what all the cloak and dagger stuff had been about – not even after they got home.

As she passed the kitchen, she stuck her head in and called '*Ya soo*' to Ariadne, who had her back to the door. The old woman jumped violently, dropping one of the small medicine bottles she was carefully extracting from an ancient clay storage jar. It smashed to smithereens on the flagstone floor. Corrie recalled smelling the pungent, malodorous herbal contents of these bottles when she had been in charge of the cooking and hoped Ariadne wasn't planning to use them to enhance tonight's goat casserole. She sniffed the air and was surprised that the glutinous liquid now seeping between the cracked slabs had no smell at all. Trust Ariadne to have destroyed one of her least revolting concoc- tions. The old woman turned and cursed vociferously, showing black uneven teeth. Then she began to scratch at a blistery rash on the back of her hand.

Yanni and Charon had gone to St Sophia to spend a hot, lazy after- noon outside the *kafeneíon*, clicking their worry beads, drinking ouzo and playing cards with their cronies. Maria had made her weekly trip to the market to stock up on provisions and gossip. It was an established and easy-going Friday ritual. Tina and Marjorie were missing too. Tina, pale and unhappy, needed to visit her relatives possibly for the last time before she was taken into custody. Marjorie wanted to buy more presents for Dan and also to visit the Church of St Sophia, intending to light a candle to the saint – in thanks, presumably, for her swift and decisive service.

Professor Gordon had left at dawn in search of the Whistling Lily. It was audible, he said, only when a fresh breeze was blowing, so Corrie didn't reckon much for his chances because there wasn't a breath of air. That left only Diana. When Corrie passed the vine-covered pergola, she saw her sitting alone, very solemn and drinking orange juice – all indications that she was not herself. She seemed to have an underlying pallor beneath her tan and the dazzling emerald eyes were cloudy and red-rimmed beneath the perfectly applied make-up. Even in that state, she looked astoundingly beautiful in well-cut shorts and a crisp, white shirt. She had her chin in her hands, and her mane of tousled hair tumbled forward, obscuring her drawn face. Although they had little in common, Corrie felt sorry to see her looking so down in the mouth. Dead envious though she was, she acknowledged that Diana had added a touch of exotic glamour to an otherwise ghastly fortnight. It would hardly matter to Jack if she went across and chatted to her for a few moments.

'Hi Diana.' She sat down next to her at the big olive-wood table.

Diana looked up, surprised. 'Corrie, what are you doing here? I thought Jack said you'd be spending the day in town.'

'I'm just on my way but I thought I'd stop and say hello.'

'Oh … right. Hello.' Diana became restless, fidgeting, probably bored and anxious to return home to England and the life of jet-setting luxury that Cuthbert provided her with.

The vines were heady with the scent of overripe grapes, sickly and intoxicating. Corrie began to chatter, divulging confidences as people often do at the end of a holiday when they know they'll never see each other again.

'I don't know about you but I'll be glad to get back to the sanity of south London after all the lunacy that's been going on here. Violent storms, no communications, people dropping like flies – first Maria, then Ellie and the terrible business with Ambrose Dobson. Believe it or not, we were supposed to be on honeymoon, Jack and me. "You'll love Katastrophos," he said, "it's the ideal 'get away from it all' destination. Loads of peace and quiet and relief from the stress of modern day living."

Huh! It's been two weeks of total mayhem. Half the time, he's been preoccupied with some job he's on when – silly me – I thought he was off duty.' She paused for breath but Diana did not seem inclined to join in. 'He's a policeman. I expect you already knew that. Policemen are never off duty, apparently. Not even on honeymoon. I suppose it's been as bad for you. The professor seems to have been working the whole time you've been here.'

'Yeah, right.'

Corrie coughed discreetly. 'I expect you'll miss Sidney. We all will. He's terrific fun, isn't he?'

'Yep. He's a great guy.'

Corrie wondered why Diana looked so miserable. She wasn't doing a great job of cheering her up. Perhaps the professor had at last found out what she and Sidney had been up to and was coming the heavy husband. Hard to imagine but not impossible. It had just taken him longer than most men to catch on. Maybe he wanted rid of her. With his wealth, he could afford to make her a very generous settlement and Diana struck Corrie as the type of young woman who would take it and run. On the other hand, a world-famous professor of botany, as Cuthbert undoubtedly would be when he took over at the university in Switzerland, probably needed a beautiful young wife to handle the social side of things. And from her point of view, he was an infinite source of the good life which she might not want to give up so easily.

'Will it take you long to get home?' asked Corrie, lamely running out of small talk.

'It depends. I haven't figured out which home I'll go to, yet.'

'Do you have more than one, then?' asked Corrie enviously.

'We have a penthouse apartment in Mayfair, a beach house in Malibu and a townhouse in Manhattan.' She said it wearily, as if owning expensive real estate was a tedious chore. 'And I guess we probably have a ten-bedroom chalet in the Swiss Alps by now, if Cuthbert has returned the papers.'

'Phew! A botany professor must be very well paid.'

Diana hesitated, wondering if she should reply then decided it didn't matter who knew now. 'They all belong to me, actually. Cuthbert doesn't have a nickel.'

'What?' Corrie's squeak of astonishment was crass and she knew it. 'I'm ... er ... sorry. That was rude. But I'd sort of assumed ...'

Diana sighed. 'It's OK, Corrie. You don't need to apologize. I know that when people look at Cuthbert and me, they see a rich sugar-daddy and his blonde bimbo and I don't do anything to correct that because I guess it's none of their damn business. But what they're actually looking at is a nutty professor and a dumb heiress – real dumb.'

'You do seem a very colourful and – er – unusual couple compared to boring folk like the rest of us.'

'You're not boring, Corrie, you're very lucky.'

'Does Sidney know you're an heiress?'

'God no. A straight-up guy like him would run a mile. Look, I don't want to seem rude but shouldn't you be on your way now?' She kept glancing sideways towards the olive groves.

'It's all right. I've got plenty of time.' Corrie had forgotten all about her resolution not to be inquisitive and poke her nose into other people's affairs. This was fascinating gossip of the very best kind. She couldn't wait to share it with Jack. 'So where did you and Cuthbert meet?'

'At university in England. I was real wild when I was a girl and my folks thought a British education would straighten me out. Cuthbert was my faculty head. He proposed halfway through my first semester.'

'How romantic. Were you madly in love with him?'

'I guess it was more of a crush. He could be very charming when he wanted. My folks were dead keen. Dad owns half Manhattan – the loaded half – and a good chunk of Europe and the Middle East. He thought marriage to a real professor would protect me from gold diggers. Even better than marrying a lord, he said. Boy, was he wrong!'

Corrie's theory about the professor threatening to divorce Diana because of her infidelity had gone right out of the window now. He couldn't afford to! All the same, her bitterness seemed a bit excessive. After all, she and Cuthbert didn't appear to have an unhappy relationship apart from his lack of attention when he was absorbed in his work. If you ignored his eccentricity, he seemed affectionate, kind and gave every impression of worshipping her, despite her promiscuous behaviour with other men, because Corrie was certain Sid hadn't been the first. Diana was young, intelligent, drop-dead gorgeous and now it turned out she was filthy rich as well. Some women, thought Corrie, are never satisfied.

'I understand now what you meant when you said Cuthbert couldn't go to Switzerland without you. I suppose he needs your money to set up the Gordon Research Scholarships?'

'You're damn right he does. They won't make him master without it and they're leaning on him hard for the dough. But after what your homicide detective husband told me today, I've decided Cuthbert isn't getting one cent out of me. I told him this morning that when I get back to the States, I'm going to call my lawyers and start divorce proceedings.' She glanced anxiously at the olive grove. 'Look, Corrie, honey, I appreciate the chat but I really think you should split now.'

'Yes, all right. I'm just going.' Corrie couldn't resist gnawing the bone a bit longer. 'But if you divorce him, won't he be able to claim huge amounts of alimony or whatever you call it?'

'Nope. I may be dumb but my dad surely isn't. He had a watertight "pre-nup" drawn up and made Cuthbert sign it. If we divorce, Cuthbert gets a big fat zero. Nada, zilch, diddly-squat.' She took a long slug of juice and Corrie realized then that there was something a lot stronger in it than oranges. 'The only way he benefits is if I die first. The old guy's got twenty-five years' start on me so I never figured that would happen – until now.' She took another swig. 'Thank Jesus we never had the kids I wanted.'

If Corrie had been thinking clearly, if her 'masterly intuition' hadn't been anaesthetized by the dreamy effect of the island, if she hadn't spent much of the last two weeks drifting in and out of a parallel universe of ancient myth and superstition, maybe her sense of self-preservation would have kicked in at that moment and she would have legged it fast to St Sophia and avoided the most terrifying experience of her life.

CHAPTER EIGHTEEN

'Speaking of kids, wouldn't it be great if Maria and Yanni had a baby?' Unwilling to end their fascinating conversation until Diana had dished absolutely all of the dirt, Corrie decided it would be safer if she shifted on to less controversial territory than the Gordons' potential divorce. 'Maria's so desperate for a child but they seem to pin all their hopes on St Sophia and the annual pilgrimage up to the monastery.'

'Yeah. She told me when we were climbing those god-awful steps. They've done all the fertility stuff at a hospital in Greece and all the tests said there's no physical reason why she shouldn't get pregnant – it just hasn't happened. So now I guess they're depending on some spiritual help from St Sophia. Maria really believes in all that crap. That's why I traded lamps with her.' Diana stared pointedly at Corrie. 'Didn't you just say you were leaving? Better hurry, the shops will be closed. They shut early here and everyone hits the sack until evening. It's been great chatting. 'Bye.'

'What do you mean, you traded lamps?'

Diana sighed impatiently. 'You remember. The whole geeky show depended on your lamp still being alight when you got to the bottom of the steps or you didn't get pregnant. Maria said her lamp was unlucky. It was the same one she carried on last year's pilgrimage and back then, it had fizzled out halfway down. She figured that's why she hadn't conceived.'

'So you swapped it for yours on the way up?'

'Sure I did. I said, "What the heck, I won't tell St Sophia if you don't" – and we traded lamps. No big deal. It was hardly going to make a whole heap of difference to me, was it? I mean – you do have to get it together with a guy before even the miraculous St Sophia can do her stuff and

179

Cuthbert is no longer active in that department.' She laughed mirthlessly. 'Maybe if I had a stigma and smelled like a hibiscus, he would have gotten around to putting some of his pollen in my direction but it's too late now – way too late.' She looked wistful and whatever alcohol was in the orange juice was making her maudlin. 'Darn thing was, my lamp stayed alight – until Maria had that seizure and chucked it down the side of the mountain.'

Corrie's torpid intuition began to warm up – very gradually – accompanied by a paradoxically cold, clammy feeling clutching at the pit of her stomach. She remembered how the ritual had required them all to eat a piece of the wick from their lamps in order to consume St Sophia's blessing. This meant Maria had swallowed the wick originally attached to Diana's lamp. But surely that wasn't significant because the lamps had to be distributed at random, didn't they? That was part of the ceremony. Everyone took pot luck and St Sophia decided who would be blessed. She tried desperately to remember who had given out the lamps on that fateful, stormy night.

'Ladies! How lucky I am to happen upon not one, but two beautiful damsels all alone and in need of male company. How about some liquid refreshment? I don't know about you, but I'm simply sweltering in this heat.' Professor Gordon, bluff, affable and extremely red in the face appeared at the entrance to the pergola carrying a tray of glasses, a bottle of ouzo and a jug of iced water. It was that precise image that jogged Corrie's memory and now she recalled exactly who had rushed around that night, hyped up and with eyes popping, 'randomly' giving out the lamps.

'Hi Cuthbert,' said Diana, in a languid voice edged with boredom. 'Corrie's just leaving, aren't you Corrie? She has some chores to do in town. But I'll have some of your ouzo-boozo – you can get real sick of orange juice, even laced with vodka.'

'Surely you'll stay for a last drink, Coriander? Before we all go our separate ways tomorrow.' Cuthbert poured three glasses of the strong liqueur and mixed them with ice and water. He picked up one of the glasses, held it up to the sunlight and swirled the contents. 'An excellent drink – ouzo. Such a distinctive flavour thanks to the *Pimpinella anisum*, a herbaceous, flowering plant that gives the drink its unique, aniseed taste. Have you ever wondered why the clear liquid turns milky with the addition of ice and water? It's because oil of anise is soluble in alcohol but not in water, so when we dilute the spirit, it separates and becomes an emulsion. See how the fine droplets scatter the light.'

Diana yawned. 'Dear God, Cuthbert, you're so bloody boring. Can't we even have a drink without one of your dreary plant lectures?'

'In some parts of Greece,' continued the professor, ignoring his wife, 'they add other flavourings, such as cinnamon, cloves and – dare I say it? – even coriander. So I insist you stay and enjoy your drink, my dear.' He put the glass firmly in Corrie's hand.

'Did you find your whistling weed, darling?' asked Diana, sarcastically. She picked up her glass and gulped down half the contents.

For a mad, illogical moment, Corrie had to fight the impulse to knock the drink out of her hand. Her intuition was racing out of control now – red-hot and throbbing. She pulled herself together. This was absurd – surreal almost. Even if Jack had been right all along about the professor purposely poisoning people, he would never harm Diana. He adored her, didn't he? But she was forgetting what she had just learned – Diana was the one with the money. Millions of dollars that would never fund Cuthbert's scholarships if she divorced him as she threatened – only if she died. Corrie thought she was going to be sick. Pull yourself together and think calmly, she urged silently. Even if Cuthbert did intend to harm Diana, suppose he *had* doctored the wick of her lamp – and the idea was still preposterous – he wouldn't try again here, in broad daylight with a witness. Besides, she'd watched him pour all their drinks from the same bottle. She was overreacting. It was the disturbing influence of this sinister island! It could drive you crackers in time. Make you imagine that everyone was evil. Look how she had suspected poor, innocent Marjorie of bumping off Ambrose. All the same, her perspective on the dynamics of the Gordons' relationship had shifted radically in the last half-hour and she was very uneasy. There was no way she was going to leave Diana alone despite her promise to Jack.

'No, I'm afraid I didn't find the Whistling Lily, my darling.' The professor beamed, either ignoring or unaware of her mocking tone. 'But I did find a perfect specimen of *pancratium maritimum*. The sand lily,' he explained, turning to Corrie. 'Beautifully scented white flowers and quite rare on this island. But I'm sure Diana's right and you're not interested in my dreary old plants. Have you girls been having an enjoyable gossip?'

'We sure have!' Diana drained her glass and Cuthbert immediately poured her another. Corrie hadn't touched hers and neither had the professor. 'I've been telling Corrie how I'm sick to my stomach of you and your insane obsession with plants. I've also told her about that little matter of divorce we discussed this morning, but she really isn't interested in our marital problems and now she's fed up with us both. Can't wait to leave, can you Corrie? So long, hon. See ya!' Diana looked her straight in the eye and nodded very obviously towards the exit from the pergola.

Corrie didn't move. She was very uncomfortable about where this was leading but was confident nothing awful would happen while she was there and she intended to sit it out until Jack returned, if necessary. It was becoming clear now why he had asked her to keep an eye on Diana. She had thought it was because he suspected Diana was up to something but obviously, it was for her own protection. If only he'd told me what was going on, Corrie ranted silently.

'It's the end of the line for you, Cuthbert. How's that for a juicy bit of gossip?' Diana stuck her face belligerently into his, more than a little drunk. 'You're a busted flush, sweetheart. A waste of space. Go screw yourself – better still, go screw a hibiscus!'

His vague, amiable expression did not change, only his bristling ginger eyebrows betrayed his inner rage. 'Now, now Diana. You know you don't mean that, my angel. You're just hot and a little emotional.' He turned to Corrie, as if some explanation was required. 'She'll be fine once we get to Switzerland, of course.'

Corrie sensed a terrible, pent-up fury bubbling beneath the surface, waiting to erupt into violence. He kept fidgeting and glancing at the Rolex on his wrist. Suddenly, Corrie was scared – really scared. She had the panicky urge to run and fetch help. Then she realized with an icy shock that there wasn't anyone to fetch. Yanni, Maria, Charon, Tina and Marjorie were in town all day and Jack and Sid were drifting about in a boat, somewhere on Katastrophos Bay. She silently cursed Jack for leaving her to go fishing, just when she most needed him. What could he have been thinking about, pushing off like that when he must have at least suspected something appalling might happen? It was so unlike him. She had a sudden idea. It was pretty pathetic but worth a try. Maybe if she went down to the hotel beach she could signal to him on the boat. Jump up and down and wave her hat or something. Light a bonfire, even. She stood up.

'Well, it's been nice chatting to you both.' She indicated the swimsuit and towel in her beach bag. 'I think I'll just go and have a last swim. See you later ...'

'Nonsense, my dear.' Instantly, the professor rose from his chair, his six-foot frame effectively blocking her exit, challenging her to physically shove him out of the way. 'You haven't touched your drink yet, Coriander, and I mixed it specially.' He picked up her glass and put it in her hand again. She sat down, thinking fast, and pretended to take a sip. Then, as he turned back to Diana, she quickly chucked all but a dribble of it over her shoulder into the vines. Diana on the other hand had knocked back another full glass and was actually holding it out for a refill. Corrie prayed indiscriminately. Please God, St Sophia, Santa Claus, my Fairy Godmother, anyone! What should I do?

Diana was clearly very drunk and her speech was badly slurred. 'You still here?' She struggled to focus on Corrie's face. 'Well, let me tell you something before you go. This guy you see before you, this smart-arse professor, has a screw loose – in fact, *all* his screws are loose.' She stood up, circling him unsteadily, taunting and poking him. 'He thinks he's a great genius. A botanical giant among intellectual pygmies – that's what you said, didn't you, darlin'? And yet this "genius" believes I'm going to give him a million bucks just so he can set up some stupid scholarships and play the big dude, the number one head honcho, using *my* dough. That's pretty damn dumb for a flat-broke genius, isn't it?' She was speaking to Corrie but confronting Cuthbert head on, staggering slightly and jabbing him hard in the chest.

The professor looked at his watch again. 'Diana, my dear,' he was dangerously, coldly calm, 'whether or not you are prepared to fund the Gordon Research Scholarships voluntarily is a matter of complete indifference to me now, but I can assure you that they *will* go ahead and I *shall* become internationally revered.'

Diana ignored this completely and continued to goad him. It was almost as if it was deliberate, provoking him into violence, retaliation. Despite his calm pretence, he was bright scarlet in the face and kept clenching and unclenching his big, bony fists. Corrie noticed, as if through a dreamlike mist, that he had bad blistery rashes amongst the ginger hair on the backs of both his hands – exactly like Sidney's.

'If this old guy was as potent and powerful as he thinks,' Diana renewed her vicious harangue, 'you'd expect him to have given me at least one kid sometime in the last ten years, wouldn't you, Corrie? But no, he's too busy arranging goddam flowers.' She turned to Corrie and pretended to speak confidentially in a hoarse, stage whisper. 'He did it once, you know that? He got one of his students pregnant. His stamens worked OK that time. But not me – he couldn't do it for me!' She was shouting now.

'How did you know about that?' The professor grabbed both her arms, shaking her and glaring angrily. She laughed in his face.

'You don't think my daddy would have let me marry you without having you checked out first, do you, Cuthbert? He had a private eye dig up the dirt on you but he didn't find much.' She began to count on her fingers. 'You got busted for growing your own wacky weed, you once threw a brick through the window of a vegetarian restaurant and you put one of your students in the club. The girl didn't want to complain and the university didn't want any scandal so it was hushed up and you got away with it. I didn't care – at least I knew you were fertile and I wanted babies. Not that your ageing pollen has done this hibiscus much good, has it, my angel?'

'My dearest Diana.' The professor refilled her glass. 'You really are quite as obtuse as my poor lamented sister. I'm not to blame for any of this. It's hardly my fault if neither of you had the intelligence to understand the immense importance of my work. Even the bureaucrats were too stupid to give me the knighthood I deserved. But soon my work will be made available to the whole world. It is my destiny to become a living legend in my field, so you must see how futile it is to try to stop me. In Switzerland, I shall finally be recognized as the greatest botanist of our time.'

It was at that moment, when he laughed out loud, his bulging eyes glittering wildly, that Corrie realized the awful truth. In her parallel, mythological world, this man had been Zeus, god of the sky and thunder, his power symbolized by the eagle, the bull and the thunderbolt. This was the ruler of Mount Olympus to whom mortals and animals were sacrificed indiscriminately and to whom the olive tree was sacred. But Zeus the King, alias Professor Cuthbert Gordon, was completely and irredeemably insane.

Diana burst into raucous drunken laughter. 'Switzerland, baby, is right where you belong – in a country full of cuckoo clocks! Because that's just what you are – cuckoo.' She shoved him hard in the chest and began shrieking, 'Cuckoo! Cuckoo! Cuck ...' The shrill jibe turned into a harsh, choking sound. Diana's vivid emerald eyes widened in surprise. She clutched at her stomach and staggered backwards, retching horribly, then fell across the olive-wood table and slid to the ground, screaming and writhing with pain. For a split second Corrie was paralysed – unable to move a muscle. It was Maria and Ellie all over again. The same terrible symptoms – gasping for breath, delirious fits and intolerable, disabling pain. Diana seemed unable to focus and began twitching violently. Corrie was jolted out of her trauma.

'Oh, Diana, no!' She fell to her knees on the rough stone slabs and tried to help Diana sit up, but she thrashed about wildly, fighting her off. Although gagging painfully, she still hadn't been sick. Remembering how Tina had made Maria vomit up the poison, Corrie scrambled to her feet and reached for the salt cellar, still on the table. She was about to grab the water jug when a bony hand seized her wrist in an iron grip.

'Leave her,' ordered the professor. 'It's quite useless. She's had enough poison to kill an elephant. There's nothing anyone can do to save her.' His tone was matter-of-fact, conversational even, as if commenting on unfortunate weather.

Diana lay on the ground, jerking and convulsing, her flawless features now distorted in agony. For a brief moment, Corrie thought it was a nightmare – that kaleidoscope hell where fact and fantasy whirl together, indistinguishable. In a minute, she would wake up in the real world with Jack snoring beside her and Diana safe in her room with a sane, loving husband.

Suddenly, the heartrending screams stopped and Diana lay still, the flashing green eyes closed for ever. Corrie cradled her head, feeling her golden curls damp with sweat. Her perfume drifted up, still heady and vibrant. Even in death, she looked breathtakingly beautiful. It was a wicked, wilful destruction of life. Corrie heard herself weeping hysterically. If only she had listened to Jack instead of arrogantly thinking she knew better. She might have warned Diana, got her away, saved her life.

'Diana, I'm so sorry.' She sobbed bitterly over the body she had so envied, now limp and unresponsive. 'It's all my fault. If only I'd listened.'

Then the red mist descended – thick and blinding. Corrie seethed with boiling, churning rage. The flood of adrenaline pumping through her veins made her dizzy. It was a case of 'fight or flight' and foolishly, Corrie chose fight. She stood up and faced the professor, hot tears still pouring down her face.

'You bastard. You murdering, heartless, evil bastard. Don't imagine for a moment that you're going to get away with this. Jack's already on to you and I shall tell him everything, give him the evidence with your fingerprints all over it and they'll lock you away for the rest of your life – you'll never see your precious plants ever again!'

'I don't think you will,' he replied, reasonably, picking up Corrie's empty glass. 'Of course, you haven't consumed as much poison as my lovely wife over there, but you've swallowed more then enough to silence you long before your bungling husband returns.'

'Oh no I haven't! I threw it in the …' Corrie blurted it, unthinking and in white-hot temper. She knew it was a fatal, mindless mistake before the words were even out. Gordon grabbed her hard around the throat, forcing her backwards into the vines. She could smell the bunches of sticky, overripe grapes as they squashed around her head. In a different situation, her generous proportions might have given her an edge over his spindly frame, but now his strength was astounding and took her completely by surprise. He shoved her down into one of the rustic chairs, pulling her arms behind her. Then he whipped a length of cord from his pocket and tied her wrists.

'I wasn't expecting you to be here, Coriander, you are an irritating complication but luckily I came prepared. Soft cord you will observe – I don't want them to find marks on your wrists after you're dead. Now, I think perhaps you had better take a little more refreshment, my dear.' He reached for Diana's half-empty glass and, squeezing Corrie's cheeks, he forced the rim against her teeth. She could taste the bitter, aniseed liquid pouring into her mouth and tried desperately not to swallow but she was choking and gulped it down involuntarily. She knew, in that single defining moment, that she was going to die agonizingly, callously murdered, but even worse, without Jack to comfort her. The hotel was deserted, there was no one to come to her aid. Then, in a miraculous flash of lucidity, she remembered Tim. He hadn't gone to town with the others, he was exhausted from his rough, overnight ferry trip and had gone up to his room to rest. It was worth a try. He might hear her as the afternoon was so still and silent. She took as deep a breath as her panicking lungs would allow and screamed, 'Tim! Tim! Help me!'

'You're wasting the last of your precious breath, my dear.' The professor was matter of fact. 'Watkins's room is round at the back of the hotel, on the top floor. He's fast asleep, thanks to a little valerian in his tea, and will hear nothing. I made sure when I found out he had returned to the island with some meddlesome message from that silly wife of his.'

'You tried to kill her, too, didn't you, you bastard?' Corrie felt she had nothing to lose by making the maniac confess; unlike poor Diana she felt no ill effects yet, apart from abject terror, so maybe there was a slim chance she might stay alive long enough to tell someone. She stuck out her trembling chin, belligerently. 'What went wrong? Did your brilliant research turn out to be not so brilliant after all? Did you get the dose wrong?'

The professor sighed. 'Of course I didn't try to kill the stupid child, although it would have been no loss to mankind for all the use she was as an intelligent human being. It wasn't my fault, Coriander. None of this is my fault. You do understand, don't you?' His voice was earnest, concerned that she should believe him and seemingly wanting her to stay conscious long enough for him to defend his indefensible crimes. 'People kept interfering. First it was Maria, so desperate to become pregnant that she exchanged lamps with Diana. How was I supposed to have anticipated that? Naturally, I had already applied concentrated poison to Diana's wick but Maria chewed it instead. Not a sufficient dose, as it turned out, because as you know, Maria survived. A useful test of the potency of my newly developed toxin, however. Rats are all very well but no substitute for a human guinea pig. Then that vacuous child, Ellie, drank Diana's wine. How could I be held responsible for that? If she had remained at her usual place at table instead of fidgeting about, Diana would have been dead days ago and none of this unpleasantness would be necessary.' He stood up and began pacing about, puzzled that Corrie was not yet showing any inclination to die. Irritably, he grasped a handful of her hair, forced her head back and poured more ouzo down her throat.

Corrie gagged but through the cotton wool that was now her brain, the clues began to fall into place like the mandatory last scene in the library at the end of an Agatha Christie mystery. She recalled Ellie, dim, besotted Ellie, that night at the dinner party. She had moved into Diana's seat when Diana got up to dance with Sid, partly to avoid sitting close to the smelly *kokorétsi* but mainly to be on Tim's left, so they could hold hands while they ate. She had absent-mindedly picked up Diana's wine glass and drunk from it.

Corrie struggled to speak. 'Are you saying you actually watched Ellie drink Diana's wine, knowing it had your filthy poison in it, and you didn't stop her?'

'I had no choice. You must see that. If I'd stopped her, it would have aroused suspicion and I knew that dull-witted, flat-footed husband of yours was already watching me. Anyway, she only sipped it in that silly, simpering way of hers. Diana would have gulped it down and then it would all have been over. That meddling nurse couldn't have saved her.'

The glass he held was empty now so he reached behind him for the bottle of neat ouzo. In that instant, Corrie glimpsed possible salvation. Over his shoulder she saw a familiar figure bashing an octopus against the kitchen tree-stump to soften it up for dinner. Ariadne. Thank God! Thank St Sophia! She still had no stomach cramps and no vision disturbance, apart from the alcoholic effects of the ouzo. There might still be a chance. She screeched with all the breath she had left. 'Ariadne! Ariadne! Help me!'

Ariadne looked up, alarmed, and was about to scamper across but the professor shouted urgently to her in Greek. To Corrie's horror, she squealed, threw her apron over her head and scuttled back into her kitchen.

'Ariadne won't help you. I told her the devil had possessed you. She believes it is the curse of St Sophia and she ran for her life. Clever of me, isn't it, to make use of an old woman's fear and superstition? She's very loyal, Ariadne. Knows when to keep her mouth shut. She helped me to poison Diana's picnic lunch but that bloated buffoon Dobson ate it instead. Interference, you see? More interference. If only people would mind their own business and allow me to get on with mine, life would be so much simpler. All the same, I'm glad Dobson died the way he did. There was a certain poetic irony about it, don't you think? It was a plant that kept him alive and a plant that finally killed him.' He laughed, his eyes now mad and staring. Corrie was nothing if not feisty and although terrified, she was determined not to let him think he had won so easily. Kicking out with her feet, she tried to tip her chair over and clawed helplessly at the cord binding her wrists. Gordon put his hands around her throat.

'Please don't struggle, Coriander. There's really no point and I don't want to leave finger marks on your throat. Strangulation is clumsy and uncouth and not part of my plan.'

'They'll know it was you when the post mortem finds your poison in our bodies,' she choked.

His cackle this time was unquestionably that of an incurably deranged man.

'Ah but they won't, you see. That's the beauty of it. The sheer, unerring brilliance of my research into toxins. I keep trying to tell you, Coriander, plants are so much more intelligent than human beings. They outsmart us at every level. Only plants, our very origins, have any relevance to our lives and our future. Let me explain before you die. The toxin that is currently effecting dangerous changes to your heart rhythm and will eventually induce vomiting, psychoses and death is distilled from the bulb of a genetically modified *urginea maritima* – the sea squill. Through my incomparable skills, I have been able to cultivate a hybrid of the red and white varieties, both potentially poisonous in their original itera-tions. I have called my hybrid *urginea Gordonea*. Toxin distilled from this plant is not only deadly and with no known antidote but it has an additional and invaluable property as a murder weapon – it decomposes in the body in a matter of hours. By the time the incompetent idiots in pathology get you and my lovely wife, Diana, on their slab, it will be totally undetectable.'

Corrie drew a shuddering breath. 'You can't be sure of that! The only post mortems you've done have been on rats.'

The professor smiled triumphantly. 'Why do you suppose they couldn't find any traces of poison in my dear, departed sister, Lavinia?'

'Lavinia? Lavinia Braithwaite? She was your sister? Oh my god!' Corrie slumped in her chair, beaten at last by his shocking and unemo-tional revelation.

'Oh I know they suspected me. Pulled me in for questioning on several occasions – but they couldn't prove a thing, because I'm so much smarter than the police. No evidence of poisoning and not even a motive, as it turned out, because the senile old bitch left all her money to some scrounging charity instead of me. So you see, I had no choice then. I had to get rid of Diana. Rather a pity in a way, she was an exquisite creature, but it couldn't be helped.' He spoke impassively as if he had just dispatched a favourite, exotic parrot. 'When your nosy husband returns from his fishing trip, he'll find two bodies, claimed by the same myste-rious food bacterium that attacked the others. Detective Inspector Dawes and I will, of course, be distraught widowers, united in our grief – except that I shall be very, very rich.' Impatient now, he poured neat ouzo into Corrie's mouth straight from the bottle and shook her like a Jack Russell shakes a rat to make her swallow. 'Naturally, he'll be suspicious, like the other policemen, but it will do him no good. Ariadne will swear that I spent all day on the far side of the island among the olive groves. There will be no proof, no opportunity, no evidence and only one witness to your death, my dear Coriander. Me.'

'And me, Cuthbert, baby,' drawled a familiar voice. 'Don't forget me.'

Diana was standing just behind him, calm, poised and surprisingly beautiful, belying the fact that just minutes ago, she had been thrashing around in the dust, screaming. Her face was flushed, her hair tangled but she was very much alive.

At the sound of her voice, the professor's florid face drained of colour. He turned very slowly and froze, transfixed with horror. Corrie gasped, unable to speak for the first time in her life. Gordon began to back away from his resurrected wife, shaking his head in disbelief, his slack mouth opening and closing like a landed goldfish, bug-eyes wide with fear. If he had watched Diana rise, zombie-like, from the grave of the undead, he could not have been more traumatized. He stumbled backwards, his gaze never leaving her, clinging desperately to the vines for support. When he reached the entrance to the pergola, he turned to run but a muscular arm snaked out, locking him firmly around the throat.

CHAPTER NINETEEN

'Hold it right there, Prof.' The grim owner of the restraining arm showed not a glimmer of his usual lighthouse smile. 'Detective Inspector Dawes wants a word with you.'

'Christ, Sidney, you took your time!' Diana collapsed on to the nearest chair and pushed trembling fingers through her mane of hair.

Sidney had expected – had hoped – that the professor would struggle, try to resist arrest. Sid was not a violent man, very rarely got into a temper about anything, but now he ached to smash his fist into Gordon's face. Make him feel some of the fear and pain he had so pitilessly inflicted on others. But the professor was already a broken man. The shock of discovering he was not an invincible genius, that something had gone radically wrong with his faultlessly brilliant research had finally tipped him over the edge of reason into total, vacant insanity. He neither moved nor spoke as Jack jerked his arms behind his back and snapped on the handcuffs.

'Cuthbert Delauncey Gordon, I'm arresting you for the murder of Lavinia Delphine Braithwaite and Ambrose Aubrey Dobson and the attempted murder of Maria Stasinopoulos, Eleanor Lucy Watkins, Diana Marilyn Gordon and ... Corrie?'

Jack spotted his wife for the first time, hidden in the far corner of the pergola, still tied to her chair and trembling with terror and shock. She tried to speak, to tell him she'd been poisoned and probably only had minutes to live but could only gibber incoherently through chattering teeth. Leaving Sidney holding Gordon, Jack strode across and untied her, scooping her up into his arms and holding her tight. He whispered 'Oh Corrie, Corrie,' over and over in her ear and kissed her hair tenderly. Then he held her abruptly away from him.

'What the bloody hell are you doing here?' Through the rushing noise in her ears, she could hear him yelling at her, his fright and relief exploding into anger. 'What did you think you were playing at? I distinctly told you to stay out of the way. You were supposed to be in town, out of danger. You promised me. Will you never learn to do as you're told and stop interfering? You could have been killed if this operation had gone wrong!'

Indignant, Corrie opened her mouth to protest – and threw up all over his shoes.

That night, the group's last dinner on Katastrophos was a long and solemn affair. Of the ten 'hopeful travellers' who had assembled around the big olive-wood table at that first dinner two weeks before, only seven remained, hunched morosely down at one end. No one had much of an appetite, which was just as well since Ariadne had taken to her bed, heartbroken, when Professor Gordon had been led away in handcuffs, and both Yanni and Maria were deeply shocked at the disturbing turn of events taking place on their peaceful little island. Gordon was docile and bewildered, muttering plant formulae to himself and shaking his head in disbelief. Jack had simply locked him in his room. Communications with the mainland were now restored and Jack had summoned a police launch which would arrive the next morning, With a bit of luck and some persuasion on Jack's part, it would take everyone back to the mainland.

When they searched Cuthbert Gordon's sample-case, they found, among other things, a single airline ticket to Switzerland. As Sid had wryly pointed out, he had hardly intended to use it just to nip over and get the Rolex cleaned. It was his planned escape route. He had also opened a Swiss bank account – presumably to deposit the millions he was confident he would inherit after Diana's death.

'Jack, I wish you'd told me poor Lavinia was Cuthbert Gordon's sister. It was such a shock finding out like that.' Corrie was still dazed and her stomach was churning volcanically but they had managed to persuade her that neither she nor Diana had been poisoned and now, like everyone else, she was trying to make sense of the whole ghastly nightmare. 'She was such a lovely lady – warm and generous. He told us why he killed her and why they couldn't find any poison in her body at the autopsy but *how* did he do it? She died at a charity luncheon. I prepared all the food myself.'

'And Gordon had a cast-iron alibi. He was in Leicester, lecturing to a hundred botany students when she died. Wasn't there anything that only she ate?' Jack asked.

'No, I served everyone the same meal. Terrine of trout, confit of duck béarnaise and raspberry pavlova, except the poor soul keeled over with stomach pains before she got to the dessert. At first I thought the duck might have been too fatty for her. She'd had her gall bladder out, you see, and always took a dose of medicine before a rich luncheon so it wouldn't …' She looked at Jack, horrified. 'The bastard put it in her medicine.'

'Almost certainly, only we'll never get him to admit it now. He's having trouble remembering his name.'

'Cuthbert was so certain he'd get Lavinia's money when she died because he was her only living relative,' Diana said quietly. 'He was furious when he found she'd left it to charity. Said she was too stubborn to understand that his research was much more important than giving handouts to scroungers but he wasn't about to let her stupidity prevent the world from benefiting from his genius.'

'Now I understand why you came to Lavinia's funeral,' Corrie said to Jack. 'You wanted to see if Cuthbert had the nerve to turn up.'

'Murderers often do attend the funeral of their victims. He didn't, of course. By then, he'd moved swiftly on to plan B and was plotting his next murder – you, Diana. The DI who headed up the investigation into Lavinia's death was positive Gordon had poisoned her but he couldn't prove it. There was nothing traceable in her system, no motive because he didn't get her cash and he was miles away when she died. But the DI was convinced from Gordon's bolshie, arrogant attitude when he was being interviewed that he was completely without remorse and determined to get his scholarship money from somewhere. When we checked your financial situation, Diana, and found out the terms of your pre-nuptial agreement, you were favourite to be his next victim. Then after we discovered he'd booked the trip to Katastrophos, his own private plant reserve, we were really concerned for your safety. But you can't arrest someone on the grounds that you suspect he might be going to commit a crime. Our hands were more or less tied unless we could catch him in the act.'

Diana nodded. 'Yeah, I can see that. It was when the Swiss uni started to lean on Cuthbert to hand over the bucks for the research scholarships that he arranged the holiday on Katastrophos. Said he needed to do some final urgent experiments and he needed me to go with him. Now I know what his final urgent "experiment" was going to be.'

'Why did he want to go to Switzerland particularly?' Sid wanted to know, thinking only of skiing in freezing snow and a fairly indifferent football team.

'Because Swiss universities and colleges are linked through the Swiss Science Network which is connected to the European and American networks, so Swiss universities can exchange knowledge at both national and international level. That's how Cuthbert figured he'd become world famous.' She glanced at Jack from beneath long lashes. 'I guess I'm real lucky you were on my case, DI Dawes.'

'Yes, DI Dawes, it was lucky, wasn't it?' Corrie eyeballed him, her tone dangerous. 'Perhaps now you'd be kind enough to explain which particular piece of luck selected you to take Diana's case instead of someone else on the squad? Especially when you swore to me you were off duty. Do you remember what you said? "I've chosen Katastrophos for our honeymoon, darling, because I know you'll love it. It's a romantic island paradise where we can be alone and relax at last". It's been about as romantic as a fortnight on Alacatraz!'

'Actually, Alcatraz is real popular these days.' Unwisely, Diana hoped to distract Corrie from beating up Jack to whom she felt she owed her life. It was like trying to divert a charging rhino with a carrot. 'You can go on tours of the Golden Gate Recreation Area. You just get the ferry from San Francisco and—'

'Shut up, Diana!' Corrie's glare silenced her. 'Go on, Jack. Explain how we fetched up on Katastrophos the exact same fortnight as the professor and Diana? Of course, I might just have believed it was intuition, that you were acting on a hunch, except you don't believe in all that touchy-feely stuff, do you? Intuition's unreliable – that's what you said. The inconsequential fancies of impressionable women.'

Jack looked sheepish. 'It was the chief super's idea, sweetheart,' he protested lamely. 'He saw I'd put in for two weeks' leave and suggested it would be a good idea if I spent it on Katastrophos.'

'Don't be such a wimp! You could have refused.'

'But darling, when the DCS "suggests" something, it more or less amounts to an order. I was the obvious choice because Gordon had never seen me. I'd been working on ... well, another case when he was being pulled in for questioning.' He carefully avoided Tina's eye. 'The DCS reckoned it was an ideal opportunity to get close to him, find out how he was making the toxins and get samples, so the forensic lads could have a go at them. That was all I planned to do at first. I was convinced he'd set up some kind of lab in the monastery. When it turned out just to be Yanni's wine scam, I followed Gordon round the island, watched what he did, examined all his samples, there was nothing incriminating. I searched everywhere for the poison we knew he was manufacturing. Except, of course, Ariadne's ancient clay storage jars. It was only this morning on the beach when Diana told me he went missing from their room most nights and she'd found him in the kitchen a couple of times that I realized where he'd worked on the distillation. That kitchen is such a dump, it never occurred to me it might be suitable for scientific experiments. Of course, Ariadne knew all about it and covered for him. Hid everything away. He told her she was a vital part of his important research and she worshipped him. Sid and I found his stash of poison this morning. We caught Ariadne getting it out of the jar and gibbering on about how the professor was coming soon to collect it.'

'But I found it the first Tuesday we were here when I took over the cooking!' Corrie said with horror. 'And I found the burned-out pots. He must have been boiling stuff up in them for hours.'

'Explains why nobody got poisoned while you were in charge,' Sid said grimly. 'Must have slowed him down a bit, not being able to get into the kitchen and without Ariadne to cover his tracks.'

'I just thought they were little old bottles of concentrated herbs, something every Greek housewife kept in her store cupboard,' said Corrie. 'They smelled disgusting, like rotting vegetables.'

'Bloody good job you never tasted any of them,' said Sidney.

'Or put it in our food,' added Tim. 'Although that didn't help poor Ellie. The hospital said she's lucky to be alive. And we've you to thank for that, Sky.'

'Please call me Tina. And I'm glad to have been able to help.' She pushed the untouched food around her plate. She hadn't looked healthy when she arrived and now she was sallow, silent and very thin, waiting for the police launch next morning and the moment when DI Dawes would snap the handcuffs on her, too. She supposed she should be grateful not to have been confined to her room under house arrest, like the professor.

'Corrie, why on earth didn't you tell me you'd found bottles of something odd at the time?' asked Jack, exasperated at all the time he'd wasted.

'Because you didn't tell me you were looking for them! It's what happens when you keep me in the dark. How was I supposed to guess

what was going on? I'm intuitive – not clairvoyant! It's your own fault.'
Corrie's stomach rumbled audibly, still suffering from the after effects of
all the ouzo forced down her throat.

Sid poured everyone some red wine – rich, fruity and at room temper-
ature. Ironically, he was just starting to get the hang of Diana's posh life
style and now he had to give it up. They were all edgy and in need of a
medicinal sedative to get over the shock. Sid needed it to get over Diana.
They drank gratefully, even Tina, so he topped them up again.

''Course, it was the perfect place for the prof to bump off Diana when
you think about it. A plentiful supply of that bulb thing he'd been cross-
cultivating for years; no police presence on the island, just a very old
priest in charge, and a long enough trip to the mainland for the poison
to decompose in the body even when the phones were working and you
could call for assistance. The storm was a real bonus. He must have
thought Corrie's Greek gods had blessed him.' Sid's expression was bitter.
'The worst part for me was that he showed absolutely no reaction or
guilt when Maria, Ellie and Dobson got poisoned by accident. He just
kept on trying. Sorry, Diana, but he was a real callous bastard. If it was
down to me, he'd be put away for the rest of his life.'

Everyone had noticed how Sid's relationship with Diana had changed
subtly since he found out she was an heiress and enormously rich. He
obviously still adored her but now he was distant, even cool with her. She
had been through a terrible, shattering experience and he longed to
comfort her, declare his feelings, but now with her husband about to be
tried for murder, it would be both presumptuous and crass. People would
draw the wrong conclusions – that Sid was after her money. Couldn't
blame them – he'd probably think the same himself. But the worst thing
would be if Diana thought it. He couldn't bear that – wouldn't risk it.
Tomorrow they would go their separate ways and he'd get over her –
eventually.

'What I don't understand,' said Marjorie, 'and please forgive me,
Diana, this must be awful for you, but why didn't Professor Gordon just
– er – well, do it somewhere private? I mean, he could easily have slipped
some poison into his wife's morning tea when they were in their room
instead of risking other people swallowing it by mistake.'

'He daren't chance it, Marjorie,' said Jack. 'He found out I was a
policeman when we arrived because Tina told everyone and he must have
realized, eventually, that I was watching him rather more closely than a
casual interest in botany warranted. It's hard to be unobtrusive on such

a small island. But he was encouraged by how easily he'd got away with Lavinia's murder and decided he'd be safe if Diana died somewhere where he couldn't possible be a suspect, such as up in the monastery, or at dinner where we all helped ourselves from the same dishes, or when she was on the other side of the island eating her picnic lunch. He was cunning, very clever and—'

'Nuts,' finished Diana. She was very flushed and her eyes were unnaturally bright. 'He isn't a genius, he's a fruit-cake – a total basket case. But I was even nuttier. D'you wanna know why? I'd decided to tell him I was going to give him the money for his dumb scholarships. I'd even have played the part of a respectable master's wife – some of the time. He was my husband and I believed, deep down, that he loved me even if he didn't fancy me any more. But then Jack told me he'd killed his own sister in cold blood.' Her voice wavered. 'She was such a great old lady, I was real fond of her ...' She stopped and blew her nose. 'When I realized he was also responsible for Maria, Ellie and your husband, Marjorie, I knew it was the end of the line – he had to be stopped.' Her voice broke altogether and instinctively Sid made as if to put his arm around her but hesitated and drew very slightly away. Corrie noticed and was sorry. It was a shame. No wonder Professor Gordon hadn't cared about his wife carrying on with Sid – you wouldn't if you were planning to murder her anyway.

'I'm sorry I had to put you through such an ordeal, Diana, it isn't normal practice in the murder squad to use civilians as bait but I had to force Gordon's hand. Time was running out and I needed evidence and, with a bit of luck, a confession, before you both left Katastrophos. By then, it would have been too late and we couldn't have protected you.'

'You guys certainly cut it pretty fine!' Diana blew her nose. 'I was expecting you to grab him as soon as I hit the deck. I was terrified he'd check my pulse – guess I was shamming.'

Sid was full of apologies. 'We couldn't help it, Di. The wind dropped and it took us longer than we planned to sail back to shore. Believe me, when Jack and I first found that filthy jollop where the prof had hidden it, I didn't want to let him anywhere near you. I was so angry I wanted to wring the bastard's neck, but Jack said that wouldn't get a confession out of him and I'd just finish up behind bars instead of him.'

'Right,' agreed Jack. 'And we had to let Gordon see us actually go out on the boat because he was checking that everybody had left the hotel to make sure he had the place to himself. He took a huge risk but as he saw it, he'd run out of options. The university was threatening to give the job to another botanist so he had to find the cash, fast. You did a great acting job, Diana. Very convincing.'

She laughed mirthlessly. 'Didn't I tell you? I flunked botany soon after Cuthbert took over my class. I switched subjects and majored in performing arts.'

Corrie looked difficult. She had been listening to the explanations and gradually things were becoming clearer.

'Let me get this straight, Jack. You set up a high-risk operation to catch a man you knew was a ruthless murderer and you didn't think to mention it to me?'

'Sorry, Corrie, but you weren't even supposed to be there. I told you to stay in town.'

'And you were in on it, too, Sidney?'

'Sorry, Corrie.'

'And you, Diana. You let me think you'd been poisoned – that we'd both been poisoned?'

'Sorry, Corrie.'

'Will you all please stop saying that!' She glared angrily at them, control ebbing away. 'Have you any idea what I went through today? I was tied to that chair having what I believed was deadly poison poured down my throat and I really believed Diana and I were done for. It was terrifying. I'll probably need counselling – therapy, even. I'll be surprised if I don't get post-traumatic stress … thingummy. Why on earth didn't you tell me what was going on, Jack?'

He looked contrite. 'You know what you're like, dumpling. If I'd given you the slightest hint about the operation, you'd have been hopping about like Miss Marple with a bat up her nightgown – desperate to inter-fere. You're hopeless at keeping secrets and you're a lousy liar. Gordon would have guessed straight off that it was a set-up and we'd never have got a confession.' He put a cautious arm around her. 'Diana said you were amazing – really feisty and brave, and you wouldn't leave her even though she kept telling you to go. I'm so proud of you – but you shouldn't have put yourself at risk, sweetheart.' He tried to kiss her on the cheek but she shoved him away. A sudden unpleasant thought struck her.

'I assume you snatched the bottle of ouzo he'd poisoned and switched it for a safe one?'

Jack shook his head. 'We couldn't, there wasn't time. The boat was so slow sailing back, by the time we got there, Gordon had already poured his toxin into the bottle and fed it to you and Diana.'

'It was OK, though,' assured Sid, cheerfully. 'Before we left to go fishing, we got Maria to keep Ariadne out of the way and we replaced the poison in her bottles with something else, double quick, before the prof arrived to collect it. You were quite safe.'

'Oh, were we?' said Corrie, nastily. 'Were we, really? And what if he'd had extra supplies hidden in other places – such as his sample case, or Yanni's cellar, or his anorak pocket, for example? What would have happened if he'd used some of that instead of the stash in Ariadne's kitchen?'

Jack and Sid looked at each other uncomfortably. Sid shuffled his feet nervously and swore under his breath – something deeply obscene.

'I heard that, Sidney Foskett! And as for you ...' Corrie shot her husband a look far worse than anything Medusa might have conjured up. But she was denied the satisfaction of telling him exactly what she thought of him because her stomach gave another ferocious growl and she knew she needed to leave the table urgently. A glance at Diana confirmed that she, too, was not without discomfort. Ignoring Jack, Corrie fixed Sidney with a terrible eye, considering him the more vulnerable of the two.

'What exactly did you replace the poison with, Sidney?'

'Yeah, what was in that bottle besides ouzo?' gasped Diana, between cramps.

Sid hesitated, glancing helplessly at Jack. 'You have to believe me, ladies, we didn't have much time and—'

'What was it?'

'... we had to find something that looked and smelled more or less the same so he wouldn't spot the switch—'

'Sidney!'

'It was squirty cucumber juice.'

'Not at all poisonous, my darling, they use it on the island to make medicine,' reassured Jack. 'It's just that it's a bit ... well, I suppose it's a lot, really ...' He swallowed hard. 'It's a very ... potent ... purgative.' But Corrie had already left with Diana hard on her heels. A turbulent end to a turbulent day.

CHAPTER TWENTY

Saturday morning, the day of departure, was even bleaker than the previous evening. Everyone had run out of things to say. They huddled around the now depressing olive-wood table for the last time, deep in their own thoughts and willing the Greek police launch to arrive and return them to normality although it would be a long time before anything felt normal again. The dramatic events of the last fortnight – a lifetime ago – now seemed unreal – impossible for even the most resilient of them to absorb. Mostly, people seemed to have turned in on themselves, searching their battered senses for some sort of under-standing.

Sidney, in an unusually sombre mood, was bracing himself for the inevitable parting from his lovely, unattainable Diana and trying to work out why fate had brought them together, given him a brief taste of joy and then kicked him hard in the balls. Unable to endure the oppressive silence, he broke it, sharing his confused thoughts.

'Wasn't it a strange coincidence the way we all arrived on Katastrophos at the same time?'

They looked up, puzzled, waiting for further clarification.

'What I mean is, this island doesn't have ten visitors in a year, never mind in a fortnight. The odds against us all choosing it for the same two weeks must be astronomical.'

It remained quiet for a long time while they considered this, then Corrie put a hand on his arm. 'Maybe the hypnotic atmosphere has befuddled my brain like the professor told us it would, but I don't think it was coincidence that brought us all to Katastrophos.'

Sid frowned. 'Sorry, Corrie. I don't understand, love. What else could it have been?'

'This island is tiny, remote and isolated – not even on the tourist map. You're right, Sid, under normal circumstances, none of us would have even found it, let alone chosen it as a holiday destination. But something powerful and compelling – something outside the boundaries of logic – drew us all here. I don't believe it was an accident. I believe it was for a reason.'

'Sweetheart ...' ventured Jack, 'you've had a very traumatic experience. We all have. You mustn't let it put strange ideas into your—'

'I thought that, too, Corrie,' Marjorie broke in, 'but I couldn't make any sense of it. The ten of us couldn't be more diverse. Different age groups, professions and backgrounds – a real hotchpotch of personalities. What do we have in common that has pulled us together like this?' Corrie wasn't the only one who had fallen under the sinister spell of the place – sensed its control over them. Marjorie felt it intensely and was curious to grasp its significance.

Corrie didn't answer for some moments. It was a toss-up whether to keep quiet and simply let them go on thinking she was a bit odd or share her theory and confirm their suspicions that she was totally unhinged.

'I think Lavinia Braithwaite is the reason we're on Katastrophos,' she replied eventually.

'Corrie, I really don't think it's healthy to start imagining ...' Jack began, helplessly.

She continued, undaunted, as he knew she would. 'I've been aware of it for some time. It's strange we haven't discussed our connections to Lavinia before now. But then, I suppose you don't talk about dead people, do you? Not on holiday.'

'Corrie, we don't all have connections to Lavinia Braithwaite,' said Jack, still trying to bring her back down to earth.

'Don't we? I wonder.' Corrie was resolute. 'Your connection, Jack, was that you were the copper tasked with arresting her murderer, which you've done. My connection was that I did the catering for all her charity luncheons. I liked her a lot and I was concerned that I might unintentionally have had some kind of responsibility for her death. Diana, you were her sister-in-law and also very fond of her, never suspecting for a moment that she had been murdered by your husband – her own brother. Marjorie, you helped to raise funds for her charities, didn't you? Lavinia was kind and generous and gave you something worthwhile to cling to, knowing that your life with Ambrose was increasingly intolerable. It was her legacy that enabled you to come to Katastrophos where ...' she hesitated, unsure how to put it, '... the cause of your unhappiness was removed.'

'OK, so what about Sid?' Jack was sceptical as ever. 'He didn't have any connection to Lavinia Braithwaite at all.'

'Actually, I think I did,' said Sidney. 'If she was the same Mrs Braithwaite who lived near Richmond Park in a posh, mock Tudor mansion with a pond and lime trees down her drive, then it was me who put in her new luxury bathroom. Top of the range pastel suite in Byzantine Twilight, "the elegant charm of a bygone era", with a set of gold basin mixers with little dolphins on the taps. A real nice lady, she was. Passed on my business card to her friends and I made a lot of good contacts, got some big orders. Terrible to think the poor soul's dead – murdered in the middle of her lunch. I'm just glad I was able to help catch the bugger who did it.'

'And before you ask,' said Tina, 'I had a connection too. I nursed Mrs Braithwaite after she was rushed to hospital for an emergency gall bladder operation. She was so kind. She had only ever had private treatment before but she wrote a letter to the hospital saying that my care had speeded up her recovery.'

'Blimey,' breathed Sid. 'Spooky, innit? Like the Twilight Zone.'

'That just leaves Ellie and me,' said Tim, 'and I'm afraid we blow your theory out of the water, Corrie. Neither of us has ever heard of Lavinia Braithwaite and we've never even been to Richmond Park. We're the exceptions to your hypothesis – no connections to the lady at all. Sorry.'

Jack was wrestling with a quandary. Common sense and good police practice told him he should keep quiet – say nothing. Nobody else knew and if he stayed silent, this ridiculous conversation would just fizzle out and Corrie's theory would slink back to where it belonged – in her shadowy, intermittent world of gods and demons. But for some reason, it wasn't that easy. Something kept niggling at the back of his mind in a fanciful, rarely used brain cell lurking behind the logical, coherent mass that served him so well as a hard-nosed copper. The niggle wouldn't leave him alone, nagged at him to tell the truth. But if he spoke now, it would open up not one can of worms but a whole truck load. Eventually he made a decision, or rather, the decision was somehow made for him. He was far from sure it was the right one but he felt compelled to carry it through.

'Actually, Tim, you probably have a stronger connection than any of us – or at least, Ellie does.'

'But that's impossible. Ellie has never mentioned any Lavinia Braithwaite, not all the time I've known her. If she'd been a close friend she'd have been invited to our wedding. You're wrong, DI Dawes. You must be.'

Still driven by his indefinable niggle, Jack looked across the table at Diana. 'Last night, when you said your husband was Lavinia's only living relative, that wasn't entirely accurate, was it? Lavinia had a niece.'

Diana's face was pained. 'I didn't know the baby was a girl. Did Cuthbert know?'

'Yes. Her mother wrote and told him when the baby was born. She didn't want any trouble or money from him but she did follow his career, kept up with where he was living and working, in case her daughter asked about her father one day. He never replied to her letters, not even the one inviting him to the wedding.'

'That figures,' said Diana. 'He didn't mention any of it to me. I'd never have known he had a kid at all if Daddy's private eye hadn't found out.'

Corrie had been struggling to make sense of this exchange. Now the fog was gradually starting to lift. She recalled that ghastly moment when Diana had purposely goaded Cuthbert, the taunts about how he had made one of his students pregnant many years ago, then abandoned her with a baby. But surely that baby couldn't be …

'Just a minute,' Tim stood up, flushed. 'What are you saying? What has all this got to do with Ellie? I don't understand. Will someone please explain?'

Jack looked at Diana but she was clearly reluctant to speak. He took a deep breath.

'Tim, I'm not sure I'm the one who should be telling you this. In fact, I'm not sure I should be discussing it at all. But having got this far, I can see that only the truth will do, now. Police investigations into Professor Gordon's past revealed that he had a brief association with one of his students some twenty years ago. The result was that she became pregnant and had a baby – a little girl. Tim, that little girl was Ellie.'

There were sharp intakes of breath. Just when everyone believed there was nothing left that could shock them, there was this unbelievable revelation with all its terrible implications. Tim paled and sank back into his chair.

'My God. Are you sure?'

'Positive.'

'Ellie never knew who her father was – never wanted to know. She loves her mum very much and would never ask her. How am I going to tell her that her own father nearly poisoned her to death?' He gulped. 'Did Professor Gordon know Ellie was his daughter?'

Jack shook his head. 'He knew he had a daughter, knew she was getting married. Ellie's mum wrote and told him, thinking he might at last want to acknowledge her, come to her wedding. But as we know, he was only interested in his own self-importance, getting his hands on the money to fund his research. He never replied to the letter, probably binned it without even reading it. I'd been keeping a close eye on Ellie – we thought she might be at risk – so when she was poisoned, I was stunned. I really thought Gordon had traced her identity through her mum's letter and tried to kill her.'

'I can just about see why he mightn't want to meet his daughter after all these years, but I don't understand why he would want to harm her.'

'The position of master, as well as requiring academic excellence, carried with it a responsibility for personal integrity and honourable behaviour. Gordon was not above getting rid of Ellie if he believed for one moment that the existence of a daughter born as the result of an illicit liaison with one of his students might jeopardize his future position at the Swiss university. It was all he cared about and he would have been quite ruthless in dispatching her if he deemed it necessary. You have to remember, we're not dealing with a sane man here. Gordon had no conscience. Nothing was to get in the way of the world recognizing his genius. But in the event, he didn't know who Ellie was, had never bothered to trace her, and she was poisoned only because she drank wine intended for Diana.'

'Sane or not, the man's a monster,' said Marjorie quietly. 'I hope you throw the book at him, Jack.'

'How on earth am I going to tell Ellie?' Tim moaned again.

'Do you have to tell her, son?' asked Sidney. 'What has she got to gain by finding out her dad's a murdering psycho? At the moment, she doesn't know him and he doesn't know her. Why don't you just leave it like that?'

'I want to, believe me. We were so happy before we came to this horrible island and this awful nightmare happened to us. But what if she asks about her father in the future?'

'Then you just get her mum to explain that she once fell in love with a very clever teacher and Ellie was born. Tell her that's probably why she's so good at teaching kiddies herself. Then her mum and the teacher sensibly decided to move on and not interfere in each other's lives. They were poles apart and it would never have worked if they'd got together. Something like that.' He glanced obliquely at Diana. 'After all, just because someone is way out of your reach, almost on a different planet, it doesn't stop you falling in love with them.'

Diana leant forward suddenly and took his hands. Her face was flushed, her emerald eyes brilliant. Loose blonde curls spilled over her shoulders and firm, tanned breasts swelled up from her low-cut dress. He could smell her, feel her warmth. It was too much. He stood up abruptly and strode to the other end of the table on the pretence of pouring himself more coffee.

Tim turned anxiously to Jack. 'But won't the police have to tell Ellie? Won't everything come out at the professor's trial?'

'I don't see why it should. Ellie's relationship to Gordon is completely irrelevant to the case as neither of them knew about the other. Their names are different, he isn't on her birth certificate, and there's no reason why anyone should make the connection. Except Ellie's mum, of course. She'll know. But I can't see her wanting to upset Ellie by telling her, can you?'

'No. I'm sure she won't.' He relaxed slightly. 'Thank you. I'm grateful.'

'So that's the final piece of our jigsaw,' said Corrie, still relentlessly pursuing her theory. 'Ellie was Cuthbert's daughter – which makes her Lavinia's niece. That's her connection.'

'But assuming you're right and we're all here because of Mrs Braithwaite, what was the point of it all?' asked Sidney.

'Nemesis.'

They looked in surprise at Tina, who had, until this moment, remained distant and withdrawn. In England she was a model nurse, methodical and down to earth, tending the sick with competence and compassion, her skills based on sound scientific knowledge. But here on Katastrophos, the place of her birth, she had absorbed mystery and superstition from the womb and now the deep convictions of her childhood resurfaced, strong and unshakable.

'Do you remember what I told you that first morning after we arrived?'

Nobody answered, recalling that a fortnight ago they had simply dismissed her as weird.

'I could feel the powerful synergy of vengeance and reprisal all around us.' Once more, she was almost whispering, her eyes half-closed. Her soft accent with the Greek lisp made her words even more compelling. 'St Sophia does not rule Katastrophos. Sophia is a superficial saint, a frivolous collector of trinkets and candles. It is Nemesis, winged balancer of life, dark-faced goddess and daughter of justice who holds deadly court here. She is the spirit of divine retribution from whom there is no escape – the true avenger of crime and hubris. At first I believed she was urging me to seek revenge for my own resentment. I was wrong, and Nemesis ensured I did not succeed.' She glanced briefly at the cut on Jack's head, now virtually healed. 'It was then that I realized that the injustice for which Nemesis had beckoned me was much greater than a personal grudge, it was something for which more than one person must atone. I had no understanding of it until now but I knew Nemesis would show us when she was ready.'

Corrie was fascinated, mesmerized, succumbing readily to the world of myth and mystery that she had been unable to resist since she arrived.

'Are you saying that Nemesis summoned us here to avenge Lavinia's death?'

'Of course. Nemesis is vengeful fate, personified as a remorseless goddess, the implacable executrix of justice – she could not allow it to pass unpunished. On Katastrophos we believe the dead have the power to punish the living if atonement for their death has in any way been neglected. We all owed Mrs Braithwaite a debt in some way. Now those debts are paid and her murder is avenged – and everyone played their part in it.'

'Yes, I suppose we did,' mused Corrie. 'Diana and I tricked her murderer and forced his confession. Jack and Sid arrested him. Tina saved Ellie's life so she was able to send us, via Tim, valuable forensic information about the toxin before it decomposed, and Marjorie sadly witnessed her husband's death from the same poison – but provided more incriminating evidence to ensure the murderer is convicted.'

'Leave off, you two. You're giving me the creeps.' Sid shivered. 'You don't believe all that divine vengeance stuff, do you Jack?'

Jack shrugged. 'I believe there are more layers to life and people than just what you see on top. And I believe coppers like me are put here to stop murderers like Cuthbert Gordon. Whether Nemesis has a hand in it depends on your personal beliefs, I guess.'

'What the hell's "hubris" when it's at home?' asked Sid.

'Hubris is exaggerated, overbearing pride,' answered Corrie. 'Professor Gordon certainly had plenty of that.' Corrie knew little about

Nemesis, certainly not as much as Tina, but one fact had stuck in her mind – Nemesis had been dealing out her brand of justice on Olympus long before Zeus arrived.

'A toast is called for, I think,' said Sid, raising his coffee cup. 'To Nemesis!'

'Nemesis!' they echoed.

Tina drank then solemnly threw a few drops in the dust as a libation to the divine settler of scores.

Two Greek policemen came to escort Professor Gordon on to the police launch. The young officers had never been to Katastrophos but had heard many imaginative and disturbing rumours about it. They were formal, efficient and wary. Gordon, incongruous in an immaculate Ossie Clark suit and handcuffs, was meek and compliant – no sign of hubris now. As they led him up the gangplank, Ariadne scuttled up out of nowhere and pushed a flowering hibiscus plant into his manacled hands. The fact that he had been responsible for the near fatal poisoning of her daughter, Maria, on the monastery steps was totally beyond her comprehension and she still regarded him with abject adoration. A blissful smile spread across the professor's face and, ignoring Ariadne, he began to talk lovingly to the flowers.

A small crowd of Katastrophans had assembled on the quay, silent and grim-faced, no doubt wanting to witness the exodus of the troublesome visitors from their island. Some of the younger ones had never seen a police launch – or a uniformed policeman, come to that. Tina was in the crowd, accompanied by a large contingent from the Stephanides family. Releasing herself gently from her mother's tearful embrace, she stepped forward and approached Jack, holding out her wrists bravely. She looked him in the eyes, unflinching.

'You will want to put the handcuffs on me now, Detective Inspector. I have said goodbye to my family and I am ready to come with you.'

Jack took both her hands in his. 'I don't think so, Tina. No real harm was done and I can't think of any good that will be served by arresting you and taking you back for trial. I'm supposed to be very careful about the appropriate use of public funds.' He smiled at her.

Her expression was a mixture of doubt and relief. Tears sprang into her eyes and she brushed them away. 'Does that mean I am free to stay here, on Katastrophos?'

'If that's what you want.'

'It is. This island badly needs a nurse – especially for the children.'

'Sounds like an excellent idea.'

'I shall try to run weekly surgeries, obtain some basic medical supplies. The priest may allow me to use the small ante-room in the church.'

Jack was glad to see she was already planning a more positive future.

'I guess I could help there.' Diana strode down the gangplank on four-inch heels, sassy and magnificent, like a supermodel on the catwalk. 'I seem to have a few spare bucks that I figured I'd be spending on ... well, something else.' She swallowed hard then looked up, resolutely cheerful. 'Why don't I build you a health centre? This island could sure use one!'

'You would do that?' Tina was astonished.

'Sure. Why not? Sid's coming back home to the States with me. He'll help set it up with my lawyers, won't you, baby?'

Sidney had been plodding morosely behind her, carrying her luggage. He perked up instantly. This was the first he'd heard about going to Manhattan with Diana. Dared he hope it was a chance to spend just a few more precious days with her? Then he descended rapidly into depression again. It sounded like she just wanted him to work for her. A hired help, along with the hundreds of others her 'daddy' must employ. His instinct was to say no, he had too many plumbing jobs waiting in the UK. He had his pride. On the other hand, it would be churlish to refuse to help build a badly needed health centre and he'd always wanted to see America. He'd go over at his own expense and only stay for as long as it took to organize the work. He wouldn't plan on anything beyond that and he wouldn't take any liberties with her. The holiday was over.

'Sure, Di. Be glad to help. Just tell me what you want done.'

'There you go, hon,' said Diana cheerfully to Tina. 'With Sidney on the job, it'll be built before you know it.'

For the first time in many weeks, Tina smiled. It transformed her face. '*Efharistó*,' she said. 'Thank you very much.'

CHAPTER TWENTY-ONE

The crossing to the mainland on the police launch was much quicker and less stomach-churning than the trip out on old Charon's ferry had been. It was also quieter and less smelly. Jack was even able to dispense with the paper bag long enough to hold a decent conversation.

'Dead rats,' said Corrie, thoughtfully.

'Pardon?'

'The dead rats that we kept seeing around that awful tree stump that Ariadne used as a chopping block. And the mad one that bit Sidney in the olive grove. That was the professor experimenting with the strength of his new, improved toxin. He admitted it.'

'I expect Ariadne was given the job of feeding it to them. It wouldn't have done for someone to see Gordon doing it. Might have raised suspicion, whereas nobody would have thought twice about Ariadne doing a bit of vermin control.'

'Mm. Mad old Ariadne must have helped him a lot without realizing what she was doing. I noticed she had the same blistery rash on the back of her hands that the professor and Sidney had. Side effects of handling plants without surgical gloves, I suppose.'

'Plants can be vicious. Look at stinging nettles, for example. Do you remember I asked Gordon about the rash on his hand when we were seeing Ellie and Tim on to the ferry. He said he'd nicked a hole in his glove. He didn't have any more with him and you can't buy them on the island so he had to do the rest of his work without any protection. With any luck, that means we'll find his fingerprints on the phials of poison.'

'Do you need fingerprints? Diana and I heard him confess to everything – *modus operandi*, the lot.'

'Belt and braces, love. You can never have too much evidence. A clever brief might try to claim entrapment or confession under duress, that's if he ever gets to trial, which I doubt. My guess is they'll find him unfit to plead.'

Not for the first time, Corrie was impressed by the precision and orderliness of her husband's approach to his job, no matter how distressing the circumstances and despite the fact that they were supposed to be honeymooning. No guess-work policing for him. It all had to be strictly by the book. She would be surprised if he hadn't been keeping a daily written record of events. By contrast, her own instinctive nature – whilst an asset to something creative, like catering – would make her a lousy copper. And as for her masterly intuition – it had gone into overdrive on Katastrophos, freefalling into something much more sinister and controlling. It might easily have got her killed. She shuddered.

'I wonder how Sid got the rash.' Corrie needed all the loose ends to be tied in her mind.

'It was on the first Monday we were here. Sid and I went to the olive groves to watch Gordon taking his samples. I was trying to work out what plants he used to make his poisons. He'd just harvested a very large sea squill bulb, one of the mutated varieties he'd been cultivating for some time during previous visits. Sid lifted it out of his sample case to look at it. Handling fresh squill, particularly the onion-like bulbs, can cause blistering and rashes in some people. Gordon tried to put me off the track by pretending Sid's rash was due to the squirting cucumber, but it was the wrong hand.' Jack frowned. 'It was probably toxin distilled from that very bulb that nearly killed Maria and Ellie and caused Dobson's death.'

'How do you know? The professor hasn't made a statement, has he?'

'Good Lord, no. I don't suppose he ever will. He hasn't spoken a word since I arrested him. Once the telephones were restored, I made a few phone calls, found out a lot of useful information. The professor had already told me that peasants on the island made rat poison from the red squill and that the white squill could be used pharmaceutically as a heart stimulant. It didn't take a botanical genius to work out that if he'd managed to genetically engineer a hybrid containing both properties and concentrate its essence, it could make a very effective poison. Of course, I only suspected, what Gordon knew for certain, that it decomposes in the body very rapidly leaving no trace. Then Tim came back with Ellie's message from the hospital and confirmed it.'

'The perfect murder weapon. It certainly worked on Lavinia.' Corrie shuddered again. 'And he'd obviously refined his latest batch. The one Ariadne dropped by accident was colourless and had no smell, unlike the first lot. They stank like a compost heap. And even if it had a bitter taste, you probably wouldn't notice it in strong red wine or ouzo.'

'Or on an oily lampwick,' added Jack. 'When Gordon came roaring in after the women came down from the monastery he saw someone lying on the ground wearing an orange shawl. He naturally expected it to be Diana, hence the exaggerated marital concern. When he realized it was Maria, he covered his confusion very cunningly and tried to put me off the scent by saying it was due to a rotten egg. I knew then it wouldn't be long before he tried again but I hadn't expected the next victim to be Ellie.' Jack was still beating himself up about that. 'It shouldn't have been Ellie.'

'It explains why the professor became slightly agitated when Charon arrived earlier than expected and took her to hospital. He wasn't entirely sure that the time lapse would be long enough for all the poison to have vanished.'

'Because he hadn't had as long as he would have liked to finish testing his product. Time was running out and the Swiss university was threatening to give his job to another professor – his closest rival. As it turned out, there was still a little poison left in Ellie's system for the hospital to trace. I spoke to the toxicologist on the phone and he also explained why Dobson died so quickly after swallowing the poison Gordon put in Diana's lunch. Do you remember Dobson telling us he took digoxin?'

'Difficult to forget. He always made such a performance of insisting Marjorie prepared the exact dose at the exact same times every day.'

'He was right, in a way, although I agree he didn't have to be so pompous about it. Digoxin is used primarily to improve the pumping ability of the heart in congestive heart failure. You have to be careful about doses because there's very little margin between a therapeutically beneficial level of digoxin and a toxic level, which is why Dobson couldn't drink coffee. Even a small amount of caffeine could upset the balance. Squill has an effect on the heart similar to that of digoxin.'

'So if Ambrose ingested both of them together ...'

'Exactly. Chemicals found in squill have been proved to increase the rate of heartbeats and worsen several kinds of heart disease. Large oral doses of it have resulted in seizures, intense vomiting, heart stoppage and death. The victim often experiences vision disturbance and hallucinations. Sound familiar? Symptoms that were all displayed by Lavinia, Maria, Ellie and Dobson. The toxicologist told me that squill is not recommended in any form for medical purposes.'

'I'm not surprised. I'm glad it exonerates Marjorie, though. It was nothing she or St Sophia did that precipitated Ambrose's death. Her conscience is clear.'

'I took a gamble that she wasn't responsible in any way when I agreed to his burial without an inquiry.'

Corrie leapt back in mock amazement. 'You took a gamble, Jack? I thought that was the prerogative of scatter-brained women who run catering businesses.'

'Shut up or I'll chuck you over the side and you can swim the rest of the way.'

On the port side of the launch Tim was telling Marjorie how much he was looking forward to seeing Ellie again. If he had felt protective of her before this latest shocking revelation, his urge to shield her from anything that might make her unhappy was now even stronger. Marjorie in return was telling Tim about her son, Dan, and how she hoped to see more of him now that Ambrose wasn't there to prevent it.

The conversation to starboard was of an entirely different nature. Sidney, whilst secretly delighted at the prospect of more time in Diana's company, was nevertheless apprehensive and at great pains to ensure she didn't think he was after her money.

'Naturally, I'll have to get the necessary paperwork sorted out, visas and that, but I'm happy to come to the States and help out with the planning. I haven't much experience in building health centres, although I have plumbed in one or two in my time, but I like to think of myself as a sound businessman who knows the value of an investment. I imagine I'll be working with your financial team, will I? Just until the job's done. Then I'll go back home to ...' He was unable to continue because Diana wrapped both arms and one sinuous thigh around him and kissed him, long and hard. When she'd finished, Sid felt as if he had just surfaced after a long spell under water in the clutches of a very sexy octopus.

'Sidney, don't be a klutz. You won't be working for me – not in any capacity. We have enough technical guys in our companies to design and build a hundred health centres.'

'Well, what do you want me to do, then?'

She kissed him again. Longer and harder – grinding her groin into his crotch in a way that caused the Greek policemen to look away and study the horizon.

'I see,' he said eventually. 'You're just after my body. You're not interested in my brain at all.' He pretended to be offended and pursed his lips, primly. She giggled. Something she realized she hadn't done since Cuthbert had tried to murder her.

'Seriously, Diana, are you sure about this? I mean, there'll be loads of handsome millionaires in Manhattan trampling each other to get to you now that you're … well, you know … on your own. It was a terrible thing that the prof did and you must be shocked and hurt and I shouldn't want you to make any rash decisions while you're still upset.' He looked into her passionate green eyes and felt himself weaken. Sod it, he'd do anything she asked, go anywhere she wanted him to, never mind the consequences. British gallantry, however, demanded that he had one last try at reasoning with her.

'I don't mind admitting I'm a bit shaken up myself. Unless you're an out-and-out cowboy, a rogue trader, plumbing is generally a murder free profession. It was a bit of a stretch to witness a brilliant academic, a respected botanist, going around poisoning people. Maybe we should wait until we've both recovered – calmed down a bit.'

She was wildly excited now, unstoppable. 'But I don't want to calm down, my darling! I've spent the last ten years being so calm I've had to take my own pulse to make sure I was still alive. I want to go on being thrilled, laughing, having fun. For the last two weeks, you believed I was a penniless blonde living off a rich sugar daddy, but despite that you still cared about me – and I loved you because of it. You wouldn't believe the number of guys who hang around me with one eye on my breasts and the other on my bank balance.' She grasped the front of his jacket and pulled him close. 'Sid, this is me, Diana, the lady who jumped you in the Cave of Nymphs. I don't recall you wanting to make a federal case out of it then. Since I met you, I've been happier than I've been in my whole life, and I'm not letting you go. God help me, I'll even charter a plane so you can go back home and watch your beloved Arsenal!'

That clinched it, really. How could a man resist? Sidney still couldn't believe his luck, but he was a beaten man. Brace yourself, Sidney Arthur Foskett, he thought as Diana slipped her fingers inside his shirt and kissed his mouth again. Looks like you're going to be a love slave.

*

From a distance, Corrie had noticed the exchange between Sidney and Diana and was inordinately happy for them. Maybe one good thing had come out of the last hideous fortnight.

'I think Sidney and Diana are planning to stay together,' she said to Jack, putting her arm through his, 'at least for a while.'

'You're just a sad old romantic. I hope you're right though. I think they complement each other. Like tin and tang.'

'I think you mean yin and yang, but I agree.' She looked at his weary face. 'I suppose this arrest is a pretty good result for you?'

'Not really,' said Jack, ruefully. 'Maria and Ellie could so easily have died and Ambrose Dobson actually did. Not what I would call a successful, well-run police operation – one stiff and two near misses.'

'But you got your man – and the evidence. And you stopped him before he did what he came to do, murder his wife. As for Ambrose, you don't know that he might not have died anyway after all that rowing. He was a victim of his own beastly lust.'

'Maybe, sweetheart. We'll never know.'

'The really frightening part for me is how plausible and kind Cuthbert seemed. I had some fascinating conversations with him and he appeared to adore Diana. How can a man so gifted and intelligent be so crafty and evil?'

'I'm no psychologist, Corrie, but I can recognize a psychopath when I meet one and it's often a very fine demarcation between genius and insanity. Gordon is a text-book example. He's a callous predator, he uses charm, manipulation and violence to satisfy his own selfish demands. He has no conscience or feelings for others, he just takes whatever he wants without guilt or remorse. In other words, what's missing in his person-ality are the very qualities that make the rest of us relatively decent human beings. Mind you, not all psychopaths are violent offenders. Some have become dynamic leaders in a highly competitive business world, using their manipulative skills to get quick results for themselves and their corporations. Eventually, though, they cause long-term damage to colleagues and their companies because although they're enterprising, they're also deceitful, abusive and fraudulent.'

'I can think of a few chief executives like that. You can't help feeling sorry for Diana, though. Cuthbert didn't want a wife – just access to her money. But he must have convinced her and her father that he loved her when they were married.'

'Very probably. A psychopath's real emotions are superficial at best, that's if they exist at all. They're incapable of forming lasting relationships or showing any kind of meaningful love and they never perform any action unless they consider it beneficial to themselves. The reason he was able to fool Diana and her father, and even you, into thinking he was a nice, caring bloke is because he watched normal people and mimicked their feelings and behaviour when it suited his needs.'

'That's awful – so cold and calculated. But I still don't understand how he could murder his own sister.'

'You're forgetting – he doesn't feel any emotional attachment to the people he harms. What did for him in the end – the reason he failed – was that he had no real sense of the potential consequences of his crimes, not only for his victims, but also for himself. He considered himself invincible and couldn't accept that there was a risk of being caught as a result of what he'd done.'

'What will happen to him?'

'Well, he won't go to prison. Once the mindbenders get hold of him, he'll probably end up detained indefinitely in a secure hospital for the criminally insane. I doubt they'll ever let him loose again – not if they've got any sense.'

Corrie had her own views on the subject of avoiding responsibility for your actions. Technically, Professor Gordon might be pronounced criminally insane but he'd been smart enough to concoct a premeditated plan to murder for money – twice – and prepare an escape route.

'I hope you've stopped drifting off into your nether world of Greek spirits now we're off that weird island,' said Jack.

'Of course I have. It was just that being in a deeply superstitious community seemed somehow to conjure up the ancient mythology that must have been lying dormant in my brain all these years.'

'Sometimes I worry about what's lying dormant in your brain.'

'Did you notice those three old crones in white, sitting in the crowd that gathered on the quay to see us off?'

'No. Why?'

'They were sewing.'

'So what?'

'They looked just like the Moirae – the three Fates. Clotho spun the thread of your life, Lachesis measured its length with her rod and Atropos cut it off with her shears when your time was up. She also chose how you died. They were psychopaths – cold, remorseless and unfeeling.

Even Zeus feared the Fates. Mind you, he was a psychopath, himself. He could …'

Jack sighed. 'Thank goodness. We're pulling into the harbour. Let's go home.'

EPILOGUE

Now all the rest, as many as had escaped sheer destruction, were at home, safe ...

The Odyssey Book I – Homer

The travellers – such as were left – had said their goodbyes at the airport. There were no promises to keep in touch, no invitations to 'call in if you're ever in our neck of the woods' and most definitely no expressions of interest in returning to Katastrophos – ever.

Six Months Later

THE CLERK AND THE NANNY

Tim Watkins looked at the scan of his baby son, safe and warm in Ellie's womb and silent tears of joy streamed down his face. Memories of their ordeal on Katastrophos had at last begun to recede, driven away by this beautiful child waiting to be born. It seemed like a miracle to them both as Ellie, never robust, had been fragile for some weeks after they returned home. Now she looked radiant and so happy.

Tim had spoken to Ellie's mother as soon as he could about the true identity of Ellie's poisoner. She had been deeply shocked but agreed there was no question of telling Ellie, especially now, in her condition. Thanks to Jack, the necessary statements to the police had been handled sensitively and with a minimum of distress. All that mattered now was the safe delivery of Tim and Ellie's son and their future together as a family.

Some weeks later Ellie accidentally discovered the identity of her father. She had gone round to her mum's house, rooting in the bureau for some family snaps for the baby book she was making for her unborn son. In an inner recess, she found an old crumpled photo that her mother had kept hidden away, tucked inside her birth certificate. There was also a panoramic photograph of everyone in her mother's last year at college with Professor Gordon, in his cap and gown, seated in the middle, beaming. He must have been in his thirties when it was taken, but she recognized him instantly. Somehow, finding out had not been the bomb-shell she might have expected. Maybe she had been subconsciously aware of a relationship between them on that dreadful island. For some time she studied his face quite calmly and philosophically, seeing aspects of her own features that she hadn't noticed on Katastrophos. How tragic to think she might have died at her own father's hands.

She put everything carefully back in the bureau so that her mother wouldn't know she had found it. She had never asked questions and now she would never mention any of it to her mum or Tim. It would be too upsetting for them. Of course, she would have to think of something to tell her son if he ever asked about his grandfather. But there was plenty of time for that. She wondered if he would be born with wispy ginger hair.

THE MERRY WIDOW

Marjorie Dobson sat on the deck of the cruise liner sipping her rum punch and watching the sun set over the Caribbean Sea. Dan was below deck in the games room, playing pool with his partner, Jeff. Such a nice young man and they'd both been so considerate, promising to keep in touch more often now she was a widow. They didn't want her to be lonely. How could she ever explain that becoming a widow was the first time she hadn't felt lonely since she married Ambrose? She'd passed her driving test, found herself a very absorbing part-time job and made lots of good friends. She worked because she enjoyed it, not for the money. She had plenty of that. Ambrose's insurance company had paid up unusually promptly once they had translated all the Greek documents. They'd been very sympathetic and offered their sincere condolences, saying how tragic it was for her, losing her husband on holiday abroad and on their thirtieth anniversary, but they supposed it could have happened at any time given his weak heart.

Marjorie smiled quietly to herself. Only she knew exactly what had happened in St Sophia's sacred grotto. She couldn't help but enjoy the irony of the situation when she found out that Professor Gordon had already poisoned the picnic. She had nursed the basket all the way to the grotto, stopped it from falling into the sea when the boat capsized and carried it carefully into the cave, knowing that Ambrose would take it from her and greedily wolf everything down. How particularly expedient that the professor's poison had exactly the same effect as the double dose of digoxin she had put into the orange juice.

The people on the cruise were such jolly fun, cheerful and friendly. She'd danced until dawn, played tennis and laughed and cheered at the live shows with Dan and Jeff. She smiled again, thinking how much Ambrose would have hated it.

THE PLAYGIRL AND THE PLUMBER

Exactly how Diana's 'daddy' felt about his lovely daughter going on holiday with a professor and coming back with a plumber, Sidney never really discovered. Naturally her father was devastated when he found out her husband had tried to murder her and there was even talk of sending over a team of his crack lawyers to ensure the man was dealt with properly. Ideally, he'd have liked him extradited to the States but apparently there were lengthy legal problems with that and anyway, Diana was adamant, Cuthbert was British and so were both his murder victims. It was only right he should be tried in the UK – and, not unreasonably, she wanted him kept as far away from her as possible.

Now, six months on, it was sufficient for her father to see that she was so obviously happier than she had ever been. When the news first broke that she was going to have Sidney's baby, her enormous, extensive family welcomed him with open arms and he thought the party would never end. Sid was unrepentant about her having become pregnant so soon after they got together. As he pointed out, if she insisted on shagging him senseless every night, it was pretty well inevitable. She asked if he would still fancy her when she looked like a humungous muffin. He said he was a brave chap and he'd do his best.

'Daddy' put the crack lawyers to work arranging a quickie divorce and Diana and Sidney were married on the seashore in front of their Malibu beach house. When he discovered one of the showers in the marble bathroom was dripping, he whipped off the jacket of his morning suit and set about fixing it. Diana sat on the floor in her Emanuel wedding gown, her amazing legs crossed beneath her, and laughed from sheer joy.

THE PROFESSOR

The nice criminal psychologist told him he was doing very well. There had been no delusions of divine genius for several weeks now. She was an earnest young woman, with a modern, compassionate attitude to psychopathy, and she really believed that the revolutionary Tibetan approach she had been studying was working. Once she had coaxed him out of his profound silence, Professor Gordon had impressed her with his coherence and sincere remorse. Whilst he hadn't made any excuses, accepting that what he'd done was indefensible, he believed it had been overwork that had driven him into a breakdown during which the unforgivable crimes had been committed. She was putting him through a course of new, cognitive behaviour therapy and he was responding so well, she told him, that it was a real possibility that her colleagues' prognoses had been unnecessarily pessimistic and he might, with her support, be considered for some type of experimental parole and rehabilitation in the very near future.

'Don't worry, my dear,' he whispered, after the nice lady psychologist had gathered up her papers and left. 'You and I will soon be out of here. She's a monumentally dim-witted young woman even for a psychologist. I can make her believe anything I choose. Once we're free, my darling, we'll disappear, back to Katastrophos to replenish my stocks. Then all we need is someone with a lot of money who can be persuaded to leave it to me. Once they're dead, I shall be able to carry on my research without interference from stupid, nosy people who don't understand my genius. Just wait a little longer until the simple-minded doctors are convinced I'm cured.' He looked at his watch. 'Time for a drink before dinner, I think, sweetheart.' He picked up the watering can and sprinkled the hibiscus, growing in a pot on the windowsill.

THE NURSE

The Katastrophos Health Centre was almost finished. Rather than embark on a completely new building, they had taken over an empty mini-market in the centre of St Sophia and refurbished it. The result was a clean, efficient, sterile clinic that would have been a credit to any small town. Tina was quietly amazed and gratified.

It had become imperative that the centre was built quickly, since most of the women who had made the pilgrimage to the monastery had become pregnant shortly afterwards. It was not considered in the least surprising that so many women were expecting babies at the same time, simply that St Sophia had been particularly pleased with her Katastrophans that year – probably because they had effectively ejected the disruptive foreigners. All, that is, except the one who was currently nourishing several trees in the olive grove and would be of no further trouble to anyone.

Tina thought frequently of Mark. She was no longer bitter and festering with unrequited vengeance, accepting that the law had taken its course and even Nemesis must acknowledge it. There was an appeal pending against the Draconian sentence he had been given. She hoped it would be successful but remained pragmatic about the outcome. One day he would be free and she had written to him, often, suggesting he might want to join her. Although he could no longer be a doctor, he had skills that would be invaluable to her. And maybe, in time, St Sophia would smile upon them, too.

THE COP AND THE CATERER

It was a crisp Saturday night in late January with a sprinkle of snowflakes floating down from the clear, midnight sky. Corrie and Jack sat up in bed sharing a box of chocolates and a bottle of red wine that reminded Corrie very strongly of the illicit *Agiorgitiko* they had glugged in such awe-inspiring quantities on Katastrophos. She and Jack hadn't discussed their fateful honeymoon at any length, Jack believing discretion was the better part of staying in one piece. The police evidence and witness statements had been dealt with remarkably efficiently and, as Jack had predicted, once the mindbenders took over, Professor Gordon's prosecution and punishment became a mere formality as the medical profession took over from the judicial system.

He surreptitiously sneaked an orange cream – Corrie's favourite – and chewed it, thoughtfully.

'I bet none of them got pregnant afterwards.'

'Pardon?' Corrie looked up from her food magazine.

'Those women on Katastrophos. They were a superstitious bunch, weren't they? All that mumbo-jumbo about St Sophia and fruitfulness and traipsing up to that monastery every year.'

'How do you know it was mumbo-jumbo?'

''Course it was. Couldn't have been anything else. Chewing a bit of oily wick won't put you in the club.'

'Well, that's just where you're wrong, smarty-pants. I happen to know that several of us became pregnant after making the pilgrimage up the mountain.' She carried on turning the pages of her magazine.

Jack paled and beads of sweat began to form on his clammy forehead. He poured another glass of wine, took a stiffening slug and braced himself.

'Corrie, sweetheart, you don't mean ... you're not trying to tell me ...'

She looked at his stricken face. 'Oh for goodness sake, not me, you idiot! And you'd better breathe out. That sigh of relief you're holding in is making you go a very funny colour.'

They both laughed. 'I had a postcard from Sid,' said Corrie. 'He and Diana are Greek Island hopping on her father's yacht. Diana's pregnant and they're both ecstatic. It's a girl and they're planning to call her Calypso after the nymph who seduced Odysseus and kept him a captive of love on her island for seven years. Isn't that just so romantic after Sid and Diana first ... well, got it together in the Cave of Nymphs on Katastrophos? Anyway, they stopped off very briefly to see how the health centre was progressing and it seems Maria and lots of the other women are pregnant, too. Isn't it wonderful?'

'It's bloody scary,' said Jack, feeling a sudden icy shiver through his veins. 'I happened across the file containing a copy of the Watkins's statement yesterday. The detective constable who took it mentioned that Ellie was pregnant, too.'

'Well, there you are then,' said Corrie, decisively.

They were silent for a bit – each occupied with their own thoughts. Then Jack asked cautiously.

'Am I completely forgiven now, dumpling? It was a lousy trick, pretending we were on honeymoon when I was really on a case. It must have been terrifying for you at the end.'

'It bloody well was! But I knew you were a single-minded, workaholic flatfoot when I married you and I've no time for women who marry a bloke then set about trying to change him into something different. And it wasn't entirely your fault. I was to blame as well. I should have listened – done what you told me instead of interfering.'

'Can I have that in writing?'

Corrie cuffed him. 'One thing that did surprise me, though. The way you blurted out to Tim and everyone that Ellie was the professor's daughter. Normally, you're such a tight-lipped old codger. What happened to the "leaked information jeopardizes convictions, you can only reveal certain facts on a need-to-know basis" and all that old cobblers. I'd have put next month's profits on you keeping it very quiet.'

'I most certainly would have if I'd been at home on my own patch. But it was that blessed island. It was as if I couldn't help it. It was a very creepy feeling and not one I'd care to repeat or even admit to anyone but you. And if you say one word about Nemesis and divine retribution, I'll guzzle the rest of the orange creams.'

'Nemesis or not, poor Lavinia's death was terrible but I'm so relieved the truth came out about how she died. Coriander's Cuisine has never had so many orders. It's as if people feel guilty that they suspected my food.'

'Tell you what,' said Jack, sitting up suddenly. 'As you're so well off and I'm owed some leave, why don't we book another honeymoon? Somewhere remote and peaceful that isn't in the tourist guides, where we can retreat from the stress of our jobs – absolutely no catering or murders …'

'Stop right there. We'll have our honeymoon – on our silver wedding anniversary.'

'Why wait so long?'

'Because by then, DI Dawes, you'll be retired and that's the only way I can be sure you're not on duty.'